Dodger Down Under

(The Further Adventures of the Artful Dodger)

1827-1832

David Weston

This edition published in 2013 by:
Thistle Publishing
36 Great Smith Street
London
SW1P 3BU

ISBN-13: 978-1-909609-43-3
ISBN-10: 1-909609-43-9

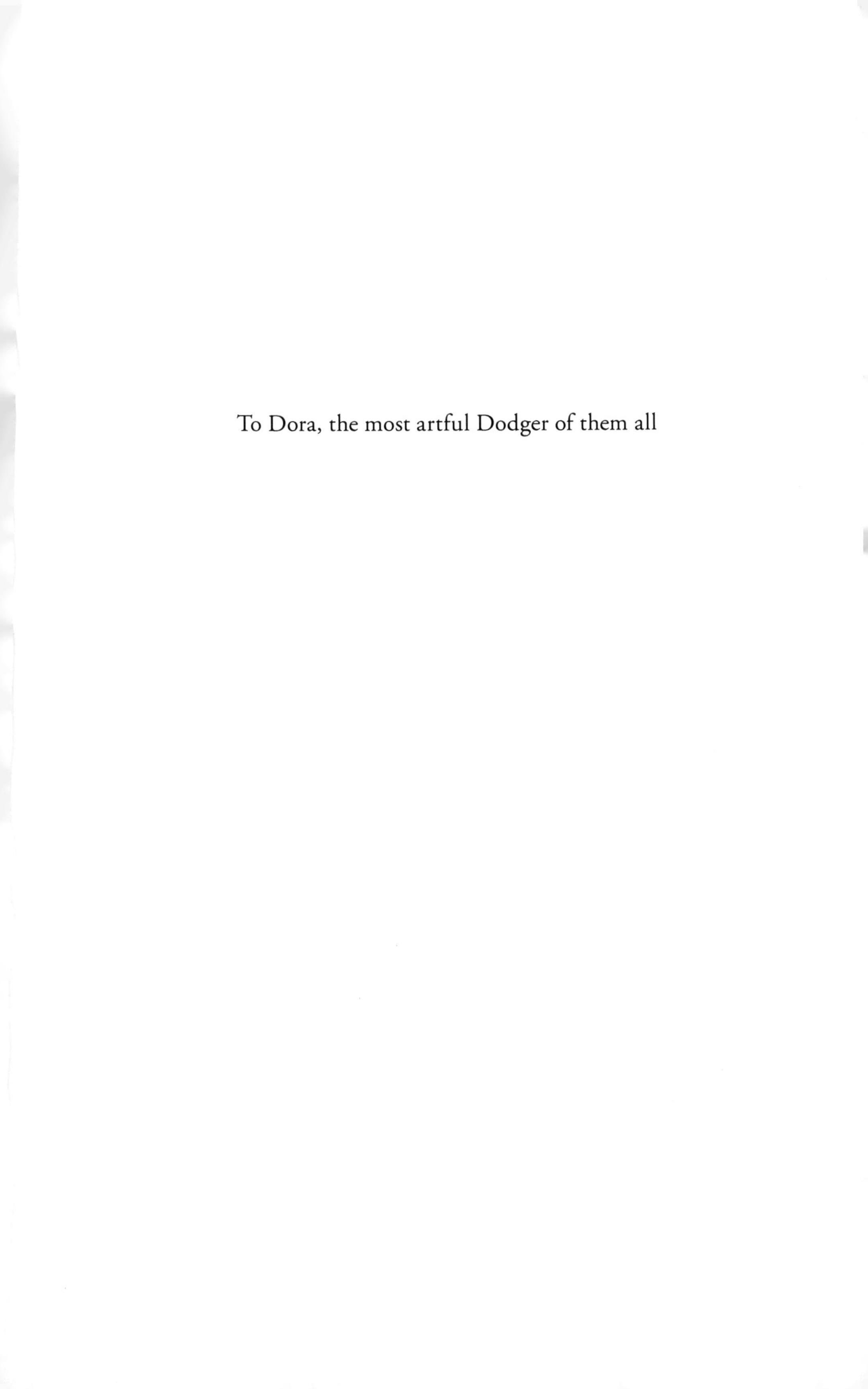

To Dora, the most artful Dodger of them all

These documents, tied tightly in old brown paper with "Reminiscences of Jack Dawkins" scrawled on it in faded ink were recently discovered in a trunk at a country house clearance in Shropshire. They are believed to have been the property of Lieutenant Peter Freeman, a nephew of Sir Raymond Stiles, the owner of the estate in the early years of the last century.

Wessels Springs Laager, Mafeking.

5th May 1900
My dear Uncle Raymond,

One morning last September an old Englishman staggered through our lines, delirious and weak with fever. He called himself Jack Dawkins and claimed to be a diamond merchant who had been caught up by the Boer advance. He was of a hardy constitution and recovered his health within a few days. I found him an engaging, if somewhat unsavoury and unreliable companion, and took down his extraordinary story to while away the long nights of the recent siege. I have put it all down, warts and all, although I appreciate that the more salacious and obscene passages will have to be removed.

I have promised Mr Dawkins to do all I can to publish his extraordinary story on my return to England at the end of the present war. If I fail to return, the Boer is a clever and deadly enemy with plenty of fight still in him, I bequeath these papers to you, knowing of your love of the immortal works of Dickens, and trust you will endeavour to affect a publication. If you are successful, it is Mr Dawkins' wish that any resulting royalties should be forwarded to The Waifs and Strays, a charity close to his heart.

Wishing you health and happiness,
Your loving nephew,
Peter

Contents

Chapter 1: Farewell to Fagin	1
Chapter 2: The Hulk	13
Chapter 3: The Enterprise	32
Chapter 4: The Voyage Begins	53
Chapter 5: At Sea	74
Chapter 6: Across The Southern Ocean	118
Chapter 7: Sydney	136
Chapter 8: A Wild Colonial Boy	143
Chapter 9: First Day's Play	175
Chapter 10: Second Day	201
Chapter 11: Repercussions	217
Chapter 12: Into The Outback	228
Chapter 13: Change of Plan	248
Chapter 14: The True History Of Private Robert Skinner	266
Chapter 15: The District Magistrate and The Settlers from Yarmouth	274
Chapter 16: Back To Sydney	295
Chapter 17: London Again	317
Acknowledgements	338
NOTES	338
About the Author	343

1. Farewell to Fagin

"They were the dregs of life. I paint them in all their deformity, in all the squalid misery of their lives, to show them as they really were, forever sulking uneasily through the dirtiest paths of life.... It is true. It is emphatically God's truth, for it is the truth he leaves in such depraved and miserable breasts...."

Miserable? We were never miserable apart from the times the runners and traps were down on us. It wasn't the best of bleedin' times but it certainly wasn't the worst, but then the 'inimitable' Charles Dickens, or 'Boz' as he called his self when I first knew him, could always bend the truth to suit himself. You read his books and you'd never believe that people firk and fart, and believe me we boys had tail winds aplenty with those rotten sausages Fagin fed us on. But I'm getting ahead of meself. How de doo and all the bloomin' rest of it. I am not a going for to tell you my life, like a song or a story-book, but give it you short and handy. My name is Jack Dawkins erstwhile known as the Dodger. I was born in 1815 at the end of Boney's war, and have fornicated and fought through far more than I care to remember, from the blazing heat of Calcutta to the freezing cold of Sebastopol and back again; and here I am in 1899 up to my old privates in another. My earliest memories are of the workhouse at Barnet, where in that summer of Waterloo I'd first seen the light of day. I can still recall the sneering face of the keeper's wife telling me my mother was a trollop who'd abandoned me and had scarpered off to Flanders to join some soldier who'd knocked her up. Neither of them ever came back for me, no matter how often I wished that they would. Didn't you ever wonder, when you were reading old

Dickens' book, what on earth I was doing in Barnet that morning when I first met Oliver Twist? Or should I say Oliver Leeford to give him his proper name? But I'll explain about that later.

In many ways my beginnings were similar to Oliver's although I never had his posh connections. Nevertheless I've supped with the highest in the land and drunk with the lowest villains on God's earth; I've loved many women and turned out the lights on a good few men, lost and won, and seen countries and sights Oliver Leeford never dreamed of. I've gone through eighty-four years and outlived the bloody lot of 'em. Even the 'immortal' Dickens himself, who stole my story and used it in some of the greatest novels man has ever written, and paid me not a brass farthing. But all that was years ahead when we first crossed paths in 1827, that morning I spoke up to the beaks, before I was transported to Botany Bay.

I remember it all crystal clear. I waited in the well of the court in Bow Street as judgment was passed in the case before mine, cursing myself for being nabbed for a common two-ha-penny sneeze box. I wouldn't have minded so much if it had been for a gold ticker and chain. I was twelve years old, only a bit older than that little prig Oliver, but doing all I could to show I wasn't scared of any of 'em. Even after a few days in the remand cell, the courtroom smelt close and insalubrious. I looked up and perceived the walls were streaked with greasy dirt, the ceiling black. There was an old smoky bust over the mantel-shelf, and a dusty clock ticked above. I became aware of the drooling voice of some lawyer pleading mercy for his client on account of his youth and breeding and the fact that he'd been misled by his older companion, a hardened criminal. I heard the wheezy voice of some magistrate passing sentences of seven and fourteen year's hard labour; then a fierce, terrible voice crying out: "Liar! Once out of this court I'll smash that face of yourn!" There was grappling and a sort of posh voice screaming frantically: "Please protect me! I beg you! Chain him! He'll kill me else!" It now sounded like a mighty scuffle was going on. Four big Bow Street Runners pushed past me, their truncheons at the ready. I saw distorted, struggling shadows on the wall and heard savage thumps of wood on flesh, the cracking of skull or bone, before a huge, ugly brute was dragged down the stairs with blooded head. His arms were tightly manacled behind his back. One of his small dark eyes opened as they tugged him past me – it had the same hopeless look as I'd seen in many a bullock on the way to be slaughtered in Smithfield. He was followed by a terrified, curly-haired younger man, dressed in smart black clothes.

The jailer prodded me and I shuffled up, my big coat sleeves tucked up as usual, one hand in my pocket, holding my hat in the other. I looked in vain for a dirty red beard, but there was no sign of Fagin, nor the big-wig lawyer he'd promised me - I guessed he knew I'd never grass on my mates. The only face I recognized was that copper's nark, Noah Claypole, or Bolter, or whatever he called himself, leaning over the rail. Two wizened old magistrates were seated above me; one was signing the sentences he had just pronounced, the other looked to be fast asleep.

I decided to put on a show: "Why am I placed in this here disgraceful situation?" I demanded in a superior tone.

"Hold your tongue, will you?" hissed the jailer, who wasn't such a bad fellow really.

"What is this?" inquired the magistrate, laying aside his pen. He had a particularly sour face, and peered at me through his spectacles as if I were something exceptionally unwholesome.

"A pick-pocketing case, your worship."

"Has the boy ever been here before?

"He ought to have been, a many times," replied the jailer. "He has been pretty well everywhere else. I know him well, your worship."

"Oh! You know me, do you?" I cried, pretending to make a note on my sleeve, although at that time I couldn't write or read. "Very good. That's a case of deformation of character, anyway."

There was laughter in the gallery and a cry for silence, which woke the other magistrate.

"Now then, where are the witnesses?" he queried, blinking his watery eyes.

"That's right," I added. "Where are they? I should like to see 'em." I was banking on there not being any. I'd lifted the snuff-box months ago outside Drury Lane - I was certain no-one had seen me. That would mean only a summary conviction and I'd be back with the boys within six weeks.

A parish constable stepped into the witness box and identified me as the young person he'd seen lift a handkerchief from a gentleman's gropus*.

"I only borrowed the wiper to blow my nose. I put it back as soon as I'd used it," I protested.

"Silence!" said the clerk.

The constable further testified that on arresting me, he'd found upon my person, a silver snuff-box with a gentleman's name engraved on it, and pointed out some cove as being willing to swear that he was its rightful owner. I knew then that I was being stitched up - he wasn't the gent I'd stolen it from, I'd never seen the rogue before.

"Have you anything to ask this witness, boy?" said old sour face.

"I wouldn't abase myself by descending to hold no conversation with him."

"Have you anything to say at all?"

I folded my arms and shook my head, in what I thought was a heroic pose: if I was going to be sent down, I wanted to ensure my going would be noticed.

"Do you hear his Worship ask if you've anything to say?" inquired the jailer, nudging me with his elbow.

"I beg your pardon," I replied, looking up with an air of distraction. "Did you redress yourself to me, my fellow?"

The whole gallery was now in fits. It was then that I saw him - scribbling away, his long brown hair falling over his forehead, little more than a boy himself. He looked up and caught my eye and seemed to see right through me. It was as if he were reading my very soul. "Who's the cove what's scribbling?" I whispered to the jailer.

"Goes by the name of Dickens. Comes here most afternoons, takes down the most bloodthirsty and beguiling stories. They say he can put it to paper as fast you can talk."*

I continued staring at him and hardly heard the clerk's wheedling voice passing sentence: "It is therefore ordered and adjudged by this Court that you be transported upon the seas, beyond the seas, to such place as His Majesty, on the advice of his Privy Council, shall think fit to direct and appoint, for the term of your natural life."

I fought back my tears and decided to make one final show of defiance. I'd seen the Newgate Calendar enacted in many a penny gaff,* and always fancied one day I'd be portrayed as one of its legends, alongside Dick Turpin and Moll Cutpurse; but I suspect I might have done it specially for young Dickens. I turned to those two selfish old bastards, fearfully sniffing their nosegays of rosemary:

"You do well to look frightened: I won't show you mercy, not a ha'porth of it. *You'll* pay for this, my fine fellers. I wouldn't be you for anything! I wouldn't go free now, if you was to fall on your knees and beg me. Here, carry me off to prison! Take me away!"

I stuck out my tongue; the jailer clipped me round the ear, quite gently, and led me off by the collar. I looked back at Dickens, he was still scribbling. I thought I saw a trace of pity on his face.

And that's the last mention Charles Dickens gives me. At the end of *Oliver Twist* he tells what happened to almost everyone: even minor characters, who no one gives a toss about - but me - the most engaging character in his entire god-damn book - not a bloody word! Apart from an afterthought in the very last chapter, when he says the chief remaining members of Fagin's gang died far from home. Well, he was wrong there if he meant me. I asked him to amend it - but he thought his bloody books were sacrosanct like the Bible, and wouldn't change or add another sentence. Not for me at any rate.

The jailer took me down to a cellar below the court where the prisoners were waiting before being carted off There was a grate high up in the wall and I could just make out heads and faces looking down, crying their farewells to friends and loved ones. I didn't bother to look up – I didn't suppose anyone would come for me.

"Dodger! Dodger!"

You could have knocked me down with a feather. I squinted into the pale sunlight and saw my comrade in thievery, good old Charley Bates, with tears streaming down his face. Despite the heavy shackle round my ankle I leapt up and clung to the bars, polishing King George's iron with my eyebrows.

"Don't you worry Charley, they won't keep me long."

"It ain't you I'm weeping for Dodger - it's Nance. Bill's gone and murdered her."

"What?" I couldn't believe it. "Murdered? Nance murdered? Never!" Across Bow Street I could see the Theatre Royal, where only a few weeks before, Nance and me had pissed ourselves laughing at Grimaldi playing Squire Bugle in *Mother Goose.* I could still hear Nance's jolly voice joining in the chorus of Hot Codlins, Grimaldi's favourite ditty:

'And this little old woman who codlins sold
Though her codlins were hot, she felt herself cold
So to keep herself warm, she thought it not sin
To fetch for herself a quart of gin…'

But there was more. Lots more. Charley rattled on. I could hardly take it all in: "Fagin's been taken - they say he'll swing within the week. Me and Tom Chitling only made our 'lucky' by climbing up the chimney. We waited till it was dark and went down to Jacob's Island where we knew Toby Crackit was hiding out. But then Bill came, followed by his dog, and then hundreds of people, running and shouting with lights and ladders. Bill tried to escape by the roof; he had a rope around his neck. He tied it to a chimney stack, but he fell and hanged his bloody self with his own noose. He swung outside the window, right before me. His eyes bulged and he pissed himself. I'll never forget it. There was such excitement when they cut him down, that even though they took Tom and Toby, no one bothered about me. I crept away. Bill's dog followed me - he's here with me now - I suppose he's got no one else to follow now Bill's gone…."

Yes, I know that Dickens says the dog hit his head against a stone and dashed out his brains. Is that likely? Have you ever heard of a dog doing that? No, there was a lot Dickens didn't know. He got most of that story from Fagin's trial and the papers and the things I told him later, but I swear Bill's dog, Bull's-Eye, lived and remained with Charley till the end of his days. That dog, despite its ferocity was one of us. He'd never grass on his mates - he wouldn't so much have barked in the witness box, not if you tied him up in one and left him there without vittles for a fortnight.

Charley's news took away what strength I had; I let go of the bars and dropped to the dirty straw on the stone floor

There was no transport sailing for Botany Bay for a month or two, so I was temporarily ensconced in Newgate. Back at Fagin's, I would sketch the ground-plan of Newgate on the table with a piece of chalk, calling it the 'family hotel' for a laugh. But that was just swank. I'd no idea what a terrible place it was. It stunk of stale piss and worse. Fagin had always promised me beer every day and money in my pocket if ever I went inside - said I would be kept like a gentleman. He was probably lying but I knew he couldn't do that now. I cursed myself for picking up Oliver that morning in Barnet. He was the reason everything had gone wrong. If Bill had taken me on the raid to Chertsey, I wouldn't have panicked, and we would have come back safe with our swag. If it wasn't for bleedin' Nolly Twist, poor Nance would be alive and so would Bill; and me and the boys would still have been picking pockets for Fagin. The enormity of my sentence began to dawn on me - sent to the end of the earth for the length of my natural life. I felt I'd nothing to live for.

On my third miserable night in Newgate I was awakened by a key turning in the lock, the door creaked open slowly and a dark form, wrapped in a long, hooded cloak, stood against the dim light in the corridor. I couldn't see a face. Something about it filled me with dread.

"Are you what they call the Dodger?" it whispered, in a dry, dead voice.

"What if I am?"

"Shut your lip and follow me."

I got up, with my legs trembling beneath me, and shuffled along, following the shadow down dank, dark corridors. Slime dripped from the very walls. From behind many doors we passed came screams, lamentations, snatches of sad songs, or cries of pain. It was as if I'd been summoned by a demon, who was conducting me to the depths of hell. He spoke never a word as he opened three strong gates with his big ring of keys and led the way into Newgate's very bowels. We descended two flights of slippery stone stairs before he finally stopped and rapped four times on a rusty iron door. I caught sight of his hand in the faint glow of a lantern. It was white as a maggot. The door was unbolted from within, and there, sitting on an old mattress, his grizzled red beard torn and twisted into knots, a dirty bandage round his head, rocking himself from side to side as if saying one of his strange Hebrew prayers, was my old master, Fagin. The two turnkeys who were with him looked fearfully at my escort. He beckoned with a thin white finger and, without a word, they got up and followed him into the passage outside. Fagin and me were alone. We stared at each other, contemplating the fate that awaited us both. He was the nearest thing to a father I'd ever known, vile and ugly as he was.

"You was always my top-sawyer, my best hand, Dodger," he said at last in a low voice. "I gave Blacknell the last piece of gold I had to bring you."

"Blacknell?"

"The chief cuffin* of all Newgate - never sees the light of day. A bigger villain than you or I, my dear."

"Uncommon of you to spend money like that."

He gave a little chuckle before the mournful look returned to his face. "How did this happen, my dear? Eh? No one could touch you, Jack, or come near you on any scent."

"I got careless. I'd a silver sneeze box on me when they took me. Lifted it weeks before. Kept it for my personal use - as you know, I'm partial to snuff."

"You was worth fifty boxes, my dear."

"Well, now I'm lagged for life."

"Life...Life is a wonderful thing, Dodger. As long as you have life you have hope." A bluebottle buzzed out of the chamber pot and flew up into the darkness of the ceiling where it escaped through some long forgotten hole. Fagin watched it enviously and a tear glistened in his blood-shot eye, "I'm an old man - an old man. What rights have they to butcher me?"

"They say you told Bill to butcher Nance."

"I never did, my dear. I told him not to be too violent. I told him to be crafty, not too bold. I only wanted him to frighten her so she wouldn't peach us all. If only you had been there, Dodger, you would have stopped her. You would have made her see reason." A distant church bell chimed eleven. He gnawed his grimy knuckles and looked at the fetid straw on the floor. "I'll swing in the morning. Rabbis, priests of my people, came to pray with me; but I cursed them and sent them away. I have no religion. I cannot pray. But I have something I must tell you before I go." He sipped some water from the cup by his bed. "It was just a few months after I found you, my dear, about three years past. I was waiting for Bill in the parlour of the Cripples, in my usual place, in the high-backed settle in the corner. A soldier came in - a poor soldier, his uniform was patched and torn, he only had money for half a pint of ale, although I could tell he had a thirst for more. He told Barney, the waiter, he was looking for a boy - a boy named Jack from Barnet Workhouse."

"What?" My heart skipped a beat. I'd never let on to Fagin, but I'd often scudded off to Barnet, in the hope that one day my father would come back, looking for me. That was the reason I was in Barnet the morning I found Oliver Twist. I'd always felt a grudge against my mother for deserting me, but my father, in my juvenile imagination, had been something of a hero. But many boys were called Jack. "Did the boy have any other name?"

"No. Only Jack - the name the workhouse had given him. The soldier said the boy had been apprenticed to a sweep, but had run off with gypsies."

My heart was now beating fast. I remembered the horror of the hot, choking chimneys and the cruel bugger of a sweep that forced me up them. I still bore the scars of the even crueller beatings the gypsies gave me.

"Somehow he'd found out the gypsies lost the boy at Bartholomew's Fair."

"Bartlemey's Fair?"

"Yes. Where I found you, my dear."

That had to be the final proof. "What did you say to him?"

"I did not say a word."

I stared at him in disbelief. "Why ever not?"

"I didn't want to lose you. You were so promising Dodger, a real fine wirer*, you were worth thousands of pounds to me and the soldier was poor. He made no offer of a reward. He said he was sailing to Botany Bay with his regiment and did not intend to return. He was going to make a new life there and wanted to see the boy before he left."

I was close to tears. "What was his name?"

"He did not say, my dear."

"What did he look like?"

"You know me Dodger, my dear. I was on business; I do not like to be observed. My head was tucked in the darkest corner, behind the curve of the settle - I did not see his face - only the frayed sleeves of his tunic and his scarred hands." He tapped my knee with his dirty fingers, "Who knows, eh? - Perchance he was not your father, but these last days it has troubled me. That was why I sent for you. Maybe you will find him when you get to Botany Bay."

"You're a damned old villain, Fagin. Have you ever done a good thing?"

"Did I not take care of you boys? Where would you all have been without me? I gave you your education, my dear. When you are a great man in Botany Bay, Dodger, as great man you will be, remember that. You will show yourself Dodger and not disgrace your old pals and teachers - the world will know what a clever fellow you are - one day they'll say: 'You should have known the Dodger, my dear, you should have known the Dodger.'"

I hated him at that moment: his fawning and flattery no longer affected me. I wanted to stab him in the nearest region to his mean old heart. He'd no son or family but there was something I knew he held more precious than blood.

"What happened to your box of pretty things? What you was keeping for your old age?"

His dirty face whitened. "Do not talk of them. They are my secret."

"Are they still stowed under the trap in the top room?"

"You knew?" His ugly old face was distorted in fear.

"We all knew," I laughed. "Don't you fret yourself on that score. One of the boys will have been back and lifted them by now."

He didn't reply but his eyes betrayed something that I couldn't then understand. We sat together in painful silence for a few more minutes before Blacknell appeared like a ghost, to summon me away. I didn't say goodbye. I'd a few shillings sewn into the left sleeve of my coat - that was why I always had 'em turned up. I managed to unpick them as we made our way back. As Blacknell stopped at the door of my cell I opened my palm. The silver shone in the dim light.

"Let me see him hang."

I saw Blacknell's face for the first time. It was as thin and white as a skull. He took the money in his claw-like hand but said not a word.

Next morning, just before nine, Blacknell came and led me, in silence, to a window on an upper floor overlooking the Debtor's Gate. Just outside stood what we used to call a 'top-up fair' - a makeshift gallows with a collapsible platform. A strong barrier, painted black, had been thrown across the road to break the pressure of the huge crowd, of all sorts and ages, waiting behind it, eating, drinking like there was no tomorrow. Even the hangman was full up to the knocker - the mob were passing him up bottles and flagons as if it were a wedding. When Saint Paul's clock struck the hour there was a moment of silence anticipation before the gate opened and Fagin was led out, looking very small. The mob gave a mighty cheer and surged over the barrier chucking stones, dead cats and horse dung. They were never averse to throwing abuse and worse at a Jew, whoever he was. Fagin sent out cry after cry that penetrated even Newgate's massive walls. He shook his fist and spat on his tormentors and struggled with the power of desperation as the screws dragged him towards the crossbeam and the rope. The hangman pinched and prodded him, like he were dead meat already.

"What's he doing that for?" I asked.

Blacknell made a dry, cruel sound, which may have been a chuckle. "To guess his weight for the length of rope required. If he guesses right the old rogue will die quickly - but that fool is too drunk. He'll guess wrong."

Blacknell was right: Fagin danced in the noose for several minutes before he finally choked. I'd wasted my money - it gave me no satisfaction.

As I turned away I caught sight of young Dickens, in the midst of the mob, still writing in his little book............

I learned, years later, Fagin did one good deed on that last morning of his wicked life. He was visited in his cell by Oliver and Mr Brownlow, the old cove whose pocket I picked outside the bookshop in Clerkenwell. Brownlow begged Fagin to tell him where he'd hidden the papers that would help Oliver claim his inheritance. Fagin whispered in Oliver's ear they were in a little canvas bag, in a little hole up the chimney in the top front room. Now, he didn't have to tell him that did he? I've often wondered why he did.

2. The Hulk

A few days after Fagin danced the Paddington Frisk, Newgate became so overcrowded that they decided to send me and a pack of fellow unfortunates down river to a prison ship - an old hulk - until the next transport sailed. It was December - near Christmas, although a fat lot we knew about Christmas then. They say Dickens invented Christmas - old Fezziwig's Ball and all that Christmas Carol muck-load of cobblers. I knew Scrooge well - remained a miserable old bugger to the end of his days.

As dawn broke, we convicts were led to a closed wagon in the courtyard, our prison numbers round our necks like condemned cattle - I still remember mine - 4102. I made sure I had a place by the door so I could get a last glance of good old London before I left it.

"Move your arse, you little devil or I'll cut your throat."

I looked up to see a giant towering above me. It took me a moment to recognize the fierce man in the dock at Bow Street. He now looked so frightening that even Bill wouldn't have wanted to cross him. His clothes were filthy, his shoes were broken and his head was shaved, making him even uglier. I shifted along the wooden bench as he flopped down beside me. Then, as the jailers were attaching his heavy leg-iron to the wagon's chain, he suddenly spied his adversary the younger man being dragged towards the wagon. The giant lunged forward as fiercely as old Bull's-Eye after a bitch.

"Damn you - you villain - you liar - I'll have your heart and liver!"

"Don't put me near him! He'll murder me." He cowered in fear: I'd rarely seen anyone so terrified.

"I'll smash your lying face in. You devil! You get away with seven years and they've given me fourteen...You're a liar born and a liar you'll die!"

His big scarred hands were around the other's throat as a soldier's musket butt smashed on his skull. He slumped senseless beside me as his intended victim was taken to safety at the far end of the wagon. The door was slammed and bolted and we lurched forward. Through the dirty glass of the small round window I could just make out the Old Bailey, Ludgate Hill and Blackfriars, my old familiar haunts. I looked in vain for Charley or some of the other boys, but it was too early - the streets were deserted and lifeless. We jolted our way down to Puddle Dock where a large wherry awaited us. The jailers unchained us and pulled us from the wagon and handed us over to the charge of a fresh-faced Navy Lieutenant. Armed red-coated marines hauled my still stunned companion aboard and pushed him and the rest of us, eighteen all told, on to a narrow bench that went the length of the open boat. We were made secure by chains which ran through the shackles on our ankles. My short legs dangled in mid-air, but I still could feel the icy water through the planks.

It was a grey, miserable morning - 'rimy' was Dickens' word. The river was the colour of lead, as a dozen stout seamen rowed us downstream with the Lieutenant at the tiller and the muskets of four marines trained at our breasts. The river was swollen, and became a foaming flood as we shot beneath a small arch of old London Bridge, which was indeed on the point of falling down. Workmen were busy sinking the piles of John Rennie's new one. I smelt the stink of the fish in Billingsgate and gazed at the Dome of St Paul's and then the smoke-blackened walls of the Tower as they disappeared round the bend of the river, and wondered if I'd ever see or smell 'em again. I didn't believe I ever would. We passed thick forests of masts of innumerable tall ships anchored in the Pool, and the stacks of countless warehouses, full of the world's riches which I thought then I'd never enjoy. The oars rattled in the rowlocks as the sailors pulled us past the smoke of the lead mills, the stench of the tanneries, and the warm malt-laden air of the breweries. I screwed round my head and saw Jacob's Island on the south bank, surrounded by its muddy ditch and its ramshackle wooden bridges. I spied the empty roofless building - our old hideout where Bill copped it - I even made out the chimney stack where he'd dangled, watering his breeches. We rowed past crumbling, filthy, tenements, half tumbling into the slimy waters of old Father Thames. Repulsive and loathsome some may have called it - but it was home to me. The nearest beings to friends I had ever known lived here, and now I was leaving it all, on my way to the far end of the earth. I thought of the poor soldier, looking for the boy from Barnet. What hope did I have of ever finding him? I put my head down into the collar of my coat and pretended not to cry.

Despite the cold, the easy motion of the oars sent me to sleep for most of the morning. When I woke I found myself leaning against the rough woolen coat of the fearsome man next to me. He'd recovered his senses and had tied an old rag around his bloody head. He was surveying the bleak marshlands around us, sniffing the air like an animal. His small dark eyes flickered, noting every detail - every house - every little hamlet - every lonesome church. I'd never seen country like it. It was a dark flat wilderness, intersected with dykes and mounds; the only signs of life were scattered miserable-looking sheep and cattle. He became aware of me staring at him.

"I wish I was a frog; or an eel." There was a strange click in his throat.

Suddenly a pistol cracked out behind me. I saw a dark hulk laying a little way from the mud of the shore: the Lieutenant was giving warning of our approach. The hulk was moored fast by massive rusty chains, each link bigger than me: it looked as much a forlorn and helpless prisoner as we were. The masts were stumps, the gun ports covered with iron grills, the figure-head unpainted and battered. A skirt of sewage and waste floated on the water around her. I spied a white bundle bobbing amongst the stinking flotsam.

The grizzled sailor nearest me turned his head and chewed on a plug of black tobacco. "Poor bugger won't sink. Too mean to waste a cannon ball." My stomach tightened with fear as I made out the outline of a corpse sewn into a hammock. My informant spat into the murky water: "The old *Indefatigable*. An unlucky ship. She was a foul old wreck when Nelson was a midshipman - look at her now."

The ship stunk of bilge - it was seeping out of her ancient ill-sealed timbers. Above I could see a swarm of men lining the ship's sides - red coats of soldiers mingling with jailers' black and gray. A ladder was dropped down; the Lieutenant navigated our wherry alongside it. Our shackles were unchained and we were prodded up by the long bayonets of the marines.

The wherry, as if reluctant to stay near so foul a place, was already on its way back upstream as the last of us clambered aboard. Soldiers, directed by a fat, florid-cheeked sergeant, forced us into an enclosed pen in the middle of the deck. Stout oak walls towered above me - at least five feet high with sharp iron spikes embedded on the top. An open hatch led to the dark quarters below. No sooner were we all in, when the gate of the pen was slammed shut and a corporal quickly scribbled our numbers in a tally book. An odd stomping sound preceded the appearance of a wooden-legged man in an old tri-cornered hat on the quarter deck above.

The sergeant sprang to attention: "Silence, you rum culls! Bow your heads in the presence of your Commander!"

The one-legged man surveyed us coldly. His naval coat was worn and green with age; his face was blotched and swollen with drink. He cleared his throat and spat before he spoke. "My name is Captain Wentworth." His speech was slurred. "I have commanded worthy ships and have led brave men into battle for the honour of England and her King. I lost a leg at Copenhagen and I would gladly lose the other before I'd allow a criminal to escape this sorry vessel. Some of you are bound for transportation - England is well rid of you - but most of you villains will serve your sentence aboard this hulk. You and your labour are the property of the Crown. When you are not working you will be kept below, chained together, six at a time. The hatches are secured fast by cross bars, bolts and locks. You will be summoned to a daily roll call and eat your meals within this enclosed area - yesterday a felon attempted to climb the wall during breakfast. The fool was shot and his body rots in the river. Never forget Sergeant Syper has armed guards posted day and night."

The red-cheeked sergeant nodded enthusiastically.

"You are vermin-infected jail sweepings," the Captain continued, wiping his nose with a blue handkerchief, "but I will allow no vermin here. Vermin spread disease and disease spreads nowhere quicker than aboard a ship. There are another hundred and fifty like you below, but this hulk will be kept as sweet as any parlour in England." His bloated lips twisted into a cruel smile. "Strip off your filthy rags."

"Strip off your filthy rags!" Sergeant Syper repeated with great enthusiasm.

Shirts and coats were easy enough, but a long and complicated process began as each man struggled to pull his breeches over the iron on his leg. When they were stripped naked, Wentworth watched approvingly from above as the soldiers threw buckets of icy Thames water over thin and dirty bodies. The discarded rags were then burnt in an open brazier on the deck, as the Quartermaster handed the convicts coarse linen shirts, canvas trousers and gray jackets made of thin kersey. The men were shivering with cold, hugging their shuddering bodies as if they were holding themselves together.

The fierce man was toward the end of the line. When the Quartermaster came for his clothes he pushed him away. "I'll keep my own coat. It stinks but it's warm. Those garments ain't fit for winter. We'll freeze to death."

"You'll be flogged on the iron if you refuse." Sergeant Syper pointed to a cruel-looking triangle. "Shall he have a dozen lashes to warm him up, Captain?"

The Captain ignored him. "Heavy wool attracts lice, and lice encourage typhus. You'll be better cold than dead. Strip, you rogue." His left hand began to tremble - he stuffed it in the breast of his coat, like a peg-legged Napoleon.

A soldier prodded the fierce man with his bayonet until a spot of blood appeared on his dark hairy chest. Two muskets were trained on him before he reluctantly stripped off his clothes. He extracted a small, black book from his pocket and held it carefully in his veiny hand as he endured the indignity of the icy water. His entire body was covered with gruesome scars, welts and bruises. Now and then he glowered across the deck at his adversary, the younger man, who seemed only too keen to rid himself of his silk shirt, well-cut black jacket, breeches and boots, as if seeking safety in the anonymity of the grey convicts' uniform.

"Don't burn those. Pass them to my steward."

The Captain had taken note of the quality of the young man's attire. The Quartermaster shot a knowing look at Sergeant Syper before grudgingly handing the finery to a surly man at the Captain's side. Wentworth snatched the shirt and felt the quality of the silk between his fingers as he disappeared into the poop.

I'd managed to make myself as inconspicuous as possible and eventually all were stripped of their own clothes but me. I still had a few pennies, my special pack of cards, a knife and a bent nail hidden in the lining of my coat, and was desperate not to lose them. I knew a hidden knife would be punished with the lash, but I'd heard what happened to boys when men were starved of women; I'd met mollies and 'fluters' aplenty in London, and I meant to protect my youthful virtue as long as I could.

A soldier with very few teeth pulled me forward. "What about him?"

The Quartermaster frowned down on me. "He's too small to fit anything we have. Just soak him in Thames water. It'll be the cleanest water he's ever washed in."

I gritted my teeth, but was thankful, as I was drenched in icy brown water.

The fierce man had become quiet and subdued, but as the soldiers began to marshal us towards the hatches the young man passed in front of him, averting his eyes. At once he sprang forward again, with savage energy. "I'll kill you, you dog! I'll drag you by the hair to hell!"

"Help me! He'll murder me!"

The younger man turned his head imploringly towards the sergeant, whilst his opponent furiously pummeled him about the face, yelling all the while: "Turn your eyes and look at me. I defy you to look at me! That's how it was when we were tried together in the dock. You never looked at me."

The sergeant nodded and four soldiers threw themselves upon the assailant and pulled him down on the deck where they gave him a thorough kicking with their heavy boots, before manacling his arms behind him and throwing him down the steps to the prison deck below. He was sprawled in an untidy heap when the rest of us followed him down into the blackness. If the ship smelt foul from the outside it was nothing to the stench below - a mixture of stinking bodies and the acid, gut-wrenching smell of piss and spew. In the dim light I could see large cradles, like flat table-tops, suspended from the low roof running the entire length of the ship. On each cradle lay about half a dozen men; the dampness from their breath shone from the beams above in the light of the sergeant's lantern. Heads were raised and dull eyes looked up, inspecting the latest arrivals to their hell.

The sergeant began to count us off in groups of six, whilst an old grey-haired soldier threaded a heavy chain through the ankle shackles, and the Quartermaster handed each convict a thin blanket.

"You'll be fettered at eight every evening and unfettered each morning at six. In the night you use the bucket - the rest of the time you can squat at the heads at the bow."

The fierce man, still stunned by his latest beating, was dragged to his feet as his leg iron was threaded on the chain. I thought the fight had been finally beaten out of him until a soldier pulled the terrified object of his hatred towards him. Immediately he bared his teeth and strained on the chain with all his strength.

The other turned frantically towards the sergeant, his handsome features distorted with terror. "Please I beg you! Don't put me next to him. He'll murder me in my sleep."

Sergeant Syper nodded. "We don't want trouble over Christmas. Chain 'em separately - keep the buggers apart."

Each cradle had a chain stapled fast to the timbers of the ship, which was padlocked to another iron staple on the deck. The old soldier fettered the fierce man to the cradle nearest the stairs, whilst the younger man was taken to the far end at the prow. Soon all were chained up and accounted for, apart from me. I hung in the shadows, hoping to be overlooked, but the old soldier had sharp eyes.

"What about him? The little 'un?"

"Chain him next to the ugly brute." Syper smiled maliciously. "Perhaps he'll eat him."

The Quartermaster laughed. "I know what I'll be eating. Look lively, tomorrow's Christmas Eve, I've got us extra drink and grub tonight."

The sergeant clapped his hands. "Musical glasses! The top of mine to the foot of yours." They departed cheerily to join the others in their warm quarters above.

The grey-haired soldier lifted me upon the cradle and locked me next to the bleeding man, who sat like a trussed turkey. His head drooped and his arms were manacled cruelly behind his back. The old man looked at him and quietly unlocked the manacles: "You'll not get very far with that ankle bracelet."

I sensed he might be a friend and inquired, "Were you ever acquainted with a soldier from Barnet?"

"Can't say that I was. Knew a sergeant from Barnsley though - poor sod had his head blown off at Salamanca." He put a blanket round my shoulders and went up to join his comrades. For a while all was quiet as the sounds of comfort and merriment, sounds we all were once familiar with, seeped through the thin, worn timbers of the wreck.

"When do we eat?" asked one of the new arrivals.

"You'll get a lump of rock-hard salt beef and a spoonful of pease in the morning, before they take us off to work on the dykes." A soft voice came out of the darkness. "But chances are they won't take us working tomorrow - being Christmas Eve."

Then there was silence. The convicts seemed dead and drained of life. Perhaps they were remembering Christmases past and dreading Christmases yet to come. I wrapped the thin, damp blanket around myself and yearned for the smell of Fagin's sausages, a pipe of black tobacco and the sharp taste of a piece of Double Gloucester. I fell asleep and dreamt of rabbit pie with bones so tender they melted in my mouth, washed down with a flagon of gin and hot water.

I was awoken by the shaking of the chain on my foot. In the gloom I could just make out the fierce man silently pulling on it with all his strength. His ankle was dark and wet with blood. He had the instincts of an animal and knew I was watching. "You young dog. What fat cheeks you have. Darn me if I couldn't eat them." He growled softly.

I hoped he was joking.

He raised his head and listened to the sounds of drinking and revelry still continuing above: "If I were free of this chain I could escape this god forsaken hulk. I know these marshes. I was born on the Essex side." The click was back in his voice.

"How would you get to the shore? You'd drown with the weight of that iron."

"It's low tide this time of night. I told you, I know this river. It's not more than a fifty yard swim to the Kent shore. I'm a good swimmer and diver. I'd make it."

I don't know why I did it. Up to that point I'd never pitied anyone apart from Nance in my entire life. But I fumbled in the bottom of the lining of my coat and found my bent nail. I don't think he even noticed as I slipped it in the lock and felt for the lever just like Fagin had taught me - he always said I'd make a fine cracksman - I felt the lever spring back and carefully pulled the chain free. The leg iron was a different matter - it would need a strong blacksmith's file at least.

He still didn't seem to realise what I'd done. He said nothing as he rubbed life back into his bloody ankle. He looked around, made sure all the rest were asleep, and then crept towards the pitch darkness at the prow. I silently freed myself of the chain and followed in his wake. He pushed open a door and we were standing in the cold night air, at the very front of the ship, on a plank with three squat holes. He looked upwards and checked no sentry was watching from the forecastle above. He fumbled in his pocket and took out something small and black and shiny.

"Swear on this book you won't dare to say a word. If you do, I'll tear your liver out and eat it."

I think it was the first holy tract I'd ever touched. It was smooth and warm from the heat of his body. My mouth was dry. I could hardly whisper "I swear."

He stowed the book back carefully, gave me one more dreadful look, before he took in a huge breath of air, clasped his hand tightly over his bent and broken nose, and dropped through the nearest hole. There was a quiet splash. The weight of his leg iron took him deep below the dark surface, it was a long time until his head bobbed up about twenty yards from the ship, and he began to strike out strongly with his arms. I watched until he disappeared in the cold mist. If I could have swum I might have gone with him.

I cursed myself for what I'd done. Fagin had taught me never to be soft - only think of number one. I'd risked being flogged on that fearsome triangle and I hadn't got a bleedin' thing to show for it. I felt quite ashamed and went back inside to return to my cradle.

Suddenly a hand reached out of the blackness and held my wrist in a frantic grip. Another hand pulled down me head by me hair and a voice whispered in my ear: "What are you doing free? You've got a lock picker. Unchain me, else I'll yell so loud I'll bring that sergeant and all his men down on you."

It was the younger man. He'd just woken up and hadn't seen me pass by him with his assailant. He twisted my wrist so that it hurt: "That brute will kill me if I stay here. I'll see you flogged till the flesh is cut from your back if you don't give me that key."

I thought quickly. If he called down the guards I was a goner for sure. My only hope was to get rid of him quickly. All at once the solution was as plain as the nose on my face.

"Can you swim?"

He nodded.

"You can drop down through the shit hole - it's only a few yards to shore."

With that I stuck my nail in his lock, unchained him and led him outside. He looked at the hole and the murky, cold, water beneath and seemed to have second thoughts. I wanted him out of the way. If he knew I'd helped the other bloke escape - he'd grass on me for sure.

"I was born near here. It's low tide. If you can swim; it's easy pickings. Only twenty yards and you can wade the rest. They can't keep that rogue off you forever."

He nodded fearfully but still seemed undecided. I made up his mind for him by giving him a sharp push in the back. I hoped he'd sink where he'd dropped, but he was a floater. He bobbed up and splashed off frenziedly in the same direction as the man he was so desperate to get away from. I began to see the funny side of it.

I went inside and crept back to my cradle. I'd already decided on my story: the fierce man had a lock picker and released himself and the other bloke whilst I was asleep. I pulled my hat down tight on my head, curled up in a ball and tried to keep warm.

The soft voice in the dark had been right. No one came to unchain us at six. The convicts slumbered in their cold sleep as the faint winter dawn crept through the cracks between the hatches. I began to make out where the soft voice had come from - a tousled blonde head sticking out of a grimy blanket on the cradle on the other side of the aisle. I wondered how much he'd seen or heard. After another half an hour or so he got up and began to pee noisily in his bucket. He was young, about twenty-four or five, with round red cheeks like apples. He saw me watching him and grinned.

"Good morning, you young villain. What have you done with your pal?"

I feigned surprise and looked around. "Gone has he? There's a lucky thing! He was the devil himself. He scared the shit out of me."

"I thought I saw you going to the heads with him in the middle of the night. I couldn't understand how you could have got free."

My story was shot to pieces - he'd seen everything. I changed tack.

"He had a lock picker. Forced me to go outside with him - said he'd murder me else. Unlocked his pal as well. That fight was all a sham - they'd planned it all along. They both went over the side together and swam."

"You better have a story to explain why you didn't report it as soon as they were gone. What's your trade?"

"Pickpocket. I'd scorn to be anything else."

"What's your name?"

"Jack Dawkins, but people call me Dodger. The Artful One. You'd have to get up very early in the morning to catch me, indeed you'd have to go to bed with your boots on."

He laughed. "Well you're not so Artful that you end up in this hell hole."

"Don't fret your eyelids on that score." I fumbled at the bottom of my coat lining and took out my special pack of cards. "Cut any way you like for the first picture card at a shilling a time."

He cut low three times. I turned over a Queen, a King and a Jack.

He laughed. "I owe you three shillings, if I had 'em. I'll pay you when I get to Botany Bay."

"I'll want guarantees. What's your name and trade?"

"Warne - Thomas Warne. They call me Warnie. Hampshire fisherman, turned smuggler. Resisted the excise men. Sentenced to swing but was reprieved. Seven years transportation."

"So we're going to be shipmates on a long voyage to Hell."

"I hear it need not be so bad a place, if a man can keep his wits about him - use his nouse. You work for a few years, get your ticket of leave and then you're free to do what you wish. Even buy land if you have the cash. The important thing is not to lose your spirit like most of these here." He looked over his shoulders at the dead-eyed men slowly rising from their cradles. "You seem a bright lad, perhaps you and me should be pals."

I wasn't quite sure what he meant by 'pals' but gave him the benefit of the doubt. "Toor rul lol loo, gammon and spinach." I put out my hand.

He took it. "Right. Those two have probably drowned by now but if they haven't, we've got to give 'em as much time as possible before those fools up above realise they've gone. The buggers never count properly. It's more difficult for 'em if everyone keeps moving. I'll pass the word."

"Won't they grass?"

"No. It's the convicts' catechism to pray every escaper makes it. It gives 'em all a little victory."

He turned and began to whisper to a thin man next to him.

By the time the old soldier, looking weak and doddery, came down to unchain us, the entire deck was in the know. As he came to unlock my cradle Warnie pulled him by the sleeve. "Unchain me first, I've got to use the bucket or I'll befoul the deck. Mustn't do that. The Captain wants it kept as sweet as any English parlour."

The old soldier turned and failed to notice I was already unchained. I couldn't resist picking his back pocket but extracted no silk foogle*

- only a snotty rag. I'd put it back before Warnie's lock had been opened. As each cradle was freed the convicts swarmed about, never standing still, so that the old man failed to notice the two absentees. Another hour passed before more guards appeared to take the convicts assigned to cooking, on deck to prepare our breakfast. It was past mid-day and the pale watery sun was high above as we came up for our food. The beef was as rock-hard and salty as Warnie had predicted, but I was so hungry I devoured it as eagerly as fresh ham and mustard in a hot roll. As I ate I scoured the lonely and disconsolate landscape of the marshes, but the only sign of life was the turning sails of a distant windmill. I began to believe the fierce man may have got away.

We were locked below again. Another hour or so passed - the short winter's day was already drawing to its close. I went out to the squat hole to get a better view of the long black horizontal line of the shore. Warnie came out and squatted down beside me.

"Can't hide it much longer. We'll have the daily count at three bells. Old Wentworth is still sober at this hour - can't fool him."

A moment later the tattoo of a drum summoned us up above, where the soldiers pushed us into lines of twenty. I shuffled into the rear row next to Warnie, kept my head down, and studied the rings on the warped oak planks on the deck.

When the lines were in some sort of order Syper shouted: "Convicts ready for counting!"

Wentworth emerged from his cabin above, wearing his new silk shirt. He regarded us contemptuously with blood-shot eyes. "Proceed with the count, sergeant."

"Sir!" Syper's fleshy lips trembled as he counted, before finally proclaiming, "Five rows of twenty, plus fifteen and a boy, Captain."

Wentworth scowled and focused his eyes on the tally book in his hand.

"That's only one hundred and sixteen. I've got one hundred and eighteen listed here. There's two missing. Count the blaggards again, you damn'd fool!"

Syper repeated his count with even more trembling of his lips, but came up with the same result: "Five rows of twenty, plus fifteen and a boy, Captain."

Wentworth's florid face became the colour of an over-ripe plum: "Where are they in God's name? Search the ship. Look sharp."

Four soldiers trained their muskets upon us as the rest hurried below. It was becoming bitter cold.

In ten minutes Sergeant Syper returned: "The buggers have gone, Captain. There's not even a stink of 'em."

Wentworth's face darkened even more. "Give signal to the fort on shore. Convicts escaped. Fire the cannon."

Syper and three gunners ran to the prow, whilst a soldier climbed the rigging to a platform on the main mast with semaphore flags.

Wentworth now turned his wrath upon us. "You scum know how they escaped, but I promise you they will not get far, and you will stand here, without food or drink, waiting to welcome them back. All night and all tomorrow if need be."

With that the cannon began to boom out it's warning over the dark and gloomy land and the signaler waved his bright flags against the darkening sky.

We stood shivering, becoming colder and hungrier by the minute. We heard more cannon boom along both the Kent and Essex shores, and as the December night rapidly fell, beacons were lit like Christmas bonfires, warning the peaceful citizens of the dangerous felons in their midst. I stood next to Warnie and leant against him, finding some warmth through his thin kersey jacket. The guards watched us constantly from the quarterdeck deck above - there were no more than a dozen of them guarding a hundred and sixteen of us.

"Do you think we could rush 'em, Trumper?" Warnie whispered to the pale but good- looking convict to his left.

"We'd have to climb the wall and spikes with leg irons - they would shoot down half of us before we got near 'em."

After an hour or so Wentworth and Syper re-appeared above. Wentworth had a cup of steaming punch in his hand. The aroma wafted warm and sweet in the cold night air. "There will be patrols after them at first light. Which bank did they make for? Did they intend to swim to Kent or Essex? Tell me and I'll order the guards to feed you. I am a Christian man and it is Christmas Eve. A cup of hot punch for the first man to speak up."

There was silence. The convicts stood still in their lines.

"I command you in the King's name to tell me what you know. One of you dogs must have seen them unlock their chains. I'll flog the back off any man who knows and is keeping silent."

I was trembling with cold and fear. I cursed myself for what I'd done. I looked up at Warnie who was frowning pensively and thought for a moment he was going to grass on me.

"Why are you protecting those dogs?" Wentworth bellowed. "I'll make sure every man of you will suffer. There is no honour among such villains as you."

I swear that a star twinkled above at that moment and the convict in front of me began to sing in a frail but tuneful voice:

"God rest ye merry, gentlemen..."

"It's Trumper," Warnie whispered, "he used to sing in his church choir in Dorset."

"Let nothing you dismay..."

Wentworth looked as though he couldn't believe his own ears: "Silence!"

"Remember Christ our saviour
Was born on Christmas day,"

Syper's jaws wobbled in fury. "Stop that unholy row. Bow your heads. Show respect to the Captain."

But several voices were now singing:

"To save us all from Satan's power
When we were gone astray...."

"Stop this blasphemy!" Wentworth's face was black with rage. He looked like Satan himself: "This is sacrilege. I'll hear no more of this profanity!" He threw the remnants of his steaming punch over the head of the nearest convict and stomped back to his cabin as more voices joined in:

"O tidings of comfort and joy
Comfort and joy
O tidings of comfort and joy."

We weren't merry - we certainly weren't gentleman, but the words seemed appropriate to those lost men I stood among:

"Now to the lord sing praises
And you within this place
And with true love and brotherhood
Each other now embrace...."

'True love and brotherhood' I didn't know what that meant but I felt as if I really wanted it.

Syper seized a musket from one of the guards and fired it into the air: "Silence! In the King's name!"

"This holy tide of Christmas
All other doth deface...."

"I'll flog every dog among you!"

We knew nothing of comfort and joy but nearly every convict, even me, sang the last lines:

"O tidings of comfort and joy,
Comfort and joy
O tidings of comfort and joy!"

Trumper sang many carols that night but '*God rest you merry, gentlemen*' has always been my favourite.

We stood for hours, asleep on our feet, until the black sky above began to be shot with streaks of grey and angry red lines appeared in the east. I realised it was Christmas Day. We were numb with cold and damp from the heavy mist that rose from the river. I looked yearningly towards the smoke coming from lonely cottage chimneys and envied the folk inside being warmed by their fires, but the most agonising thing of all was the smell of frying bacon coming from the soldiers' quarters in the fo'c'sle.

Soon Syper appeared above wiping his greasy mouth with the back of his hand. The gate was unlocked and he entered our enclosure with two soldiers - their pieces cocked and leveled. Four other muskets were trained on us above. The Sergeant began to walk down our lines as if he were King bleedin' George himself, inspecting his guards at Windsor Castle.

"I'm taking a patrol ashore and we'll have those runaways back trussed and tightly bound sooner than they can count on. I promise you they'll never want to run away again. I'm going to pick the strongest of you to row the long boats. If I tap your back go to the bulwark and get down the steps lively, but mind you don't fall in the water, you'll sink like a millstone with those bracelets on your legs."

He seemed to find this funny. As he strutted along the line in front of me, like a great red turkey, I noticed his handcuffs hanging from the back of his belt above his wobbling bum. I had my lock picker clasped in my hand.

"For God's sake help me.... I'm so cold and famished...." I fell forward forcing the nail firmly into the handcuffs' lock. I spiked them as firmly as any French gun at Waterloo. It would take a good blacksmith to have them working again.

"He's got to have some food. He's only a kid." Warnie knelt down beside me, resting my head on his knee.

"Take him up above and give him a cup of gruel." Syper said reluctantly, watching his chosen convicts, shuffling with their heavy irons and clambering over the side. "Remember you dogs. You dip your oars and begin to row when I give the order!"

He didn't see the wink I gave Warnie.

Warnie took me to the galley and managed to get some hot gruel into his own empty belly. When we returned to the deck we found the convicts being locked in their quarters below.

"Only a handful of guards left to watch us - they're not taking any risks," Warnie whispered. But nobody seemed to bother with the two of us, as we watched the two boats being rowed towards a wooden hut at a landing place made of rough stakes and stones. In the distance we could see the scarlet coats of other soldiers fanning out into the dismal wilderness. Warnie spat into the wind. "Poor devils. Out there all night. With a light head and a light stomach, perishing of cold and want. The redcoats are forming a circle - they'll trap 'em in the middle." I hoped my spiking of the handcuffs might yet help the fierce man escape.

The hours passed the sky began to darken into yet another long night. A bitter sleet came rattling up the river on the east wind like the shudder of the dying day. The only sound was of faint sheep bells. I began to believe that perhaps he'd managed to get away.

Then all at once a long shout wafted across the black water: "Convicts! Runaways!"

We saw torches being lit and a melee of redcoats. Then we spied two grey figures being dragged from a ditch. Four soldiers fired their muskets twice into the air. Three cannon roared their response from the far-off fort. Warnie and I looked sorrowfully at each other: they'd been taken. We felt defeated. We watched as flickering lights came back to the wooden hut and the landing stage. Other lights followed after, dropping blotches of fire as they came. We could see the fugitives being pushed into the boats, their hands manacled behind their backs. Had someone managed to repair the handcuffs? Torches were flung blazing into the water and the boats made their way slowly back towards us.

Wentworth had appeared on the poop deck above and was observing all with a look of triumph on his face. As the first boat came alongside I saw the fierce man was more bloody and beaten than ever. He looked up and spied both me and Wentworth watching him.

"I wish to say something regarding this escape. I want no person laying under suspicion but me. I escaped from your black hell hole alone. I did it all myself and I could have got clear of those death cold flats - do you see any iron on my leg?" I looked and indeed his ankle was torn and bleeding but there was no fetter on it. "I could have got free if I hadn't made the discovery that he was free as well." He jerked his head towards the other boat where his enemy sat, with a flat, broad-brimmed, low-crowned, felt hat pulled over his face - as if to hide the terrible beating he'd suffered. I don't know where he got that hat from. "He's a gentleman, if you please, this villain. Now you've got this gentleman back through me. I couldn't let him go free, after what he's done to me and mine. I took him! I dragged him back to you. Mind that! I dragged him down like a bloodhound. I'd have swum back to you towing him by the hair and if I had died in that river you would have found him safe in my hold."

"You may well wish you had died in the river, Magwitch." Wentworth smirked. "You'll be tried again. You had fourteen years before - now I'll make sure you're transported for life."

I cursed myself once more. It was my fault. I should never have released him or let his enemy escape. Again I had been the cause of great misfortune...

3. The Enterprise

I'll skip the next month or so...nothing much happened on that rotten hulk, except that me and Warnie and Trumper got to know each other better.

Those were bad times in England. The gaols were full and overflowing what with the discontent and poverty. The Tories were so shit-scared of a revolution like they'd had in France, that they passed all these harsh laws to keep the people down - the poor were treated worse than they treat the Kaffirs out here in the Cape. The landowners had enclosed the commons and open fields, the farm labourers were driven off the land, and the weavers could no longer compete against the new machines. There was no work except in the factories, potteries and mines, where men, women and children worked underground from dawn to dusk in twelve-hour shifts, and the pay was such that you did little better than starve. Our life with old Fagey was paradise to that.

I stayed on the hulk when the convicts left each morning to work on the ditches, and helped the cook in the galley. The food was little better than pig's swill, but I was never hungry, and usually managed to sneak the odd extra piece of bread or meat for Warnie and Trumper.

One evening in early March, it was 1828, there was just a hint of spring in the air, Trumper, me and Warnie, were sharing a pipe full of the tobacco I'd managed to win from the cook. Thank God for those cards - I don't know where I'd have been without 'em.

"One of the soldiers told me we'll be taken to Tilbury tomorrow. There's a transport for us at last." Warnie looked over towards Essex. "It's a miserable looking place, but that may be the last we'll see of dear old England."

Trumper sighed sadly as he sucked on my pipe. He liked a smoke but I never ever saw him touch a drop of drink.

"What did a God-fearing man like you do to get lagged?" I asked him.

"Threshing machines brought it upon me. Worked on the same Dorset land as my father and his father before him. Me and Sarah and the little ones could live with full bellies on ten shillings a week. Then threshing machines came. They worked by steam and one machine could do the work of a hundred men. Lord Julian didn't need labourers any more. He dropped my wages to eight shillings and we could still just about get by. Then he dropped them down to six. That was too much. Bess begged me not to, but I joined Captain Swing."

"Who the hell is he?"

"He don't exist. It were a band of us that went round the county burning ricks and wrecking the threshing machines. Lord Julian came out with the Yeomanry and rode us down - it were as simple as that. I should have listened to Sarah. God knows what will happen to her and the boys."

His eyes filled with tears. We were silent for a while.

Warnie watched a small yacht sail past. "I had a little fishing boat in Langstone harbour. Farmer I knew persuaded me to take some wool out to a French ship off Selsey Bill - he didn't want to pay the duty on it. The cruel narks caught me coming back with a barrel of brandy. Seven years transportation." He took the pipe from Trumper and had a long pull on it. "But I'll never come back. I've no family here. Thank God I didn't get hammered for life with one girl - I liked 'em all. There's no future in this land if you ain't a gentleman. Besides," he chuckled, "Australia will be the finest country in the world - its people have all been picked by the finest judges in England."

"Won't you miss England?" I asked.

"I'll miss watching the cricket at Hambledon. Drinking a pot of ale outside the Bat and Ball on Broadhalfpenny Down."

"What's cricket? Some kind of flea?" I joked - I'd often seen the game being played on Golders' Green on my way to Barnet - but Warnie took me seriously.

"It's a game, Dodger. But it's an art more than a sport and Hambledon is its cradle. They don't have stuck-up toffs playing there as at the grand grounds in London. Just ordinary blokes like you and me. Yes I'll miss cricket, but not England."

"I'll miss the birds." Trumper looked up at the grey sky as a large flock of feathered things past overhead. "Black Tern and Spotted Redshank and a pair of Marsh Harriers," he noted with great affection. "I know all their names as well as I know the Bible. Could always tell the seasons by the birds - when they come and when they go. They say swallows fly all the way to Africa and back. I wonder if the birds are the same where we are bound?"

"I've heard they've got giant birds that can run faster than a thoroughbred. A whole family can breakfast on one of their eggs. What about you, Dodger? What will you miss?"

"I'll miss London, Warnie. It was the only home I ever had."

"What about your father and mother?"

"Never knew 'em. Don't even know their names. Don't even know my own - the only name I was given was the name Barnet workhouse gave me - Jack. My father was a soldier - still is for all I know. My mother left me at the workhouse and went to find him. Strange thing is - I only learned it in Newgate - there was a soldier bound for Botany Bay looking for someone of my description. It was a few years ago, but perhaps I'll find him there."

"How did you become a thief?"

"I was never a common thief. I scorn the word," I retorted indignantly. "I was a fine wirer – a top pickpocket, well-acquainted with all the lurks of the trade. When I was about five or six they took me out of the workhouse and apprenticed me to a chimney sweep. He chose me on account of my size. The bastard could push me up the smallest, tightest, hottest chimneys. One day I couldn't stand it any longer and ran away. I fell in with some gypsies - or rather they took me up. Taught me the art of the deft and slippery hand - made me swear allegiance to the Tawny Prince. Even gave me a Romany name - Jack Daw - on account of my aptitude for picking up bright shiny things. I'd pick the gentlemen's pockets whilst the gypsy women held their hands and told their fortunes. One day in London at Bartlemey time...."

"Bartlemey time? What Pagan festival is that?

"My eyes, how green you are Warnie. Never heard of Bartholomew Fair? The whole world goes there - even the Lord Mayor himself. For three days you get the richest pickings of the year. Anyway I'd just lifted a fine foogle and ticker with seals* when an old rogue called Fagin spied what I was doing. Offered me lodgings for nothing and said he would never ask for change - promised he'd make me a great man. Took him at his word and changed my name to Dawkins - but he soon started calling me the Dodger."

Warnie laughed, "Who knows? We're starting off in a new land, full of nothing but rogues and thieves. You might yet be a great man there, Dodger."

Next morning we three, and half a dozen others, were taken by long-boat to a graceful, three-masted, three-decker anchored off Tilbury. She looked to be heavily armed: the barrels of two black cannon glinted from her quarter deck and gun ports lined her upper and middle decks; but as we drew nearer, to my astonishment, I could see that they were only painted dummies.

Warnie ran an appraising eye over her: "An old East Indian. From a distance she looks like a man-of-war. Scares off pirates in the China seas. Plenty of room below for us on the way out, and tons of tea, cotton and silk on the way back."

Armed sailors ushered us aboard in our chains. The main deck, devoid of guns, was large and spacious, and as busy and noisy as Smithfield on a Friday. Little wooden shacks and pens had been erected, containing sheep, pigs and cattle; Trumper seemed to cheer up as soon as he saw 'em. Female convicts, wearing striped jackets and petticoats, wandered about freely with their children. One girl stood out from the rest. I couldn't tell whether she was child or woman. She was small like me and her hair, the colour of fresh shiny chestnuts, hung round her face in ringlets. Her pale blue eyes seemed filled with sorrow. Until that moment I hadn't realised there was such a thing as beauty. To my profound disappointment she was all too quickly swallowed up in the throng. Then I noticed another girl, slightly older, who looked vaguely familiar. She had a good deal of hair, not very neatly turned up behind, and was rather untidy about the shoes and stockings. She wasn't exactly pretty, but had a great deal of colour in her face and looked quite hearty. She was talking to some sailors and seemed remarkably free and agreeable in her manners.

"Bet!"

Betsy turned and recognised me at once.

"Dodger!" She ran through the crowd and kissed me. "Dear old Dodger. We heard what you gave those beaks at Bow Street. You were the toast of the Three Cripples. You told 'em where to put it. You done us all proud."

She smiled. Her teeth were turning green and black.

"Bet, what happened? How did you end up here?"

Her smile faded. "I had to identify poor Nance's body. It was dreadful what that cruel bastard Bill had done to her. I went off mad, screaming and raving, beating me head against the floorboards - they put a strait-westcoat on me and took me to the hospital. They kept me there for days - when I came out, I had no one. Fagin had swung; even Tommy Chitling was doing time. I had nowhere else to go but to her."

She pointed across the crowded deck to a stout woman who had somehow managed to still be wearing a green silk dress. It took me a moment to recognise Madame Greere, who ran the best knocking shop in Cable Street.

"She worked us day and night. She had this special client who was the friend of a judge. Didn't want to pay his bill. The bastard claimed one of us stole his watch. The Runners closed the place down. Madame Greere, me and two other girls were sentenced to seven years lagging."

Warnie was showing a keen interest: "The girls are aboard? When are they open for business?"

A marine shoved us on before she could reply. But there was another surprise:

"Sam!" A fine looking woman with two young boys pushed through the mob and flew into Trumper's arms, whilst the kids hugged his fettered legs.

Trumper could hardly speak with amazement and burst into tears. "Sarah! I prayed every night we'd be together again."

She tossed her head proudly: "Prayer didn't do it. The parish didn't know the meaning of charity. Lord Julian forbade them to show any clemency to a rick burner's family. The doctor were the only one who tried to help, gave me a letter of introduction to a London lawyer, called Mr Jaggers. So I took the boys to London - it were a fearful place - but not as fearful as Mr Jaggers. He looked so fierce and contemptuous, but to my bewilderment he took up my case and got us aboard. The Captain, Captain Boswell, is a decent man - he says you will not be chained once we are at sea. You'll be able to visit us on the women's deck."

The marine shoved Trumper with the butt of his musket. "No talking. Get below."

I returned the courtesy by dipping my hand into the side pocket of his red coat and purloining half a crown.

Sam Trumper seemed a new man as we shuffled past big brick ovens and down the hatchway. The upper deck, once a gun deck, had been taken over by the women; the middle deck accommodated the crew, our quarters were on the lower deck, below the water line, the orlop deck they called it. Beneath us were the hold and the brig. In contrast to the gloom of the hulk, the walls had been washed with whitewash and quicklime. Four lines of sleeping cradles ran the length of the ship, most of which were already occupied. There was precious little room - each man had about eighteen inches. Warnie, me and Trumper made sure we were chained on one together. I still had my twirler, my lock picker hidden in my coat.

Later we were led back up to the main deck for a meal of flapjacks and a porridge of mashed peas with small flakes of salted beef. As we ate, a stout, dapper naval officer appeared on the quarter deck. His face was pock-marked and one eye did not move.

"Captain Boswell," someone whispered.

Boswell cleared his throat and began to address us in a stern but kindly voice: "King George has paid my employers the sum of seventeen pounds, seventeen shillings and sixpence for every soul we carry to

New South Wales, for that is the name of this new English dominion to which we are bound. I would not be a traitor and waste the good King's money, so it is my intention to get as many of you there safely, as is God's will. Our journey will be long and arduous - it could take more than half a year, but once we are at sea your conditions will be eased. I am a fair man. Some of you are villains born and bred, so expect no softness from me. Others have been unfortunate and led astray. You will find me a just master. Tomorrow we take on board officers and men of the 57th Regiment, then our voyage will begin. May God preserve you all."

His good eye squinted down at the tally book in his hand. "Samuel Trumper?"

Sam raised his hand with trepidation. "Sir?"

"I read here you are an agricultural labourer. Were you a shepherd or herdsman?"

"I was both and more sir."

"Good. We have livestock aboard. Some will provide fresh meat on our long voyage; others are to be added to the colony's breeding stock. They are in your care." I was standing next to Trumper. The little captain ran his one sharp eye over me: "My cabin boy jumped ship. I need a new one. You don't look like much, but you'll have to do."

That night I settled down on the cradle between Trumper and Warnie, more hopeful and contented than I'd been since the morning of my arrest. I was no longer lonely: besides my two convict pals I now had Betsy, an acquaintance from the old days in London with me. There was also the beautiful girl. Dickens was wrong again when he described me as being snub-nosed, flat-browed, common-faced, with bow legs and little sharp ugly eyes. True - I wasn't a golden haired cherub like Oliver, but I knew I had a winsome manner and began to fantasise that she might like me. The Captain seemed a fair man; I had what seemed to be an agreeable job. Due to my yet undiscovered duties, I wasn't even chained. On the deck below our cradle lay a clean set of clothes, the previous cabin boy had left behind. Ball, the captain's steward and a kindly old fellow, had considered my corduroy trousers, shirt and waistcoat, to be alive with vermin and had burnt them, although I managed to preserve my old coat and hat. I thought my luck had changed at last - but that was before Patrick Napier came aboard.

Next morning, having served Captain Boswell his breakfast, which Ball had cooked in the galley, I watched from the fo'c'sle as our ship, *Enterprise*, sailed across to the new iron pier at Gravesend. The steam ferry was just leaving for London. The convicts were chained below, but Sam, helped by his two boys, was watering the livestock. The ship's timbers shook with the thud of hammers, as carpenters constructed thick bulkheads, from port to starboard below the mainmast on the top two decks, to accommodate the soldiers. They'd marched down from the barracks in the town, and I could see 'em standing in a long red line waiting to come aboard, together with piles of equipment, a carriage and several officers and horses.

"The 57th - they were a fine regiment. Known as the 'Die Hards' after Albuera - bloodiest battle in the entire Peninsular Campaign." I turned my head and saw Boswell watching with Crowe, the ship's surgeon, beside him. "Now they're known as the 'steel backs' - their officers inflict more lashings on their men than any other regiment in the King's army."

As we drew nearer I spied a slender, elegant-looking officer striking his polished boot impatiently with his whip. His uniform appeared to be covered with gold embroidery - his forage cap positively glistened. His lips were thin and slightly twisted beneath his trimmed moustache. A handsome young woman stood by his side. It was obvious from her belly she was with child. Boswell watched them both intently:

"That will be Captain Patrick Napier. Gained quite a reputation in Ireland, putting down the rebels. His wife's Irish - Protestant of course. His uncle is Under-Secretary at the Home Office. The contractors have warned me to handle him gently."

I'd managed to sneak a slice of bacon from Boswell's plate and took it down to Warnie. I found him watching the loading through a port-hole.

"See that?"

I looked and saw some long bags and what looked like wooden clubs being hoisted up in a rope net.

"See what?"

His face broke into one big smile: "Cricket bags. We'll play cricket in Australia yet."

It took several hours to get all aboard, especially Napier's two black thoroughbreds, that were hoisted, kicking furiously, into the hold; and his wife's piano which had to be manhandled up the gangplank and carefully squeezed into their small cabin. The pale sun had begun to set and the steam ferry had returned from London, before the anchor was raised and the March wind wafted the *Enterprise* on her course.

Later that evening, as we passed Sheerness and made our way into the Channel, it was my duty to assist Ball, the old white-haired steward, in serving dinner at the captain's table. It seemed easy: all I had to do was carry the dishes from the galley. There were five guests: Crowe, Napier and his pretty wife, whom I'd heard him call Leticia, Lieutenant Attenborough and Ensign Crawley.

Napier was in a foul mood as he chomped his whitebait. "The quarters you have provided are not fit for a lady of my wife's gentility. Convict women are on the same deck. We can smell their stinking breath and hear their foul language."

"We have a long voyage ahead of us; it is better not to make mountains out of mole hills," replied Boswell, genially.

Napier glanced at his wife, who was demurely studying the pattern on the Captain's china. "I do not consider my wife's health to be a mole hill. Her condition is delicate."

"Your wife is in safe hands. Mr Crowe is an excellent surgeon. He will have two assistants, medical students, joining us, and I am sure there are skilled midwives aplenty among the convict women. Besides, Mr Crowe has taken every precaution against disease. Every deck has been whitewashed with lime - he has even exploded small doses of gunpowder to disperse any vapours of infection."

Mr Crowe nodded at Mrs Napier reassuringly.

Napier frowned, reluctant to concede a point. "Our quarters are too cramped. I demand more room."

"Captain Napier, I have seventy-three crew aboard this ship together with two hundred and forty-three convicts, seventy-five female convicts, and one hundred and three of your soldiers. More convicts await us at Portsmouth and two young surgeons at Plymouth. I have no more room to give you."

Napier sipped his claret. "Give the convicts less space. I want them securely chained throughout the voyage. With my wife aboard we cannot risk a mutiny."

Boswell was a Scot and had a Scot's temper. "I am master of this ship and the supervision of the convicts is my responsibility."

Napier's face flushed. "They are the property of Sir Ralph Darling, Governor of New South Wales. He is my commanding officer; they are part of my command."

"Not on my ship."

Everyone had stopped eating. Napier wiped his mouth with his napkin. "You clearly have not been informed of the new Government policy. The gaols of England are overflowing like an ill-made cesspit: transportation is no longer a fear. Word has got back to the criminal classes of the easy life that awaits them in Australia. Governor Macquarie was a disaster - giving convicts rights - what rights do they deserve? No more than those cursed rebels in Ireland. We crushed them all there - White boys, Ribbon Men - call 'em what you will - by using the most severe means. It's the only treatment that rebels and convicts understand. My uncle, Lord Poole, is sending me out to assist Sir Ralph Darling in restoring some sort of order. We will put more iron on their legs and more lashes on their backs."

Boswell glared at him defiantly and repeated: "Not on my ship."

I put my dirty thumb in Napier's soup and spat in it as I brought it up from the galley.

It was our first night at sea and the Channel was choppy. At first we could hear the delicate sound of the piano drifting down from Napier's cabin. I caught Warnie listening to it with a wistful look on his face, but then the wind stiffened, the mainmast groaned, the timbers strained, and the music ceased. We were tossed about for several hours, as the tub that served as our sole latrine spilled over the deck and mingled with the spew. I was exceedingly glad, when dawn broke, to be able to clamber up to the fresh air of the heaving deck, where Trumper and his boys were already busy watering the livestock.

We were past Spithead, approaching Portsmouth harbour, and all along the shore I could see gun emplacements, castles and fortifications. Warnie had told me it was the most powerful naval port in the entire world. Boswell was at the binnacle, busy navigating us in, and had no time for his breakfast; so I scrounged a cup of hot coffee from the cook and gazed at the town from the main deck. I didn't know it then, but I was probably looking at the very house where Charles Dickens had been born sixteen years before.

Something sharp stung my arm. "You, you young laggard, fetch my wife her breakfast. Look lively else you'll feel more of my crop." Napier, a cold smile on his stuck-up face, was tapping his riding whip in his open palm. I put on my saturnine expression and scudded to the galley like the wind.

We'd anchored off the Point when I came back on deck with some fresh coffee and rolls. I spied Napier getting out of a longboat and clambering up the Hard. He hurried past some mournful-looking convicts standing fettered under guard, and made his way towards a high square tower on top of which was a mast with odd-looking pieces of wood, which were swinging jerkily from vertical to horizontal and back again.

Ball had come out of the galley to throw out some slops to the shrieking sea-gulls. He stopped and watched with a worried frown.

"What's that place Napier's going to?" I asked him.

"That be the semaphore tower, there's a chain of stations from there all the way to the Admiralty in London."

"They can get a message to the First Sea Lord within the hour." Captain Boswell stood behind us, watching through his spy glass.

The coffee was getting cold. I made my way down to the noisy frenzy of the women's deck, hoping to get a glimpse of the beautiful young girl. Some of the women were calling out to sailors on the nearby ships and waving to others on shore. Betsy had pulled up her striped skirt and was waggling her bare bum out of the porthole at a passing man-of-war. A sailor saw it and almost fell out of the rigging.

I thrust my tongue into my cheek, slapped the bridge of my nose some half dozen times, put on a familiar but expressive manner and knocked on the door of Mrs Napier's cabin.

"Come in." She was brushing her long raven-black hair as I put the tray upon a small polished table. She was very pale. I suppose she had been suffering from the motion of the ship on top of her delicate condition. She gave me a sad smile. "Thank you."

Nobody had ever thanked me so gently before. I ruminated how comforting it would have been to have had a mother like that.

The new convicts were brought aboard - there were fifteen of them from the Guildford Assizes. They'd come down overnight, across the Devil's Punchbowl, chained to the outside of a coach. They were in a pitiable condition, most of 'em had chilblains. Crowe, the surgeon, spent the afternoon treating them with some purple concoction. His assistants hadn't yet arrived, so I held the bowl for him, and my small agile fingers were useful in tying the bandages. After taking on more provisions from the dockyard we sailed out on the evening tide; but an easterly wind was blowing up the Channel and we spent the night in the Solent tacking backwards and forwards between the Isle of Wight.

The wind was beginning to change the following morning, and we were passing the Needles as I came up from below. Trumper waved cheerily to me from the pig pen - he was truly as happy as a pig in shit. Napier was on the quarterdeck with a sturdy-looking corporal, who was carefully holding two highly-polished mahogany cases before him. I watched Napier open the top case and take out a brace of long slender-barrelled pistols with silver mountings. He frowned as he looked up at a flock of seabirds flying overhead, then raised the pistol in his right hand and fired - almost immediately, bird dropped into the sea. Trumper looked up from his pigs whilst Napier raised his left hand and casually dispatched another bird. The birds wheeled, cried and circled, uncertain from whence the danger came.

"Quick, Bradman, you numbskull, give me the second pair."

Before Napier had put the discharged pistols back into their open case, Trumper had rushed over: "Please sir, do not shoot them birds. They're very rare."

A look of blank amazement spread over Napier's face. "Are you addressing me?"

"I'm sorry sir, but they be Sabine Gulls - you can tell by the way they fly and their forked tails - they've flown down all the way from the Arctic seas- it's a pity to kill them."

Napier took the second brace of pistols, felt the weight of them in each hand and fired both simultaneously into the flock above. Two more Sabines dropped into the sea.

"Don't you ever dare have the effrontery to speak to me again. If you do I'll have you flogged until the white of your backbone sees the light of day."

Napier turned and went below whilst Trumper sadly shook his head.

Bradman gave him a wink before following with the pistols.

I hurried off to the galley to fetch the captain's breakfast. No sooner had I placed his eggs and bacon before him, when Napier stormed into the cabin.

"Your lack of discipline will put all our lives in peril. You allow an insubordinate rogue to wander around the quarterdeck as he pleases, insulting officers holding the King's Commission. I demand you put him in irons with the others below."

Boswell wiped his mouth with his napkin: "Who and what are you referring to?"

"The felon who reeks of pig had the nerve and impudence to upbraid me for shooting a bird."

"I am inclined to agree with him. It seems a waste of shot and a waste of one of God's creatures."

Napier's eyes flashed. "You are deliberately insulting my honour. No man does that"

Two mornings later we sailed past Smeaton's lighthouse and could see the wretched convicts building the huge stone breakwater out in the waters of the Sound, before going up the river Tamar to Devonport,

Plymouth's great arsenal and dockyard. It was a city in itself - the smoke of forty-eight forges blackened the sky. Hundreds of great anchors and chains were piled on the quay. There were huge sheds overflowing with immense ropes, thick cables and lofty masts, and all around men were heaving and lifting, straining and sweating. I understood that day how Britannia ruled the waves. As we tied up in the new North Dock I spied two convicts standing in chains. One was a huge black man - the biggest I'd ever seen. He was also the ugliest - he looked like a gargoyle, his features seemed to have been battered by a hammer into grotesque shapes. The other was Magwitch. I could see dark hair was beginning to grow on his shaven head and his wounds and bruises were healing, but he looked as fearsome as ever. Beside the two convicts stood a secretive-looking man in a dark green coat with leg-of-mutton sleeves. He held his head all on one side and wore a flapping broad-brimmed traveller's hat and under it, a handkerchief tied over his head in the manner of a cap.

Boswell looked at Crowe and groaned: "Chivers, the Agency representative. I wonder what he has in store for us?"

I was soon serving Chivers a glass of rum and water in Boswell's cabin. He had a cunning expression and one of his eyes was half shut, as if he were taking aim at something with an invisible gun. He gave a comfortable grunt and lit his pipe, then spoke in a half laugh as he stirred his rum and water, not with the spoon I'd given him, but with a small file. "I've brought you two big brutes down from Dartmoor. Better keep an eye on Magwitch - the white one - fourteen years transportation - he's a noted runaway."

Boswell took a pinch of snuff. He hadn't noticed I'd been having regular sniffs from the packet he kept in his bureau. "Who is the great black heathen? I doubt if we have room on board for him."

Chivers swirled the rum around inside his mouth. "Samuel Harper, a noted pugilist, real gamecock, went thirty-five rounds with Tom Cannon, the Great Gun of Windsor.* Would have beat him too and upset the odds, if the blacklegs hadn't thrown pepper in his eyes. Took a terrible pounding - rattled what brains he had - hasn't been the same since - struck dumb. Didn't lose his terrible thirst for drink though - got drunk in Exeter and hit a gentleman, nearly killed him - transported for seven years."

"He'll feel at home in Botany Bay. There are black fellows aplenty there. I hope to sail tomorrow."

"You'll have to delay for another day or two." Chivers fumbled in his breast pocket and took out a warrant with a red seal. "I have more livestock for you: nineteen Irish rebels recently sentenced in Dublin. Held up by storms in the Irish Sea. Mr Crowe's assistant surgeons are with them."

Boswell took the warrant and studied it closely. "This is outrageous. I have no more room. Overcrowding will endanger the ship. I refuse to take any more."

Mr Chivers wiped his lips with the back of his hand. "I'm afraid you have no choice. A complaint has been filed against you - it came yesterday by the telegraph from London. It took a great deal of persuading on my part to stop the Agency replacing you."

Boswell's face flushed and a big vein stood out on his forehead. "A complaint? What complaint? Have I not always done my duty to the best of my ability? Who the Devil has complained about me?"

"It is not my place to say. Just follow your orders Captain Boswell, and the matter will be forgotten."

I went to the galley, managed to slip a few hunks of bread and cheese into my pocket and went down to the convicts' deck. Magwitch and the black giant had been chained to a cradle at the prow. They were so big that the two of them spilled over the cradle intended for six.

Magwitch was reading from his little book, no longer shiny and much warped with muddy Thames water. He looked up in surprise as I approached. His small dark eyes were incredibly sad. I heard the familiar click, like a clock about to strike: "You young villain - you deceiving imp - what do you here?"

I palmed him the bread and cheese. "Thought you might need some wittles."

He grabbed the food and began to cram it in his mouth. He took strong sharp sudden bites, just like a dog, looking sideways, here and there while he ate, as if he thought there was danger in every direction of somebody's coming to take his bread away. It was plain he had no intention of sharing it with his companion.

"Next time I'll bring some for him."

He turned and looked at the black, who was sitting head bowed - a picture of utter desolation. "Don't bother with wittles for him. Rum is what he wants. Get him some rum."

Next morning Napier went into Plymouth with the other officers, and trusted members of the crew and the soldiers were granted shore leave. Mrs Napier remained in her cabin, playing what I later learned was a nocturne by Chopin. The convicts, firmly locked below, listened to the sweet, lilting music, as did the women, confined to their deck. It was a peaceful interlude before another storm.

In the afternoon I'd just brought the Captain and Mr Crowe their tea, when Napier burst into the cabin, his gloves in his hand. Boswell looked up from his cup. "It is the custom to knock on the captain's door before you enter."

"You are a great scoundrel, sir. I do not knock on the door of scoundrels." Napier wiped his moustache with the back of his hand. "I met an acquaintance in the Assembly rooms - a naval officer who is also a gentleman - attached to the Admiral's office. He informed me you had the audacity to request the Admiral to have me thrown off this ship."

"I merely play your game, sir. I know you wrote to your uncle demanding I be replaced from my command. Besides, I would find your company tedious on so long a voyage."

Napier gnawed his lip in fury. "I have settled greater men than you."

"You are welcome to try to settle me whenever you wish."

Napier flicked Boswell's face with his gloves; "Very well let us settle this like gentlemen - although I doubt you know the meaning of the word. Shall we say pistols? My second, Lieutenant Attenborough, will inform you of the time and place."

Crowe placed himself between them, breaking his customary silence. "I beg you both to stop this. Duelling is illegal."

Napier shook his head. “My regimental code forbids me to submit to opprobrious expressions.”

I managed to spill hot tea over his polished boots as he stormed out.

Boswell drained his cup. “Well James, you’d better come along in a double capacity as second and doctor.”

“Don’t try him, Captain,” I frantically interjected. “I’ve seen how he can shoot. The rogue will kill you if he can.”

Boswell looked up at me in surprise. “Thank you for your concern, Mr Dawkins, but I trust I can take care of myself.”

“The boy’s right. My cabin is next to Attenborough’s and Crawley’s, I’ve heard them talking at night. Napier is a noted ‘blazer’ - he duels to give a sharp edge to his reputation. Moreover, he’s a seasoned campaigner - fought in Spain, France and America. Your eyesight is not good. You have a responsibility to the ship. I’ll go and refuse the challenge on your behalf.”

“In God’s name you will not. Besides, James, pistols are notoriously inaccurate - they are great equalisers. They leave no inequality between combatants but that of intrepidity. Tell him I accept his challenge. We will meet this afternoon at four o’clock on the Hoe.”

I was helping the cook in the galley, feeling very apprehensive, when a sailor told me that Mr Crowe wanted me to report to his cabin. I found him packing his medical bag.

“Dawkins, my assistants have not yet arrived. You had better come with me.”

I think he’d forgotten I was a convict, but nevertheless I gratefully grabbed my coat and hat and tagged along. Captain Boswell was waiting on the deck and I followed him and Mr Crowe down the gangplank past the armed guards and into a closed carriage. As we made our way through the busy streets up to the Hoe, I looked at the thin unlocked door and thought how easy it would be to open it and run.

Our journey was short - we climbed a hill and soon stepped out of the carriage on to a great green open space. Large tiers of dark, heavy clouds, which had been gradually overspreading the sky, now formed one black mass overhead. The grey sea lay before us, dotted with the white sails of ships seeking haven in the harbour for the night. Napier, Attenborough and Crawley were waiting for us in a tight cluster of scarlet and white.

Attenborough came forward with a box of Napier's cursed pistols. "Choose your weapon, Captain."

Crowe took out a pistol and examined it on Boswell's behalf. "Percussion capped and rifled barrelled. Fore and rear sights - why these are weapons of murder."

Attenborough smirked. "Shall I inform Captain Napier that his challenge is refused?"

"Like Hell you will," Boswell snorted. "How many paces?"

"Shall twenty be to your liking?"

"Make it a dozen." Boswell replied carelessly, handing me his coat.

I desperately racked my brains to give him some advice: "Stand sideways, Captain. Present a slimmer target."

He laughed. "Why Mr Dawkins, I'm as thick one way as the other."

Crowe took the pistol over to Attenborough to supervise the loading. I followed behind, my bent nail clasped between my fingers, hoping I might be able to spike Napier's pistol, but to my chagrin it remained firmly in Attenborough's grip.

The loading done Attenborough called the protagonists to the mark. They stood back to back - the tall, slim, Napier towering over the squat Boswell.

Attenborough had an unpleasant, lazy way of speaking. "Gentleman I shall count twelve paces. On twelve, turn and fire. Are you ready?"

They nodded and Attenborough began to count. "One...Two..." A seagull flew overhead and shat a white streak on Attenborough's shoulder. I looked up to see if it was one of Trumper's Sabines taking revenge, but there was no forked tail. "Three...Four...Five..." Several carriages had stopped on the Hoe. Gentlemen and their ladies had descended to watch the spectacle. I suppose they wanted blood - same as the mob at Fagin's hanging..."Six...Seven ...Eight..." Napier and Boswell were getting further and further apart. I hoped the distance would be too great and Napier would miss, but then remembered how high and how fast the Sabines had flown. "Nine, Ten..." Boswell was taking as big strides as his little legs would allow - now wishing he'd accepted twenty paces and was endeavouring to get as far as possible from Napier's deadly aim. He was pathetic but at the same time bloody brave... "Eleven..." I closed my eyes.... "Twelve!" I heard a solitary shot: I saw Boswell standing, smoke coming from his barrel. He'd missed. Napier raised his pistol and took careful aim. He held his fire for several seconds, enjoying the torment of his opponent, tempting him to run.

Crowe stepped forward: "The matter is closed. Discharge your pistol in the air."

Napier smiled as he fired. The crack of the pistol mingled with a cry and Boswell lay on the greensward, the right sleeve of his white shirt rapidly turning crimson.

Mr Crowe ran over with his bag and I followed at his heels.

Boswell looked up at us with gritted teeth: "The damn'd rogue's holed me in the upper deck."

Crowe cut the blood soaked linen from the wound: "The bone of your arm is shot through. Pass the laudanum, Dawkins." Thank God he pointed to the bottle, because at that time I couldn't read. I uncorked it with my teeth, gave it him and he poured a long draught down Boswell's throat.

"Now give me a bandage. I'm going to tie it tightly around his arm above the wound to staunch the flow of blood."

Napier swaggered over, followed by his seconds: "I trust his hurt is not fatal?"

I'd never seen Crowe angry till that moment: "If it is I'll see you tried for murder."

Boswell affected nonchalance despite his agony - he'd have made a bloomin' fortune on the stage. "I've been shot at by French twenty-pounders - it would take more than your Purdy's pop gun to finish me. Give me some brandy, Dawkins." I rummaged through the bag and passed him the flask.

"I think it's time to quit the field." Attenborough pointed towards the far end of the Hoe, where a parish constable had appeared, and was asking questions among the spectators.

A twinge of concern crossed Napier's smirking face. "I leave him in your capable hands, Mr Crowe." He melted away with Attenborough and Crawley at his heels.

Large drops of rain began to fall. Crowe was tightening the tourniquet: "Call over our carriage, Dawkins. We must get Captain Boswell to the Naval Hospital immediately."

I scudded over at a rapid pace but the driver was reluctant. It was only a hack cabriolet but he was loathe to have his seat stained with blood.

"The surgeon says there is an extra guinea for you if we get him there in time," I lied.

The 'mabber' nodded sourly, cracked his whip and we trotted over. Crowe and a couple of bystanders lifted Boswell, now nearly delirious with brandy and laudanum, gently inside. I fussed around, with Boswell's coat over my arm and, with steady assiduity, managed to rifle a silver ticker and chain from a gentleman's canary waistcoat. The constable was striding purposely towards us as Crowe and I clambered up beside Boswell, but we were away in an instant, with the rain pattering against the windows. The Hackney had terrible springs, and as we galloped along Union Street to the Royal Naval Hospital at Stonehouse, poor old Boswell was jolted about something dreadful. The slightest movement was agony for him.

Crowe pressed a fresh swab of bandage around the wound. "My friend, Jack Lambert, is staff-surgeon. I'm afraid you will lose your right arm, but Jack is the best and quickest amputater in the entire Navy."

Boswell opened his eye: "Damn my arm. That bastard has lost me my ship."

It was nearly dark when we drove through big stone gates, the nag's hoofs clattering on the uneven paving of the yard. Orderlies came running towards us with glimmering torches. Crowe took command: "Bring a stretcher. Call Staff-Surgeon Lambert and make ready the operating table. Look alive there." He took the coat from me and draped it around Boswell's shoulders. There was so much noise and bustle as Boswell was taken out of the carriage that he and Crowe and all the orderlies were inside the building before the coachman had a chance to demand his extra guinea.

"What about my money?"

I whistled, took off my hat and scratched my head: "The frog he wouldn't and high cockolurum. Lord strike me dead! What money?"

"You, young dog!" He swung his whip at me but I wasn't called Dodger for nothing. He missed me by a mile. "Young gallows! May you rot in Hell!" He pulled his nag savagely around and was gone.

I walked out through the gates and realised I was alone. The hospital was on the very edge of town on the banks of a small river. I could see open country on the other side of the nearby bridge. The road led up over the moor and two hundred miles away was London and freedom. They would never find me there. How my life might have changed if I'd taken that road. But something held me back: Fagin, Nance and all the others were gone. The only friends I had were on the *Enterprise:* Warnie, Trumper, Betsy, Mr Crowe and Captain Boswell - if he lived. There was also the girl, whose name I still did not know; and perhaps, in Botany Bay, I'd find the poor soldier from Barnet. Besides I wanted to try my luck in this new country - this land populated by thieves like me.

I turned away from the bridge and made my way back to the ship. In Chapel Street I came upon a drunken sailor lying in the gutter. I helped him to his feet but, so as not to disgrace my old pals and teachers, I played the bug hunter and drew two gold sovereigns from his inside pocket.

4. The Voyage Begins

Boswell lost his right arm and never came back to the ship. The worse for us. Mr Crowe got him a job at his old school, Rugby, teaching geography. Boswell gave Flashman the biggest thrashing the bastard ever had - and with his left arm too.

We didn't sail for another week, while we waited for our new Captain. I continued with my duties as cabin boy - nobody questioned my situation. I decided to purloin Boswell's snuff and a several bottles of his best rum and brandy, which I deposited, together with my newly acquired watch and sovereigns, beneath a loose plank under a cupboard in the galley. Crowe came back and told me Boswell would live, and there was talk of a magistrate's inquiry over the duel - but nothing happened and Napier got away Scot-free. After a day or two he and his pretty wife moved into a hotel in town; Attenborough and Crawley went with them. We sorely missed her music. As Crowe was Surgeon-Superintendent, the only government appointed official on board, he assumed temporary command and immediately ordered that the convicts should be allowed exercise on deck - they'd been locked below for days. Some had family and friends waiting on the quay for final messages or tokens of love. I watched pitiful scenes as they made their farewells, old parents throwing gifts and mementoes, women holding up children to remember their father's faces, knowing they'd never see them again. Then I saw the girl. She was leaning over the bulwark with tears streaming down her cheeks, waving to a man on the dockside. He looked weak and feeble and could barely manage to wave back.

Bet was also watching. Like me, she had no farewells to take.

"Who is the girl?" I asked.

"Molly Chapman. A factory hand from Manchester. Accused of stealing from her employer. Lagged for seven years. That's her poor old father down there. Looks as if he's on his last legs."

I watched and wondered what I would feel if the soldier from Barnet was down there waving goodbye to me. I was glad that I'd been spared that heartache and remembered Fagin's words: "Some conjurors say that number three is the magic number, and some say number seven. It's neither. It's number one."

I thought then he was right.

At that moment a familiar figure made his way past the guards up the gangplank on to the quarterdeck. It was Chivers from the agency. He searched about, with his head all on one side, before he spied me. He took his pipe from his mouth after slowly blowing all the smoke away, looked hard at me and nodded. I nodded back and he nodded again.

"You, you young parcel of bones, what's your name?"

"Jack Dawkins, sir, though some folks call me the Dodger."

"Dodger? What the Blue Blazes? That's not a name. Talking of names, d'you know the whereabouts of a convict called Magwitch?"

"I do sir. And a fearsome brute he is."

"I've got a bright new shilling somewhere in my pocket - if you take me to him you shall have it."

I needed no further persuading and led him down to the convicts' deck. Nobody minded him. He worked for the agency and had every right to be there. He followed me to the darkest corner at the prow where Magwitch and Harper lay like two beached whales. Harper didn't flicker an eyelid, but Magwitch got up excitedly and took his visitor as far away as his chain would allow. They whispered together in a corner of a bulkhead. My ears were sharp but I couldn't make out much. 'A lonely church… right out on the marshes…with the graves round it… a blacksmith's boy,' was all that I remember. I thought once I caught the glint of silver and a rustle of paper. After a minute or so their business was complete and I led Chivers back onto the deck. He gave me a look with his aiming eye as if swearing me to silence, before tossing me a shining shilling.

"Yours!" was all he said and he was gone.

The following day Captain Gervase Deplidge arrived to take over the ship, together with the contractor's steward, a miserly little man called Farrington. Deplidge was a hawk-nosed martinet without an ounce of humour; his cheeks were so hollow that he seemed to be always sucking them in. The sun and wind had turned his complexion, not a wholesome red or brown, but dirty yellow. He was as crooked as my bent nail. It takes a thief to know a thief, and I knew what he was from the moment I laid eyes on him. The packet from Dublin finally docked that afternoon. On board were Crowe's assistants, Adair and Hampton, two medical students from St Patrick's Hospital, Dublin, who would take up posts at the hospital in Sydney when we arrived in New South Wales. They had a swaggering and facetious manner about them and I disliked them instantly. With them came a bunch of the wildest-looking Irish 'Croppies' I'd ever seen. I noticed Napier, who'd returned to the *Enterprise,* scouring their faces intently as they shuffled up the gangplank.

That night, whilst Mrs Napier played sad Irish airs on her piano, her husband and Deplidge dined alone - Crowe was at the hospital, taking his farewell of good old Boswell. I served the table as before. My training with Fagin had taught me to affect so shadowy a presence as to be invisible, and they talked freely.

"I gather from the Agency that there was a dispute between my predecessor and you over the ultimate command of the convicts aboard this ship." Deplidge searched in his pocket and threw a ring of heavy keys upon the table. "Those will open any lock on the convict deck. You can do what you like with the brutes, providing you leave the commercial aspects of this voyage to me."

Napier reached out and eagerly snatched the keys. "I've always considered trade an unfitting occupation for a gentleman."

Later I took a bottle of Boswell's brandy from my secret store and crept down to Magwitch. He lay trembling on his back looking at the deck only a few feet above. He turned his head quickly as I approached and saw the bottle in my hand.

"What's in the bottle, boy? Rum?"

"Brandy."

"So much the better."

He snatched it from me, pulled out the cork and held the bottle to his lips as it rattled against his teeth.

"I think you have the ague," I whispered.

"I'm much of your opinion boy. I thought those marshes were aguish but Dartmoor was worse." He passed the brandy to Harper. The smell of the alcohol had woken him from his stupor and he was staring at the bottle like a dog waiting for his bone.

"I'll report your condition to Mr Crowe when he comes aboard. He's a fine surgeon - he'll soon have you better."

"Better? That's right. I must get well. Must work and earn my fortune. Luck changes, perhaps even mine. I lost my wife and little daughter through my sin. Must help Pip. Must help that dear boy. I have no one else...."

We weighed anchor at dawn on the seventh day of April 1828, and sailed out of Plymouth flying a red and white pennant from the mizzen, proclaiming us a convict transport. As soon as we were on the open sea a different atmosphere took hold of the entire ship. It was if everyone aboard sensed we were now bound together until the very end of our voyage, wherever that might be. Although the male convicts remained chained and were kept below in their stinking quarters for much of the day, the women were allowed almost complete freedom. Some of them couldn't wait to sell their bodies, or give them freely, to the soldiers and the crew. Some did it for money or favours, but others were desperate to become sea-wives and procure a protector. Squeals and cries and thumps of ecstasy penetrated to the convicts' deck and added to the misery of the men below. I bored a blimp hole in a bulkhead with my lock-picker and watched the women at their sport, so beginning my life-long study of pleasuring the female in all its subtle variations. Madame Greere drove her girls particularly hard - I noticed Betsy accommodating a soldier and a sailor at the same time, but her heart didn't seem to be in it although the rest of her person was very actively engaged. Eventually I'd had enough and I went up on deck looking for Molly, hoping against hope I wouldn't find her with a soldier between her legs. Sarah Trumper had made a haven for herself and her sons in one of the little outhouses. I watched Trumper, after making sure his boys were busy with the cattle, gently take his wife by the hand and slip inside. That tender act reminded me that not all women were whores. Mrs Napier had noticed too, and looked wistfully towards them as she walked up and down the quarterdeck, her belly full-blown as the sails above. At that moment a group of convicts, assigned to galley fatigues, were ushered up on deck. Warnie was among them and as soon as he spied Mrs Napier, he stopped and gazed, despite the prod of a soldier's musket. She met Warnie's eye and gave the faintest of smiles before looking away.

Sex seemed everyone's main preoccupation and I was therefore very relieved when I eventually found Molly, sitting on the deck at the fore-peak, innocently sewing. She looked up and smiled when she saw me. I whistled and put my arms in my coat pocket as far as my big sleeves would let me, and put on all the airs and manners of a gentleman.

"Here's a jolly life." I offered her my pipe. "Fancy blowing a cloud?"

She smiled. It was the first time I'd seen her smile, but she shook her head. "I don't like it."

"I'm at a low-water-mark myself, but you shall have all else I've got to offer." I took a somewhat dirty stick of Deplidge's brown sugar from my pocket.

"Thank you, you are very kind." She popped it into her pretty mouth.

"You sound more Irish than English."

"Tis how we speak in Manchester."

"Manchester? I'm a London man myself. What's Manchester like? Are there good pickings to be had there?"

She frowned, as if in fear. "Tis a dreadful place, surrounded by a circle of fire." She spoke strangely - there was something fairylike about her. "Smoke trails in the sky like a giant black serpent that goes on and on forever. There is not a blade of grass or tree - even the river is purple with dye. I was born in the country, my father was a weaver," her pretty eyes softened, "he had his own loom, was proud of his craft, but could not compete against the mills."

"Mills? We have mills a plenty in Newgate. Shin-scrapers - everlasting staircases - tread-mills. Poor souls tread 'em night and day."

She gave me a look that led me to believe that she had not quite understood the drift of my meaning: "My mother died and we left our cottage to find work in the factories. We lived in one room with one foul bed. When I was seven years old I began working at Medlock Mill…" She paused as anguish crept over her face. "The noise of the machinery was dreadful - the steam engine rattled the windows and made the whole building tremble. Because I was small they made me crawl beneath the looms and pick up the waste cotton. The machinery clashed back and forth above me - it never stopped - I dared not raise my head, lest it be crushed. I crawled for twelve hours, day after day; I have knock knees because of it." She lifted her skirt to show me. I still thought they were pretty.

"Your mills are far worse than those in London. How could you endure such a place? They tried to make me sweep chimneys. I ran away."

"I could not leave my father - besides I did not know where to go. I would have starved. It is hard to believe but there are even worse places. In the mines, boys and girls, some only five years old, work underground for sixteen hours every day and never see the sun. They work in blackness in foul air in which a candle will not burn, dragging loads of coal, tied to them on an iron girdle and chain."

My life with Fagin seemed better every minute. "How come you were lagged?"

"My father worked in a pottery and breathed flint-dust every day. He became ill and I had to find money for a doctor and medicine. I stole some cotton, only a few yards, but the overseer caught me. The judge would have hanged me but the jury showed mercy - if you call seven years transportation mercy. I'll never see my poor father again - he begged his way from Manchester to bid me goodbye. He'll die in the street."

She began to cry. I decided to change the subject.

"How old are you?"

"Fifteen."

"I'm sixteen." I lied.

"You look much younger."

"Don't fret your eyelids on that score. I'm just short, four feet six in my bluchers.* Runs in the family."

"What did you do in London?"

"I was an honest traveller. On the lay. A dip. A top-sawyer. Decided to make my fortune in New South Wales. Will you be my pal?"

She gave another smile, even more beautiful than the first. "Yes."

As the day wore on I got to know more of the other convicts, such as George Lindwall, a tall Lincolnshire poacher, and a so-called gentleman, handsome D'Arcy Miller, whose means of business had been two pops and a galloper, or highwayman to put it more mundanely. I talked with Nicholas Kidman, a young lawyer's clerk, who told me he'd been transported for fourteen years for distributing seditious papers among the poor; although I didn't understand at the time what that meant. I also conversed with James, a funny little fat fellow, who seemed to be asleep most of the time. He was already going bald though he was not much older than me. He claimed he'd been a pageboy, but had been transported after being falsely accused of stealing from his master. Most of the others were country bumpkins, 'Johnny Raws', who appeared to have done nothing except snatch something that would feed them or their hungry children. Joseph Simpson was sentenced to seven years for stealing a pair of shoes; Ann Clark: seven years for five bonnets; Fred Lawson: seven years for stealing two sheepskins; Mary Hague: seven years for three pounds of cheese; old Daniel Thorpe, a discharged manservant: fourteen years for stealing a silver spoon - there was hardly a 'buzz-gloak' or 'rum-hustler' amongst them.* I was thankful that at least I'd been sentenced for something worthwhile. I was a thief and proud of it, a true son of St Peter with every finger a fish hook.

That night I again waited on Deplidge's table where he dined with Napier and Crowe.

"We are due to call into Corunna," said Deplidge, pouring Crowe a glass of Madeira, "so pick up what remaining stores you need there - it will be a long haul down to Cape Town."

Crowe frowned. "The normal route is to sail to Rio on the southeast trades and then cross back on the westerlies."

"I see no point in crossing the Atlantic twice. The company believes it is more economical to sail straight down the West Coast of Africa."

"If we can find a wind. Ships can be becalmed for weeks."

"It is my responsibility as Captain to find the wind."

"I think it will cause the convicts unnecessary suffering."

"They are here to suffer, Mr Crowe," snarled Napier. "This is not a cruise for their health."

Crowe threw down his napkin and left the cabin without another word. I served the other two their dinner and left them drinking brandy, becoming as thick as the thieves they most certainly were. Mrs Napier's piano was playing a bright, tinkling tune, when I went up to the quarterdeck to find Mr Crowe. His bulky frame was leaning against the bulwark, gazing at a far distant headland.

"Shall I bring your dinner to your cabin, sir?"

He turned and smiled. "Thank you, Dawkins. Just looking at the old enemy - remembering old times. That tune she's playing, it's known as *The Emperor Concerto* - Beethoven wrote it in honour of Napoleon when he still considered him a hero. Everything was much simpler then. I was just a little older than you, a midshipman in the Royal Navy. Served under Admiral Cornwallis in the Channel Fleet. We blockaded this French coast for more than twenty years. Spent my youth in these waters - shipwrecked off Cherbourg in the winter of 1811." He lit his pipe. "The entire crew were taken prisoner. The French marched us through the snow for forty miles to a filthy prison in Caen, where we rotted for more than two years until Napoleon fell in 1814. I learnt then that men, whatever their condition, all have the same feelings and passions. Decided I wanted to understand them better. When I returned to England I decided to quit the Navy and study medicine." He looked at me kindly. "I didn't think we'd see you again, Dawkins. Gave you the chance to cut and run outside the hospital in Plymouth."

"Thought about it sir, but decided you couldn't manage without me."

He laughed. "You may be right. I think I'll need all the allies I can muster on this ship. I noticed the other day you hesitated when I asked you to pass me the laudanum. A smart young lad like you should be able to read and write. Would you like me to teach you?"

I nodded - for once I couldn't think of anything to say.

Later I retrieved another bottle of Boswell's brandy from my little hoard and smuggled it below. After Warnie had had his fill I crept along to Magwitch and Harper. They were sitting motionless in the gloom like two giant statues. Magwitch's little dark eyes flickered as I proffered him the bottle.

"Let the dumb wretch have it. He has more need even than I."

The black man grabbed the bottle and poured the brandy down his pink throat. Magwitch watched him before turning back to me. I expected him to thank me but he didn't.

"What do they call you, boy?"

"Jack Dawkins, but people call me the Dodger."

"Magwitch is my name. Abel Magwitch. A cursed name since the day I was born."

"What happened to the other man? The one you were taken with?"

The terrible anger returned to his face. "Compeyson? That coward? That villain that ruined my life and destroyed the only things I held dear? He's a smooth talker and has a dab at the ways of gentlefolk - went to a public boarding school. He pleaded in court he'd only escaped because he was half-wild with terror of me. The judge took pity on him and he'll be walking free in England in six years, but I'm to be transported to the end of the world for the rest of my days." He snatched the bottle from Harper, drunk hungrily and swirled the brandy around in his mouth, quenching his rage.

"Warnie, my friend, says it need not be so bad. After four years you get your ticket of leave and then are free to sell your labour where you wish. You can even buy land - many convicts are now free men and rich."

He spread his scarred hands broader on his knees, and lifted them off and put them on again, then looked at me, with a smile that was like a frown, and with a frown that was like a smile. "Aye, boy, I've heard that too - it's the only thing that keeps me sane. Upon my soul, I am determined to labour and prosper - I must earn money for Pip."

"Who's Pip?" I enquired.

His gimlet eyes softened, "The dear boy that helped me in those marshes. I will make him a gentleman - I will work hard so he will be above work. Every guinea I earn shall go to him. Lord strike me dead if it don't."

The next morning we entered the Bay of Biscay. The ship's timbers groaned, as if protesting in pain, as we ploughed through rolling abysses, between high, watery walls, which broke through the gun ports and washed us from our cradles into the filth and spew which covered the deck.

Only Deplidge and Napier could eat their dinner that evening, and Napier was very green about the gills. There was no music. Mrs Napier was confined to her bed and Crowe was attending her.

Deplidge passed Napier a copy of his orders. "We put into Corunna in the morning. There is a consignment of Merino sheep that Chivers, the agent in England, has arranged to be taken aboard. The ship's carpenters have built pens in the hold."

Napier frowned: "Hope they don't upset my thoroughbreds."

"Have no fear: a separate bulkhead is being built as we speak. They won't bother your horses or your grooms."

"What do we need Dago sheep for anyway?"

"Our good English sheep do not flourish in the barbarous land to which we are bound. These Merinos can forage in the driest country and produce an abundance of fine soft wool. Fortunes have already been made. Chivers says the flock he has acquired are of a particular hardy breed. I have made a partial investment in them myself."

Napier began to forget his seasickness. "If it's that good a proposition include me as well. I spent the greater part of my inheritance on buying my Captaincy and need all the capital I can get. I intend to use my wife's money to acquire as much land in that God forsaken place as possible - my uncle has arranged favourable terms for me. Put me down for a hundred guineas worth of mutton." He was on the verge of heaving up as he said it.

"They'll need special care. None of the crew are capable of such a task. I've noticed that convict on the deck tends the livestock well."

"Him? Yes, he's an insolent dog but he knows animals. That's the only reason I have not clapped him in irons. He'll need help of course."

Deplidge tapped the tally book which lay on the table beside him. "I'll go through this in the morning. All the villains' occupations are listed. I'll pick out the shepherds amongst them."

"While you're about it - my wife needs a mature lady's maid, with some knowledge of midwifery. Check if there's a decent one aboard."

The tally book was still on the table when I cleared the dishes. No one noticed as I tucked it up my sleeve.

It was soon in the hands of William Cummins, a talented forger - transported for drawing the King's picture on notes without Royal Assent. His thin fingers flicked through the dog-eared pages.

"What am I to do with this?"

I took out a quill and inkpot I'd borrowed from Deplidge's desk. "I've two ounces of Boswell's best snuff if you turn a couple of those coves into shepherds and a woman into a lady's midwife."

Within an hour the tally book was back on the Captain's table with 'Head Shepherd' alongside the names of Warne and Magwitch. I'd considered doing the same for Harper, but thought better of it: there were black sheep aplenty in England, but I was certain nary a black shepherd. The occupations of the three genuine shepherds on board had been changed to pot man, ostler and sweep. Mrs Trumper was listed as having attended to the labours of the Duchess of Portland herself.

Two mornings later we sailed into a green lush bay in which, behind high fortified walls, lay the town of Corunna. I watched from the main deck entranced: it was the first foreign city I'd ever seen.

"Never thought I'd set my eyes on that blasted place again after we scuttled out in 1809." Corporal Bradman was leaning against the bulwark beside me. Officers apart, I've always enjoyed the conviviality of the military.

"You've docked here before?"

"We did more than dock, you young villain. Have you never heard of Sir John Moore? Better General than Wellington himself. Only decent officer I ever knew. He held off Soult, one of Boney's finest Marshals, and got us clean away."

"My father was a soldier. Never came back from Waterloo." I looked at the rapidly approaching town with fresh interest. "Perhaps he was here."

"He'd have a tale to tell you if he was. I was in the 9th of Foot then. We were the last to leave after burying Sir John up on those ramparts. Don't you know the poem?"

I was about to confess that at that stage in my life my knowledge of poetry was as scanty as the hairs on my chin, when he began to intone in his deep Norfolk voice:

"Not a drum was heard, not a funeral note...."
As his corse to the rampart we carried,
Not a soldier discharged his farewell shot
O'er the grave where our hero lies buried.".

My education was taking off apace: women, medicine, writing, reading, now history and poetry. I'd be a great man yet.

We sailed past an ancient stone tower and entered the harbour, teeming with weird- looking fishing boats, and tied up at the jetty, on which stood a large flock of sheep with the thickest fleeces I'd ever seen.

Crowe came on deck, dressed in his old Royal Navy blue. He had long out-grown it and his big frame seemed to be bursting out at the seams.

"I like your togs, Mr Crowe. Superfine cloth and the heavy swell cut."

He laughed. Thank God he found me amusing. "A uniform carries a lot of weight in this country." He put his cocked hat on his head at a jaunty angle. "Fancy a stroll round the market, Dawkins?"

"Here's a jolly life!" I said and followed him ashore.

It was busier and noisier than Billingsgate and all in Spanish. Everywhere fishermen were shouting, selling varieties of fish which were foreign to me then - squid, giant shrimps, octopus and tuna. Behind them were stalls with fruit, vegetables, huge casks of wine, evil-smelling cheeses, hams, sausages: so long, pink and juicy that they made the ones that Fagin used to feed us look as meagre as a parson's pizzle. Many of the soldiers and crew were already bargaining with the Dagos for extra provisions for the long haul ahead. I noticed several veterans, such as Bradman, speaking fluent Spanish, which they'd picked up during Wellington's long Peninsular Campaign. It was the first time I'd been in a busy crowd since my arrest and I could spy thick pockets and shining tickers all around - easy pickings. I was sorely tempted to lift a purse from a swarthy Spaniard in a plum coloured coat - but forced myself to resist, remembering I was in Crowe's company. Perhaps he guessed my intentions because he kept a firm hand on my shoulder.

"I am going to purchase a large supply of limes - limes are the best antidote to scurvy."

"What's scurvy?"

"It's the curse of all long voyages. The salt meat diet and lack of vegetables can make your gums swell and bleed, give you such terrible pains in your joints that you are unable to stand, and eventually your internal organs rupture. The Navy now insists that every man has a daily issue of grog - rum mixed with lime juice and water. The convicts confined and chained as they are, will need extra doses of fresh lime juice."

It was as if he were teaching me already. I took his advice and immediately began helping myself to bright green limes from every stall we passed, secreting them in the depths of my coat.

Crowe eventually found a merchant to his liking. After much bartering he paid for two dozen huge baskets of limes and ordered them to be taken to *Enterprise*. Then we went to a vintner where he bought three great casks of port wine, telling me: "I think a nightly half-pint of fortified wine will also help keep scurvy at bay – at the worst it will fortify the spirits of the poor wretches." I began to like him more and more. On our way back we spied Farrington, the contractor's steward, at a farrier's, buying large quantities of horseflesh. It looked green and rotten. Crowe shook his head: "He should be buying good fresh beef. There is villainy aboard our ship. But we must do all we can to prevent it, Dawkins."

When we got back to *Enterprise* all was disorder. The Merinos - there must have been about fifty of the beasts, were swarming around the deck, as Trumper and his boys endeavoured to put the big clumsy brutes in rope netting and lower them into the hold, where Napier's two thoroughbreds were kicking and screaming in their stalls. Sheep shit was flying everywhere. Warne and Magwitch had been brought up from the convict's deck and were running about aimlessly, as fast as their shackles would allow, waving their arms and whistling. I hadn't told them of my intervention on their behalf, and they'd no idea why they were there. Napier and Deplidge were standing on the poop, jealously guarding their investment. I noticed Mrs Napier and Sarah Trumper watching from the fo'c'sle. A particularly pugnacious ram put down his head and made a charge for a gap in the bulwark; Warnie threw himself in front of it, was tossed high in the air and went yelling down into the struggling mass of wool and mutton in the hold.

"Take care of those beasts of I'll have the skin off your back!" A furious Napier dashed down from the poop, but in his anger, failed to notice a pile of steaming sheep dung. I watched gleefully as he slipped and his glittering forage cap flew off his pomaded locks onto the soiled deck. Affecting much concern, I immediately ran and picked it up for him, managing to rub a large piece of ordure on the inside.

Napier's face contorted in rage. "That cap was made by Buckmaster himself - the finest military tailor in London. It's ruined." Poor Warnie's muck-covered face popped up through the flock and grinned feebly. Napier turned to Deplidge. "Shepherds! They know less about sheep than my arse!"

"These are a peculiar breed. We'll soon get used to them." Trumper seemed happier than ever. He now had as much sheep shit on him as pig. "David, go below and help him."

Trumper's eldest boy, a bit younger than me, slid down a rope into the hold and began to help Warnie drive the bleating, frenzied sheep into their various pens. Meanwhile Magwitch began lifting the large beasts and wrestling them into the rope netting. Trumper used his natural calming influence and slowly the Merinos were stowed below.

"We may well end up eating most of those." Crowe had waited until he had Deplidge's unqualified attention.

"What in damnation do you mean? Those sheep are private property."

"I have just seen Farrington buying rotten horseflesh. Was that with your authority?"

"Indeed it was my authority," snapped Napier, trying to clean his cap with a handful of straw. "My orders are to purge England of excrement as cheaply as possible. One does not throw good food into a sewer."

Mrs Napier and Sarah had moved closer and were listening intently.

"The convicts are still British citizens under law - our duty is to help them redress their so-called crimes and work their way to freedom."

"A thief will always be a thief - unworthy of trust. You are sounding like a Radical. Men have been transported for less. You have fellow-thinkers aplenty below."

"I am not a Radical, Captain Napier. I am a Liberal. There are a growing number in England who think as I do. We have no God-given right to cast these poor people away forever."

"You waste your time trying to reform the likes of them. Christ himself was a reformer, and even he made a mess of it and ended up being hanged. Wellington is now Prime Minister, and his policy is to think less about a felon's dubious redemption and more about present punishment. It will make for less crime in England."

"That does not mean we should feed them rotten horse flesh."

"Why not? The population is rising and so is crime, even Peel's new-fangled Metropolitan Police will never be able to cope. We have too many useless mouths to feed. If we feed the convicts too well they will breed. Let the brutes starve and they'll find their natural level."

Crowe was so angry, he was lost for words.

Deplidge suddenly caught sight of a stream of Spaniards struggling up the gangplank bearing heavy sacks of limes. "Who in damnation ordered those?"

"I did." Crowe exploded at last.

"Whatever for?" Deplidge's Adam's apple twitched and jerked up in his throat. "Farrington assures me we have a plentiful supply of grog."

"I am the official medical officer and government agent aboard this ship, with full power to exercise my judgement, without being liable to the control of any ship's captain. Because I fear this may be a protracted passage, I have purchased the limes, together with several casks of the local wine, as an extra preventive to scurvy. If scurvy takes hold we will all suffer. I need not remind you of your wife's condition, Captain Napier. If you refuse to pay, Captain Deplidge, it is no matter. I have a receipt and will send my bill to the Agency on my return to London, together with a report on the conduct of this voyage." Deplidge was about to protest, but Crowe had already turned back to Napier: "The convicts are under your command but their health is my responsibility. As well as fresh food, they require fresh air and exercise. Tomorrow we enter blue water. May I remind you that it is the custom to allow them on deck once we lose sight of land?"

Napier twirled his finger angrily through his moustache: "Very well. I will address all felons on deck tomorrow. They shall have exercise - but they shall have it with severity. This ship will be converted into a place of punishment."

Fresh supplies of water, oranges, melons, onions and wine were safely stowed, all the soldiers and crew were back aboard and as the sun began to set our sails rose with the wind, and we wafted on our course out of Corunna. I was enjoying a quiet smoke on our cradle, wondering what new torments Napier had in store for us, when two soldiers brought down a bruised and battered Warnie and dumped him beside me. He lay on his face groaning - his ankles raw and bleeding where the iron shackles had rubbed against them. I wasn't sure how grateful he'd be if he knew his condition was all down to me. I decided to say nothing and be my normal convivial self.

"Hello, my Covey! What's the row?"

"What the fuck had I done to that bastard Deplidge? Why did he pick me?"

"At least you'll get fresh air - being on the deck all day with the animals like Trumper."

"Fresh air my arse! Magwitch and me are going to spend twelve hours at a stretch in that stinking hold. I hate bloody sheep – can't even bear the taste of mutton."

Once again my best intentions had gone awry. All I could do was wrap some rags round his shackles to ease the rubbing.

After supper I climbed down to the hold to take Magwitch some scraps from Deplidge's table. The Merinos had been divided into small groups in separate pens and fresh straw had been put down on the deck, but it was already damp and stinking of bilge. I found Magwitch sitting in a pen nursing a ewe that had slipped out of the netting and damaged a leg. He held the animal as tenderly as if it were his own child, his small dark eyes soft with pity. They reverted to their normal hardness as soon as he saw me. He snatched the bread and cheese I offered and as before, crammed it in his mouth with strong sharp bites, his head on one side like a dog.

I tried to break the ice: "This ain't the place for justice, is it?"

"Justice? I had a daughter once. A beautiful child. I lost her - I know not if she be alive or dead. Mayhap we get the justice we deserve."

"What do you mean?"

The click came into his throat again. "I must have my smoke. I'll go as melancholy mad as these sheep if I don't have my smoke." I passed him my pipe which I'd filled with Deplidge's best tobacco. He lit it and sucked on it noisily. After a minute or two he took the pipe from his mouth and dropped his jaw, as if feeling the pain of his past. "That villain Compeyson envied me my happiness - my wife and child. It was the only thing I possessed that he had not. But the devil knew my weakness. He put another woman in my way. A woman who would do anything for Compeyson's gold. I sinned with her and then he told my wife what I had done - she who had stuck with me through all my troubles - who had always been faithful and loving to me." He looked down at his big scarred hands and fought back his tears. "My wife had a terrible anger. She told me she would kill the woman I had sinned with and that she would also kill my child - she loathed anything that was part of me - even her own daughter. She killed the woman and I never saw my daughter again. I had no one. No one to love and no one showed me any kindness, until that young lad, stole food and drink for me when I was on the marshes." One of Napier's horses neighed in anger and kicked frantically against the bulkhead. Magwitch nodded his head appraisingly: "That boy on the marshes shall be a gentleman and have horses. Horses to ride and horses to drive - blood-'uns like those. He'll show those officers and gentlemen another pair of shoes."

The following morning, to the rattling of drums and the whistling of pipes, both male and female convicts were mustered from below, to be confronted with the gaping black muzzles of two of the ship's cannon, together with the muskets and bayonets of Corporal Bradman and a squad of soldiers. The bemused prisoners waited in anxious anticipation as the ship's crew watched from the masts and rigging above. After the bosun had piped that all were assembled, Napier and his officers came out of the poop followed by Deplidge and Crowe. Napier was dressed in his finest uniform - his epaulettes glittering, his sword sparkled. A new forage cap was on his head. His finery and elegance were in complete contrast to the squalor and raggedness of the massed men and women before him. He regarded them with cold distain.

"The Duke of Wellington has ordered that you be transported to the far side of the world at great expense, to earn your redemption through hard labour. I am the representative of Lord Darling, Governor of New South Wales, who has complete and absolute power over you. I have heard talk amongst you of expectations of a good life in this new colony. There has even been talk of 'convict rights'. I must tell you that I, like Governor Darling, care little for 'convict rights'. In the past convict scum such as you, have been allowed to purchase land, some have grown rich. I promise you that will not happen again. There are now as many honest free settlers in the colony as convicts. In future the land will be owned by gentlemen such as myself, as it is in England. There will be no more easy life for such as you. You will remain in shackles whilst aboard this ship and you will work in chained labour gangs when you arrive. There are public works and roads to be built across the wilderness, and that will be your task." He paused and seemed to relish the forlorn faces before him. "As to the present, against my better judgement, you will be allowed some daily exercise on deck. I will point out that there will be ten solders with primed muskets on guard day and night. The cannon are loaded with grapeshot - which can inflict the most deadly of injuries - they will fire on you at the slightest sign of disorder. You will show me, my officers, and my men, the utmost respect. You will tip your cap or knuckle your forehead whenever we pass. Anyone who fails to show this respect will be flogged on the triangle." He turned to the Irish, who were clustered sullenly together towards the rear: "As for you rebels, I will not grace you with the appellation of men; you are the most wild and savage race that were ever favoured with the light of civilisation. Let me remind you that I crushed you and your brethren in that bog you call a country and will delight in hanging any one of you who sees fit to rebel again."

Hope is a precious fuel - while it burns a man's spirit can endure almost anything; Napier had brutally sought to extinguish its flame. The convicts looked as mortified as if they'd been sentenced afresh - the Irish more desperate than ever. The women were as disconsolate as the men, some, including poor Bet, began to weep. Even Mrs Napier, standing on the forecastle with Sarah Trumper, looked shocked and distraught. Warnie, leaning against the bulwark, shook his head and spat into the wind. Only Harper, black and alone, appeared unmoved. The bosun was about to pipe 'dismiss' when Mr Crowe stepped forward.

"I am the Surgeon-Superintendent aboard this vessel and your health and wellbeing is my responsibility. To that end, and to prevent scurvy, in addition to your grog, I will be issuing you all with a daily cup of port wine."

In the depths of despair the smallest expectation can shine as bright as August sun. The convicts, led by Warnie, took off what caps they had and cheered.

Napier's face darkened, "Silence! Or I'll ensure you'll never cheer again."

As if in answer Warnie began to stamp his feet in a clinking beat - others around him took it up immediately. It was a sound such as I'd never heard before - the chains dragged and clanked like Marley's ghost, but slowly, through sheer force of will, they adopted a defiant and merry sound. Within a minute the entire glum assembly, even the Irish, had been transformed into a jovial, jigging throng.

Napier looked in vain for the perpetrator of the defiance: "Corporal Bradman - order your men to load their muskets." Bradman gave the order and in a matter of moments, cartridges were bitten open, pans were primed and charges poured down the barrels. Wadded cartridge papers were thrust into the muzzles, the bullets spat in on top, and ramrods plied to drive all home.

Still the jig continued - the chains rattling even louder.

"Corporal Bradman, order your men to level their weapons."

Bradman complied reluctantly: "Front rank, take aim.". Several of his men lifted their Brown Besses even more unwillingly, aiming at a breast they'd been fondling a few hours before.

The women moved fearfully to the rear, but the jig grew more frenzied. The sheer weight of the shackles caused parts of the deck to buckle.

Napier was black with fury: "Gunners - fire at my command!" The gun crews knelt at their posts, lanyards in hand. Most of them were looking down at the deck, not wishing to behold the slaughter they were about to inflict. It was a terrible moment. Napier was crazy enough to massacre them all - the convicts knew that - but felt they'd nothing to lose. They'd been presented with the prospect of a living death. Mrs Napier and Sarah turned their heads away. I desperately looked for Molly but couldn't see her.

"Stop!" Crowe had moved in front of a cannon's mouth, waving his arms in a pacifying gesture. I was certain that Napier had passed the edge of reason, and would order the cannon to blow Crowe's broad back asunder. But, to my profound relief, the men stopped jigging and the clanking ceased.

Napier seemed disappointed to have been deprived of his bloodbath. "You see what comes from undermining my authority, Mr Crowe. Give that scum an ounce of mercy and they lose all their fear and respect."

"I believe you earn a man's respect through his belly not his back."

"I'll put that to proof." Napier turned again to the assembly. "For that insubordination you damned scoundrels will be chained below with no food until noon tomorrow. The next time I am disobeyed all offenders will be triced to a grating, so tight that they cannot cringe, and their spines will open up with a few dozen strokes of the cat."

That night fornication, lewdness, debauchery, name it what you will, was rampant all over the ship. The women desperately sought means of easing their hopeless condition with the only thing they had. Even the decent ones, with husbands and children back in England, gave themselves willingly to any man with the meanest rank of authority. There were so many dirty legs and feet dancing in the air that even I grew tired of watching.

I decided to concentrate on my duties, and crept into Deplidge's cabin with blacking and brush to jepan his trotter-cases.* To my surprise there were grunts and groans coming from behind the curtain that divided the cabin. I scudded stealthily over and took a peep through a chink. On the bed, Deplidge's bony, spotted arse was plunging up and down, as quick and frantic as Nancy dancing a reel. Beneath him was something smooth and white and beautiful, the first naked woman I'd ever seen. Her chestnut hair was spread over the pillow, her breasts were firm and white, but her fists were clenched, her eyes pressed tight, either in ecstasy or agony, I could not tell. It was my Molly.

5. At Sea

Your first wound in battle is the most painful, and so is your first heartbreak. Although I'd never even kissed Molly, in my childish fantasies I'd begun to dream she would be mine. If I'd lost her to Warnie, or to any ordinary sailor or soldier, I could have borne it, but to see her being ravished by that odious villain drove me close to madness. Even though I yearned to explore every inch of her body, I couldn't bear to watch. I ran up on deck and paced frantically up and down. A new sensation, I'd never felt before, pounded in my heart: hatred - violent hatred of Deplidge. I knew then, whatever the cost, I would find a way to kill him. Eventually I ceased my pacing, lit my pipe and leant against the bulwark, looking up at the brightest stars I'd ever seen.

"Give us a smoke, Dodger," whispered a soft voice.

I turned and saw Bet silhouetted against the moon. I passed her my pipe. "Thought you'd be busy tonight, my girl. Why don't you find yourself a regular bloke and free yourself from that old cow Greere?"

"None of them want me. A whore is a whore. That's what I'll always be now. Besides Greere gives most of what I earn to that lousy scoundrel, Deplidge; he'll never allow anyone to have me for free."

"That bastard is having Molly for free as we speak. I thought there was more to her than that."

"The poor girl had no choice. If she'd refused him, he'd have turned her over to Greere. She would've ended up the same as me."

I don't know why, but that made me feel a little better.

"The world's a cruel place, Bet."

"Tis certainly that, Dodger. I often wish that Bill had done me in as well as Nance."

I put my arm round her. "Don't think that, Bet. Things will get better, I'm sure."

But it was hard to see how.

Within an hour or so a plan had begun to form in my mind and I made my way towards Mr Crowe's cabin. As I passed Attenborough and Crawley's door I spied a light spilling beneath and heard the familiar sounds of coupling. I knelt down and squinted through the lock and beheld four dirty legs waving in the air. The young officers and gentlemen were grinding away at Till Flower and May Rooney, trollops from Liverpool, two of the filthiest females aboard. Even at that early stage of my sexual education I could see that the cold fish didn't have a clue. It was as plain as the snub nose on my face that those particular ladies preferred a private's privates to an officer's baton.

I'd soon seen enough and knocked upon Mr Crowe's door.

"Come in." He was sitting writing at his table, his medical books around him. "What can I do for you, Mr Dawkins?"

I adopted an incorrigible air. "Beg your pardon Mr Crowe, sir, but I wish to inform you that after due consideration, I've decided to withdraw my services from Captain Deplidge, sir."

Crowe's face broke into an amused smile. "May I ask the reason, Mr Dawkins?"

"Between you and me sir, I do not consider him to be a gentleman, sir."

"You realise you will lose certain privileges by this withdrawal?"

"I do sir. But I am an honest traveller, Mr Crowe. I cannot abase myself by descending to serve such a rogue."

"Take heed, Mr Dawkins. That could be considered as slanderous mutiny. Have I fallen from your favour as well?"

"Oh, my eye! No sir. You are the most gentrified and genivine of gentlemen. You are the downiest one of the lot."

"Very well, Mr Dawkins. I have need of an extra pair of hands. Henceforward you will assist my assistants. I will inform Captain Deplidge."

Good old Crowe didn't know it - but that was just what I'd schemed.

Next morning I came up on deck and was surprised to see several of the old tars up in the rigging, standing still and silent with their straw hats held before their chests.

"What's up with them?" I asked a young sailor, holystoning the deck.

"We're sailing past Cape Trafalgar where Lord Nelson fell - they're rending passing honours. The old salts still love him. There was no flogging in his fleet."

"Napier wouldn't have liked that then, would he?"

I went to the galley to collect a pot of coffee for Mr Crowe and passed Molly coming out with Deplidge's breakfast. She avoided my eyes.

I found Crowe in his cabin together with his assistants, Adair and Hampton, who didn't look too pleased to see me; but Crowe gave me his usual friendly smile:

"Good morning, Mr Dawkins."

I thrust my tongue into my cheek and poured him a cup of coffee. I think Adair and Hampton expected one too, but I was damned if I was going to wait on the likes of them. "We are discussing the convict's fitness. It is imperative that they get as much fresh air and exercise as possible. I am going to suggest to Captain Deplidge that he lets them take over some of the menial duties of the crew - such as swabbing and scrubbing; the women are already laundering - have you any suggestions?"

I whistled, scratched my head and nodded thrice. "I thought the jig was an excellent exercise - very good for their spirits too."

"Yes Dawkins, but we can hardly call them to jig at Assembly every day. I am loathe to provoke Captain Napier. I do not wish to seek the bubble reputation in the cannon's mouth again."

"I beg your pardon, sir?"

"Shakespeare, Mr Dawkins, I'll tell you more of him some other day." It was the first time I'd heard the name - little did I know then how often I would suffer from the old bore in the years to come.

"I was thinking of the issue of the port ration, sir." I pointed to the three huge casks which now occupied much of the cabin. "The mere mention of it occasioned a lively and animated appearance in the men. To celebrate the first issue, could they not jig in to the cask, partake of their ration, and then jig out? It would occasion an overflow of their ardent spirits."

Adair and Hampton snorted derisively at my suggestion, but Crowe sensed the possibilities. "Yes, Dawkins, perhaps we could award an extra ration for the most inventive steps."

"Ball, the steward, can conjure up a lively tune for them with his fiddle."

"Excellent idea, my boy. Make sure Mr Ball is present. The issuing of the port wine will be your special responsibility. The need for you to master the art of reading and writing is even more imperative."

At noon, as the hungry and despondent convicts were released on deck for their long-awaited meal, I spread the word of the jigging contest. Their enthusiasm was quickly aroused, and some immediately began to practice long-forgotten steps. Harper was one of the last to appear. He had become even more withdrawn and melancholy since Magwitch had left him to tend the Merinos.

I tried to cheer him up: "Look lively, this evening, my old covey. If you dance well enough at Mr Crowe's parade, you'll win an extra cup of grog to put down that thirsty black throat."

But he didn't seem to understand.

That evening when the convicts assembled on the main deck, with their tin cups and rags tied around their ankles, they found Corporal Bradman and the armed guard in position on the quarterdeck and the crews crouching in readiness by the two guns. Ball stood by the foot of the steps tuning his fiddle like fifty stomach-aches. The sailors watched from the rigging, the women and the remaining soldiers clustered on the poop, Napier, his wife, and the other officers were standing about the binnacle. Deplidge was nowhere to be seen - I tried not to think what he might be doing with Molly.

Bradman called the roll: all were present apart from Magwitch, who was down in the hold with his Merinos. The Corporal then pulled back his shoulders and barked in his finest military voice: "You will file up to Mr Crowe's cabin, one by one in an orderly manner, for the issue of your daily dose of port wine. Once it is in your cup you will return to your present positions."

As the first convict put his fettered foot upon the bottom step, Ball struck up a reel, the shackles clanked and rattled, and, to the consternation of Napier and his fellow officers, the jigging began. Some convicts were shy, some were bold, some were graceful, many were awkward, some pushed on the man before them, some tripped on a step and fell back, pulling at the shirt of the man in front, but they all jigged, anyhow and every how. Some went up alone, others went up in pairs, and nine went up together in a Nine Man Morris. Some did the sailor's hornpipe, some stripped the willow, there were Mad Robins, Figures of Eight, Back to Backs, Cast Offs, Cast Ups, and several versions of Sir Roger de Coverley. The Scotch did their reels, the Irish hopped up with their arms straight down like headless chickens, the men from Lancashire performed a clog dance without clogs, even fat little James managed to leap up the steps in an imitation of the Lancers, but pride of place went to Warnie, who attempted a particularly delicate Pousette. A positive light appeared to issue from his calves - you couldn't predict what would become of them next. He appeared to wink with his legs and the women squealed with delight. All the while more than two hundred and fifty chains swung to the rhythm of the music which Ball, who knew his business better than I could have told him, scraped from his bow. The crew and soldiers applauded and hissed as if they were at a pantomime, the women blew kisses and some flashed their tits as a distraction, but every convict danced into Crowe's cabin to receive the ration, which I assiduously poured into every cup, and danced back again without spilling a precious drop. Napier alone glowered from the binnacle.

The sun was beginning to set far over the yard arm before I finished pouring the two hundred and fifty measures. Harper was the last to come up. He was the only one who didn't dance. He shambled up the steps, uncertain where he was, and stood before us helplessly. He'd forgotten to bring a cup.

Crowe observed him closely and shook his head. "Prize fighting is a brutal sport. Give him his ration in my pint pot, Dawkins."

I sedulously filled Crowe's pot to the brim. Harper grabbed it and drank it as greedily as if he were dying of thirst. He turned without a nod of thanks, and clanked his way back to the deck. I refilled the pot and handed it to Crowe who stepped out onto the quarter deck to a resounding cheer from the sweating multitude. He raised his hand and the jigging ceased. Ball plunged his hot face into a pot of porter which I had especially provided for that purpose.

"I hope you find the exercise as beneficial as the wine." Crowe looked towards the grim-faced Napier and his wife. "I did not have the opportunity of observing all the dances. I wonder if our much appreciated pianist, Mrs Napier, will condescend to choose the best dancer?" Napier bit his lip whilst his pretty wife blushed. He turned as if to forbid her to speak, but she was already looking at Warnie, who looked back at her with a face flushed either from his exertions or plain bashfulness. She was about to point to him when she caught the fury in her husband's eye.

"Give it to him." She fearfully turned her head and pointed at James who, having already drunk his ration, was slumped half dozing on the deck.

Crowe handed me the cup. The convicts were somewhat mystified by the choice, but nevertheless, cheered once more and renewed their stamping. I pushed my way through them and handed the prize to the fat boy, who, much surprised, swallowed it in a single gulp and promptly dozed off again. I looked back towards Mrs Napier, but her husband had already dragged her into their cabin.

Warnie was gazing after her.

The hold was dark and damp apart from the golden glow around a solitary lantern, in which Magwitch was sitting amongst the sheep, reading his little black book.

"You missed a fine display of dancing but I've brought you your ration of grog."

His small dark eyes sparkled in the faint light. "Thank 'ee, kindly." He took the cup and sipped it with relish: "Port wine. I was always partial to it."

"Do you mind being down here?"

He shook his head. "The sheep give me peace; I know each one and have given them all names. Every creature should have a name. Names don't lie - when I was a boy all I knew was my name - Magwitch, christened Abel. How did I know it? Much as I know'd the birds' names in the hedges to be chaffinch, sparrow and thrush. Everything else was lies, only the birds' names came out true." He paused and seemed lost in a long-forgotten dream. His eyes flickered down to his little book: "Besides, I have plenty of time to read of the Good Shepherd, who will lead me to green pastures. I shall not want and everything I have will go to that dear boy."

Something had been puzzling me since Plymouth. "What dealings did Mr Chivers have with you?"

His throat clicked. "Look 'ee here, Chivers is a rogue, but a rogue you can do business with. I met a man in Dartmoor who owed me a favour. I'd done time on his behalf. He gave me ten guineas, part of what he owed me. On the journey down to Plymouth I learned Chivers often had dealings in Chatham - close to where that dear boy lives. I offered him five guineas to take the other five to Pip. I made him swear he wouldn't mention where it come from. Chivers is a greedy villain, he'll keep most of it himself - but he'll give Pip something. The first payment of the fortune he'll have one day that'll make him a gentleman."

Magwitch drained the cup: "Best poison a man can drink."

"What's the best poison to kill a man?"

"I've never tried it, lad. Poison was never my style, but I've heard there's no better way than arsenic."

I now had an urgent need to learn to read, and came on apace under Crowe's tutelage. I also became acquainted with the natures of the poisons and potions in his cabin, which in some ways resembled a small laboratory. I pretended to be fascinated by chemistry and Crowe let me have free range of his equipment. He kept large quantities of arsenic for the treatment of syphilis, which was already breaking out among female convicts, soldiers and crew. I secreted small quantities of it each day and deposited them amongst my other treasures beneath the loose plank in the galley. At the same time I craftily went about learning the quantity required for a fatal dose and the best way to administer it. I learnt that the most lethal form was a compound of arsenic trioxide, which could be easily incorporated into food and drink and, at that time, was untraceable in the body. I was glad to discover that death would be slow and painful and the symptoms indiscernible from cholera. I planned to slip it in Deplidge's drink as we neared Cape Town, I couldn't risk putting it in his food lest Molly ate it, but I knew she never touched alcohol. I then intended to jump ship and sail on to Australia at a later date. I'd heard from the sailors that the Cape was a pleasant enough place, with opportunities aplenty for a smart fellow like me. I hoped I might persuade Molly to come with me.

Crowe had had his way and, for the sake of their health, the convicts were given menial tasks - they were only too grateful to get out of the convict deck, which was now little better than an oven. They holystoned the decks, swabbed, cleaned, repaired and polished, as well as manning the bilge pumps night and day. The females laundered and sewed but, to my deep consternation, I hardly ever caught a glimpse of Molly. She sometimes emerged, white and pale, from Deplidge's clutches, and paced up and down the quarterdeck, gazing sadly at the distant coast of Africa. Depildge, himself, appeared to be completely besotted with her and left much of the daily running of the *Enterprise* to Farrington and Stride, the mate. I hated Deplidge more each time I saw his thin, pinched face, but comforted myself in imagining the agony of his death. Napier, on the other hand, was all too evident, strutting about the deck in malicious mood. He banned any further jigging contests, so Crowe made it my special duty to go round the convicts cradles each evening with their daily issue of port. My ears and eyes were as sharp as ever, and I flattered myself that little happened aboard *Enterprise* that I didn't know.

But life is full of surprises. One morning I came up on deck and beheld an extraordinary spectacle. Netting was hanging around the rigging on the quarterdeck, as if someone was hoping to catch flying-fish; and Napier was standing in front of the foremast waving something that resembled a wooden club, which I discerned to be a cricket bat. Attenborough stood by the bowsprit carelessly throwing a hard red ball from hand to hand; whilst Crawley, Bradman, and half a dozen soldiers were scattered about, gazing intently at Napier's bat, with a hand on each knee, stooping as if making a back for some beginner at leap-frog.

Suddenly Attenborough cried "Play!" The ball flew from his hand straight and swift towards Napier, who thwacked it furiously up towards the crow's nest, where it became enmeshed in the netting.

"Well played!" exclaimed Crawley. A soldier dutifully scrambled up the rigging to retrieve the ball, whilst Napier jogged between the foremast and bowsprit and back again. The soldier, having recovered the ball, threw it down to Attenborough, who cried "Play!" again, and hurled it back at Napier, who thwacked it up into the rigging once more. This tedious exercise continued for several minutes as Napier hit the ball harder and harder, and waved his bat in ever more elaborate swings, obviously very pleased with his style and accomplishment.

Attenborough was sweating under the burning sun and did not seem to be enjoying his task but as he took the ball in his hand for the umpteenth time, a sharp shout, almost an order, came from the other side of the deck.

"Bowl him a slower one!"

Attenborough automatically obeyed and tossed the ball gently. Napier already into his stroke misjudged the speed and it flew off his bat in my direction. I was aware of a red thing flying toward me - Fagin had trained my hands to be quick - I put them up to protect my face and felt a sharp sting in my palms as I held on to the ball.

"Well caught! How's that?"

"Not out!" Napier bellowed before turning in fury to behold Warnie leaning against the bulwark. "Your cry distracted me. What the Devil d'you think you're doing?"

Warnie's rosy cheeks rounded into a cheery smile. "Just giving a bit of advice to the bowler. He looked as though he had need of it."

"How dare you interfere with my game, you insolent dog. Is that how you address an officer?"

Warnie dutifully raised his knuckles to his forehead.

Napier glared at him contemptuously. "What does an oaf like you know about Cricket?"

"Watched it at Hambledon since I was a boy."

"Hambledon? Country bumpkins playing on a village green. Cricket is played by gentlemen at Mr Lord's establishment in Marylebone."

"The bumpkins of Hambledon beat the gentlemen of all England on more than one occasion."

"Pshaw. That was before the game became an art. The boys at Eton could thrash the drunken clods of Hambledon with an innings to spare."

"I'd like to have a wager on that."

A savage glint was in Napier's eye. "You've been asking for a flogging since this voyage began. Damn your eyes, I'll teach you to show some respect." He threw his bat to Crawley. "Bradman, assemble all convicts to witness punishment. Put the villain on the iron." Bradman nodded at two soldiers who seized Warnie, non-too enthusiastically, and pulled him towards the iron triangle, whilst pipes and drum mustered everyone to the deck.

"You can't flog me for nothing," Warnie protested as his arms were tightly bound to the triangle above his head.

"You are a damned convict and I'll have you flogged as often as I like. You are the property of the Crown to be used as I think fit - not even the hair on your damn'd head is your own."

The convicts sullenly clanked up the stairs and formed their ranks. The women clustered at the forecastle; Crowe joined the other officers standing on the poop. The remaining soldiers and crew watched from the rigging and along the bulwarks. Even Deplidge came out of his cabin with a pale-faced Molly at his side. Warnie's shirt was ripped from his white back, and Bradman took off his tunic and slowly rolled up the sleeves of his shirt. I noticed his forearms were thick and strong. The nine tails of the cat twitched angrily in his hand.

Mrs Napier, leaning on Sarah's arm, was the last to emerge. She gasped when she saw Warnie hanging helplessly by his wrists. Napier noticed and relished the moment even more.

"Despite my previous warnings, lack of respect and lack of discipline are flourishing aboard this ship. I have therefore decided to make an example - a light example - to remind you all that you are being transported to be severely punished and no mercy will be shown any of you until the last day of your sentences has expired." He smiled malevolently at Warnie, who was watching him with defiance written all over his face. "Bradman, scratch the rogue's back - open up his carcass with forty lashes."

Bradman put a leather bit in poor Warnie's mouth. "Bite hard. There's hardly a man in the regiment that has not gone through this. No hard feelings."

"Commence punishment. Lieutenant Attenborough, call out the strokes, at half-minute time." Napier was extending the punishment and pain as long as possible.

Bradman swung the cat and it whistled through the air and struck Warnie's flesh with a dull crack. Warnie shuddered at the impact but bit hard and uttered not a sound. I desperately tried to think of some way of stopping it - I looked towards Crowe but he had a look of distressed resignation on his face. By the fifth lash Warnie's back was bleeding and his skin lacerated, but he pulled doggedly on the straps by his wrists and remained silent. I could see Napier was determined to break his spirit:

"Thinks he's an iron man, does he? We'll have him blubbering yet. Lay on harder, Bradman!"

Bradman complied, but he did not relish his task. Mrs Napier had turned away and was sobbing with Sarah's arms about her. I was leeward of Bradman, and bits of Warnie's skin and flesh hit my face as they flew off the cat. Attenborough counted twelve, but Warnie still remained stoically quiet. Napier shot a glance at his weeping wife, who at that very moment lifted her head from Sarah's bosom and stole a fearful glance back at Warnie. Warnie was already looking at her and I'll swear he gave her a reassuring wink. Thank God Napier didn't see it. "Twenty!" he was half way there. Warnie's back was now quivering, weals ran across it in deep ridges from which blood flowed freely into a crimson puddle on the white holystoned deck.

Napier was now beside himself in fury: "You damn'd scoundrel! How do you like it?"

Warnie merely looked at him with disdain, and stayed silent despite the battering pain. Crowe had turned away in disgust - Molly and several other women had joined Mrs Napier in their tears. "Thirty!" Bradman's back was dark with sweat. His face and the front of his shirt presented the appearance of a mincemeat chopper.

Warnie's back now resembled bullocks' liver, but still Napier wasn't satisfied: "Another half-pound off the beggar's ribs, if you please, Corporal Bradman."

I vowed then that I would kill Napier as well, but Warnie seemed to be possessed by an inflexible obstinacy and still hung silently on.

"He's a game one...a real pebble, he'll show his stripes with pride," a soldier muttered beside me.

At last Attenborough called the 'domino', the fortieth and final lash. Bradman dropped his arm and rubbed it vigorously, whilst a soldier cut Warnie from his torment. Warnie's knees sagged but he refused to fall. Instead he jabbed his elbow in the pit of Bradman's stomach with all his remaining strength, knocking him back against the bulwark.

"No hard feelings," he muttered.

I ran towards him with a cup full of port, hoping to ease his pain, but was pushed aside by Adair and Hampton, laden with buckets of seawater which they threw over Warnie's bleeding, steaming back.

"Take him to my cabin." Crowe had come down to the main deck.

"Like hell he will. He'll go straight in the hold to take care of my sheep."

"Captain Napier, I concede that you have full authority over the punishments meted out on this vessel, but I am responsible for the health of all who sail in her. This man needs hog's fat applied to his wounds and I am going to insure that is done immediately. He will not be fit for any duties for several days."

As Adair and Hampton assisted Warnie up the stairs to the quarterdeck, past the glowering Napier, a convict began to stamp his feet, the chains rattled, and in an instant a hundred others were stamping in unison. Warnie's indomitable spirit had put courage in them all - but that night the piano did not play.

The following morning, after Mrs Trumper reported that her mistress was feeling delicate and ill, I knocked on Mrs Napier's cabin door with the tonic Crowe had prescribed.

"Come in." She was brushing her long hair. It shone like a raven's wing.

"Beg pardon, Ma'am. Mr Crowe says this should make you better."

She smiled gently. "He's very kind."

I put the bottle on her table and turned to go.

"How is Thomas Warne?"

I stopped in surprise. "Warnie? You know his name?"

She blushed. "I learnt it from Mrs Trumper. How is he?"

"He's lying face down in Mr Crowe's cabin with the fat of half a pig on his back."

"Would you give him my sincerest wishes towards a speedy recovery?"

"Don't you fret about that, Ma'am. Mr Crowe says Warnie has a hide on him like a rhinoceros - I wouldn't know as I've never seen one - but he promises he'll quickly mend."

She smiled again. "I will pray that he does."

As I came out on deck I met Sarah Trumper bringing some newly-washed linen.

"Poor, dear girl. Married to a brute. Married her and took all her money. She's completely in his power - she stood up to him last night, though - refused him her bed. He's moved in with the other officers."

I went to Crowe's cabin and found Warnie lying face down, with his head resting on his folded arms. I gave him Mrs Napier's message. I also added what Sarah had told me. He didn't look at me, but murmured softly: "Thank her."

The weather became hotter as we sailed south along the West Coast of Africa. The sun above us blazed down and melted the pitch between the planks, which dripped from the seams and burnt the flesh of those on which it fell. Crowe had sails fitted over the hatches, which he hoped would scoop up the wind and blow it down below; but the wind seemed to have died and the air became ever more stifling. There was only one word spoken or thought - one yearning desire in every convict's fantasy - not women or freedom or riches - but water. Cool, fresh, sweet water. Buckets of it, gallons of it - not the three pints of putrid, blood-warm liquid that Farrington dished out each day. The only relief was Mrs Napier's tinkling music, sounding as refreshing as a mountain stream. Mr Crowe told me it was called *The Trout Quintet*.

I'm not sure it was the music that inspired him, but as Warnie began to recover he returned to his old occupation - fishing. He had no net or line but invented a new method of angling by trolling hooks with strips of canvas, soaked in the hog's fat he was now all too familiar with. He soon became very skilful at it and began to haul in all varieties from the scuppers. I helped Crowe extract certain oils and juices from their slimy guts, which he assured me would prove beneficial to the general health of the ship, but the seamen and soldiers preferred Farrington's mouldy meat to fresh fish, and most of the catch ended up on the officers' table, where it was so appreciated that Warnie became the ship's unofficial fisherman and never returned to the hold, where Magwitch coped well enough on his own.

We were a hundred miles off the coast of Gambia one airless morning, and Warnie had just hauled in a fat, dark-striped Bonito, when the cry of "Sail Ho!" came from the crow's-nest. Most of the convicts were manacled below, but the women, soldiers and crew, scurried excitedly to the deck. A three-master, carrying a large area of sail had appeared on the horizon; as it drew nearer we saw it was flying an American flag. Deplidge had been called from his cabin to join the other officers at the binnacle. Molly followed - her face whiter than ever, contrasting with the dark rings around her sad eyes.

Deplidge's eye was blood-shot as he put his telescope to it:

"A clipper. Probably a slaver. Coming out of Africa with a cargo of black ivory."

"We must apprehend her - it is our duty as Britons," interjected Crowe.*

"That is best left to the ships of the West Africa Squadron, Mr Crowe," Deplidge snapped. "I would point out that she has a full deck of guns - unlike ours they are not painted show - see how the sun glistens on their barrels."

"We have more than a hundred soldiers on board - we can grapple and board her - it would be cowardice not to do so," Crowe protested.

"We will do no such thing," Napier snapped. "In 1812 I fought the rebels in America without a qualm, burnt Washington to a cinder, but it is madness to go into action with more than two hundred felons at our backs. They would mutiny at the first sight of the American flag - the accursed Stars and Stripes always awakens seditious thoughts of revolution. Besides, my men are replacements - not trained soldiers. Some were recruited in Ireland, God help us."

Deplidge was still focussing his glass on the clipper. "She's signalling her captain is coming over in the jollyboat."

"You're surely not thinking of entertaining a slaver?"

"Mr Crowe - we are not at war with the United States - it is the custom for captains at sea to exchange greetings and trade any surplus supplies."

As the clipper drew ever nearer we became aware of a foul stench wafting from her. *Enterprise* smelt bad enough, but this was a stench such as cannot be imagined or described. At the same time a strange dirge-like song, in some heathen language, drifted across the placid ocean. It made the hairs at the back of my neck tingle - it sounded like the lament of lost souls on their way to hell.

Harper had been honey-stoning the deck but on hearing the song he rose to his feet and gazed fearfully at the ship across the water. Tears began to stream down his dark cheeks, making them all the blacker. He shook his head and put his hands to his ears as if trying to keep the song from his fuddled brain.

Napier was on him immediately. "Get back to work, you black dog. Bradman give him a taste of the lash."

Bradman flicked at Harper's broad back. To everyone's amazement the black brute turned in fury and snatched the cat by its tails from Bradman's grip.

"Let him alone," expostulated Crowe. "He was probably taken from Africa as a child on such a hell ship."

"Insubordinate dog!" Napier exploded. "Put him on the triangle. Summon the felons to witness punishment."

Harper turned towards Bradman and the soldiers around him and raised his fists. It was the first time I'd ever seen him do that. It was an awesome sight. They were huge and looked hard as rocks. Bradman backed away, staring intently into Harper's eyes, holding his attention, whilst half a dozen soldiers edged behind him, then suddenly threw themselves onto the Negro's back, and by sheer force of numbers wrestled him to the ground.

"Leave the brute till later," remonstrated Deplidge. "Gag him and tie him to the foremast."

Napier was about to protest, but the bosun yelled that the jollyboat was fast approaching, and Deplidge hurried to bulwark. I followed, wishing I could push the foul rogue overboard. In the water below was a small boat rowed by eight of the cruellest, roughest villains I'd ever seen. At the stern stood a stout man, in a broad-brimmed white hat, with a long, fat cigar protruding from beneath his thick black moustache. He looked up at us, revealing a dazzling set of munchers. Cunning and deceit oozed from him like fat from a roasting goose. "Captain Pollipus Hammond, of the *Liberty*, out of Charleston. May I have your permission sir, to come aboard?"

Crowe jostled Deplidge aside: "You are a slaver, sir. We consider you a pirate. We will have no dealings with you."

Hammond continued to smile: "I come on a mission of mercy, sir. It is a common courtesy of the sea."

Deplidge asserted his authority: "I am master of this vessel. You may come aboard, Captain Hammond. Bosun, lower the ladder."

Hammond clambered up the steps and stole a look at the women gathered at the prow. "You have a fair cargo, sir. Sweeter than the black devils aboard my ship."

"What is this mission of mercy?" demanded Crowe impatiently.

"My ship's doctor contracted yellow jack, or something like it. He died two days ago and now the Congos in my hold are dying faster than flies. I expect to lose one in ten on any voyage - the black rogues get homesick for their benighted country - but if they continue dying at this rate, I'll have none left by the time I get to Charleston."

"I thought the American Congress had declared such voyages as yours illegal?" demanded Crowe.

The slaver lost his smile. "The Yankee Government in Washington made Congress sign a bill, but Southern gentlemen will never comply with such an iniquity."

"What exactly do you need?" asked Deplidge.

"I wondered if I might borrow your surgeon for a few hours? Give me some advice - show me which ones ain't going to make it, so I can get rid of them before they infect the others."

Napier had been silent until now. "I am no lover of your country, sir. What can we expect in return for such aid as we may give you?"

"Some good Yankee gold and as much rum as you can drink. Rum's the only commodity the King of Dahomey will take for his slaves. Made a good deal with him - got plenty of rum to spare."

"I'll gladly use my medical knowledge to assist those poor souls on your ship, but I'll never contaminate my hands with money earned from such an iniquitous trade."

"Speak for yourself Mr Crowe," Deplidge exclaimed. "My employers can't afford to lose time and money for your misplaced acts of charity. Captain Hammond, we are well supplied with rum. The fee will be a hundred dollars in gold for four hours of Mr Crowe's time."

Hammond glanced at Harper who was now straining at the mast - his eyes bulging like a pug dog. "Throw in that big buck and I'll make it a hundred and twenty-five."

"He is not a slave," exploded Crowe.

"You could've fooled me," retorted Hammond. "I reckon you've got more slaves aboard this ship than I have on the *Liberty*, and mine are black savages not my fellow countrymen."

"The convicted felons below forfeited their freedom. They are being transported to Australia to make amends for their crimes," snapped Napier.

"Sure, I've heard that song your sailors sing about Britons, never, never, never being slaves," said Hammond with an ironic smirk.

"It's a fine song. Better than that heathen row emanating from your hold," Napier retorted.

Hammond ignored him. "Well, Mr Crowe, may I avail myself of your services?

Crowe nodded and turned to Adair who was listening anxiously nearby. "You'll be coming with me. Fetch my bag from my cabin and tell Hampton I'll need him as well."

"Mayn't I go, Mr Crowe? I'm sure I'd be able to assist." I don't know why I volunteered, just curiosity, I expect.

"Dawkins, there will be sights aboard that infernal ship that will haunt you for the rest of your days."

"I've been in Newgate, Mr Crowe - I've seen awful sights all my life."

"Very well, but you must tie a scarf that I'll prepare across your mouth - be careful not to breathe in any infection."

Hammond was counting out gold coins into Deplidge's open palm.

"Is there anything else you are in need of?" Deplidge asked.

"Now you mention it, Captain, many of my crew, when they come to eating chicken, prefer white meat." He gave an appraising glance at the cluster of women, "Can I hire a few of your girls at the same rate as the surgeon?"

"Do you infer we are pimps?" protested Crowe. "I refuse to be part of such a depraved transaction."

Deplidge shot a glance at Napier, who nodded his assent. "Mr Crowe, I am in sole charge of the financial arrangements aboard this ship." He turned back to the American: "Make it a hundred and fifty, Captain Hammond, and Madame Greere will send over three of her best girls."

"What about that little beauty there?" Hammond pointed to Molly. "I'd give you two hundred for her."

Molly looked petrified as Deplidge hesitated. My hand clasped the knife in the lining of my coat which I still wore even though it was such a stifling day. I was prepared to stab Deplidge there and then, and to hell with the consequences; but to my relief Deplidge shook his head:

"She's worth more than that. Besides, she's a dish reserved for the Captain's table."

A few moments later, as our own jollyboat was being lowered into the water and we were clambering over the bulwark, I turned and looked back at poor Harper, still straining at the mast. He reminded me of a picture I'd seen in one of Crowe's books about Greek heroes. The one about the cove they tied to a mast, to prevent him jumping overboard, because some witch's song had enchanted him. But Harper was not enchanted - he looked as if his heart was broken. As I went down the stairs, convicts were looking out of the portholes, gazing disbelievingly at a ship where beings suffered even more than they. I climbed into the back of the boat next to Betsy; the other two girls were sitting fearfully beside her. Crowe, Hampton and Adair, were facing us at the prow, and between us six strong sailors were at the oars. Hammond was already on his way - we followed in his wake.

Crowe looked completely crestfallen. "I'm sorry ladies; I will make a full report of this scandalous conduct on my return to England."

"Fat lot that will do for us," said Betsy, "we'll be dead by then. Why do you help them, Mr Crowe?"

"I took an oath when I became a doctor, to do the meanest office if it would assist those in need of my services. I fear there are many desperately in need on yonder ship."

The *Enterprise* and *Liberty* tacked in the faintest of breezes, keeping a few hundred yards apart. As we drew nearer, we became aware of dark shapes circling round the *Liberty* and sharp fins cutting above the water. Suddenly something naked and black was thrown from the aft of the clipper; the dark shapes were upon it almost as it hit the sea and it disappeared into a mass of blood and foam.

"They must be the fattest sharks God made," muttered the tar in front of me.

When we reached the slaver's stairs, the stench was even more appalling. Crowe handed me and his assistants pieces of white linen. "I've soaked them in a special preparation of chlorine and lime water. Tie them round your mouths and noses when you go below. It should prevent you being infected." Our sailors couldn't wait to turn the boat around and get back to the *Enterprise* which smelt like roses by comparison.

Hammond laughed at the sight of us when we clambered aboard: "Few men are fit for these voyages but them that are bred to it." He gestured towards his crew, all big, hard, sun-burnt men, who were gazing awe-struck at Bet and her companions. Some grinned lasciviously and one, to my astonishment took out his member and began to rub it as if it were Aladdin's Lamp. I wondered if this was a common American way of greeting. Bet whimpered with fear.

Hammond took control: "Behave like Southern Gentlemen and uphold the honour of the great state of Carolina. I've arranged for you to have the privileged use of these fair English ladies for four hours. The price is five dollars a throw for ten minutes of their valuable time, paid to me in advance. Don't overstay your welcome. The mate will time you with his watch - any overtime must be paid in full."

"This is iniquitous," protested Crowe. "These women are human beings not animals."

"This is my ship and I call the rules..." Hammond broke off as a young black girl, naked except for a skimpy piece of coloured cloth around her lower parts, appeared on the poop above. He noticed the disapproval on Crowe's face. "Yes, Mr Crowe, I do not care whether my meat is dark or white, provided it is fresh." He looked at me for the first time with his small twinkling eyes. He had a singular expression, which was not a frown, nor a leer, and yet might have been taken at first glance for either.

"And what meat do you prefer, Mr Crowe? Have you a taste for young cock?"

I almost choked with indignation. I caught Hampton and Adair exchanging knowing looks. Crowe's face reddened - I am not entirely sure if it was with anger. "Confound it, sir. Are you inferring I am a pederast? That is a slanderous accusation - I am only concerned with this boy's education - I would sue you if we were under any provenance of law."

"I'm the law on this ship," Hammond replied disdainfully. "No doubt you wish to attend to the savages below - I'm paying enough for your services."

As Bet and the girls were dragged towards the crew's quarters, a surly sailor pulled up a hatchway and we descended into the hold. I had never dreamt, in my foulest nightmares, that I would ever behold such sights.

The deck was covered with naked black bodies, lying in their own filth. The men were shackled in pairs - wrist to wrist or ankle to ankle. Some had heavy spiked iron collars around their necks;, others wore iron muzzles such as you wouldn't put on the fiercest dog. Several lay dead and motionless in the filth lapping about them. The women sat with their heads on their knees - they had no space to lie down. Only their long, sagging breasts told me they were women, their heads were shaved from a point on the crown to the back part of either ear. Some looked up in terror as we came down behind a lantern and stared at us open-mouthed, revealing teeth, filed and sharpened to a point.

Crowe knelt to examine some poor black bastard before rounding furiously on Hammond who had followed us down. "This is an abomination. What have you been giving these poor souls to drink?"

"Why, the bilge water. Always been good enough before. They have different stomachs to us - like dogs."

"They are suffering from dysentery - the bloody flux - call it what you will. If you want any of these to be alive when they reach your accursed country, get them up on deck into fresh air immediately, and give them all the clean water they can drink. If you've not enough on board, embrace the first fair wind and sail back to Africa. Empty your rum into the sand and fill the casks with clean, sweet, water. It's their only hope." He turned to Hampton and Adair, who'd been hovering reluctantly in the gloom: "Start carrying them up now - start with the women - but be gentle."

We spent the afternoon carrying the poor wretches up to the deck. Some were dead before they got there and, to the delight of the sharks, were thrown immediately into the sea. A few were not quite dead as they went over the side. Crowe tried to prevent it, but the slavers only laughed at him - there was nothing he could do - and perhaps the poor bastards welcomed a quick, clean death.

At last a signal came from *Enterprise* that the four hours were up and the jollyboat returned. Bet and the girls crawled out of the crew's quarters - they could not stand - and had to be carried down the steps. The mate handed Hammond, who'd spent most of the past four hours with his black beauty, a bag heavy with the silver dollars the girls had earned. He slipped it into the pocket of his coat. I edged closer to him.

Crowe surveyed the deck, overflowing with suffering, and shook his head: "Captain Hammond, you have more blood on your hands than any pirate. We will meet on some future occasion, in some place where the rule of law is recognised, and I swear that I will do everything in my power to bring you to justice."

Hammond leered arrogantly. "It will take more than you and the entire British Navy."

I'd had more than my fill of him. I stepped forward and tugged at his coat: "I would inform you that I am neither a molly nor a punk, and that Mr Crowe is the most honourable man I've ever had the pleasure to encounter."

It was one of my most delicate lifts: the bag of dollars was out of the scoundrel's pocket in an instant. I didn't wait for his reply and scudded down the stairs into our boat. I was mightily relieved when the others piled in behind me and the sailors pulled lustily away. I held the bag tight under my arm and wondered how long it would be before Hammond discovered his loss. I didn't relax until we were under the shadow of *Enterprise's* hull. I now had enough cash to set me up in Cape Town, and would make sure that poor Bet had not toiled for nothing and, most importantly, I'd taken ample revenge on that foul rogue for his shameful slur on me and Mr Crowe.

Harper was still tied to the foremast as we scrambled on deck - still gazing desolately at *Liberty*, drifting away on the evening breeze. Mr Crowe ignored Deplidge and Napier, took a scalpel from his medical case and cut him free.

"He has endured all that we have seen today. In the name of Christ he has suffered enough."

Harper slid down the mast and squatted on the deck. Bet - poor, bedraggled, ill-used, Bet, sat beside him and tried to comfort him, putting her arm around his wide shoulders.

Our voyage south continued in fits and starts. Deplidge locked Molly in his cabin and spent more time at the barnacle, tacking east and west striving to snatch the faintest breeze. The bastard was a good sailor - I'll say that for him - he could trap a seagull's fart in his sails. Everyone grew crazy in the heat as we neared the Equator. For two days old Ball, the steward, paced the deck as Neptune himself, sewn into the flayed skin of a dolphin and stinking to heaven under the vertical sun, with a mop on his head for a wig, a bristled broom as his trident, and an oakum* beard entangled with shells and dried starfish, whilst the old tars initiated the young sailors, those who'd never crossed the line before, with all kinds of degrading and injurious tricks. The soldiers, women and convicts gaped as the poor lads were forced to crawl through tubs of rotting garbage, or beaten with wet ropes, or even flung overboard and dragged from the stern. Some were stripped naked and, to the delight of the women, shaved all over; others had gallons of seawater poured down their throats. For once the convicts were glad to remain safe in their sweltering, stinking quarters, with only the dulcet notes of Mrs Napier's piano to remind them of the civilised world they'd left behind.

By now most of the women had become sea wives with regular protectors - apart from those too old and Madame Greere and her whores - Deplidge insisted they would not open their legs for free. In any case

Bet now seemed to spend most of her time in Harper's company. So over a hundred of the soldiers and sailors and practically all the convicts were forced into sexual abstinence, which was the normal lot of all sailors, but this was not a normal voyage. At night, groans of wantonness echoed from *Enterprise's* every nook and cranny, only adding to the frustration of those who went without. Sodomy was punishable by death and there was little privacy for such an act, even so I kept my knife razor-sharp and to hand.

We finally crossed the Equator on the evening of the second day. That night as I passed the bulkhead by the crew's quarters, I heard wild music and raucous cries coming through the thin timbers. I put my eye to the nearest blimp-hole and beheld what I would later learn was termed a 'ballum rancum'. It was a sight such as I'd never dreamt of in all my childish fantasies. The women were supposed to be mermaids, and were dancing outrageously to the jig old Ball was scraping from his fiddle. They were entirely naked except for the fishtails tied around their waists, which flapped up and down over their bums. The sailors, drinking rum by the gallon, cried out instructions to their chosen women to perform evermore grotesque and unbelievable acts. I'd never imagined that females came in such a variety of shapes and colours and sizes. My little Dick Turpin stood and delivered.

I thought after that I'd seen everything but, being a city boy, there was one act I'd not bargained for. Later, as I returned from reading *Robinson Crusoe* with Mr Crowe, growls of fury and screams of terror erupted from the depths of the hold. Trumper was on deck feeding the pigs and heard it too. He grabbed his lantern and we hastened down the hatchway together. There, in the faint light, we beheld Magwitch with his hands around a soldier's throat.

"You vile rogue - I'll tear your liver out."

Trumper threw himself at Magwitch, put his arms around his chest and pulled him away: "Easy now, old fellow. What's he done?"

"He was trying to violate Stella. I caught him in the very act. She's little more than a lamb - never been tupped."

The soldier, who I now recognised as Private Evans, a sallow little chap with sunken cheeks, fell to the floor rubbing his throat and shaking with fear. "I'm sorry – I meant no harm by it - we did it in the village when we were lads when we wanted a woman."

Magwitch's hairy black nostrils dilated: "You damned villain - would you corrupt an innocent beast? An honest creature that gives nothing but everlasting love?" He raised his fist as if to land a mighty blow."

Trumper tugged him back again: "No, Abel. If you harm him they will lock you in the brig - who will tend your sheep then?" At that Magwitch dropped his fist, nodded his ugly head and looked down lovingly upon his flock.

I began to smell a way to profit from this. "Listen good, my flash companion," I whispered into the petrified Welsh lughole, "if Captain Napier learns you've been milling with his Merinos - he'll flog the hide off your back. We'll keep quiet about it, don't you worry, so long as you improve your habits and don't do it again. And remember to return favour for favour if ever we've a mind to call it in."

Evans nodded gratefully.

Sexual caperings abated somewhat during the following week as the heat grew ever more unbearable. Napier and his officers took to drink, quarrelled vehemently in the confines of their mess, and woke each morning with splitting heads and queasy bellies. Rats, cockroaches and lice grew ever more prevalent and added to the general misery. As I went about the ship distributing the port wine, I heard constant mutterings, complaining that we should have taken the trade winds to Rio: stories were told of the rum and women and the good times to be had there. Grievances grew as we began to grow increasingly short of fresh water. The daily allowance of everyone onboard was cut from three pints to two. The crew and soldiers resented the fact that they were given no more water than the convicts, and were even more aggrieved when they learned Napier had insisted there would be no reduction in the ration for his horses and sheep. Washing had to be done with seawater; some simply hung their dirty clothes from ropes and dragged them along in our wake. One soldier lost his best white breeches to a shark - morale was not improved when Napier sentenced him to a dozen lashes for abusing his uniform. The Irish seemed to grow ever closer, whispering to each other in their outlandish native tongue. I sometimes caught them murmuring earnestly with certain members of the crew and a few of the Irish soldiers, but they always fell silent whenever I approached. I took scant notice of them; there was much on my mind. I had concocted what I thought was a fatal dose of arsenic and now had money enough to survive in the Cape Colony; but I was growing ever more fond of good Mr Crowe and was loathe to leave him. I saw less and less of Molly - some days I wondered if she were still alive.

It was late one evening - Crowe was reading Southey's *Life of Nelson* to me in his study - he was a good teacher and I'd already begun my life-long love of literature in all it various forms - when Bradman knocked at the door and informed him all officers were summoned immediately to the captain's cabin. I automatically followed at Crowe's heels, hoping to catch a glimpse of Molly.

Evans was on guard outside Deplidge's door. He looked at me sheepishly. "Make sure on your life, nobody hears what is said inside," Bradman hissed at him as we entered.

Napier was standing by the big window with his hands clasped behind his back, his sword in its scabbard and a cased pistol on his belt. Attenborough and a nervous looking Crawley were similarly armed. Deplidge was seated at his table, Farrington, Stride the mate and Curram the bosun, were standing either side of him with folded arms. There was no sign of Molly, but the curtains were drawn around the bed.

Napier waited whilst Bradman shut the door and leant against it.

"Gentlemen, I have called this emergency meeting because an informer has warned me of a mutinous plot by the Irish. They plan to free the convicts this very night - they have made counterfeit keys and hidden them throughout the ship - they then intend to murder every man present in this cabin. They have already persuaded some of the Irish soldiers and crew to adhere to their foul cause and intend to coerce the recruits and crew to join them - and believe me they will do it. I have witnessed all too often how they mutilate limbs and gouge out eyes to persuade doubters. The fools think they have knowledge enough to sail to Brazil. We must act tonight to crush this serpent's egg in its shell."

"What proof is there of this - beyond the word of your informer?" demanded Crowe.

"I've used him in the past when I was serving in Sligo. I have a hold over him that he dares not break. His information has always been sound."

"How many men can we rely on?" Farrington reminded me of a cornered rat.

I'll say this for him, Napier was a good soldier. He was calm and in perfect control, revelling at the prospect of the action that was about to explode. "Bradman is the only non-commissioned officer I've got, but he's a good one. Corporal…" Bradman clicked to attention at the door, "pick twenty men you are certain of and relieve the guard. If any protest, we'll know they're rebels, so clap 'em in irons immediately. If you're convinced the rest are loyal let them join us. Captain Deplidge, the ship's officers will have to man the cannon. Load with grapeshot and have 'em aimed at the hatchways - don't fire until ordered. We will make the poop our redoubt. My wife and her maid had better take refuge in here with your slut, Captain Deplidge." He waved his hand contemptuously towards the curtained bed. "I suggest the crew are locked in their quarters until this has been put down. Once we have secured the cannon and relieved the guard, I will commence arresting the mutineers and traitors." He pulled a sheaf of paper from his pocket, "I have a full list of names."

I suddenly thought of Warnie - had he joined the rebels? He'd reason enough after his flogging - besides I knew how he felt about Mrs Napier - he might see this as a way to win her. I was uncertain which side I was on. I was only too happy that the mutineers intended to murder Deplidge - that would save me the trouble - I had no qualms about Napier - but they wanted to kill Mr Crowe too, and he was my dear friend; but so was Warnie.

Events were moving fast. Bradman was already below picking his men. Napier was now seated at the table giving Attenborough and Crawley their final orders. Deplidge had unlocked the weapons cabinet and was handing out cutlasses and muskets to Crowe, Farrington, Stride and Curram. He hesitated when he came to me.

Crowe noticed at once: "He's loyal - I'll stake my life on it,"

"On your own head be it, Mr Crowe," Deplidge reluctantly handed me a small pistol, little guessing how much I desired to fire it at his breast, "but I suppose we need every hand we can muster. Put it in your pocket, boy. Go to the galley and fetch Bell and the cook."

Evans was still guarding the door. I could not resist whispering *Baa, Baa, Black Sheep* as I passed him - which made him look more sheepish than ever. I'd almost reached the galley when I caught sight of a dark figure on the deck; lurking behind the main mast - the moon shone on fair hair - it was Warnie.

I made sure the sentries were half dozing, looking out to the placid sea, and scudded stealthily down to him. "Are you planning to mutiny? Don't be a fool. Napier knows everything."

To my relief he shook his head. "No. I wouldn't do anything to harm her. I knew about it, but I couldn't nark."

"What are you doing here - they'll shoot you if they see you on deck."

"I'm keeping an eye on her - I know what they'll do to an officer's wife. Especially if she's a Belfast Protestant."

"How did you manage to get free?"

He opened his palm to reveal a key. "I knew where one was hidden."

"Go back below - Napier's about to take her to Deplidge's cabin - she'll be safe there."

At that a crack of light came down from Deplidge's door and Napier came out and crossed to his cabin. We heard frantic whispers, then watched as he pulled his wife out by her arm, Sarah Trumper followed. Almost immediately Bradman and his chosen men came up the hatchway to take their positions on the poop. There was a hiatus as the sentries began to be relieved:

"Get below. And don't leave your cradle. She's safe now."

Warnie turned reluctantly and disappeared into the gloom. I hurried to the galley and conducted Ball and the cook to Deplidge, who eyed me even more skeptically.

"What kept you so long?"

"Went with great circumcision, sir."

Crowe laughed. I thought it was the right word - picked it up from Fagin.

Napier checked we were all armed. "Right, take your positions on the poop. Mr Crowe, stay here with that brat and guard the women. If we fail to overcome this mutiny, I rely on you to prevent my wife falling into their hands. Death is better than dishonour."

With that the pompous fool led the others out, closing the door. I went over and listened through the thin wood.

"Bradman are the guns secure?"

"Yes, sir. They're ready: primed with grape and aimed at the hatchways."

"Can you rely on the sentries you relieved?"

"They're all sound, sir. Not an Irishman amongst them."

"Are the crew and the other recruits locked below?"

"Yes, sir. I've placed an armed man on each door."

"Very well, pick your best ten men and come below with me. Attenborough, you take command here until I return. Be ready to open fire if anything goes wrong."

I heard whispered commands and the noise of boots scraping the deck. Then silence. I turned and looked back into the dimly lit cabin at Crowe and the women. He'd laid his loaded musket on the table and was administering one of his comforting draughts to Mrs Napier. Sarah Trumper looked distraught.

"What is going on? What will happen to Sam and my boys?"

"Don't worry. The Irish have planned a mutiny - your husband and sons will not be involved."

"Is Mr Warne part of it?" Mrs Napier asked Crowe fearfully.

"No, milady. He'd never do anything to put you in danger," I answered.

She blushed. The bed curtains were pulled aside and Molly was staring at me. I stole over to her. Her arms were black with bruises - like Nancy's after a violent night with Bill. I tried to take her hand.

"Don't touch me," she hissed.

"What have I done?"

"I heard everything," she whispered vehemently. "You're no better than the overseers in the mill - you only care for yourself. You've sided with them - with Deplidge - I thought you at least would try to help me."

"It is a crazy and desperate scheme, Molly. Napier knows everything - it would never succeed..."

I wanted so much to tell her of my plans for Deplidge - how I would exact revenge for all that she'd suffered - but harsh shouts and orders began to come from below. A shot was fired. Mrs Napier trembled; Sarah took her in her arms. Mr Crowe picked up the musket and pointed it towards the door.

The sounds of scuffles and cries, violent blows and bitter curses went on for several hours, but as dawn began to break the bosun's whistle piped all hands, and nineteen Irish rebels, three soldiers and five seamen were dragged to the deck, tightly handcuffed and with rigid leg irons round their ankles. Napier, flanked by Attenborough and Crawley, sat behind a large drum on the poop, on which was draped a Union Jack. Crowe and I watched from the binnacle with Deplidge and the ship's officers - the soldiers, crew and convicts assembled in rigid lines on the deck, looking fearfully at a pair of nooses swinging gently from the yardarm. The women, as usual, clustered at the prow. There was no sign of Mrs Napier or Molly.

Napier began the proceedings. "Thanks to the diligence of my officers, a most nefarious mutiny has been put down. The culprits and their ringleaders are here in chains. Their guilt and evil intent is manifest: their punishment inevitable." He cast a glance over the paper before him. "Ryan, O'Brian and Dooley," the three wretched soldiers hung their cruelly-beaten heads. "You have taken the King's shilling and wear his coat - you are traitors and will be executed forthwith." Dooley began to blub.

Crowe stepped forward and spoke urgently in Napier's ear. "Surely they are entitled to have someone speak in their defence?"

"They have forfeited that right. This is a drumhead court-martial. In the power invested in me by the King, I am judge and jury."

Crowe sighed, shook his head, clasped his hands behind his back and came back to the binnacle.

Napier was positively enjoying himself. He turned to the five sailors: "You are guilty of mutiny - the seaman's foulest crime - you will remain in irons in the brig until we reach New South Wales, where you will be consigned to labour in punishment gangs as long as the Governor sees fit." He finally set his sights on the Irish rebels, who were still staring defiantly at him beneath their bloody brows. "You have already been sentenced for rebellion and are only alive due to the King's mercy. You have violated that mercy and can expect none now.........."

"Liberty or death! 'Tis all one to us." cried a black-bearded man with a great mass of forehead.

"You shall have death, John Hogan, and so will you, Paul Brannon."

A badly-beaten man swayed on his feet - I noticed they were of unusually large proportion. "Do what you will, old Ireland will be free."

"You two were the ringleaders and will hang forthwith, before you spread any more seditious pestilence," Napier continued. "The rest will have your backs skinned with forty lashes and then join the mutineers in the brig."

Bradman motioned four soldiers to drag Hogan and Brannon towards the ropes but one of the younger rebels threw himself in their path, crying up to Napier: "I was trained as a priest - may I not at least give these men absolution before they die?"

Napier shook his head peevishly. "I will not countenance Popery. It is nothing but vile superstition - destitute of every principle of morality."

"For pity's sake - show some humanity!"

All eyes looked behind Napier to where his wife stood, wide-eyed and distraught. Crowe hurried over to her; Warnie just prevented himself from doing the same.

Napier flushed with anger and embarrassment, but growled reluctantly: "Very well - but make haste with your nonsense."

The young man, who I later discovered was called Donovan, hastily chanted as much of his rigmarole as he could remember. It seemed to comfort the two condemned men as Bradman stood them on stools and fixed halters about their necks. On Napier's signal Bradman kicked the stools away, the yardarm was swung out, and the pair of them danced and gurgled the 'Paddington Frisk' over the blue Atlantic. Brannon's large feet flapped like the flippers of a walrus. Donovan repeated his dirge before the three unfortunate soldiers were dispatched in like manner from the other side of the ship.

Then the flogging began. Forty strokes each for the remaining seventeen rebels - six hundred and eighty in total. Not even Bradman's strong arm could manage that alone. The Irish were strapped up in pairs whilst four of the most robust soldiers administered the flogging, two at a time. Some endured silently like Warnie, but others blubbered and screamed from the first lash. One remarkably big soldier called Carter seemed to particularly relish his task. He would step back a couple of paces then bound forward with his arm uplifted, take a jump and come down with the whole weight of his body upon his unfortunate victim. We stood and watched for more than two hours, until the final lash had been delivered and the last man had been cut down from the triangle.

Crowe was fuming with impatience and anger. "Hampton and Adair fetch the buckets of sea water; Dawkins make ready the hog's fat."

Napier stopped us with a wave of his hand. "These men do not deserve your attention, Mr Crowe. Corporal Bradman!"

A weary Bradman clipped to attention, "Sir?"

"Handcuff them again and throw them all in the brig. They won't see daylight until we reach Australia. Lieutenant Attenborough, dismiss punishment parade and then join me for a celebratory toast to the King."

He turned and swaggered off to the officers' cabin. Crowe hurried after and followed him in. I surreptitiously listened at the door in best Fagin fashion.

"If their wounds are not cleaned they will become gangrenous in the filth and stench of the brig," Crowe expostulated.

"They would have killed us all - their welfare is no concern of mine."

Crowe's voice was little more than a whisper. "You said one of them is your informer. Why do you punish him with the rest?"

I heard Napier's cruel chuckle. "How little you know of duplicity and subterfuge, Mr Crowe. If I gave my man better treatment the murderous traitors would suspect him - I am saving his life by giving him the lash."

"I tell you this Captain Napier, the spirit of enlightenment will not always be suppressed by the power of cruelty."

Crowe came out of the cabin with tears in his eyes.

Warnie was sitting on the end of his cradle, looking melancholic when I came with his port that evening. "Have you still got yer knife, Dodger?" he asked softly.

I gave him the nod - it was safe in the lining of my coat.

"I can't bear to see those poor bastards swinging. Their eyes are everlastingly fixed on me when I'm fishing in the scuppers. I'm going to cut them down."

"Don't be a fool, Warnie. Think what Napier will do if you're caught. What about the sentries?"

"They won't see me - not if they're drinking one of your bottles of rum. Meet me on deck at midnight." He opened his hand to show me he still had his key.

"Why risk everything? You and me have got easy stations now."

"I can't let that butcher Napier win every hand."

As the ship's bell began to strike midnight I waited in the shadow of the main mast, hugging a bottle of rum under my coat. It was a cloudless night; every star was in the sky - illuminating the five hanging bodies, swaying in a macabre dance: spinning around with the motion of the ship, their tongues hanging from their mouths like exhausted dogs.

Warnie's blonde head appeared at the top of the hatchway on the tenth peal of the tinkler. I signalled all was clear, he crept over to join me, and I handed him my knife, freshly sharpened on Bell's whetstone in the galley. A throaty chuckle came from the poop - I could see bright little balls of flame where the sentries puffed on their pipes.

"How will you cut both sides down without 'em seeing you? You'll have to cross the deck. You'll show up clear as day."

"You keep 'em busy, Dodger. Give 'em your card tricks."

I waited behind the mast, until Warnie had crawled along in the shadow of the bulwark to below where the two Irish rebels were swinging, then took a deep breath, gripped the bottle in my right hand and stepped onto the deck in my lazy saunter.

"Who goes there?"

I recognised the voice. "Hold your noise - you Welsh rogue." I whispered.

The other soldiers turned questioningly. "It's only the kid," said Evans softly.

I scudded up the steps and joined them on the poop. Evans regarded me anxiously, as if frightened I was about to reveal his dirty little secret.

"What do you want?"

"A sociable call, my covey. I bring salutations." I held up my hand - the bottle sparkled in the starlight.

The other soldiers clustered eagerly about me as I pulled out the cork with my teeth; I edged round so that they had their backs to the deck. I could see Warnie climbing into the rigging above the swinging bodies. A thirsty soldier made a grab for the bottle.

"Stow the gammon. You ain't going to have it for nothing." I took the cards out of my pocket and laid them on top of a hatch. I'll play you for a swig. - I lose, you drink free - you lose, you pay me a penny."

They pressed closer, ever up for a wager. Warnie was reaching out and cutting at a halter. "I'll cut any gentlemen in the company, for the first picture card."

"I'll have that!" Somebody put a penny on the hatch.

I deliberately turned over a three and gave him Queen of Hearts.

"I win," he made a grab for the bottle - I held on to it for a brief moment until I saw that Warnie had almost cut through the rope. They were all engrossed, watching their fellow put the bottle to his lips, and failed to hear the first body splash into the water. The others couldn't wait to lay their pennies down. Big brutal Carter was next. He drew a five - I showed King of Diamonds and gladly pocketed his penny.

Carter was a bad loser. "Give me another turn, young gallows." He slapped another penny down on the hatch.

I didn't think it wise to aggravate him. Warnie was now hacking at the second rope. I took my time cutting the pack. "Toor rul lol loo, gammon and spinach…"

"Hold your noise, give me my bleedin' card."

Warnie had almost cut through. I gave Carter the Knave of Clubs - an extremely suitable choice. He yelled in triumph as the second body dropped into the ocean. Carter deliberately swallowed two large draughts to make up for his lost penny. Warnie was now creeping across the deck behind the main mast, making for the safety of the other bulwark. Evans turned his head a fraction and I knew in that moment he'd seen him.

"Let's have a glim, Taffy." I demanded, looking meaningfully into his eyes. He understood my meaning and dutifully struck me a match; I made great play of lighting my pipe with it.

I let the next two punters win as Warnie climbed up into the rigging above the three dead soldiers. All the sentries were now totally riveted - I was certain that Warnie would accomplish his task - when suddenly a shaft of light came from a cabin door opening behind me and someone stepped out on to the poop. Warnie flattened himself in the rigging, tight against the nearest swinging body but I knew whoever was on the deck behind me could not fail to spot his blonde head.

The soldiers were all now looking fearfully at the intruder. The man who'd been about to drink, hastily put the bottle down on the hatch. I was expecting to hear Napier's sneering voice, order his men to fire into the rigging, when a hand rested gently on my shoulder.

"Entertaining the troops, are we, Mr Dawkins?"

It was Crowe - good, old, gentle Crowe.

The soldiers all came to attention. Crowe picked up the bottle.

"An excellent idea, Mr Dawkins - to give the sentries an extra ration of rum. They've earned it after their exertions in the past twenty-four hours." He coughed to cover the sound of a body slipping beneath the waves. He took a flask from his coat pocket. "I'll think I'll join you. Shall we have a toast to the King?"

They murmured, "The King!" as another body hit the water. There was only one left. "Mr Dawkins, I suggest you pass the bottle to the men. Let's all drink to the 57th - to the Die-Hards."

There was much agitation and ado as they all tried to grab the bottle, hoping to toast their regiment before all the liquor had gone. Warnie meanwhile had cut free the last dead soldier and was stealing back towards the hatchway. The last drop of rum was slipping down Carter's cavernous throat as Warnie disappeared.

Crowe tapped me on the shoulder. "Now Mr Dawkins, would you be so kind as to join me in my cabin, there are some matters I wish to discuss with you."

As soon as the door was shut Mr Crowe turned upon me in fury. "Dawkins, I gave you my complete trust. I believed you were an intelligent young man and had great hopes for you; but what you and the convict Warne have accomplished this night is plain foolhardiness. Wellington may be a poor politician but he was a great general - he always chose his ground with great judiciousness before a battle, but you have blundered into a most calamitous situation, which will endanger you and cause unnecessary suffering to many more."

"I beg pardon sir. But I couldn't bear to see Captain Napier always getting the better of you."

"My hour will come, never fear. Now I have to do all I can to save those sentries from his lash. Tell your friend Warne that whatever happens, he must not admit to what he has done tonight. This time Napier will kill him."

Crowe was right. The following morning when the cut ropes were discovered, all Hell was let loose. Napier charged the sentries with neglect of duty and would have flogged all ten of them, even though Crowe pleaded their case, emphasising their exemplary conduct in putting down the previous night's mutiny. I was looking forward to seeing that brute Carter being flogged and he would have been, had not Attenborough reminded Napier they'd few enough men to rely on. Eventually Napier grudgingly conceded and merely fined them all a month's pay. There was another painstaking search of the ship for knives and keys. Having failed to uncover any, Napier ordered the convicts should be kept on half-rations until the culprit was found, and offered a reward of an instant ticket-of-leave on arrival in New South Wales to anyone who would name him. Perhaps because his informer was securely locked in the brig, no names came forth.

I thought no one had suspected my involvement, until the next morning a rough hand grabbed me by the scruff of my neck and shook me violently, like Bill's dog shaking a rat. I was swung around and found myself a few inches from Carter's ugly, scowling face. His breath was foul: "You, young devil - you duped me - almost got me flogged, damn you, and cost me a month's pay. One day you won't have your precious Mr Crowe to protect you, and I swear I'll grind your skull under the heel of my boot."

I now had added reason to jump ship in Cape Town.

After a few days on half-rations, some convicts, already malnourished, were close to starvation - even so I saw Bet giving her meagre piece of dried horse flesh and weevily biscuit to Harper, whom she was now nursing like her own child. Because they were so weak and as further safeguard against scurvy, Mr Crowe instructed me to give every convict half of a lime with their port each night. Such was their hunger that they sucked on the bitter fruit as if it were honey. All this whilst Napier, Deplidge and the other officers feasted on Warnie's fish and the remains of Trumper's livestock.

Lethargy descended on us all - even the piano stopped playing. At the end of the week, despite Mr Crowe's best efforts, old Daniel Thorpe, the genteel manservant, died in his sleep. Next morning all were paraded on the main deck for his burial. Although old Daniel had never been given the comfort of a hammock in life - he was sewn into one in death. '*He brought nothing into this world and it is certain we can take nothing out*', read Mr Crowe. I've heard those words more times than I care to remember since then, but they've never sounded more apt as when old Daniel slid into the ocean's watery embrace.

Later I found a miserable Warnie fishing at his usual place in the scuppers.

"What's the row?" I asked him.

"I won't allow anyone else to die because of me."

"Don't be a fool. Old Thorpe was on his last legs - Mr Crowe says his lungs were wasted away."

He shook his head. "It's my fault. I did what I did to spite Napier - for my own selfish reasons - because I wanted revenge for the lashing and because I envied him his pretty wife. I look at their faces down below - they know it was me and they'll never nark - but I see the accusation in their eyes. There's no telling how long this voyage will take, how many more will die...". Something ruffled his long blonde hair. He stopped to wipe it from his eyes. Something ruffled it again. We glanced at each other - not daring to speak. A faint breeze - too weak to be called a wind - was coming off the sea. Warnie sucked a finger and slowly, fearfully, held it above his head. "It's blowing south ..." We looked up, the drooping sails, ever so gently, began to swell, and *Enterprise*, like a reluctant mare, began to inch at last towards the Cape.

The atmosphere aboard changed immediately. The air became fresh, the breeze became a wind, the wind grew stronger, torpor and lethargy vanished. The sailors constantly pulled on ropes and clambered aloft to trim the sails, as Deplidge sought to gain the smallest breath of extra wind. The female convicts hung out their washing and the bedding in lines across the deck; the soldiers became good humoured again, looking forward to the good food and shore leave at Cape Town. Even the convicts were happier as cool, clean air managed to find its way into their stinking quarters and as their spirits rose, Warnie's feelings of remorse departed. Only the poor souls in the brig remained in the same pitiful state - chained together without light or air - their only solace an old Irish air floating down through the timbers. I'll never know if Mrs Napier played deliberately to fortify their spirits - even so they'd have all died if Mr Crowe hadn't disregarded her husband's orders and given them daily care.

We had a pretty spanking run along the African coast for days on end; all I could see was arid desert and shifting sand dunes - I wondered how, or if ever, I would survive in such a place. Although it was mid-June, the days became cooler and the nights cold: Mr Crowe explained it was winter down here on the bottom half of the globe.

One morning Mr Crowe was writing his diary when I brought in his coffee. He looked up at me and smiled: "Special day today, Dawkins. June 15th, anniversary of Waterloo."

A strange feeling came over me - I'd never been aware of the day before. "Nearest thing to my birthday, Mr Crowe. What year was Waterloo?"

"1815."

"What's it now?"

"1828."

I'd found out my age at last - I was thirteen.

I hadn't spoken to Molly since the night of the mutiny. She either ignored me when we passed on deck, or watched me contemptuously as I went about my business - but I was more infatuated with her than ever. One morning, as I hung around the binnacle, hoping to see her on her way to the galley, there was a shout from the crow's nest. Deplidge put his glass to his eye and focussed at a distant headland. I watched his cruel, thin mouth twisting as he squinted through his telescope. "Cape Saldanha - if the wind holds we'll reach Cape Town in another day." Whilst I had no conscience as far as thieving was concerned, killing was a different matter, but I thought of what the foul villain had done and was still doing to Molly; the brutal way he'd sold Bet and the other girls to the slavers, and convinced myself the time had come to put my plan to action.

I retrieved my bottle of poisoned rum from its hiding place, secreting it deep in the lining of my coat, and hung around the poop waiting for Molly to come out of Deplidge's cabin. After a while she appeared with a bundle of his soiled linen. She glanced at me disdainfully as she locked the door behind her and then made her way to the scuppers. I waited until she was busy laundering, then meandered up to the aforesaid door, leant against with my hands behind my back, whistling whilst I felt for the lock and turned it with my bent nail. Then, glancing round the deck and ensuring no eyes were upon me, I slipped inside.

Deplidge's bottle of rum was on the table - it had roughly the same level of liquid as mine. I crept towards it. My heart felt as if it was pumping in my throat. I'd just exchanged the bottles, when I heard footsteps outside and a murmur of voices. Someone was putting a key in the lock. I looked frantically for a hiding place; there was nothing else but to dive behind the curtains on the bed. The key rattled around - it was that brief moment that saved me.

"The stupid little bitch forgot to lock it - damn her!" I peeped through a chink: Deplidge was locking the door with Madame Greere beside him. "Let's do our business quickly." He said in a low tone, then went over and sat at the table. She stood before him. The bed smelt of his sweat and the sheets were stained with his depravity.

"That's it for this week." She threw a small bag upon the table. He opened it and a trickle of coins fell out.

"And this is all?" he asked after a close scrutiny.

"All. The men are getting short of money and I've only got the two girls on the game. Bet, stupid cow, spends all her time with that dumb black and won't work anymore. Not that anyone wants the bitch - they all think she's his woman and are terrified what he'd do if he caught 'em at it."

Deplidge drew a long breath, and poured himself a glass of rum. I realised with horror that I'd left both bottles on the table - but he didn't seem to notice. I wasn't sure now which bottle was which.

"There's a Portuguese who runs a cheap house in Cape Town who'll take her. I mean to sell my little ladybird to him, she'll fetch a good price, she's still young and fresh. I'll throw in your trollop as well, get even more." He downed his rum in a single swallow. I hoped with all my heart that is was from the poisoned chalice.

"How will you get her away from that black brute? He'll put up a fearful fight."

"I'll shoot the villain if he resists and accuse him of mutiny. My word is law upon this vessel." He got up and led the way back to the door. "I may pick up a couple of Hottentots cheap when we dock tomorrow. Slaves are still plentiful and cheap at the Cape. We'll need to replace Bet for our business venture in Australia. I'm told they're not particular down there - they're starved of women."

They went out. He locked the door behind him. I jumped from the bed and scudded over to the bottles. I sniffed them, but couldn't tell the difference. Had I poisoned the bastard already? I heard more voices outside and began to panic - my only concern now was to pad the hoof and make a swift escape. I left both bottles as they were, unlocked the door and departed unobserved, hoping Napier would join his pal for a liberal nightcap.

I watched Deplidge assiduously throughout the day, but apart from rubbing his belly once or twice and some ferocious flatulence - he appeared quite normal. Molly finished her laundry and disappeared back into the cabin. After I'd checked that my money and valuables were still in place, there was nothing to do but wait. The shoreline grew ever nearer - the land grew more hospitable; I could make out white sandy beaches with green uplands beyond. I could see that Warnie was studying it too as he fished in the scuppers.

Evening came at last. The sea was like a millpond. I was in the galley when Molly came in to fetch Deplidge's supper. There was such despair in her face it was hard to believe that she didn't know what the damned villain had in store for her. I stretched out my hand in sympathy, but she flicked it scornfully aside and went back to the cabin, for what I hoped would be her last night in his cursed company. As we were sailing so close to the shore all the convicts, even the women, were securely chained below. Mountains were now appearing in silhouette against the fading light. I'd never seen such mountains before - they made me feel very small, very lonely and quite afraid. I was glad to busy myself with the issuing of the port and limes. Magwitch remained in the hold, diligently tending his sheep - miraculously he'd kept them all alive - I filled his tin cup twice and gave his shoulder an affectionate tap as I left him, but I don't think he noticed. Poor Bet was disconsolate because she was spending the night apart from Harper; her face had become thinner, she seemed so weak and listless, she could hardly stand. She refused to take her ration and made me promise I would give it to Harper. I promised, but filled her cup anyway. I couldn't help but kiss her dirty cheek; she was my last link with my Fagin days. I poured out extra port to all my pals - Trumper, Miller, Fatty James, Lindwall and Kidman, until finally I came to Warnie. I found him picking at a bone with a needle.

"What's the business, my flash companion?" I enquired.

Just making a brooch." He looked as discomforted as Bill Sikes, caught putting money in a poor box.

"Oh my eye, whose it for? As if I didn't know."

He didn't reply. I realised how much we'd gone through. I didn't want to leave him. I made up my mind there and then.

"Have you still got your key?"

He nodded.

"When we dock tomorrow I plan to jump ship and make a run for it. Will you come with me? I've got plenty of money for the two of us - three of us if Molly comes as well."

He shook his head in disbelief. "What of Australia? That soldier from Barnet? He might be your father."

"I've no proof he ever existed. Perhaps it was just another one of Fagin's lies. I've got to get Molly out of Deplidge's clutches - he plans to sell her to a shag-house when we dock tomorrow." He looked down at the half made brooch in his hand. I thought it best not to tell him about the poison. "Come with me, Warnie."

He hesitated. I could see he was undecided, but at that very moment the piano began to play. He listened for a moment before he shook his head: "Sorry, Dodger. I can't leave Leticia." He looked at me affectionately and ruffled my hair, "Best of luck, little mate."

I had only one more farewell to make. Mr Crowe had begun to read me passages and scenes from Shakespeare and that night he chose *Macbeth*. Since then I've heard that pompous snob Macready, Sir Henry Irving, and Ira Aldridge – the best of the lot of 'em, tear that passion to tatters a hundred times, but never did I listen to those words with such horror as that night, in the dim light of a swinging lantern. Murder, guilt and retribution, seemed to be in every line. I endeavoured to comfort myself with the thought that if Deplidge did drink my poison, I would not have murdered a good, old king but a foul, damned villain who deserved everything he bloody well got.

Crowe eventually finished reading and slammed his big volume shut. I must have looked pale for he patted my knee reassuringly, "Chilling isn't it, old chap? Keats said he wouldn't like to read Macbeth alone in a house at two o'clock in the morning."

"Who's Keats?"

"John Keats. Another great poet like Shakespeare - but one from our own times. Poor, unfortunate chap, died young of consumption, but wrote superb poetry - I'll read you some tomorrow. I think *Eve of St Agnes* will be an appropriate work to start with."

Poor Crowe - I wouldn't be there to hear him read any more. He and Warnie were the best friends I had in the entire world and I was leaving them both. There was so much I wanted to tell Crowe, so much I wanted to thank him for. "I'll always be grateful for the kindnesses you've shown me," was all that I could stammer out.

The faintest hint of a tear came into his hazel eye. "Don't mention it Dawkins. You're a talented boy - I have great plans and hopes for you."

The night passed slowly. I crept out on deck just before dawn. Stride, the mate, was standing at the binnacle beside the helmsman: there was no sign of Deplidge. I stole into the galley where the cook was busy lighting the fire for breakfast. He didn't see me ease up the loose plank and retrieve my valuables. I furtively checked all was there - the ticker and other pickings from Corunna and the slaver's dollars. I was rich - at least for a while. I plunged the bag deep into my coat and went up to the poop deck.

We were approaching a town beneath a large flat mountain with thin cloud resting on top like a tablecloth. Cape Town was far smaller and much more primitive than what it is today, but it was a town - a large, busy town - a place where I knew I could survive. I kept looking towards the door of Deplidge's cabin - hoping to see Molly burst out - crying that the captain was dead - so that in the resulting hue and cry we could slip ashore and run - but to my growing consternation, the door remained firmly shut.

More sailors and soldiers were now on deck, looking excitedly at the ever-nearing harbour. Napier came out of the officer's cabin with his telescope, Attenborough and Crawley followed; Mr Crowe and Bradman were on the forecastle, with Trumper and his sons, watching some odd-looking black and white birds swimming beside us, which I was informed, were penguins; but Deplidge's door still remained closed - surely someone would come and wake him? But there was no sign of Bell. I could wait no longer. I stole across, inserted my twirler and slid inside.

All was quiet and still. The curtains were firmly closed around the bed.

"Anyone there?" I called in a hushed voice.

There was no reply. Then I heard something drip onto the floor under the bed. I looked down and saw a dark puddle. I tip-toed over, my heart beating louder than a drum. I took a deep breath, reached up and pulled the curtains apart. The sheets were red and wet with blood. Deplidge lay naked, arse-upwards, with a knife planted firmly between his shoulder blades. There was no sign of Molly.

6. Across The Southern Ocean

As we sailed into Table Bay, there was a frantic search of the ship, from bilge to crow's nest, but not the slightest trace of Molly was found. Napier conducted a full inquiry whilst we docked, seated like a beak at Deplidge's table, oblivious of the two half-empty bottles before him. I was summoned to give evidence as I'd discovered the body. In the first shock of my grief my mind seemed numb. I was almost in a trance, my eyes rarely straying from the bottles. After much deliberation Napier eventually decreed that Molly had stabbed Deplidge and thrown herself overboard: the helmsman thought he'd heard a splash in the middle of the night. I clung to the faintest of hope that she'd somehow managed to get ashore but couldn't see how. I cursed myself a thousand times for not telling her of my plan. Molly, my first love, had died without hope - believing I'd failed her.

Napier declared that he'd assume sole command of the *Enterprise*, leaving the navigation and running of the ship to Stride, the Mate. Crowe protested that we shouldn't attempt a perilous voyage across the Southern Ocean without an experienced captain: Cape Town was a naval station, and the best course would be to wait in port until a British ship came in with spare officers aboard. Napier said he wouldn't risk staying in port with a cargo of murderous brutes. Crowe then proposed that the convicts be transferred to the Governor's prison in the castle. He said many of them were weak and the salutary air of the Cape would strengthen them for the rest of the voyage. Napier obstinately refused, saying his orders were to deliver the damned felons to New South Wales by the promptest means and would sail as soon as needful repairs had been made and fresh supplies taken aboard. Even the fact that his wife was near her time and would be far more safe and comfortable delivering his child in a proper bed, could not dissuade the bastard. Eventually both Napier and Crowe stormed off to the Castle of Good Hope, to state their respective cases before Sir Galbraith Lowry Cole, the Governor. I helped Bell clear up the mess in Deplidge's cabin and surreptitiously emptied the contents of both bottles into the waters of Table Bay. I hoped I hadn't poisoned the bleedin' penguins.

I was in the deepest despair. All my plans had come to naught. Despite my deep affection for Mr Crowe and Warnie and the others, I had to get off *Enterprise* - everywhere I looked brought back memories of Molly. She'd gone - I'd lost her forever; but I could still see her standing at the bulwark, her auburn hair streaming in the wind, and still hear her voice as it was when we spoke that first day, before Deplidge violated her. We were docked in the midst of the port and a gangway led down to the busy wharf. There was incessant bustle and noise with the rattling of wheels, the clattering of hoofs, the clashing of iron and the jolting of casks and timber, as suppliers brought forth their wares - some of which were already being stowed below. A few of the crew and soldiers had been allowed ashore, the rest were looking over the bulwarks, all eyes and hair, waving to some dark-skinned girls. The convicts, of course, even the women, were firmly chained below; the lucky ones peered out of the portholes, gazing longingly at the joyous liberty they feared they'd probably never enjoy again. The local boys, browner and far bigger than my pals in London, began pelting them with oranges from the overflowing baskets on the quay, which the convicts were only too grateful to receive.

I looked more closely at the town - it seemed a pleasant place with fine houses stretching away up the mountain - but it was the dark, narrow streets around the harbour that attracted me. I felt for my bag of money and valuables: made sure they were still safe in the depths of my coat and decided to leave there and then. Farrington stood at the top of the gangway, counting the sacks of flour that coffee-coloured Hottentots were carrying aboard. I edged over towards him and waited. One little Hottentot sweated up with a leaking sack, leaving a trail of flour behind him. Farrington saw it and immediately began to furiously belabour the unfortunate fellow with his cane. Whilst the vicious rogue was thus distracted, I slipped past him down the gangplank and scudded across the wharf into the cool shade of a crowded street. It felt strange to be walking on firm land again after so long at sea, but I stumbled my way as swiftly as I could. Although it had been British for more than fourteen years, most people, apart from the red-coated soldiers of the garrison, seemed to be talking in Dutch, or Boer, call it what you like - I've never understood the God-awful language. They were a surly lot even then, already resenting British rule, and all too occupied with their own affairs to notice me.

I made my way down Slave's Walk, past the spice shops of the Cape Malays, to a fine-looking inn set in a spacious courtyard, beset with vines. I slipped inside to find a busy bar made of ancient wine casks and long tables where red coated soldiers and civilians were cramming strange looking Boer food into their mouths. I spied Hampton and Adair, Crowe's useless assistants amongst them. Hampton was picking at what looked like a boiled sheep's head (I was glad Magwitch wasn't there to see it) and Adair chewing on a pickled pork hock - there wasn't a decent bit of beef and potatoes in sight. At that very moment an eye dropped out of Hampton's sheep, he looked away in disgust and caught sight of me. "What the Devil are you doing here, Dawkins? Hadn't you better go back to your friend, Mr Crowe?" Adair wiped his greasy mouth with the back of his hand and blew me a kiss.

I pretended to be embarrassed and hurried out - I cursed myself for being careless - I should have gone further away from the port. I made my way to what I sensed was the roughest, smelliest and most delinquent part of the town. The Cape was known as the Tavern of the Seas in those days, every other building was an inn of some sort or other and they all seemed to be full of soldiers from the garrison. At last I found what I was looking for: a dirty looking establishment at the end of a closed yard - the Cape Town equivalent of *The Three Cripples.* It was crammed to the rafters with sailors from all nations - eagerly drinking away their hard-earned pay. Their pockets and purses were bulging, and on other occasions I'd have been sorely tempted to dip, but I'd other things on my mind, and besides I'd money enough for the moment. I was thirsty for my favourite salutation and bought myself a mug of strange Dutch gin from the landlord, a coarse, rough, heavily-built fellow. I took a seat in a dark corner, watching the whores lead their willing victims to the rooms upstairs, not really knowing what to do.

I noticed a big, plump man with red face and strawberry nose, sketching with a piece of charcoal on a large pad of paper. His eyes were rolling hither and thither - they seemed to see everything that was going on around him. My curiosity was as sharp as ever and I surreptitiously stole across and glanced over his shoulder. He was drawing the faces around him. I was amazed how life-like they were.

He glanced backwards and saw me watching him. "Do you want your likeness drawn? I'll do it for a shilling" He spoke with a heavy Dutch accent. There was an air of melancholy about him - but also refinement despite his worn and shabby attire.

I shook my head.

"Why not? You must have a mother somewhere." He took a large sip of gin. "You could send it to her. She would be happy to see her son looking so fine and well."

"I ain't got a mother."

"A father then? Or sister?"

I shook my head.

"A sweetheart?"

"I've no one," I said bitterly.

He turned and regarded me closely. "You have an interesting face. I collect interesting faces." He indicated a tarpaulin bag on the floor by his feet which was crammed full of sketches. "Pull up a stool and sit still - just buy me another glass of gin."

I'd money enough and was feeling very lonely, so I bought him two-penny worth of gin and sat on a stool before him. He took a fresh sheet of paper and frowned whilst he studied my face.

"It is strange - I sense that I have seen your face before."

"Can't see how, old pal. Just got off the boat this morning."

"From England? From the convict ship?"

"Oh my eye, news spreads fast around this place. Are you from this manor?"

"No, from Amsterdam - I studied art at the Conservatorium," he drew in swift, bold strokes. "I had ambitions to be a great painter, but fell out with Napoleon - at least I fell out with his police. Came to this extremity of the earth to escape prison, never had enough sense or money to get back."

"Are there no good pickings to had?"

"Not for an artist." He gave a melancholy smile then took another gulp of gin and perused what he'd sketched. "I cannot understand - every feature seems familiar. The shape of the mouth, the angle of the eye. I never forget a face…" He rummaged among the sheets in his bag and, after discarding several, pulled out a yellowing sheet. He stared at it intensely whilst shooting intermittent looks at me.

"What are you looking at?

He glanced once more upon the sheet before he turned it towards me. It was a face of a middle-aged man, worn and lined; a face that had seen the world and not thought much of it; but it was my face, even I could see that.

"Who was he?" I asked, although I already knew the answer.

"A soldier, who came in off a boat a few years ago. Bound for Botany Bay. He had no money but I drew him anyway. I think I even bought him a glass of gin. He told me many fanciful tales of the brave deeds he had done at Waterloo. Do you see the likeness?"

"I do indeed. He is my father."

I'd lost my love and found my father in the same day. I gave Jan Peeters, for that was the Dutchman's name, five Yankee dollars for the drawing of my father, folded it up tenderly and slipped it in my coat, and made my way back to *Enterprise*. My fate was decided; the die was cast. I had no other course or desire but to go on and find my father in Australia.

Napier won his case - I suspect Sir Galbraith didn't wish to bear the expense of feeding so many hungry convicts. We remained in Cape Town for another five days whilst the necessary provisions were acquired and repairs attended to. Trumper advised Napier what fodder he should purchase for his horses and the merinos; Mr Crowe replenished his stocks of port with Cape wine, and bought plentiful supplies of oranges and lemons to renew his fight against scurvy - I busied myself more than ever in his service, doing all I could to forget Molly. As there was no need of fish, Warnie remained chained below with the other convicts - pining for the daily reports I gave him on the state of Mrs Napier's health. At least Deplidge's death had spared Bet. Madame Greere had no influence on Napier - who despised her - so Bet remained onboard, doting on Harper whenever the opportunity arose.

It was the second week of July when we weighed anchor once more, and sailed south into the swirling waters off Cape Point where the Atlantic Ocean met the Indian, to begin the longest and most hazardous stage of our immense voyage. Almost six thousand miles of rough seas and stormy weather still lay between us and our final destination. We were no more than a mile or so off-shore, when huge spouts of water broke the surface. Great dark shapes leapt high out of the sea and plunged joyfully back again. Gigantic fishtails waved in the air.

Trumper looked up from tending the newly-purchased pigs: "Whales! Whales!" He ran over to the hatch and called down: "Abel, you must come and see this sight. Mating whales!"

Everyone on deck was now gazing at the awe-inspiring leviathans. Magwitch emerged slowly from the hold: his pallid face now whiter than chalk, his eyes red rimmed from the darkness. He stared at the great beasts for several minutes before whispering: "It is written in my Book: *Jonah came up from the innermost parts of the ship and the Lord prepared a great fish to swallow up Jonah, and Jonah was in the belly of the fish three days and three nights until it vomited out Jonah upon the dry land.* I have been as Jonah all my life; yet God has brought me up from the pit. I will pay in full what I have vowed."

I was the only one who understood what he meant.

Then, out of nothing, came the storm. Tremendous and mountainous seas began to lay into us and drove us towards huge rocks, higher than our mastheads. It was soon all too apparent that Stride was no match for Deplidge as a sailor, and we suffered abysmally as he sought to wear the ship and stand to the wind. The lower decks were soon awash, despite the frantic efforts of the convicts at the pumps. The wretched sailors had to climb aloft to close-reef the topsails and set the main, with *Enterprise* swinging to and fro like a cork, and the fearsome rocks drawing ever nearer. In the darkness of the storm I could see the luminosity of the surf breaking over their rugged and barnacle-crusted backs. It seemed we were lost: we would either be smashed against them, or capsize, or the masts would break; I don't suppose there was a living soul on board that expected to see the sun again. Perhaps it was the God of Magwitch and Jonah that saved us, for when disaster was barely a cable's length away, the wind miraculously turned, and against all our expectations, we rounded the rocks by a hair's breadth and battled on to the south.

The storm stayed with us for days on end - the sailors clung in mortal fear to the safety lines as they went about their fearsome duties. Stride was barely aware of our position because he couldn't take a reading on the sun. Crowe's official assistants, Adair and Hampton, terrified of being washed overboard, feigned sickness and cowered in their cabin, but I never failed to accompany him, as he did all he could to alleviate the misery and suffering. Napier, now occupying the Captain's cabin, spewed alone.

The baby began to kick its way into the world on the fourth night of the storm. Crowe and Sarah delivered it, as lightning flashed and thunder roared, almost drowning the screams of its mother. The sea broke over me, drenching me again and again, as I sat outside on the heaving deck, with my arms about my knees, trying not to listen. At last the screams ceased and amid the tumult of the tempest, I made out the faint cry of a baby. A minute or so later, a thin golden beam crept across the sodden deck as the door opened half an inch, and Crowe called out softly:

"Dawkins, tell Captain Napier his wife is safe and he has a son."

I staggered across the poop, my coat tails flying above my head, bent double against the raging wind, holding on to the safety rope with all my might, until I reached the Captain's cabin and hammered on the door.

"Come in!" Napier sat alone under a swinging lantern, his legs outstretched on the table, a half-empty bottle of arrack, newly purchased in Cape Town, before him. He raised his head and looked carving knifes at me. "What do you want?"

I knuckled my forehead and gave the villain a silent fart, although even my loudest efforts would have been drowned in that wind. "Please sir. Mr Crowe told me to inform you that the baby has come sir and your wife is well sir."

He took a big swallow of arrack. "What is it?"

I affected a saturnine disposition: "What is what, sir?"

"The baby, you numbskull. What is it?"

"A boy, sir."

He nodded then barked: "Get out."

That was all he said - he gave not a smile nor sign of happiness to greet the arrival of his son, Richard Horatio Napier, as the baby was later named. But I knew someone who would rejoice at his mother's safety. I extracted one of my few remaining bottles of rum, crept down to the stinking convict's deck, and waded through the swirling water and waste to where Warnie was picking away at Leticia's brooch.

It was another ten days before the storm finally abated and we found ourselves sailing with full sail under a bright cold sun. The weather had taken a fearful toll on the health of all onboard - the convicts were in a pitiful condition, when not manning the pumps, they'd been living with water considerably above their waists; but it was the Irish in the Brig who'd suffered most. Two had died in their chains. Once more the drum summoned us on deck for a burial, this time conducted in the Catholic manner by Donovan, who seemed to have aged ten years: his face was gaunt as a skull, his eyes dark, his lips shrunken. Napier had refused the dead the dignity of a sewn hammock and their filthy, emaciated bodies were almost naked as they dropped beneath the waves.

It seemed to get colder every day: the convicts had only been issued with thin clothes and one meagre blanket and huddled together for warmth. Mrs Napier, recovering her strength, took to her piano once more - playing the most cheerful English country airs, which to some degree, kept up their spirits. One morning I was leaning on the bulwark, blowing on my fingers, comforting myself with the thought that at least Molly wasn't suffering any more, when Bradman came alongside me and lit his pipe.

"We're making good speed: we're in the Roaring Forties now." he said, gazing up at the full blown mainsail.

"Roaring Forties? What are they?"

"They're the prevailing winds you find between forty and fifty degrees south. No land in the way to slow 'em down."

I didn't really understand but nodded as if I did. I'd been wanting to ask Bradman something since Cape Town. I felt inside my coat and drew out the carefully folded drawing. I opened it and handed it to him.

"Have you ever laid eyes on that cove?"

He screwed up his face and rubbed his arm. "I'm more acquainted with soldiers' backs than faces. He looks like you."

"I think he's my father."

He shook his head: "Never came across a Dawkins in the Army."

"He wouldn't have been called Dawkins - Dawkins is my name, the name the Gypsies gave me. I don't know what his name is. All I know is, he was bound for New South Wales."

Bradman handed me back the sketch: "Show it around the regiments when you get there. He's got a memorable face."

Later I went with Crowe into the women's quarters. He was increasingly concerned with the state of Bet's health. She was becoming ever more listless and, as Crowe examined her mouth, I noticed her gums were bleeding.

"You're showing symptoms of scurvy. Are you eating the oranges and drinking your grog?"

She shook her head. "Harper has more need of them than me."

"Harper has his own ration. You must think of your own health."

"I have no wish to live." I smelt her breath: it was foul. "What have I to look forward to apart from the life of a whore? I know what that trade does to a girl. Even your skill couldn't cure me of those diseases, Mr Crowe."

"You've no need to be a fallen woman. That Greere crone has no power over you now. You can start anew in Australia as a respectable domestic servant. I'll help you find a good position. God willing - one day you may marry some good man who will know nothing of your blighted past."

"Harper is the only husband I'd ever want."

He shook his head sadly: "Some things are the same in the New World as the Old. If you marry a Negro you'll always be considered a whore."

Nevertheless, Crowe told me to make sure she imbibed her daily ration, which I did by promising her I would give Harper double.

The seawater we'd shipped in the storm had ruined much of the animal fodder in the hold, and Magwitch was forced to feed the Merinos on flour and water. Four or five were ailing and Napier, having acquired Deplidge's share in them as well as his own, commanded Stride to make the swiftest possible speed. This he did, despite Crowe's misgivings, by sailing further and further south to lessen the mileage. We were six weeks out of Cape Town on a foggy morning, when the lookout shouted "Ice!"

Warnie was back fishing in the scuppers, his hands and feet raw with the bitter cold. He came clambering up beside me on the poop deck and we both looked incredulously towards an extended ice pack, stretching before us. I'd never seen a more beautiful or frightening sight - the sun shone through wisps of mist on huge glaciers with crystal peaks and pinnacles, reflecting a myriad of colours. But there was no time to appreciate their beauty: the wind was speeding us remorselessly towards them.

"Tell Stride to change course north-east, immediately! Drop all sail!" Warnie yelled to the helmsman, who was staring transfixed ahead, and ran over to the ship's bell and began ringing it furiously.

Stride and Curram tumbled out of the wardroom, followed by Crawley and Attenborough; Napier appeared frowning at his cabin door, Bradman came running up from the hold. Almost immediately there was a sound of tearing wood and rupturing timber and *Enterprise* was veritably lifted out of the sea. She shuddered and rolled as if in pain, before breaking free, hurling us about the deck like skittles.

"We've struck an iceberg!" Stride, a fair-weather sailor at the best of times, was ashen- faced.

"Any fool would know that. What do you propose we do?" snapped Napier, brushing his sleeve.

"We can't take to the boats - we'd never survive," Stride stammered. "Besides we've only enough for the crew - there are no boats for the soldiers and convicts."

"We'll have to fother her." Crowe had run up from below.

"Fother? What in damnation is that?" Napier growled sulkily.

"We'll wrap the hull with sail and oakum, like a bandage. Saw it done after Trafalgar - several ships sailed back to Portsmouth with holed sides. If we get the sail in the right place, the pressure of water will force it into the crack and plug the hole until we can make repairs."

Napier shot a questioning look at Stride, who shrugged his shoulders in despair:

"I don't think it can be done."

"We have no other option," Crowe replied, evenly. "Captain Napier, my youthful years in the Royal Navy qualify me to take control of this vessel. Have I your consent to do so?"

Napier chewed his lip, incandescent with fury and frustration. For a moment I thought he was going to order Crowe's arrest for mutiny. I don't know what would have happened if he'd done so, every man on deck knew Crowe was our only hope; but finally Napier, unable to find the words, nodded his reluctant acquiescence.

Crowe wasted no further time: "Mr Stride go to the binnacle and heave to under close-reefed sails."

Stride, mightily relieved to be rid of his awesome responsibility, muttered, "Aye, aye, sir," and dashed to the binnacle. Crawley and Attenborough went with him, Napier stalked after.

Crowe now addressed Bradman: "Corporal, we'll put your soldiers and the convicts to the pumps and get extra pumps in the bilge – but we must first ascertain how big a hole we have to repair."

Bradman came to attention and saluted but Crowe had already turned to Curram, who was nervously biting his fingers. "Get a foresail out of the locker: and get every spare man sewing strands of oakum to it. The convict women must help; their hands are quicker with a needle."

There was now a bedlam of activity: soldiers, sailors and convicts, men and women alike, all were only too anxious to obey - they knew how close they were to a cold and agonizing death - especially the chained Irish in the Brig, who'd be first to die.

Napier, the officers and Stride watched at the binnacle as the sailors scrambled aloft, whilst Crowe took Bradman and the ship's chief carpenter to check the inside of the hull. I scudded behind them. We pushed passed Magwitch soothing his sheep as the water seeped up around their feet; Napier's horses were whinnying pitifully in their stall - their groom had fled up above.

Crowe lifted the hatch in the forward hold and instantly we felt the icy sea pouring in beneath: "At least we know where to apply our bandage. Corporal Bradman, get some of your best men and the strongest convicts. Start pumping in here immediately; the hole must be just beneath us, just about level with the foremast." He turned to the carpenter, who was gazing down in disbelieving terror: "Get your men and tools ready. You must begin repairs from the inside of the keel as soon as the water level allows. Caulk it with white lead and oakum."

He ran back up to the deck with me at his heels. I don't think I'd ever felt real fear until that moment: "Please, Mr Crowe, don't leave me, I can't swim."

"Swimming don't matter, Dawkins. We'll all die after a few minutes in that freezing water but none of us will die if we keep the ship afloat."

When we came back on deck a foresail had been dragged out, to which sailors and women alike were frantically attaching masses of oakum - strands of old pine-tarred rope. Napier, his arrogant self again, remained at the binnacle, Stride stood by him looking helpless. Mrs Napier had come out of her cabin for the first time since the birth: Sarah Trumper was with her, holding a bundle which must have been the baby. I noticed Warnie looking at Mrs Napier's fearful face, but everyone else concentrated on Crowe. Survival was their only thought.

The sail was now covered with oakum - it looked like a gigantic rug. "Right, lads," said Crowe, "now we'll thrum her. Secure the four corners with the stoutest ropes you have." The sailors obeyed his commands unquestioningly. They worked quickly - all was done in a matter of minutes. "Next we must get it over the bows and pass it under the bottom until it is level with the foremast."

Eager hands rushed forward to lift up the dead weight. There was no time to dismantle the bowsprit, Warnie hacked it down with an axe; then, after shooting a re-assuring look at Mrs Napier, he perilously perched himself on the forepeak and guided the thrummed sail over his head with his hands. It hit the water and everyone heaved on the ropes, port and starboard, as it slid beneath the waves to make its agonising way beneath the hull. Warnie leapt over the larboard bow into the scuppers, seized a rope and pulled for all his worth as the freezing water swirled around his bare legs and feet.

"Steady, lads!" Crowe stood with his arm raised until the men heaving on the leading ropes were level with foremast. "Now! Make fast! Tie tight as you can to the bulwarks and mast."

The sailors knew all about knots - the sail was secure in less than a minute. Then I followed at Crowe's heels as he dashed back down below. Under Bradman's supervision soldiers and convicts alike were desperately manning the pumps - no sooner did one man drop off exhausted than another took his place.

"How's the water level, Bradman?"

"It's going down slowly sir. Thank God we've plenty of men. It's fearful hard work. They can't keep it up for long."

The carpenter and his crew had mixed white lead crystals with linseed oil and yet more oakum and were standing ready with fresh timber and their tools. Crowe grabbed a lantern, pushed past them and peered into the keel; I looked fearfully over his shoulder. To my relief white sail was swirling in the dark water.

"Good. The pressure has pushed it through. We are sealed for a while. More pumps down here, Corporal Bradman if you please!"

"Aye, aye, sir!" A dozen men leapt into the icy water as valiantly as the forlorn hope at Badajoz.

Crowe turned back to the carpenter: "As soon as they pump it dry, lay another skin above the hole."

I never loved Crowe more than I did at that moment - I knew he'd saved us.

We had to fother *Enterprise* three more times as we limped across the Southern Ocean; each time Warnie set an example to all by his diligence and bravery. The pumps were manned night and day: sailors, soldiers, convicts - men and women, all united in keeping the ship afloat. All distinctions were forgotten as we laboured to save our skins. Perhaps it was that that kept the convicts alive, that and the rousing music from Mrs Napier's piano. The convicts forgot the cold and their hunger: they'd no time to contemplate their fate and, despite the lack of fresh food, grew strong in their labours. Down in the freezing hold Magwitch still battled to keep his sheep alive - Trumper joined him to tend Napier's ailing stallions.

Napier was a foul rogue but he was a pragmatic one, and realized Crowe was our only chance of reaching safety; so he gave him free reign and spent most of the time in his cabin, drinking arrack and playing cards with Attenborough and Crawley. Crowe kept us under the wind with easy sail, on watch night and day, constantly navigating our course, but never neglecting his duties as surgeon. Each morning he diligently examined every soul onboard. He was obsessed that all should be brought safely to land. I was gratified when he allocated Adair and Hampton the unpleasant task of scouring the heads daily with seawater and purifying them thoroughly with oil of tar. Crowe also oversaw the fumigation of the bedding and still made sure all had their daily rations of oranges and wine. He even brought the pitiful prisoners in the Brig up on deck for wholesome air and, as soon as they were strong enough, made them take their turn on the pumps, saying the exercise would be good for their minds as well as their bodies. He treated all men as equals and was truly one of the finest men I've ever had the good fortune to know - I loved him then, I'm not ashamed to admit it.

Mrs Napier came on deck with her son every day, weather permitting. I looked at the tender care she lavished on her babe and envied it. I knew my own mother had never treated me with such affection. To her husband's disgust, Mrs Napier began to converse with the convict women, who never failed to thank her for her music; although she never exchanged a word with Warnie, who listened and worshipped from the scuppers. The brooch was long finished but he couldn't find the courage to give it her.

But despite Crowe's best efforts poor Bet grew weaker and weaker. One morning as I came round with the wine and oranges, I spied Harper kneeling by the cradle on which she lay. His dark cheeks were wet with tears. He looked up at me and opened his huge hand: his palm was surprisingly pink. I put two oranges in it.

"How are you, Bet? My dear old girl."

She opened her eyes and tried to smile: "Not so good, Dodger. I'm feeling very cold and tired." Harper had peeled the oranges and began feeding segments of them into her mouth. "Funny, ain't it? Now Harper's looking after me. No one's ever done that before."

Harper's ugly face broke into a tender smile. It was the first time I'd ever seen him respond to words.

"You know, Dodger, Harper and me have never done it," murmured Bet. "I've done it with hundreds of coves and never felt a thing for any of 'em. But I love him and he loves me, and we've never done it."

I looked down on those two lost souls - the broken prize-fighter and the sick whore - and wished with all my heart they would live and find happiness. But as I've observed in the course of my dishonest life, this is a very cruel world. Bet died in the evening of the following day and all night the ship echoed with Harper's pitiful cries. Mr Crowe determined that Bet should have a burial befitting a lady. Next morning she was sewn in a hammock with two cannon balls at her feet and placed upon a mess table under the British flag. The entire company of convicts, sailors and soldiers attended her funeral and Mr Crowe read the service. Then as: *'O God our Help in Ages Past'* resonated from the open door of Mrs Napier's cabin, Bet's poor, misused body was committed to the deep, to be turned into corruption, looking for resurrection on the day the Sea gives up its dead. It took six of the strongest soldiers to prevent Harper joining Bet as she slipped beneath the cold and restless waves.

Then, at last, on the morning of November 3rd a rocky headland was sighted - Crowe averred it was the south cape of Van Diemen's Land, on which, it was rumoured, was a punishment colony for the most violent and rebellious convicts. We wondered what sort of hell that could be - some of us would find out all too soon. A few more days and we finally reached the coast of New South Wales. Everyone lined the bulwark to gaze at sandy beaches and bold headlands, great sandstone cliffs, thick forests and distant snow- topped mountain ranges. There was a general feeling of reverence and awe - that this vast, unknown land, which we'd traversed so many thousand miles to reach, would now be our home. I did the nearest thing to pray: that my father was out there somewhere and I would find him at last. I made sure no one was looking before I wiped a tear from my eye.

Crowe stood on the poop, gazing contentedly at the shoreline with his hands behind his back, unaware that convicts, sailors, soldiers and all the women were clustered on the deck, watching him with admiration and affection.

"We would never have got here without him," muttered Warnie. "Best read it now Trumpy."

Trumper stepped forward, took a piece of paper from his pocket, cleared his throat, and began to read in a faltering voice: "Honoured sir..." Crowe turned in surprise. "It is our deep regret that we are not able to give you a greater proof of our thankfulness and respect," Trumper continued. "We can only ask you to receive our sincere thanks for the kindness, generosity and liberal treatment which you have always shown us on the long voyage here to New South Wales. May you succeed in all your future enterprises, and while we must follow our unknown fate in a far-off, inhospitable land, may the hand of the Almighty protect you and bring you back safely to a happy home."*

"God bless you, Mr Crowe!" shouted Sarah Trumper, and everyone, soldiers and sailors and all, cheered, stamped and applauded as if they were attending a cockfight in *The Three Cripples*.

Crowe raised his hands to quieten them - it took him several minutes - he was extremely moved: "That we have arrived safely is due to every one of you. When mankind works together with a universal aim, as all of you have done on this perilous voyage, there is no limit to what mankind can achieve. I trust that the same spirit will flourish in this new country. I will inform Governor Darling of your efforts in saving this ship and petition him to alleviate your sentences. Even those of you who were misguided enough to plot mutiny."

The convicts, men and women, cheered louder than ever; joy sparkled from every countenance and congratulations issued from every mouth. I think I was the only one to be aware of Napier, standing behind Crowe; his eyes filled with hate. He waited till the cheers began to subside before he pushed himself forward:

"Mr Crowe as you have successfully navigated us to our destination, I will resume command of this vessel. Corporal Bradman, ensure all felons are in fetters, then parade all hands, except those on the pumps, on deck."

In an instant wild elation had changed to dread and black despair. Bradman, after a sorrowful glance at Mr Crowe, began to bark his orders, and convicts, seamen and soldiers were comrades no more. The convicts stood glumly in their lines, looking as if they'd just been sentenced all over again. Most did not notice the serene sky, the fair wind and sparkling water as we sailed between two headlands into a huge blue bowl. It was ringed with yellow beaches; behind which were large white villas and prosperous farms, surrounded by green forests and rich ridges of vegetation.

"I thought Portsmouth was big - but this must be the finest harbour in the world," muttered Warnie. "You could get the entire Royal Navy in here alongside the French and Spanish fleets, and still have anchorage for the Dutch and the Danes."

We saw big ships riding at anchor and smaller ones trafficking busily between them. Then a sturdy white fort with a high tower from which flew the British flag and, at last, a town with church steeples and windmills and streets laid out in straight lines like a grid. There were big, grey stone buildings and a large, green park in which stood an imposing house. It was already a city.

We had arrived in Sydney.

7. Sydney

Our crossing of the Southern Ocean in a sail-wrapped keel was later hailed as one of the most epic voyages ever accomplished under the British flag. Even on that first day a huge crowd assembled on the quay to witness the final stages of our passage. Mr Crowe should have been laden with honours, his name as famous in history books as the great navigators like Cook or Bligh, but in the way of the world, it was Napier who managed to secure all the credit.

No sooner had we tied up at the Commissariat Dock, than Napier and Crowe, dashed off to report to Darling* in the Governor's House at the other end of the Circular Quay. Farrington went into the Commissariat Office with Madame Greere and her two remaining girls, whilst Bradman ordered the rest of the convicts of both sexes to parade on the quay. I patted my valuables, deep in my pocket, as they shuffled down the gangplank, clutching their pitiful belongings, I saw groups of the local blacks sitting around, half-naked, drinking rum from dirty buckets, gazing blearily at these new intruders who came in chains. Harper saw the natives too, and shook his head in pity that others had fallen the same way as he. The sailors on deck waved their farewells - some quite relieved that their sea-marriages had been duly annulled. The women now needed new protectors and had made a great deal of effort to look as presentable and alluring as possible. A mighty difficult task in the majority of cases.

Inquiring eyes were watching all around: well-dressed ladies peeped from beneath their parasols; settlers' wives stared from the balustraded balconies of sturdy brick built houses; respectable merchants, shop keepers, tradesmen, soldiers, and scarred, sun-blackened emancipists - the name given to convicts who'd worked their way to freedom - all observed us from the bustling quay. Further away I could see tough-looking men pouring out of an inn with a wooden sign on which was painted a strange beast, which I would soon know as a kangaroo. I eagerly scoured every face but none resembled my picture of the soldier from Barnet.

Farrington, wearing a greedy grin, eventually came out of the Commissariat's Office, shook hands with the Superintendent of Convicts, and made off towards the lower end of the town with Madame Greere and her girls. The Superintendent, a thin malicious-looking man with teeth like a rabbit, then spent quite a time picking out the younger, more desirable women, before ordering his constables to usher them across the quay into a stone-built storehouse. Ever inquisitive, I followed and slipped in behind the women just as the door shut. I was flabbergasted to find the building crammed to its very rafters with an assortment of sweating settlers, ex-soldiers and emancipists. I hung in the shadows and closely examined every eager, lustful visage. The Superintendent took off his hat. His hair was very flat and shiny, save at the ends, where it was brushed stiffly up from his low protruding brow. He pushed the women into the centre as the men whistled and greedily swallowed their rum.

"You trollops are to be assigned to these gentlemen as servants." He took a swig from the nearest bottle, wiped his mouth with the back of his hand, before turning back to the women, like a Smithfield butcher about to slaughter freshly bought cows: "Take off your clothes, you dirty bints. Show these lads what you're made of. They want to see their meat is sound before they bid for it."

The men cheered and applauded. Some of the women cowered, but others, mostly those who'd danced the ballum rancum, began to strip defiantly: staring brazenly into the eyes of the gaping men, as if relishing the power they sensed they had over them.

The Superintendent smiled, which gave him an expression that bordered closely on the villainous: "Now start to run around - let's see you in all your glory." He seized a crop from one of the onlookers and flicked it at the nearest buttock: the buttock's owner squealed. There were louder laughs and cheers. He struck again at another bum and then another - there were more screams and more ribald laughter from the men. I could feel lust and lechery pumping into the close air. "Come on! Race round the room! You flash pieces of mutton! The last one will feel more of this."

The women began to run in a circle - like children at a Sunday tea party, but this wasn't a game. They found moving on solid ground strange after so long at sea. Some stumbled and fell to the greater amusement of the watching men.

"I'll give ten pounds for that bleached mott, with her arse in the air," cried an old, stringy bark pointing to a blonde bunter, "as long as she can cook and sew as well." I was glad that Molly and Bet had been spared this. I could see no face resembling my father so I slipped outside into the sun to await Crowe's return. The soldiers were sitting on their packs smoking their pipes, the convicts still standing in their chains, the remaining women stealing furtive glances at the watching men. Magwitch and Trumper, under Stride's nominal supervision, were carefully leading the Merinos down the gangplank to join Napier's horses in their pens on the quay. I noticed an old, sunburnt man sitting on a large wagon, looking intently at the sheep. His face was deeply lined and bore a frightful scar, his eyes were no more than slits; his nose had been broken almost flat in some old scuffle, but he was broad-shouldered and still strong. He rose in concern as a weak sheep stumbled and fell from the gangplank onto the stone quay - it bleated pathetically, but before it could struggle to its feet, Magwitch had jumped down from the deck and cradled it tenderly in his scarred, brawny arms, making comforting sounds. The old man looked at Magwitch and opened his mouth in astonishment. He hadn't a tooth in his head.

"Abel!"

Magwitch raised his pallid face, which broke slowly into the nearest thing he had to a smile: "Lord strike me dead! Provis!"

Stride watched from above, as the old man leapt off his cart and embraced Magwitch together with the sheep: "My dear old chap, haven't seen you since Colchester gaol."

Before Magwitch could reply Stride, in an effort to reassert his clout, hurried down the gangplank and attempted to push the old man away: "Be off. You've no business here."

Provis gave Stride a look that would have struck terror in Bill Sykes himself. He pulled a piece of paper from his pocket and waved it under Stride's pointed nose: "Business? Of course I've business. I'm a man of property and have come to collect my property. Twenty-five of these poor beasts are mine - 'cept I paid for sound animals and these that you deliver me are fit only for the knackers' yard."

Magwitch looked as pained as if he had just suffered forty of Bradman's lashes: "Don't say that Provis - every one of 'em is sound. All they need is fresh grass and clean air."

"Never knew you was a shepherd, Abel," said Provis in a low tone.

"There ain't much I can't put my hand to. I've been a bit of a labourer, a bit of a wagoner, a bit of a hawker, a bit of a haymaker, a bit of most things that don't pay and lead to trouble."

Provis thoughtfully ran his tongue around his toothless gums before turning back to Stride: "In this paper here, it states I'm allowed an assigned man. I'll take him." Stride attempted to pooh-pooh the proposition, but Provis silenced him with another ferocious look. He turned back to Magwitch and pointed to the far horizon: "See those distant blue mountains, Abel? I built the first road over them mountains in the time of the good Governor Macquarie.* There was land aplenty on the other side: abounding with rich soil, ideal for tillage or pasture. Macquarie rewarded each of us that worked on the road a small grant of land. The Lord blessed me and I prospered. I acquired a taste for more land and the black folk told me of sheep runs to the east that stretch for hundreds upon hundreds of miles. It persuaded me to sell my little farm and I've just purchased a grant for thousands of acres in the new territory. The grant includes a cow, four bushels of wheat and a servant. Would you be that servant, old chap? We'll take these Merinos and a hundred others I've got already, and breed thousands more. It'll be a lonely life - you'll see no faces but the faces of sheep till you half forget what men's and women's faces are like - but you will become rich. Will you come with me?"

Magwitch smiled. This time I swear he really smiled: "I'd be very obliged, old pal."

Bradman had been listening and without waiting for Stride's assent, stepped forward with his keys and unlocked the chains from Magwitch's ankles. Magwitch lifted and shook each leg like a puppy, revelling in the sensation of finally being rid of the hated iron. Then he walked unfettered to assist Provis in lifting the weak, unresisting sheep into the cart. Evans got up to give them a hand, but Magwitch gave him a reproving look and pushed him away. When they were all safely stowed, Magwitch turned and gazed tenderly at the remaining Merinos, who were bleating feebly and blinking in the unfamiliar daylight. Trumper and his boys were already fetching water.

"Give them all your care, Trumper, they are good beasts."

"That I will, Abel, old chap. They will soon be well."

Magwitch shot a glance at Harper, who was standing forlorn in his usual fashion, "Look after that poor soul as well. I know too well the pain he bears." Then lastly he caught my eye: "Lord strike me dead, but you're a sharp young shaver. Your liquor and wittles was always welcome." He patted my shoulder then clambered up beside Provis and was gone.

The rest of us remained on the quay. Adair and Hampton came off the ship laden with their baggage and made their way towards the hospital. Then Curram disembarked and sauntered over with Stride, who'd resigned all pretence of authority, towards the contiguous inn. Warnie was sitting apart, still carving at the brooch when Leticia Napier hurried down the gangplank. She looked around anxiously, as if ascertaining her husband was out of sight, before coming tentatively towards him. Warnie saw her and attempted to rise but his chains caused him to stumble. She reached out and took his hand to steady him. They looked at each other in silence before she said softly: "I wanted to thank you, Mr Warne, before you go, for all the care you have taken of me."

He blushed and made as if to speak, but couldn't find the words. All he could do was to proffer her the brooch with his free hand.

She took it tenderly: "Thank you. I will always treasure it."

I hoped she was going to say more, but she released his hand, turned, and quickly ran back up to her cabin. He stood in his chains gazing after her.

We waited for another hour until Napier and Crowe returned. With them was a man of about thirty years. He was tall and strongly made, not stout. He had a lurking walk and as he walked constantly looked over his shoulder, in nervous manner, first on one side and then on the other. His eyes were sunk in his head, much deeper than most men's. His face was withered and haggard and dark, as were his hair and his eyes. His lips were pale and disfigured with the marks of his teeth. He even had bite marks on his pale white hands. I recognised him at once - many a time I'd seen him lurking in *The Three Cripples.* It was Fagin's crony - Monks. I thought for a moment that he'd been transported too, but that misconception was soon put right.

"Trumper!" Napier called. "I have found you a suitable position. This gentleman, Mr Monks, has recently opened a livery stable and farm by Hyde Park. I am boarding my horses and sheep with him until I acquire some land. You and your boys are to go with him."

"What about my wife, Sarah?" asked Trumper anxiously.

"Your wife is not a felon and will continue in her duties as nursemaid to my son. She will accompany Mrs Napier to the Governor's House where they will reside until I find suitable accommodation." He turned to the others with that malicious gleam in his eye. "You men are bound for the convicts' quarters in Hyde Park Barracks. You will commence hard labour in chain gangs tomorrow. Carts will convey the women to the Female Factory at Parramatta, where suitable work awaits them."

"Don't we get any remission for helping to save the ship, Mr Crowe?" called Warnie.

Crowe shifted uneasily on his feet whilst Napier's face broke into a nasty grin: "Governor Darling is of my mind that leniency is not required. You are here to be punished not forgiven - the only dispensation he has made is to suspend the death sentences on the Irish mutineers."

I spied Donovan mouthing a *'Hail Mary'*.

Crowe looked utterly downhearted; he'd clearly been defeated by Napier's family influence, but valiantly endeavoured to offer some comfort: "Do not despair. There will be a new Governor before long. I am sure you will all earn your tickets of leave."

I don't think many of the convicts believed him.

During this Monks had been examining us all, with an expression of quiet sarcasm playing on his nervous mouth. He stole a look at me, but I studied the ground and avoided his eyes. I'd no need to worry - it was Harper that intrigued him:

"You over there!" he called in a harsh, deep voice. Harper raised his sad eyes, "Yes, you, you ugly, black bully!" He gave a grim laugh and turned to Napier: "I thought so. That brute was once a noted pugilist - until he became too addicted to drink and doxies. I was a member of the Fancy and have a recollection of seeing him fib with Tom Spring on Bagshot Heath. I wagered he'd be thrashed within twenty rounds. He won me fifty guineas as I remember." He laughed again, jeeringly: "I'll take him as well - he might train up for another match. If not, I've plenty of work for the monster. His brains may be addled but he looks as if he's still got his strength." Hearing Monk's bitter voice struck up some distant memory - I couldn't place what it was or where I'd heard it - but I suspected it was to do with villainy.

Napier nodded his assent and Bradman swiftly freed Trumper and Harper of their fetters. The cruel rogue then ordered his men to form ranks and split them in two detachments at the front and rear. It was a peculiar order of march. The tattered, ragged convicts sandwiched between the red-coated soldiers, then Trumper's boys leading a stallion apiece, with Harper, Trumper, and the sheep bringing up the rear.

Crowe and me watched them go.

"What do we do?" I asked.

"*Enterprise* will be laid up in the dock for months whilst they build her a new keel. The Governor has asked me to help at the hospital - it seems to be in a bad state. You're coming there with me, my boy. You're assigned to my care as a surgeon's assistant."

8. A Wild Colonial Boy

Many things happened in those first days. Crowe and I took quarters in what was commonly called the 'Rum Hospital', as it had been financed on the proceeds of a tax on the aforesaid tincture. It was a long, two-storied building, with a cool veranda, designed by Governor Lachlan Macquarie and his wife with the help of a pattern book. Warnie and the rest were less comfortably housed in the nearby Hyde Park Barracks - a big, red-brick barn, which reminded me of the church in Covent Garden. Crowe delighted in telling me that it had been designed and built by the ex-convict Francis Greenway,* who was now the colony's foremost architect. Crowe still fervently believed there was no limit to what a reformed felon could achieve; but the days when convicts were lodged in private houses and were given free time at the end of the day to sell their labour to pay their rent, had gone. They were now locked up each night in the barracks and Governor Darling had them in chain gangs, labouring ten hours a day.

My clothes were in such a disgusting state that even Fagin would've had 'em burned, and Crowe insisted that I accompanied him to a gentleman's outfitters, where I was togged out with a smart blue jacket and white breeches and buckled shoes. I'd never looked so swell in all my life but was sorry to lose the voluminous capacity of my faithful old coat, although I took care all my ill-gotten valuables were safely stowed in a locked chest in my room. I was sorely tempted to return to my old trade as I watched drunken soldiers, settlers, sailors and emancipists staggering about the streets befuddled with rum, which appeared to be sold from every habitation in the poorer parts of the town - but I'd no immediate need of more money so decided to keep my fingers idle and my nose clean for a while.

My days were fully occupied with Crowe at the hospital, my evenings in study under his tutorage; my nights with wandering through the streets looking for any face that resembled my father. I showed the sketch to many an old soldier or emancipist but none knew him. Then one night, as I ambled down bullock tracks in George Street, I spied stepping out of the Royal Hotel, a hook-nosed gent with luxuriant red beard. He was smartly attired in plaid trousers and double breasted waistcoat, complete with gold fogler and chain. I stopped dead - and blinked my peepers. It was as if Fagin had been re-incarnated, clean and scrubbed and twenty years younger. Indeed if I'd not seen him with my own eyes, dancing at the end of that rope outside Newgate - I might have thought it was the old villain himself. The gent in question raised his beaver hat to a passing settler, revealing pomaded locks that shone like gold and, twirling his silver topped cane, progressed proudly down the street.

"Who's that cove?" I asked the recipient of his greeting.

"Him? The Jew? That's Barnet Levey."*

My heart skipped a beat: "You mean he comes from Barnet?"

"No you young numbskull. That's his bleedin' name. He owns the Royal Hotel and a great more besides. The rogue has a finger in every pie in town. If a flea jumps in this colony he knows all about it."

Throughout my life, I suppose because of my youthful acquaintance of Fagin, I've felt an affinity with those of the Hebrew race, and I determined there and then to make a friend of him - something told me that if my father was anywhere in this vast unknown land - Barnet Levey would know. All that remained was for me to find an opportunity to impress him.

That opportunity arose a few days later. Mr Crowe was deeply involved in discussions with the directors of the hospital, and I had wandered back to George Street. It was the busiest street in town - with banks and shops and markets - a happy hunting ground if I'd been in the mood for going on the lay. I waited outside the Royal Hotel, smoking my pipe, for nearly an hour until Levey finally appeared and then followed him down the street to the Bank of New South Wales. He came out, patting his back pocket, a sure sign there were rich pickings inside. I trailed him down the street as he greeted people right and left, courteously raising his hat and twirling his cane. I waited till he stopped at a greengrocer's and exchanged pleasantries with the owner, then slid past him and, in the nimble manner Fagin had taught me, extracted his thick note-case without him sensing the slightest twitch. I then watched from the other side of the street as he made his way back to the Royal Hotel. A few minutes after he'd gone in, I entered myself. It was the grandest place I'd ever visited - spacious and bright, with thick red carpets and gold painted chairs and a huge, glittering gas chandelier. Mr Levey was talking to one of the waiters - a brute of a fellow who had Newgate written all over him.

I coughed and Mr Levey turned to me with a surprised smile: "Yes, my dear young gentleman, what can I do for you?"

I did not beat about the bush. I proffered him his note-case: "Please sir, you dropped this in the street."

He took it, smiled and checked the contents. "Thank you. You are an honest boy - but why did you take it in the first place?" That quite took my breath away. I turned and saw a grinning char-black native, standing on one leg in the doorway, blocking any escape I might have attempted. Levey enjoyed my consternation. "You are a very good dip, but I am acutely sensitive as to the whereabouts and safety of my money - I strive too hard to acquire it not to guard it carefully. I always have Ben keeping an eye on me. We have a special understanding between us - we both come from nomadic tribes." The black nodded proudly. "Ben can track anything that moves - he has eyes like a hawk and a nose more sensitive than any dog - he would have followed you wherever you went. But I ask again my dear, why did you steal in order to give back?"

For a moment I was flabbergasted - but throughout my life I've never been flabbergasted for long. I thrust my hands in my new pockets and put a slight sneer on my countenance: "I wanted to meet you - it seemed the best way of affecting an introduction."

"Why did you not you just come up and introduce yourself? It would have been much simpler. Besides, my dear boy, if one of the constables had seen what you were up to, you would have been sent packing to a punishment camp with great alacrity."

"I ain't no ordinary convict - I'm an assistant surgeon, assigned to Mr Crowe at the Rum Hospital."

He raised a bushy red eyebrow. "Indeed? You must be a talented boy."

"That's right. I was trained by one of your tribe to be the finest dip in London - you had to get up very early in the morning to catch me - 'Artful' they called me."

He frowned: "I no longer consider myself to be a member of a tribe - I am an educated gentleman. Who was this man that schooled you?"

"Fagin."

He raided his other eyebrow. "Fagin? I have heard of that rogue - his trial and execution were reported at length in *The Sydney Gazette,* but I still do not understand why you should wish to converse with me. Would you like some refreshment?" He led the way over to a large, empty room full of white-clad tables, covered with silver cutlery. "A cup of tea, perhaps?"

"A glass of gin and water, if you please."

He frowned again. "I make a fortune selling alcohol but do not use it myself. It befuddles the brain - the most precious gift the Lord has endowed us with."

"Never done me no harm."

He gave me a questioning look and rang a silver bell. A pretty young woman, dressed in black with white apron and cap hurried over. He looked at her knowingly from beneath his thick red lashes. She blushed. Every man has a weakness, I knew his at that moment.

"Bring my young friend a glass of our best London Gin, my dear, and I'll have my usual lemon tea." She bobbed and returned his look. I could tell she was a willing accomplice - not like my poor Molly. He returned his penetrating gaze upon me. "Why did you wish to meet me? I am in a very different business from Mr Fagin."

I took the drawing out of my pocket and spread on the white tablecloth, smoothing down the creases: "Have you ever seen this man?"

He picked it up and examined it closely. "This is a fine piece of work. Sensitively drawn by a talented artist." He flicked his eyes at me: "I see a strong resemblance - a warning perhaps - it could be you in twenty years if you do not change your ways." The girl had returned with his tea and my gin. I sipped it nevertheless. "Who drew this?"

"An old Dutch cove in Cape Town. I think it is of my father, a soldier who was bound for here about five years ago. He was looking for me in London before he left. I've shown this likeness all over Sydney but no-one seems to have seen him."

He heaped two teaspoons of sugar into his tea. "And you think I might be able to help you?"

"I was told you knew everything that goes on here - I thought perhaps you could make a few enquiries."

"What is his name?"

"I don't know. I was born in the workhouse and the only name I've got is the one the gypsies gave me."

"And what is that?"

"Jack Dawkins."

He rubbed his well-cut beard with manicured fingers. "This is a vast, empty place, Mr Dawkins. He could have committed some misdemeanour and been sent to one of the penal settlements - they are far away and almost impossible to reach. It would be like looking inside a haystack for a needle."

I pointed towards Ben who was standing with folded arms, watching from the doorway, from beneath his long sweepy lashes: "You said he's got the eyes of a hawk and the nose of a dog, couldn't he find him?"

"He could, if your father is still alive and on mainland Australia; but he could be on Norfolk Island or Van Diemen's Land. Even Ben's senses cannot reach across the Tasman Sea. In any case, why should I help you?"

"I was Fagin's best hand - his top-sawyer - I'm a clever fellow - I would be of use to you."

His eyes twinkled as he sipped his tea. "I want no thieving from you. I told you I am a respectable business man - an entrepreneur - although, I must admit, at this moment some of my projects are being thwarted by Governor Darling. The man is a Philistine - we Jews know Philistines only too well - we have suffered at their hands throughout our history. Darling implacably counters all my attempts to establish culture in this colony. No nation can exist without culture - but that is by the by." He wiped his mouth with a white linen napkin, "Nevertheless I will help you. I can see you have talent, and talent should always be nurtured. It is a pity you do not have your father's name - then it would be simple." He rolled the drawing tightly in his hands, "I will keep this. I would gladly pay for more of the artist's work. I will have it ironed and framed and hung behind the bar. My patrons will see it - they are the most influential in the colony - if anyone knows anything of him or his whereabouts - they will. Come to the cricket match in Hyde Park on Sunday - I am furnishing the refreshments - I will have a task for you that will suit your special talents."

So began my relationship with Mr Barnet Levey, one of the most intriguing coves I've come across in the course of my eventful life.

Although it was now late December it was summer in New South Wales, the middle of the cricket season, and a match had been arranged the following Sunday between Army officers and Gentlemen settlers. Mr Crowe was taking a boat up river to inspect the medical conditions at the female factory at Parramatta and was disappointed, and I think a little hurt, when I declined to accompany him. To tell the truth I was already getting bored with my tasks at the hospital and, despite all Crowe's enthusiasms, I knew a surgeon's life was not for me. As I wandered over towards the racecourse an hour before play began, the convicts, under the bellowing commands of Corporal Bradman, were hurriedly erecting tents and a big marquee, and laying out chairs and tables for the onlookers and their ladies. Levey appeared to spare no expense in ingratiating himself with the authorities: crates of champagne and other wines, together with great cuts of cooked beef, hams, pies and roast chickens, were being unloaded from a wagon bearing his name; in the marquee I spied the pretty waitress from his hotel among the young women spreading white linen cloths on tables and laying out glasses, china plates and silver cutlery on top of them. I also spied black Ben, standing on one leg, watching intently.

It was a delightful morning, with a gentle breeze blowing in from the sea. Sheep were dotted all over the field, where they'd been grazed all week in an effort to trim the grass; some convicts were busy with scythes, others were shuffling in their fetters as they laid out the heavy rope which marked the boundary. I soon made out Trumper and his boys, together with Harper, coaxing their flock back into their pens, and the blonde head of Warnie bent over his blade in the middle of the field. I realised that I hadn't seen him since the day of our arrival.

"What you doing, big-wig?" I called, as I approached.

"Shaving the pitch so the ball will fly hard and true - the way they do it at Hambledon." He looked up and frowned - his eyes were red and sore. "Didn't expect to see you. Thought you'd forgotten your old mates."

"I'd never forget you Warnie; we're pals ain't we? How's things?"

"Not good, Dodger. We work chained, ten hours a day, covered in dust and flies, on Busby's bloody Bore."

"Busby's Bore? What's that?"

"A tunnel we're drilling. Sydney needs fresh water. So some clever cove called Busby drew up a plan to drain the Lachlan Swamps and carry the water in a two-mile pipe to a reservoir on the other side of the park. This colony is being built on the bleeding backs and bloody ankles of convicts. They put us to labour even on the Sabbath, albeit to less back-breaking tasks."

I offered him my flask of gin. He took it and drank gratefully and looked towards Elizabeth Street where coaches and open carriages were bearing ladies in bright summer dresses and bonnets towards the game. "Do you think she'll come?"

I knew who he meant but didn't answer.

White top hats were beginning to appear around the tents and marquees. The players, some of whom were dressed in white, began to practice in netting, specially hung up for the occasion - the officers wearing colourful stable belts around their middles. The military band came marching from the barracks playing '*Over the Hills and Far Away*', the colours of the 57th being given an air behind them.

I attempted to cheer Warnie up: "It should be a good day - I've met this gent called Levey - he's laid on free grub and grog. I'll make sure you get your share. Keep the flask. I've got things to do."

He nodded morosely as I scudded over to the tents where I could see Levey's tough-looking waiter sitting at a table. The brute had a leather satchel and seemed to be sorting out small white pieces of paper. I'd no time to wonder what he was doing for at that moment Levey arrived in his carriage. He stepped out, elegantly attired in a tall grey hat, mutton-shouldered grey coat, striped thunder and lightning trousers and crimson silk waistcoat. The ruby shone from the pin in his tie and diamonds sparkled from several of his fingers.

His bright eyes found me at once: "Ah, Mr Dawkins, or shall I call you Dodger? I think the Artful suits you best. I'm glad you've arrived early - that is the sign of a smart man. I have reliable servants but I always believe in checking everything myself."

"What is it you want me to do?"

He took me by the elbow and spoke in a confidential tone: "The inhabitants of this colony - especially the emancipists - are addicted to gaming. They will give odds on two flies climbing up a wall or two drips of water running down the side of a bucket. I have made it my duty to accommodate their demands. After they have partaken of my choicest wines and sumptuous viands they will feel the itch for a wager: even this so-called gentlemen's sport of cricket, they turn into a betting game. They will want to bet on the number of runs each batsmen scores - the number of wickets a bowler takes - how many catches a particular fielder will hold. Unfortunately Governor Darling will be attending. He is a simple military man - rather dull, very forbidding and totally humourless. He naturally does not approve of gaming, although his officers are among my most fervent customers. That is where you will be of use to me, my dear. As you go from table to table refilling their glasses with my champagne, you will collect their betting slips, with great subtlety and speed, and take them to my man, Croft." He gestured towards the brutish waiter.

"But how do you profit from it?"

"I have the juice, my dear, the 'vigorish'. - I charge the better each time he uses my services - the larger the wager the larger my fee. Gambling is a perilous pastime but a clever man makes money regardless of the outcome."

"Do you want me to collect cash? "I asked hopefully, beginning to smell all sorts of possibilities.

"No, my dear, my word is my bond. They will give you a chit. Croft, who for some reason has been granted a prodigious brain for mathematics - he was an accountant in the Royal Exchange before he was transported for fraud - will calculate the odds and then you return his chit to them. They will collect their winnings, or pay me what they owe me, later at the hotel."

"What if they don't pay? Ain't you afraid of them welching?"

"The officers would not dare - gambling debts are a matter of honour. As far as the others are concerned - Croft has means of ensuring they pay...." He broke off as a smart two-horse chaise approached. "Now go and report to Croft, I must attend to the distinguished guests."

He hurried over and opened the carriage door and held out his hand to Mrs Napier, who took it, smiled gently, and descended. She was followed by Napier, all in white, and Sarah Trumper carrying little Horatio.

Levey swept his grey hat from his head and bowed before Leticia Napier - his curled red locks hanging from his brow: "Welcome to our colony, dear lady. You have brought fresh beauty to it."

"Do we know you?" Napier asked unpleasantly.

Levey took out a card: "Barnet Levey, proprietor of the Royal Hotel. Honoured if I may be of service to you."

Napier did not take the card but regarded him even more coldly. "I don't think so. Levey? Strange name for an Englishman."

Levey's back straightened and his chest thrust out: "I am English nevertheless, born in the great city of London, and have freely elected to settle my fortune and endeavour in this fair colony." He turned to Leticia with a radiant smile - I could tell his weakness was getting the better of him: "Please, do me the honour of escorting you to a table out of the breeze, dear lady. I will ensure you receive everything you require by way of refreshment, whilst your gallant husband performs his feats of skill and valour on the field."

She blushed and let Levey lead her to a table laden with flowers. Sarah followed with the kid. Napier stood fuming, then caught me looking at him. I put on my most subservient expression and raised my knuckles to my brow, but the rogue was no fool:

"You always turn up like a damn'd bad penny," he rasped, "but remember, bad pennies get taken out of circulation."

"Quite aware of the fact, sir," I mumbled and hurried off to report to Croft.

I found him inside one of the tents, sitting at a table with sheaves of paper about him. He looked up at me with distaste - he'd already sniffed me to be a threat to his position:

"Yes, Mr Levey has told me all about you. Think you're a top hand, don't you? We'll see about that. Now listen, young gallows, there's chits and pencils on every table. Go round with the bottles and keep pouring - the more they drink the more reckless they bet. As soon as they write anything down pick it up and bring it straight to me."

I gave him a nod and went into the marquee where the pretty waitress was opening bottles with great aplomb. I gave her a wink; she winked back.

"Just joined the staff have yer, little 'un?"

"I ain't little in every department and small things can be very sweet. You should try sometime."

She gave a dirty laugh. I knew we would be friends.

"What's yer name, short-arse?"

"Jack, but my mates call me Dodger, sometimes Artful."

"I'll call yer Art - how about that?"

"Suits me fine. What's your title, m'lady?

"Sue. Now dodge off, I'm busy."

There was a great hoo-hah as Governor and Mrs Darling arrived with an escort of dragoons. He was a bald-headed little blighter, with that fish-like look, common to so many of the so-called upper classes. His wife* though, was young and pretty and at least twenty years younger.

Everyone stood to attention whilst the British flag was unfurled and the band played *'God Save the King.'* Then wickets were pitched, the scorers prepared to notch the runs, the umpires went to their stations, and the game began.

The military batted first. Napier was soon in and thumping the ball to all parts of the field. The spectators were clearly divided into groups. The uniformed officers and their wives - although very few Army wives had elected to venture to this extremity of the world; the smartly dressed gentlemen settlers and their ladies, who'd been offered large land grants in proportion to their wealth; the common settlers, sober folk for the most part in flannel jackets; and lastly the rough and ready emancipists - freed convicts in straw hats and their equally rough and ready wives. The Liverpool tart, May Rooney - who I'd last spied running round flapping her tired old paps in the storehouse on the Commissariat's Dock - was on the arm of an extremely ancient ex-convict. By the wicked gleam in her eye I guessed she was well on her way to making herself a widow. Fagin's old mate, Monks, had also turned up, sitting at a table alone, dressed in black, with bitten knuckles and swollen lips. Seeing him again brought back the memory of the words I'd once heard but couldn't understand. I racked my brains again trying, without success, to remember what they were, as I scudded unobtrusively between the tables, picking up the chits and returning the receipts, amid cries and shouts of "Well played - capital style - run - run you fool - catch it! - bloody idiot - are you blind?" reflecting the state of play and the fortunes of particular bets. Croft was right, for the most part, the more drink they supped, the greater their appetite for a wager grew; but Monks proved to be the exception to the rule: although he took no drink whatever, he wagered more frantically than all of 'em. I was kept very busy and went about my task diligently - so took no interest in the game- although I could tell from the applause on the officers' tables that Napier was accumulating a big score. His wife however, didn't appear to be taking much interest in his sporting skills. Each time I slipped past her she was listening intently to Levey with an amused look on her face. I wasn't the only one to notice. Warnie was standing at the rope on the far side of the field, arms folded, watching her every move.

The officer's innings eventually closed with Napier remaining undefeated on a score of 62 out of a total of 95. He walked off to great applause, with his bat raised, looking around triumphantly, as if he had been very much contradicted by someone but had got the better of him at last.

I looked across to Warnie - his arms were still folded. His face was grim.

The guests then retired into the big marquee for their lunch. The hot sun beat down on the canvas and the air was heavy with the scent of grass. Although wagering temporarily ceased, I was even busier pouring yet more wine. The Governor and his lady sat at the top table, with some of his aides, together with the Napiers and, of course, Levey their host. Levey cracked jokes and told stories, trying to get them interested in a scheme of his to import blue earth from some place called New Zealand, which he was convinced would make an excellent dye and valuable source of revenue; but they were a stuffy lot and only Mrs Napier appeared to listen or be amused.

Much more wine was drunk over the food and Governor Darling looked quite unsteady on his feet when he announced, to the obvious disappointment of his young wife, who was very much enjoying the gentlemen's attention, that he'd urgent business at Government House and would be unable to stay for the remainder of the match. I suspect his business included a good sleep, and indeed many heads nodded as the gentlemen settlers plodded through their innings that hot afternoon. The bets continued nevertheless, with far less circumspection following Darling's departure. Napier again was the centre of the action - bowling his 'trimmers' and 'shooters' - taking wickets and plunging all over the field to take what looked like impossible catches. At length, with the settlers' score notched on 53, he caught their last man on the boundary rope, and held up the ball triumphantly to the four corners of the field as the onlookers applauded vigorously. It was at that moment he spied Warnie, standing on the rope, surrounded by a group of fellow convicts. None of them were applauding, but Warnie had his arms folded and had a look of derision stamped across his face.

Napier sauntered over to him: "Ah, the oaf from Hambledon. Now you've seen how cricket should be played."

"I reckon not. I've seen the boys of Hambledon play better."

There was an icy silence. Napier grinned nastily: "If it wasn't the Sabbath and the fact that I am in good humour, I'd flog you again for insolence."

Levey, ever inquisitive, had wandered over. "Is anything wrong, Captain Napier?"

Napier shook his head: "No. Except this felon has the temerity to believe that he can play cricket."

Levey laughed: "Why not challenge him to a match? We have so little in the way of entertainment. I would be happy to furnish the refreshments."

"Gentlemen do not play with convicts. Besides there would be no contest. They have neither the skill nor the wit."

Mrs Napier had now walked over and was listening intently. Warnie saw her and could not let the insult pass: "Give us time to train and we'd match you man for man."

Napier positively snorted with derision.

"It would offer excellent opportunities for side-bets," Monks had also come across. "What odds would you offer, Levey?"

Levey winked at him and put a finger to his lips: "Tush, my dear. The Governor would not approve, but nevertheless a sporting contest in the best British tradition would be a tonic for us all."

Napier and Warnie were now eyeing each other like fighting cocks.

"Will you accept his challenge, Captain Napier?" Levey cooed softly.

"A four innings contest, over two days? Napier asked in a low voice.

Warnie nodded.

"I'll accept if you accept my terms." Napier's face was set in his most vicious smile. "At the end of next month I'm going north to take command of the punishment settlement at Moreton Bay - if you lose, which you indubitably will, you, and those foolish enough to join your team will accompany me. If you think you labour here, you do not know the meaning of the word. I intend to turn the damn'd desert into Eden. It's too cruel and hot for horses, so convicts will be my beasts of burden.

There will be no ploughs. You brutes will labour fourteen hours every day, breaking and tilling every inch of stony ground with nothing but hoes."

Mrs Napier gasped. "No! That would be inhuman."

Warnie ignored her "What if we win?"

"In that highly unlikely circumstance - I would ensure every man in your team would receive his ticket of leave in two years."

Levey clapped his hands together excitedly: "Excellent. That is what I call a wager. There is spice to it."

"The Governor would never allow it." Leticia anxiously put her hand to her throat. Her coat fell to one side and Warnie saw for the first time she was wearing his brooch.

Napier looked even smugger: "The Governor will listen to my advice. It will prove an excellent way of asserting the superiority of the gentleman and enforcing the strong discipline he requires. But the match will never take place. No one, not even the most doltish convict, would be foolish enough to volunteer for his team."

Warnie turned to Lindwall, Miller and Trumper who were clustered about him: "What about it lads? Are you up for it?" They didn't look too convinced.

Napier positively gloated: "As I thought, all bluster. They daren't accept the challenge. In that case I'll offer even better terms - if you win - every member of the team will get a ticket of leave within a year. Are you men enough to accept that?"

Warnie looked again at his fellows around him - some were hanging their heads. Attenborough, Crawley and other officers who'd witnessed the confrontation began to snigger and sneer.

Warnie's eyes met those of Mrs Napier - hers were full of pity. He took a deep breath before he held out his hand: "Very well, we accept."

Napier clasped his hands firmly behind his back and smiled triumphantly. "I do not shake hands with felons. Besides, you have not yet got a team. You'll need eleven men. I'll give you a week to find ten more idiots; we'll play four weeks from today. I'll allow you to be unshackled for an hour each evening to practice - not that it will do you any good.

A week, remember. If you fail then to take up my challenge, it will prove that you acknowledge my superiority."

As evening fell, I helped Levey's girls collect up the remains of the food and dirty crockery, whilst the convicts, under the inevitable supervision of Bradman, took down the tents and packed the tables and chairs. Warnie looked dejected. I purloined a bottle of wine and several cuts of beef and ham, tied them in a napkin and, as the convicts formed up to march back to their barracks, slipped them into his hand. "Don't worry, old pal. You'll never get ten fools to join you." He stuffed them up his shirt but didn't reply.

I made sure I clambered into the same wagon as blonde Sue, and snuggled down beside her.

"What's this short-arse? You coming home with me?"

"My secretary informs me that my diary is free of engagements for the evening. I had an appointment with the Governor but I think your cold pork has left him with the squits."

She laughed. "You have quite a way with words. Is that how folk talk in London?"

"Indubitably, my dear." I'd just picked the word up from Mr Crowe and had been waiting to use it. "You've never visited the great metropolis?"

"If you mean London, no. I was born here. My parents were transported, but they're both dead."

I spied a half-eaten chicken on a platter, broke off a leg and chewed it nonchalantly: "What they die of?"

"Starvation. It was terrible in the early days."

I threw away the chicken leg and changed the subject. "It sounds hard up in the north, where Napier's going."

"It's worse than hard - it's death - and there's no escape."

I pulled my twirler from my pocket: "I could pick any lock with this."

"It wouldn't do you any good, Art. It's surrounded by hundreds of miles of bush and fierce tribes of Aborigines. They say the 'Abbos' have eaten most of those who tried to escape. It can only be reached by sea."

I changed tack again. "How long have you worked for Levey?"

"For more than five years - since I was about fifteen. He's a kind master as long as you give him what he wants - I get comfortable lodgings at the hotel."

When we arrived back at the Royal I helped her and the other girls unload the wagons and take everything into the kitchen. It was very late by the time we'd stacked the plates and stowed the food. The other girls had already slipped away.

"Where are you sleeping tonight, Arty?" she asked with a peculiar gleam in her eye.

"Wherever you wish milady," I replied.

"Have you ever had a proper bath?"

My heart began to beat a little faster. "Not that I recall."

She looked across at a board where keys were hanging from numbered pegs. She carefully picked out number *7*. "Come upstairs."

She lit a brass candelabra and led me from the kitchen and across the deserted vestibule. Levey had been as good as his word - my father's portrait was already hanging behind the bar in a gold frame. I swear, his eyes followed me wistfully as I followed Sue up the thickly carpeted stairs to the first floor. She then led me down a long corridor and stopped at the last door. She slipped the key into the lock and eyed me once more - the gleam in her eye had now become positively wicked:

"Come in."

I entered a room such as I'd never dreamed of. A huge bed with yellow silk covers, soft Turkish carpets and rugs, comfortable leather chairs, a writing desk with pen and paper. There was even a bowl of fruit. She smiled and pushed open a small door: within was a sparkling enamelled tub with brass taps. She turned a tap and to my amazement hot water began to pour out.

"Mr Levey has all the modern conveniences. Take off your clothes."

I obeyed eagerly. She poured some sweet smelling oil into the water then turned and surveyed me with a wicked look in her eye.

"You've not got much to offer, but at least let's make sure it's clean. Get inside."

I clambered in, delighting in the unfamiliar sensation of warm water. Then she began to wash me - I'd never known a mother and I suppose that was the nearest I ever got to a baby bath. Her hands were soft and tender as she rubbed and explored all my little crevices and secret parts. When I was all pink and tingling, to my abundant gratification, she slipped out of her own clothes and joined me in the water. The tub was small and we were squashed tight together - under the cloudy water my toes brushed against her. She gave a dirty laugh and put soap on my hand and laid it on her firm round breast. I rubbed eagerly for all I was worth; and then she soaped my hand again and I rubbed the other one. I washed and rubbed her all over - and when she at last got out of the bath, the water dripping off her like some exquisite mermaid without a tail, she wrapped me in a huge white towel and carried me over to the bed. I swiftly made use of all the tricks I had learnt from my blimp-hole on the *Enterprise.*

That was the night I truly became a man.

I had duties to attend to at the hospital, so I crept out of bed as dawn was breaking and left her snoring gently in fulfilled and contented sleep. As I came down the stairs, to my consternation, a light was shining behind the frosted glass on Levey's office. I tip-toed towards the kitchen hoping to depart undetected, but the rogue appeared to have Fagin's second sense. I'd only taken a few furtive steps when his door swung open, to reveal him sitting at his desk, counting on an abacus, surrounded by heaps of betting chits.

"Did you sleep well, my dear? I should hope you did - my rooms have the softest mattresses Paris can provide."

"Indubitably - I will recommend your establishment to all of my acquaintance."

"I trust my staff satisfied all your demands? I constantly instruct them that it is their duty to keep the guests happy."

"Don't fret your eyelids on that score." I wiped my tongue over my swollen lips and changed the subject. "What are you doing up so early?"

"Going over yesterday's business - Croft tells me you did well."

"Glad to be of service. Any news of my father? I see you have his picture in place."

"I am sure I will learn something soon, my dear." He unlocked a drawer in his desk and took out an emerald brooch. "Tell me, what do you know of Mrs Napier?"

"Only that she's married to a brute and has not shared his bed since we left England."

"I thought as much." He gave a gratified smile and gazed intently at the jewel: "Beauty should never be wasted and she is indeed a beautiful lady. They are all too rare at this end of the world. Is there nothing more you can tell me?"

"Nothing - except she's very kind and Mr Crowe says she plays the piano like an angel."

"The piano, indeed...." he rubbed his beard ruminatively.

The mention of Mrs Napier reminded me of Warnie. "That cricket match must never take place. The convicts are bound to lose - if they're sent to a punishment colony under Napier - he'll kill 'em - especially my friend Warnie."

He looked at me coldly. "We will see. If it is in my interest, I am well practiced at shortening the odds."

Crowe was still away, so that evening, after executing a kinchin lay* by purloining a young kid's bouncing rubber ball, I made my way back to Hyde Park. Bradman and his guard had just led Warnie and a group of convicts out of the barracks and were busy unshackling them; Trumper and his boys had come over from Monk's stable with Harper; Black Ben was standing apart with the piece of bent wood in his hand. I said nothing but threw Warnie the ball. He'd carved something resembling a cricket bat out of a piece of wood. That was all the equipment they seemed to have. They stood silently for a minute or so - as if comprehending the enormity of the challenge that faced them.

"Well, lads, what do you say? We can't let Napier walk over us - I'm sure we can give him a game." Warnie didn't sound sure at all.

"We haven't got a bloomin' chance," someone mumbled.

"I've heard about that punishment settlement - if Napier don't flog us to death - we'll die of starvation. It's Hell on Earth, the poor devils up there cast lots to cut one another's throats," said Lindwall.

"How can we play with a soft ball, a lump of wood and no wickets?" demanded Miller.

"Napier's got us over a barrel and he knows it," moaned Kidman.

"Let's pack it in now," said Lindwall.

The rest nodded in agreement.

Warnie attempted to put on a brave show: "Let's practice for a night or two before we finally decide. At least we can run around without our chains for a while."

No one moved. He turned to me - I could see the desperation in his eyes: "Stand behind the bat, Dodger. You're small and you've got quick hands, you'll make a good wicket keeper."

"Plummy and slam!" I bounced my ball, threw it from hand to hand and sauntered to the middle of the field.

"Come on boys, might as well have a game. "Trumper picked up the piece of wood and followed me with his sons. The others slowly spread out across the park and we began to play. Each took the bat in turn whilst Warne bowled at them. Some were hopeless but Trumper and others - such as Miller and Lindwall, who'd played the game in their English villages, and Kidman who'd played at school - hit the soft ball with relish. Most of the rest, including some of the Irish, were soon chasing the ball about the field like happy schoolboys - not that I knew much about schoolboys at that time. Even Bradman took out his pipe and sat watching on the grass, with a look of contentment on his face such as I'd never seen before. Black Ben observed it all motionless on one leg. But in our hearts we all knew our efforts were hopeless. Without proper equipment we hadn't a hope in hell.

Dusk was beginning to fall when Miller thwacked a ball particularly hard - it soared high into the air before falling among a clump of long grass. Trumper's eldest boy, John, ran after it and was about to pick it up when he gave a startled cry:

"Snake!"

I could just make out a long dark brown thing inches from his hand.

"Get away, quick. Before it bites!" yelled Bradman.

But the boy stood frozen as if transfixed with fear.

"Run, John, run!" cried Trumper. The boy still didn't move, but at that moment something dark flew through the air. It struck the snake a hard blow about its neck before flying back the way it had come. We all stared amazed as Black Ben caught the thing in his hand and walked toward the writhing snake. He fearlessly put his bare foot upon it and smashed its head to pulp with a club that had been hanging from his waist.

Warnie whistled. "How did he do it? If we could do tricks like that with a ball, Napier might yet be in for a surprise."

On Crowe's return from Parramatta the following morning, I told him about the proposed match, though omitting to mention my new relationship with Levey.

He thought for a few minutes. "If Napier ever gets them into his hands at Moreton Bay, he'll surely flog them to death. He thinks he holds all the aces - we must apply tactics -give him something he doesn't expect."

"Didn't know you played cricket, Mr Crowe."

His face flushed. "There are many things you don't know about me, Mr Dawkins."

He seemed delighted at the prospect of another chance of pitting himself against Napier, but I knew Warnie could never win unless he had the proper kit to practice with - and there was only one man in the colony that would have the means to provide it.

When I had finished my tasks I made my way back to the Royal Hotel.

There was no sign of Sue but as I entered the office, Ben was leaning on the doorsill wearing a new snakeskin belt. Levey was going through his accounts with Croft. He looked up at me and smiled:

"Ah, my young friend the Artful One, Ben has been telling me of last night's doings. There is already great interest in the town. What can I do for you, my dear?"

"The convicts need some proper cricket gear to practice with."

He frowned: "That will be difficult. There is only a limited supply in the colony."

"They won't play without it - I'm sure you can lay your hands on some."

"It would be a pity if the match was cancelled - Croft is certain there is money to be made." Croft nodded his sullen agreement. "Let me think about it." Levey picked up an account receipt: "This man Monks, who chews his lips and knuckles, is a heavy gambler. Did you ever come across him in England?"

"Oh, my eye, I should think I did. He was one of old Fagin's cronies - although I've no idea what business they did together."

"An associate of Mr Fagin - I did not know Monks mingled with such exalted company. He has only been here little more than a month, and he owes me a tidy sum already. He tells me he has the management of a valuable prize-fighter and wants me to arrange a match."

"That'll be poor old Harper. Mr Crowe, the surgeon, says he's taken too many beatings and can never fight again."

"That should not be a problem if we talk him up good before he fights - I've seen the fellow, he looks big and fierce enough. There are many fools here who would be more than willing to wager on him."

Croft nodded again. "The black fool hardly knows where he is - just walks about dazed. Never speaks a word. Only thing that seems to interest him is grog."

"Then grog he shall have aplenty - he shall train on grog. Croft knows of a brute of a convict assigned to a farmer on the Hunter River, who fought in the English rings several times before he was transported here for manslaughter. It will make a good match. Don't say anything for the present - I will see what I can do about the cricket tools."

That evening Crowe accompanied me to Hyde Park. Ben was already there, carrying a bag of cricket stuff - it was very old and battered, indeed it looked as though it had come out with the First Fleet - but at least we now had stumps, proper bats and hard balls. "Present from the Boss." was all Ben said.

Most of the convicts were not sure whether they should be grateful. The mere fact that they now had proper equipment had brought them closer to playing the game with its fearful consequences. Nevertheless Warnie set up the wickets and explained some of the basic rules to the uninitiated, which I for one found very complicated. Before we began to play Mr Crowe, who'd been waiting impatiently, called us into a tight cluster:

"We crossed the ocean in a patched-up ship because we used our heads and worked together - you can do the same and win this game. Napier and his team bowl underarm - that's all they're used to - but Sussex won the county championship a couple of years ago by using a new method - round arm."

"What's that?" asked Miller.

"The bowler releases the ball higher - level with his waist - he can thus generate greater speed. The Marylebone Cricket Club amended the rules just before we sailed - luckily I have a copy," he pulled a thin yellow publication from his pocket. "The gentlemen in Napier's team won't have your strength, they'll never match you for speed, and they won't have faced anything near as fast as what you'll throw at them."

Apart from Warnie they still seemed dubious but as soon as we began to play things seemed simpler. Lindwall and Miller quickly caught hold of the new technique, the ball fairly flew out of their hands. Only Trumper and Warnie seemed capable of hitting it - the others missed completely - and my bare hands began to hurt, stopping the fast, hard ball. We were so engrossed that time flew by swiftly. Bradman was clinking his keys - indicating that the hour was almost up, when the ball fell at Harper's feet. He'd been watching intently, showing interest for the first time since Bet's death. He picked up the ball and took it to the bowler's mark. He grasped it in his huge hand as if he were squeezing an orange, then tore down the few yards to the wicket at a ferocious speed. The ball flew from his hand towards me faster than a bullet; it was as if he were throwing away all his pain - all his anger - all his humiliation. I was certain it would take off my head but to my thankful relief, it whizzed several yards past my right ear.

"That's it, Harper!" enthused Crowe. "All you've got do now is to learn to bowl straight."

Slowly over the next few nights, under Crowe's tutelage, we improved our game. The convicts ran swiftly about the field in their hardened bare feet and learned to catch the ball firmly in their calloused hands. In Warnie, Trumper, Lindwall, Miller, Harper and Kidman they had the nucleus of a team - but were still five short of giving Napier a match. Donovan and O'Neill claimed to have played the game on their masters' estates in Ireland and had a vague idea. Crowe had given me an old pair of leather gloves and after wrapping thick bandages about my palms, I'd become quite quick and agile behind the stumps, but had no intention of risking my soft position at the hospital by putting my name down to play. Ben came to watch us every evening and sometimes I'd see him showing Warnie how to hold the ball and make it spin slowly through the air. But Crowe was convinced we could only beat Napier by fast bowling and all his attention was on Lindwall, Miller and the rapidly improving Harper.

News of our progress spread through the colony and more and more ex-convicts - emancipists turned out to watch us play. One evening, towards the end of the first week, I saw Napier watching us through his spyglass on the far side of the field.

A few mornings later Bradman came into the hospital for Mr Crowe to have a look at his bunions, the result of years of marching in ill-fitting army boots. Crowe applied one of his special ointments and I wrapped Bradman's foot in one of the padded bandages I'd been using on my hands.

"I've been watching you behind the wicket, you young rogue," he said to me, "you've the makings of a good keeper."

"I've noticed you taking a keen interest - did you ever play cricket in England?" asked Crowe.

"Used to play for the Squire's team in Norfolk when I was a lad - batting was my speciality. Squire used to put me in way down the order 'cause they could never get me out. The gentlemen complained they never had a bat."

"Indeed? It's a pity you can't bat for us."

"There's something I wanted to tell you, Mr Crowe. Ain't no business of mine, but I respect you, sir, and I think you ought to know. Captain Napier has caught on to the round arm bowling business, and he's bought some of the other ranks into his team. That bully Carter, sir, as was on *Enterprise* with us, and a giant of a sergeant from the 39th called Hodson. He's teaching 'em to bowl."

Crowe knitted his brow: "At least he's taking us seriously. We must have impressed him the other night. So this is no longer purely a match between gentlemen and convicts - perhaps we should broaden the qualifications to our team."

I was now desperate for another tumble with Sue and returned to the Royal Hotel that afternoon. I found her serving drinks behind the bar to Levey and a group of tough looking coves - which was not out of order as nearly all the coves in Sydney were tough looking. To my chagrin Sue seemed to be having a good time with them. I thrust my tongue into my cheek and whistled.

Levey turned from his lemon tea: "Ah, the Artful One - the very person we were speaking of. My dear, I have news for you."

I snapped the bridge of my nose, took out my pipe and affected nonchalance:

"Proceed, my dear fellow."

"These fine men are miners from the north, who have come down to recreate themselves at my humble establishment." Levey pointed a bejewelled finger towards a bald-headed brute with a lurid red face, crisscrossed with dark blue veins: "This gentleman thinks he has seen your father."

I was dumb-founded. I must admit that I'd never really believed I'd hear those words. "What??" I stammered weakly.

"Yes - I can see his likeness in you," the hairless fellow said, giving me a disdainful glance before taking a large swallow of rum. "Bit of a short-arse like you he was as well."

Sue gave a titter at this but I quelled her with a saturnine look, though my heart was pumping fast: "Where did you see him?"

"He came off a ship that docked in Port Macquarie about four years ago. Cheerful little bastard whilst he was sober. I spent several evenings with him in the waterfront inns. He was full of great tales, he was, of his doings at Waterloo - I didn't believe a bloody word - suppose that's why I remember him. He got drunk one night and hit the Provost Sergeant who came to arrest him. I think he was sent to the punishment camp at Moreton Bay. Should still be there if he's alive."

Moreton Bay - everything seemed to lead to Moreton Bay. "How would I get there?"

"By sea of course. It's as near nigh impossible to get to by land as it is to escape. What with the desert, the heat and the hostile natives, you'd only make it with a military escort."

I turned to Levey. He shrugged: "My dear, even I cannot get you to that fearful place."

Sue was making eyes at a particularly big miner with a thick black beard. I realised that my expectations with her were negligible as far that `day was concerned. But I didn't really care. The prospect of playing cricket against Napier no longer held terrors for me. If we lost, I'd at least have a safe passage to my father in Moreton Bay.

That evening a bigger crowd than ever had gathered to watch our practice. Crowe called us into a close group before we began to play.

"Napier is no longer taking us so lightly. He's bringing in big fellows from the ranks to counter our fast bowling. We've just got to bowl faster and bat better. I'm sure you can beat them, but you must decide tonight whether to accept the challenge - otherwise Napier wins by default. Who is going to play?"

Warnie put up his hand immediately and, to everyone's surprise, mine followed. Then Harper, who now had a positive sheen on his black hide, signalled he was up for it. Lindwall, Miller and Kidman did the same.

"Would you take a brace of Irish? We want to see Napier beat as much as you do." Donovan inquired shyly. O'Neill nodded in agreement.

"What about you, Trumper? You're the best batter we've got," demanded Warnie.

Trumper hesitated. “I couldn’t risk being sent to Moreton Bay. What would Sarah and my boys do then?”

“I’m certain you would not forfeit your position,” Crowe replied reassuringly. “You are already assigned and Napier would never send you away from his sheep - your skill is too valuable.”

“In that case put me down,” said Trumper.

“There is no reason why your boys cannot play. They’re already free, so Napier has no power over them. They’re very quick in the field and will save us plenty of runs.”

To the delight of his boys, Trumper nodded his assent.

Crowe checked the numbers on his fingers: “Right! You have eleven. The match is on!”

We now had less than three weeks to prepare. Bradman had informed me that Napier’s team was practising each morning in the grounds of Government House, so next day I crept into the ‘Inner Domain’ as it was called, and crawled through the kangaroo grass and shrubbery to where I had a perfect view of the pitch. Attenborough was batting, wearing gloves with thick leather things strapped to his legs. He was facing a giant bull-necked man: I supposed was Sergeant Hodson, who was hurling a bright red shining ball at him with ferocious venom. Napier was watching in the field with his hands on his hips and a cruel sneer on his face:

“Aim for his head! The new ball will give you extra bounce. Don’t give him a chance to hit it!”

Hodson flung the ball from behind his shoulder - Attenborough ducked and it skimmed over his head.

“That’s it. Soften them up - like the artillery - weaken their resistance. Now vary your attack - go for his legs!”

This time the giant threw from his hip and it smashed into Attenborough’s padded leg. Despite the pad, Attenborough hopped and yelped at the force.

“Well aimed,” Napier cried. “They won’t have leg guards - I’ve had those made especially by a master saddler - so they’ll jump out of the way and be bowled or feel the pain. They won't be able to take many like that. This time aim for the body - try to get him in the ribs."

"Steady on, old boy! I ain't got no padding there," protested Attenborough.

After Hodson had completed his over, Carter came on at the other end to bowl at Crawley in an equally savage fashion. Crawley, without Napier's leg guards, was petrified and waved his bat about like a limp foreskin. He endured two balls, squealing like one of Trumper's pigs, as he was struck in the dumpling depot and on the shoulder. Then on the third he closed his eyes and swung in terror. By some miracle he managed to hit it - the ball soared high into the blue sky like a little red cannonball and landed in the long grass a few feet away from me. I rolled over and slipped it in my pocket and melted into the shrubbery.

I was gratified to hear Napier cursing for his lost ball as I slunk away.

I reported back to Crowe, but he didn't appear too concerned, so confident was he in the power of his own fast bowling attack. His main worry were the leg guards - he'd never heard of such things - he thought we might solve the problem by wrapping padded bandages around our batsmen's legs, but I'd seen the force of Hodson's blows and knew that would offer scant protection.

Our own practices continued. Despite the increasing heat as midsummer approached, the team became fitter each day. Crowe fortified them with tinctures of honey and other herbs he'd found in the virgin countryside. He also instilled in me how crucial my role behind the stumps was to be. If I allowed any ball to go past me the batsmen could run. For some reason they were called byes, but they counted as runs just the same. If it was a close contest any byes could well decide the outcome, with all that that entailed. I resolved that nothing would get past me. Partly thanks to the new ball I'd provided, Harper, Lindwall and Miller grew ever faster and more accurate, but my quick hands were always there and ready, no matter the pounding they took. The batting also improved: as well as Trumper and Warnie - Donovan, Miller, Kidman and yours truly were no mean performers - and the odd times he connected, Harper could easily clear the rope and run six. Tom was always there, standing on one leg, silently watching. The crowds continued to come as well, in ever-growing numbers; the match was now the main topic of Sydney conversation - some were even saying we'd a chance to win. Heavy bets were laid each night in the bar of the Royal Hotel.

I was so engrossed with the coming game that I forgot about Levey for a while, until one afternoon I spied him driving back along the Parramatta Road in his open yellow-wheeled phaeton with Mrs Napier sitting beside him. He pulled up alongside me and smiled:

"Ah, the Artful One - my little friend. How are you, my dear? Haven't seen you for several days."

"Been very busy getting prepared for the game."

"Yes, the game. Mrs Napier's husband, the Captain, is also pre-occupied with it. It is a terrible thing to neglect so beautiful a lady. I have taken it upon myself to show her some of our majestic countryside." He gave her an even bigger smile: "I suppose you became acquainted with this young gentleman on the voyage?"

She blushed, as was her wont. I noticed she was wearing Levey's emerald brooch:

"Yes, Mr Dawkins was a great source of comfort to me."

"Your piano was a great source of comfort to us all, Ma'am," I replied.

"All Sydney will soon hear it. I am about to build a concert hall behind my hotel where she will give a public recital," declared Levey airily. "I have sent to London for a grand pianoforte, from Kirkman in Golden Square, Maker to His Majesty himself. It is Mrs Napier's intention to bring the immortal tunes of Mozart and Beethoven to this cultural desert, and I have sworn that I will aid her in any way I can. Have I not, my dear?"

She blushed even more but changed the subject: "How is Mr Warnie?"

"I'd say he's choking in the dust at Busby's Bore at this moment, but he's bearing up all things considered."

"Give him my best wishes for the game."

Levey raised an eyebrow: "You wish an opponent good fortune against your own husband? A Jewish wife would not do such a thing."

"It has always been my nature to support the under-dog."

"From what my man Ben tells me, they are underdogs no more. The odds are becoming difficult to call." He shot me a sharp look, such as I'd seen Fagin give many a time. "I hear the blackamoor, Harper, is in good shape - almost fit to fib again. It seems a pity to deprive him of another chance to step up to his mark."

The following morning the Sydney Gazette printed a headline: *Convicts Hope To Win Their Freedom In Sporting Contest.* Within the hour Governor Darling had summoned Mr Crowe to Government House. I scudded along behind him. When we arrived, one of Napier's black stallions was tethered by the trough in the courtyard. Thanks to Trumper's care it had fully recovered from the months at sea and was bursting with spirit. Napier was already in the Governor's office; we could hear their conversation as we waited in the ante-room. He'd obviously fallen out of favour.

"Captain Napier, you have no right or authority to promise convicts easement of their condition. The match will not take place. You will desist immediately."

"I cannot do that, Your Excellency - I gave my word," protested Napier.

"Your word? What's your damn'd word against the interest of his Majesty's Government? If I allow this game to go ahead the colony will be covered with convicts learning to play cricket trying to inveigle tickets of leave."

"But they won't win, Your Excellency - if we cancel it will look like weakness."

"Never even contemplate weakness, Captain Napier. Convicts are like animals - you have to keep them weak - if they became strong they'd be at your throat like any French mob."

"Is not demonstrating our superiority on the cricket field an inexpensive way of keeping them down?"

We heard Darling's sigh of exasperation - then a brief silence of contemplation: "Very well - if you persist in this madness you had better win as decisively as you promise. If not, I won't give a damn for your uncle at the Home Office, I'll make sure you end your Army career at Moreton Bay. Call in that fool Crowe."

An orderly opened the door and beckoned Crowe inside. I put my ear closer to the door.

"Mr Crowe I learn you are misguided enough to be giving these criminals the benefit of your time and knowledge. I command you to cease immediately."

"I refuse to do that Your Excellency. I am a free agent and am merely attending to the men's health and well-being."

"Mr Crowe, you are an officer and a gentleman. Do you realize that if the convicts win, or at least put up a good show, every emancipist will think himself as good as a gentleman settler? It could even lead to Revolutionary nonsense such as they had in America."

"Don't you think that if they learn cricket - a gentlemen's game - they may learn other qualities as well?"

"Nonsense - absolute drivel. If you do not obey me, Mr Crowe, I'll have you instantly dismissed."

"But Your Excellency, there is much urgent work to be done at the hospital."

"The two young doctors that accompanied you on the voyage can take over your duties until a suitable replacement arrives from England."

There was a pause as Crowe considered his position. When he did speak I could hardly hear him: "Very well, I resign. A doctor is never short of occupation."

"You are both damned fools - Get out the pair of you."

I slipped from the ante-room and was waiting by Napier's horse as he came out. I made an elaborate effort of handing him the reins. He snarled and snatched them from me before thumping his bum hard upon the saddle - right upon the thistle I'd hidden beneath it. The stallion neighed with fury and reared on its hind legs, throwing an astonished Napier into the Governor's trough. He came out dripping wet and seething. I made great pretence of concern and dismay, but this time I don't think I fooled him:

"You again. It's always you. Can't even hold a horse, you damned fool. I'll see you flogged yet." He raised his crop and I put up my hand to fend off the blow - but to my relief Crowe stepped between us:

"He did nothing - he's only a boy."

"He's your damn'd boy, Crowe, and he's a villain - like all convicts. But you won't protect him much longer. I'm going to teach him, you, and all the rest of those vile rogues a lesson none of you will ever forget."

During the final week before the game Harper's speed with the ball was such, that half of Sydney turned up each night to witness it. On the Friday, as the practice finished, I spied Croft amongst the crowd taking bets left, right, and centre. I went over and slapped him on the back: "Hallo, old covey. How's business?"

He turned to me with a sullen scowl across his face. "Not good. You've become odds on favourites. Levey won't make money if things stay the way they are."

I wasn't sure what he meant.

We had our final practice the following night. Napier and some of his officers turned up to watch, as did Levey, who I spied whispering with Monks, clad as usual in Bible black. Monk's eyes were weak and he had, as yet, shown no sign of recognising me. All our team were now thoroughly fit - we could run, catch and field with the speed and energy of a pack of young dogs - and we put on a performance especially for Napier's benefit. We threw ourselves after the ball whenever it came our way, oblivious to any bruises or cuts we might sustain, and when we batted, we defended our wickets with diehard determination like the squares at Waterloo. Harper bowled faster than a lightening flash and Miller and Lindwall were not far behind. There was a feeling of comradeship amongst us - such as we'd experienced in saving *Enterprise* - only even stronger.

We were covered in sweat and some of us were bleeding when Warnie called us together at the end: "Right mates. Remember, tomorrow this is not a game - it's a bloody war. And it's a war we've got to win." With that he turned and faced Napier and his cronies and folded his arms, with the same look of defiance on his face as when Napier had first made his challenge. The rest of us: Miller, Lindwall, Kidman, Donovan, O'Neill, Trumper, his two sons, and me, even Harper, all affected the same posture. We stood bold, rebellious and united, as if we were carved from stone. The emancipists among the crowd cheered and hurried to place more bets.

Napier's face was black with fury.

Ben watched on one leg as he always did.

9. First Day's Play

It had all been going too well - knowing what I now know about life - things had to change. Crowe and I had not yet moved out of the hospital, and I was woken next morning, the day of the match, by small stones being thrown at my window. I stumbled over and opened it to see young David Trumper looking up at me. He seemed very distraught:

"Where's Mr Crowe? It's Harper!"

Mr Crowe was below in an instant as David unfolded his story: "Our master, Monks, came in the middle of the night with a gang of men and took Harper off in a wagon. Harper didn't want to go - he fought like fury - you should have seen how hard he can punch - but there were too many of them - they jumped on him and dragged him to the ground. They put chains on him and took him away."

"What?" Crook looked totally incredulous. "They can't do that."

"My father protested, but Mr Monks said Harper was assigned to him, and he could take him wherever he wants."

Crowe turned to me - he looked a broken man: "We can hardly win without him. Napier must be at the bottom of this."

I thought of the odds and knew that Levey had to be involved.

We trudged down to the racecourse with heavy hearts despite the gay bunting and excited crowds. All of Sydney seemed to be going to the match. I spied Farrington riding in a carriage with Madame Greere and her girls. The rogue had taken over from Deplidge in that department and had opened a knocking shop in the meanest part of town. Hampton and Adair, now fully-fledged doctors, sauntered along with smug smiles on their faces and cigars between their lips. Levey had again provided marquees and refreshment for the distinguished guests, but as if in fear at the prospect of a convict victory, the field was ringed with soldiers bearing loaded muskets. The large crowd was clearly divided into camps and factions. The officers, government officials and gentlemen settlers, all sat at the tables around the marquees, whilst at the opposite side of the field, the free convicts and their families sat on the grass, where Levey had put up stalls selling beer and gin. I could see Sue and the other girls already busy, plying their trade. Separating the opposing factions, were the small holders on one side and massed ranks of off-duty soldiers on the other.

When we arrived at the official tent another blow awaited us. Each team had been allowed to select an umpire of their choice. Napier's nominee, Crawley, was already there, looking as wet and useless as ever. Crowe had chosen an old shipmate, from *HMS Challenger,* at anchor in the bay. There was no sign of him.

"Have you seen my umpire, Lieutenant Rattigan?" Crowe inquired of the plump major sitting at the officials' table.

"Oh, yes," the major drawled. "He's sent you a note. Apparently, a Russian vessel has been sighted up the coast and the Governor has sent *Challenger* to investigate. I'm afraid he won't be able to fulfil his obligation."

Crowe read the note in a trembling hand. "What about my umpire? I can't officiate my own team."

"Colonel Boyle has consented to stand in for him. You're very lucky - he's a member of the Marylebone Cricket Club and is well acquainted with the rules. He's coming over now."

At that a tall, thin officer with a beak-like nose and drooping moustache sauntered up, polishing a monocle. He rammed it in his left optic and glared ferociously at Crowe: "You must be the bounder that's been giving these felons ideas above their station. Well they won't get any truck out of me I can tell you."

Crowe, looked as though the stuffing had been knocked out of him, he was about to answer when a bugler sounded a fanfare to announce the arrival of Napier and his team. The contemptuous bastard had selected the finest cricketers in the colony. Apart from Hodson and the noxious Carter, they were a mixture of officers and civilians - players from Eton, Harrow and Winchester- including the Governor's nephew, Charles Darling,* who'd been coached in Marylebone by Thomas Lord himself. They drove up in four carriages, decorated with red, white and blue bunting: the officers and gentlemen in the first three - the two huge rankers in the fourth. They alighted to tumultuous cheers from their supporters and waved confidently to all before they went to change into their sporting attire - the officers and gentlemen into a large marquee, overflowing with Levey's luxuries; Carter and Hodson into a more modest tent, well-stocked with bread, cheese and beer.

An even louder cheer erupted from the emancipists' ranks as they caught sight of Warnie and his men shuffling along Elizabeth Street in their chains. Word had obviously reached his team-mates that Harper wouldn't be playing and they looked utterly disconsolate. Warnie must have scraped the barrel for a replacement, because little fat James was waddling along uncertainly in their midst. I went over to join them with Trumper and his boys, as did Ben, who'd appeared, as was his habit, from nowhere. There was no tent for the convicts - they had no pristine white clothes or boots to change into. They simply sat on the grass whilst Bradman and Evans freed them of their fetters. At that moment Levey arrived in his carriage with Mrs Napier and Sarah Trumper, carrying little Horatio, who was growing by the week. They made their way past the seated convicts to the refreshment marquee. Warnie looked up at Leticia as she walked by him. She said nothing but surreptitiously put her hand to the brooch at her neck - not Levey's emerald, but the bone Warnie had carved. The emancipists - especially those who'd placed heavy wagers with Levey - had noticed Harper was not there and began to shout and boo - inquiring reasons for his absence, some even demanding the cancellation of their bets. Levey simply smiled and shrugged at 'em, before hastening Mrs Napier to the privacy of the marquee.

Crowe, who'd regained some of his composure, came over trying to sound cheerful: "Well, lads, we've lost Harper and I'm afraid the umpires will not show you much favour - but you can still win. Show Napier and the rest of this colony what sort of men you are."

"Who will play in place of Harper?" Lindwall demanded.

Everyone looked at fat little James who was looking decidedly nervous - in fact he was in danger of befouling his breeches.

"Him!" Warnie pointed at Ben, who, in his normal wont, was watching on one leg.

"Stow that Gammon," protested Miller. "I don't mind playing with a blacky - at least Harper's half civilised - but that bugger's a bloody savage."

"I've seen what he can do with a ball - he's taught me some of his tricks - we may need him," Warnie replied.

"We'll only beat Napier with speed," insisted Crowe. His brow more creased than I'd ever seen it on *Enterprise*. "O'Neil, you're the next fastest, you'll have to be our first change bowler." O'Neil nodded grimly.

An extremely unpleasant smell wafted from James. Unpleasant even to our nostrils which had become inured to the foulest of stenches. "I still think the black feller will be more useful than him," said Warnie, holding his nose.

"But does he want to play?" asked Crowe, beckoning Ben over.

"Do you want to play?" Warnie demanded when he arrived.

Ben's black eyes betrayed no excitement beneath his long, thick, sweepy lashes; but he nodded his head.

"Do you understand the game?" demanded Crowe.

Ben nodded again.

"Very well," Crowe sighed. "What have we got to lose?"

I didn't want to remind him. I was mightily perplexed. I believed Levey wanted to scupper our chances by getting rid of Harper - so why would he allow his man to play for us?

The band struck up *God Save the King* to herald the arrival of a sour-faced Governor Darling and his smiling lady. Napier, his team and the umpires lined up on the field to welcome him. Darling went down the line shaking each one by the hand and wishing them well. He didn't give so much a glance in our direction. Then as the Governor retired to refresh himself, the umpires summoned Napier and Warnie to the middle of the field. Colonel Boyle tossed a silver half-crown, caught it, held it tight in his palm and asked Napier to call. Napier called 'Heads'. The Colonel opened and closed his palm with surprising alacrity - indeed it would have been impossible for Warnie to have discerned anything - and pronounced Napier had called correctly. Napier smiled like the cat with the cream and elected first innings.

I pulled on Crowe's old gloves. The rest, somewhat reluctantly got to their feet.

"Best of luck, lads," said Bradman quietly. I suspect he was itching to join us.

The scorers made ready to notch the runs - a pale young man from the Judge Advocate's office stood ready with chalk to transcribe them on the blackboard that Levey had provided. The emancipists cheered again as we walked onto the field - though not as enthusiastically as before. Indeed there were some boos at the sight of the half-naked, char-black Ben. I went behind the stumps, the others to their designated positions: David Trumper and Ben deep in field to cut off boundaries; Jonathan Trumper as longstop behind me; Kidman, Warnie, Trumper, and Donovan close around the bat to snap up any catch; O'Neill and Miller, the bravest after Warnie, directly in front of the bat with orders to stop anything that came their way. They all stood ready, bent forward with a hand on each knee, just like Crowe had taught them. Lindwall, now our fastest, was pitched to bowl first. Every one of us was tight and tense as a squashed spring - I was glad my lack of inches made it unnecessary for me to bend - otherwise I might have suffered the same indignity as James.

Napier, in regimental yellow shirt, wearing the strange protection around his legs, and Darling's brother-in-law and private secretary, the Right Honourable Henry Dumaresq,* a thin, frail-looking man with a fair freckled face, walked out to their respective wickets to open the innings. Though the soldiers were essentially neutral, having no innate love for officers and gentlemen, they nevertheless felt loyalty to their regiments, so there were some cries of: "Come on the Diehards!" - even for the likes of Napier.

Boyle fumbled in his pocket, produced a much battered ball and handed it to Lindwall.

Lindwall looked at it disparagingly: "Is this the best you have? I thought we were supposed to start with a new ball."

"This ain't Marylebone. That's the best available. Get on with it," snapped Boyle, polishing his eye-glass, as he gave Napier his guard.

Lindwall threw the ball from hand to hand, taking deep breaths to engender his utmost speed. Napier tapped his bat in his mark, confidently awaiting whatever Lindwall had in store.

"Play!" Boyle bellowed. My stomach tightened.

Lindwall tore down to the wicket and hurled the ball through the air as if his life depended on it - which in many ways it did - I could see it flying straight and swift towards the centre stump. Napier, though, was ready for it, he pushed his bat forward and the ball flew off the tip, high over the head of Warnie, and sped towards the rope.

"Stop it!" yelled Lindwall.

I was so bound up and keen, that I forgot all that Crowe had taught me. I abandoned my post behind the wicket, and raced desperately after the ball at the opposite end of the field, until it was eventually cut off at the rope by young David Trumper. I turned round to see Napier's supporters in the crowd hooting their derision at my lack of finesse, whilst the rogue himself, partly handicapped by the thick protection about his legs, strolled a couple of runs, which the Judge Advocate's Assistant duly chalked up on the board.

Crowe shook his head in disgust: "You damn'd young fool! You're there to keep wicket - run for the ball only when it comes to your part of the field."

Duly chastened, I crept, cringing, back behind the stumps, like Bill's dog after a good kicking. Lindwall was furious and snatched the ball back. This time he bowled it with even greater force - it hit the ground on a bald patch a few yards in front of Napier's bat and bounced up. Napier deliberately pushed his leg forward so that the ball hit him squarely on his pad. I had a perfect view - it was plumb in front of his wicket. This was before the leg before wicket rule had been invented - as nobody wore pads you either hit the ball or got your bloody leg out of the way.

"He can't do that. The ball would have hit his wicket," Warnie protested.

Boyle sniffed and adjusted his monocle. "Nothing about it in the rules."

"Can't you see? He was deliberately standing in front of his wicket. You can't allow it!" Warnie persisted.

"How dare you question an umpire's decision? What qualification has a convicted felon to presume to understand the rules and mystery of the noble game of cricket? Bowl the next damn ball if you please."

Lindwall grabbed the ball again, but such was his anger that he lost his direction. Napier easily clipped him into the deep and ran four, and then two off the fourth and last ball of the over. (The rules were four balls an over then. Six-ball overs didn't come in until 1881. The following year, 1882, I watched old W.G. and his boys lose to the Australians at the Oval. That's when the Ashes originated, I'm the only bugger who knows what those Ashes really are, but that story comes much later.)

It was Dumaresq's turn to face Miller. He'd no leg-guards, but he'd survived Napoleon's artillery at Waterloo, and looked supremely confident as he wafted his bat in the air, practising delicate cuts. Miller paced out his mark, turned, summoned up all the strength he could muster, and sent the ball down faster than a lightning flash, dead on wicket. It hit the pitch in front of Dumaresq and shot along the ground beneath his bat, knocking over the middle stump.

"How was that, mate?" Miller nonchalantly inquired of Crawley.

There was nothing Crawley could do but mumble: "I'm afraid you're out, Dumaresq, old chap."

We exploded with joy and elation. The emancipists in the crowd cheered no less heartily: the pale young man chalked 10 for 1 on the board. "Come on, you've only got to get rid of nine more of the buggers," yelled an ancient ex-convict, as Dumaresq made his slow retreat to the marquee, shaking his head in disbelief.

Next in, to the applause of the men of the 39th, was a tall, scholarly looking man with a pea-green sash around his waist, and an old blue and white Harrovian cap perched on his sandy hair: Captain Charles Sturt.* He'd just come back from exploring the outback and discovering the Murray River. He didn't have much time to explore Miller's bowling that day - after sweeping one ball into the covers for two; he was caught by young David Trumper in the outfield: 12 for 2

We were delirious with excitement - even more delirious when we beheld Napier's scowling face.

Major Frederick Chidley Irwin* of the 63rd Regiment, future Governor of Western Australia - a stout gentleman with a round well-fed face - rubbed his spectacles as he strolled assertively to the wicket, his bat tucked under his arm. Napier came to meet him and whispered something in his ear. Irwin nodded gravely. It was plain we had 'em rattled.

Miller pawed the ground at his mark like an eager stallion, whilst Irwin painstakingly took his guard. When Boyle at last signalled play, Miller charged down to deliver his fastest yet. Irwin lost sight of it completely but waved his bat in a forlorn hope; by pure chance the ball snicked off it and went flying in the direction of Donovan.

"Run!" yelled Irwin feverously, and went flying down the pitch as fast as his bulk would allow. Napier had no choice but to run, even though he could see the ball was already in Donovan's hand.

"Throw me the bloody ball!" screamed Warnie standing by the wicket with Napier only halfway down the pitch. But for some reason, Donovan chose to throw the ball at the wicket, missed it by the width of Irwin's bum, and Napier scrambled to safety.

"In!" yelled Boyle, triumphantly, as a deep groan emanated from the massed emancipist ranks.

"Bloody, stupid Irish bastard," cursed Miller.

Napier had the batting and got a single, managing to step heavily on Miller's bare foot as he rushed into his crease.

Lindwall could not regain his accuracy and Napier began to get his eye in, scoring eight more runs off the over. It was immediately apparent when Miller bowled again, that the foot that Napier had trodden on was troubling him. He could not re-generate his top speed and Irwin played him with more assurance, even managing to get a couple of runs when Ben moved too lethargically to pick up a ball in the outfield.

Napier had taken the score to thirty when he skied a ball off Lindwall. It rose high into the air like a soaring bird. Donovan was plumb beneath it: "Catch it!" yelled Warnie. I could even hear Crowe's anguished cry of "Catch!" from the marquee. Donovan squinted up into the sun as the ball fell towards him - for a moment it seemed the ball was safe in his hands - I was about to scream in triumph when I saw it slip to the ground.

"What in damnation are you doing? How could you miss it?"Warnie could hardly believe his eyes: "You've been snapping up harder catches than that for weeks."

Donovan hung his head in shame as Napier added another two runs to his score.

Miller meanwhile had limped to the rope where Mr Crowe applied one of his soothing ointments. In the next over he seemed to have regained some of his speed. Irwin waved his bat at a particularly fast ball; I heard a distinct click before I caught it in my right hand.

"How about that, old chap?" I demanded of Crawley as Miller eyed him ferociously. Crawley reluctantly raised a well-chewed finger. 32 for 3: we were exhalant again.

The Right Honourable George Macleay,* Military Secretary to the Colony, sauntered out to bat, with a good-humoured smile on his face. He was a capable and confident batsman. That was all too apparent when he swept his first ball off Miller for four and followed it with a delicate cut for two. Miller's foot began to trouble him again, and Napier and Macleary had taken the score to over fifty, before Crowe signalled Warnie to take Miller off and bring on O'Neil. It had immediate effect. O'Neil thundered up the field and delivered a ball which literally fizzed about Macleay's ears - causing him to step back in astonishment, knocking over his wicket as he did so. Even Boyle couldn't refuse O'Neil's delirious appeal: 55 for 4! We could still do it.

Next in was Captain Chisholm Frazer of the 37th, a thin, sallow-faced chap with yellowish flaxen hair. He looked an obvious dandy, with gold braided lace on his shirt collar and about his regimental belt. He was no mean batsman though, and soon swept O'Neil for two fours. Despite our repeated protests, Napier continued to use his padded legs to divert the ball from his wicket and, as our bowlers tired, the score crept remorselessly on towards a hundred. Ben continued to move lethargically, but the rest of us ran and fielded to our utmost, despite the heat and the flies, until Frazer misjudged the pitch of a ball from Lindwall and lost his leg-stump. Again there could be no disputation: 98 for 5.

Young Charlie Darling, a cheerful looking young fellow with a ruddy complexion, ran to the wicket, practising the strokes Mr Lord had taught him. By now Lindwall was exhausted and Crowe yelled to Warnie to bring on Trumper with his medium pacers.

They were very much to Napier's liking and he scored twelve off Trumper's first over. O'Neil had also shot his bolt and young Darling played him with ease. The score had edged up to a hundred and twenty when at last, Napier, with perhaps a touch of over-confidence, skied the ball again. It hung in the air between three fielders; Kidman ran to position himself under it and seemed certain to hold it until Donovan, looking upwards at the falling ball, barged into him. They both fell and the ball fell with them.

"Look where you're going - you damned Irish bastard!" Kidman exploded, as Napier scampered yet another run.

After two more overs, in which ten more runs were added, Crowe was forced to call Kidman's underarm trundlers into the attack. Darling was circumspect and hovered watchfully at the crease, stabbing down at the battered ball, until, with his third delivery, Kidman managed to produce a daisy cutter that bumped about in a most erratic manner to find its way past the bat and, after skidding past the young man's toes, cart-wheeled his off-stump. Mr Darling left the field in a most desultory manner. We congratulated Kidman, but the score was now one hundred and thirty-one and I think most of us felt we had little chance of getting anywhere near such a total - and there were still four wickets, including that bastard Napier's, to fall.

Lieutenant Alan Nettleton of the 40th Regiment, a fine strapping, freckled, young man, came in whirling his bat like Excalibur but, as the wicket had fallen on the last ball of the over, Napier had the strike. Trumper's medium pacers had had little effect and Crowe was forced to call on the limping Miller again. Miller grabbed the ball and came tearing down towards his mark. Napier set his shoulders as if he intended to thwack him over the distant gum trees.

"Give him a slower one!"

Warnie must have suddenly remembered Napier's fallibility that morning on the boat all those months ago. It had the same effect. Miller released a slow lob that seemed to hang forever in the air; Napier mistimed his swing and the ball slipped from his bat into Warnie's eager hands. "How is he?" he screamed triumphantly at Boyle, as if it was a question not worth the asking.

"Not out."

We couldn't believe our ears.

"What? You saw me catch it." Warnie held up the ball above his head.

"It was a 'No Ball': the bowler's foot was beyond his crease," countered Boyle with utter conviction.

Caterwauling erupted from the emancipists - Warnie was near to tearing out his hair in frustration. Most of us sunk to our knees in despair.

"Don't give up, lads. Stick at it. Persevere!" Crowe pleaded in anguish from the ropes.

Miller snatched the ball and limped back to his mark. Napier edged the next ball for a single, which brought Nettleton down to face the bowling for the first time.

"Long live the Excellers!" shouted the 40th in their Somerset twang.

Nettleton responded by driving Miller above his head for four.

"Pitch him another, exactly the same," Warnie muttered softly to Miller: "I'll catch him in the long field."

I managed to divert Nettleton's attention by suggesting that the lace of his boot might be coming loose. Warnie crept to his new position behind Napier's back; whilst Nettleton bent down to adjust his trotters.

Miller's poor foot was now swollen, but he set his teeth and delivered an identical ball. Nettleton connected as before - it soared in the air and came down almost in Warnie's throat.

"How was that one?" bawled Miller.

Not even Boyle could give two blatant wrong decisions in one over, and with extreme difficulty, he managed to mumble: 'Out!' 137 for 7.

There were ironic cheers from the soldiers of the 57th as Lieutenant Attenborough walked to the wicket with great uncertainty. There didn't appear to be much of a 'Diehard' about him - and so it proved.

"Wearing any of Captain Napier's padding?" I murmured as he took his guard.

"What's that?" he asked uneasily.

"The way Miller's been sending that ball down today, you'll need all you can get. Like cannon balls they are," I said, backing away from the wicket in mock trepidation.

Attenborough gripped his bat and edged sideways from the stumps, presenting Miller a perfect target. Miller took six quick steps and swung his arm with all the power he could muster. The ball struck Attenborough's bat with the force of a hammer - it leapt from his grasp and smashed into the wicket behind. There was no need for Miller to ask anything: the pale young gentleman had already amended the score to 137 for 8!

Sergeant Hodson came menacingly to the wicket in his green regimental shirt as his comrades in the 39th shouted: "Give 'em hell, you Green Linnet!" He was indeed a fine specimen of strength and vitality - a large framed man, with forearms that looked as hard as steel. He gave Miller a savage stare, which Miller returned with interest before bowling the final ball of the over. Hodson gave a shrug of his huge shoulders and heaved the ball from outside his off-stump across to leg. It flew like a dirty brown swallow way over the ropes into the distant reaches of the race-course. In those days there was no such thing as automatic sixes and fours - all runs had to be run - and Hodson got five from that first hit. He would have got more, but Napier was by this time feeling the effects of his heavily padded legs, and went at a snail's pace. Even so, Hodson managed to ensure Miller's injured foot was made even worse by stamping on it yet again with his heavy army boot.

Hodson had kept the batting and found Kidman's underhand grubs very much to his liking - taking another nine off the over. They were now over 150 and Miller could hardly stand, so Crowe called on Lindwall for one final effort. Warnie moved in close to the point of Hodson's bat - crouching in a suicidal position which later became known as silly point.

Lindwall tore in again like a spent horse. Hodson made a wild heave and thrashed the ball directly into Warnie. It hit him clean in his family jewels. He collapsed holding them with an agonised scream. Mrs Napier rose to her feet in consternation as we gathered around him. Mr Crowe ran out on the pitch with his medical bag, and poor Warnie then suffered the indignity of having his balls rubbed with Mr Crowe's soothing ointment in front of half the population of Sydney. The emancipist women made ribald jokes, offering to take over from Mr Crowe, and I swear that some of the most distinguished ladies borrowed their husbands' spyglasses and binoculars to get a better look. As Mr Kipling so rightly points out: '*The colonel's lady and Rosie O'Grady, are sisters under their skins*'.

The ball didn't travel so no runs were taken and Lindwall prepared to bowl once more. To the amazement of everyone Warnie made his way back to the identical spot.

"Don't be foolish, Warnie. He'll kill you if he gets the chance," I pleaded.

But he took no heed. Lindwall ran in again. I watched, crouched behind the wicket, a few feet back from Hodson's great arse. I could see Warnie crouching, edging even a little bit closer. Lindwall delivered the ball with his arm well below his shoulder, it sped towards me, dead on the wicket, Hodson gave another mighty swipe - it flew like a bullet straight at Warnie again; but this time Warnie's hands moved so fast they could have snatched the bullet from the very muzzle of the gun itself.

"Got the bastard!" he bawled as he flourished the ball triumphantly in the air. 151 for 9.

Carter was never popular, so there were few cheers from the lads of the 57th as he plodded to the wicket. I think even the officers wanted to see the back of him, as lunch wouldn't be taken until the end of the innings. Napier had managed to get to the batter's end and scored another four runs in the remainder of the over.

Crowe called for O'Neil to replace Kidman. O'Neil had suffered especially from Carter's brutal flogging on *Enterprise* and was only too eager to seize the ball. Carter like all bullies was a coward at heart, and I could sense his fear as he took his guard.

"Pity you ain't got Napier's leg guards," I chaffed as I crouched behind him. "O'Neil's got a ball that can break bone. Don't fret though, old Crowe's good at amputation."

The vicious thug responded by breaking extremely noxious wind. O'Neil spat on his hands and rubbed the moisture into the old and battered ball. He glared at Carter, mumbled a prayer to his Virgin Mary, and then came hurtling towards him as relentlessly as the Light Brigade at Balaclava. Carter leapt out of the way, swung his bat in forlorn hope, missed completely and his wicket collapsed behind him. 155 all out: the Judge Advocate's assistant left the blackboard and hurried into the tent for luncheon. 155 don't sound like much in these days of Dr Grace and his centuries and sound, level pitches, but in those days it was a formidable score.

Napier strutted off the field brandishing his bat in triumph, undefeated on 83.

Whilst the officers and gentlemen enjoyed their cold cuts and champagne - the convicts rested their weary limbs and tried to regain their strength on dry bread and water, to which I added a filched pork pie and a couple of flagons of ale. The soldiers and the emancipists, those that is that hadn't brought their refreshments with them, eagerly patronised Levey's refreshment stalls, where Sue and the other girls served them at inflated prices. Levey seemed to be making money all round - swift business was also being done at the betting tent, where the soldiers were eagerly putting their money on what looked like a forgone conclusion, and some emancipists, who'd originally bet on the convicts, were now hedging their bets by doubling their original stake on Napier's team.

I spied Napier in earnest conversation with Hodson and Carter and wondered what he was planning for us - we found out only too quickly.

Trumper, our best player, opened our innings with Kidman, an obstinate bat, who Crowe instructed to stay in as long as possible. Hodson awaited them with a shiny brand-new ball. As soon as Boyle shouted '*Play*', the great brute charged down to the wicket and hurled the ball directly at Trumper's foremost leg, but Trumper skipped out of the way and clipped it past the point for two. Hodson snarled in anger and bowled again with even more force, but Trumper came forward and smothered the ball before it had time to shoot or rise or do mischief by catches, and played in this vein throughout the rest of the over without adding any more runs.

Napier tossed the ball to Carter with an ominous nod. Carter gave a vicious smile, took a dozen measured paces and hurled it at Kidman's head. It was so unexpected it took Kidman totally by surprise and struck his brow with an awesome crack. He fell as if he'd been struck by Napier's pistol. Crowe came running out with his bag to pronounce bitterly that Kidman was completely unconscious and unfit to carry on. O'Neil and Lindwall carried him from the field.

Warnie came in rubbing his tender parts and bristling defiance. He hit the first ball he received over Carter's head for four and then clipped the next for two. I could see Carter's mean little eyes grow even smaller - he measured Warnie as if he were about to make his coffin - and then deliberately hurled the ball directly at Warnie's bruised and painful privates. Warnie yelled in an anguish which was felt by every watching man and not a few women - especially Mrs Napier, who drank her glass of soda in a single swallow.

"Do you mean to kill them? It's nothing short of murder, bellowed Crowe, rushing to Warnie's aid.

Again Warnie's battered parts were exposed to public view as Crowe re-applied his balm. Warnie was white with pain but refused to retire, so Crowe padded his crotch with huge wads of bandage, provoking more ribald remarks from the lower orders of women. Play resumed and Trumper immediately thumped Hodson for what would have been at least four, but poor Warnie could hardly walk yet alone run, so they only managed two - but at least we'd reached double figures. Hodson peppered Trumper viciously to his arms, legs and shoulders, but Trumper was too good for him and scored another eight off the over.

"Fancy another one, where the last one went?" Carter taunted Warnie as he faced him again, and blatantly aimed brutally at the identical spot. Warnie desperately lifted his bat to protect himself but, to his bitter consternation, the ball flew off it into Napier's jubilant hands. The Judge Advocate's Assistant had over-indulged in Levey's champagne and scrawled 18 for 2 in a somewhat shaky hand.

"Is that the best Hambledon can do?" Napier taunted as an inconsolable Warnie made his painful way from the wicket. His anguish and humiliation increased when he caught Mrs Napier's pitying eye as she sat beside a self-satisfied Levey.

As Miller's foot was still sore and tender, O'Neil came in next to the delight of Carter. "I'll make you scream like an Irish pig, as you did when I flogged you," he whispered ominously, as O'Neil passed him on his way to the wicket.

O'Neil's dander was up and he responded with a mixture of cross-batted slogs and hot-headed cuts, which added ten quick runs to the total; but his luck couldn't last and he was soon bowled by Hodson for thirteen. The pale young man chalked up 35 for 3, as yet more emancipists made their way to the betting tent, switching their bets to Napier.

"We've still got Trumper," Crowe muttered beside me, "as long as he is there we've got some hope of getting near their score."

Donovan followed his compatriot to the crease, muttering his Roman prayers and trying to avoid Napier's intimidating eye. He was no mean bat for a would-be priest, and he defended his wicket stoutly for the remainder of the over. Trumper had added another eleven runs when he pushed forward to a low one from Hodson. The ball rolled into the covers.

"Run!" yelled Donovan.

"No!" cried Crowe by my side.

Trumper automatically obeyed Donovan's call and tore down towards the bowler's end, but the ball was already in Captain Sturt's hand and his throw shattered the wicket long before Trumper made his ground. A groan swept the emancipists' end of the field - our best man run out for twenty-two - 44 for 4.

"Why on earth did the fool call for a run?" Crowe inquired bitterly, almost to himself. We knew we were finished now. There was only Lindwall, the injured Miller, three boys and lackadaisical Ben left.

Donovan seemed chastened by his recklessness and defended his wicket without scoring during the next few overs, whilst Lindwall threw his bat at everything, ignoring the blows he took to his arms and shins, and added another nine runs to bring our score to fifty-three. Hodson began to tire and Napier took over with a mixture of underarm shooters and trimmers. His third delivery shot up off a tuft of tough kangaroo grass and sneaked past Lindwall's bat to knock out his middle stump. The pale young man rushed from the back of the marquee, where he had been answering an urgent call from dear old Mother Nature, to chalk up 53 for 5.

Miller, our last real batsman, his foot swathed in a thick padded bandage like he was suffering from acute gout, made his agonising way to the crease. He promptly smashed Napier way beyond the ropes - it should have been five or six but poor Miller could only shuffle a single and kept the bowling.

Carter smacked the ball from hand to hand: "D'you fancy another thump on yer foot?"

Miller said nothing but took his guard. Carter came rushing in but Miller wielded his bat like a sabre and swept him over the refreshment tent. The emancipists roared their approval as Miller hobbled back and forth for three. Donovan again defended for the rest of the over, leaving Miller to face Napier once more. Now Napier began aiming lobs directly on Miller's foot. Miller managed a brace of twos before Napier landed a direct hit. Miller yelled in pain, dropped his bat, and jumped about on his good foot, nursing the other, failing to notice that he had jumped out of his crease.

The wicket keeper, young Charlie Darling, seized the ball and making no allowance for Miller's discomfort, whipped off the bails: "How is that?"

"Out!" retorted a delighted Boyle. Miller was stumped: 61 for 6; but the atmosphere had changed. The soldiers were no longer cheering.

There was a sickening feeling inside my guts as I realised that I was the next man in. All I wanted was to go behind the marquee and empty my bowels. Bradman had been watching throughout the afternoon, his stone face betraying nothing, but he hastened over to me as I picked up a bat not much shorter than myself:

"Remember what the old Squire used to tell me - stand upright, keep your left shoulder well forward - keep your eye fixed on the bowler, and never lose sight of the ball from the moment it leaves his hand. Don't try to smash it - find gaps in the field. You can do it." He clapped my shoulder encouragingly: "Good luck, you young villain."

There were gasps of amazement and shouts of ridicule as I made my diminutive way to the wicket, trying to remember all that Bradman had said. (Although I should point out that at that time boys often played in major matches - the great Grace himself played against men at the age of nine - his brother, E.M. Grace, to my mind the better cricketer, played against an all-England Eleven at fourteen.) Napier gave me his superior smirk before sending down an underarm shooter; my sharp eyes easily picked it out, and I managed to push it through a gap in the field and ran a single. I kept the batting as it was the last ball of the over, which meant I had to face Carter.

"Where's yer precious Mr Crowe? He won't protect you now," the odious bludger whispered as he past me on his way to his mark.

I took my guard on the side of the wicket he bowled and held my bat loosely - all I wanted was to stop the ball, keep it away from my wicket. I watched his first one all the way - it came for my head at a frightening speed and I only managed to fend it off at the last minute.

"Steady on he's only a boy," protested Sturt, who seemed a decent fellow.

"He's playing in a man's game - he can retire if he don't fancy the bowling," purred Napier, looking smug as a bluebottle on a cow pat. The next one came directly for my head again, this time I ducked and it went flying over young Charlie behind the stumps and I scrambled two byes - the first of the day. By some miracle I saw out the over, even managing to sneak a two off the edge of the bat. It was Donovan's turn to face the barrage. I couldn't understand the meaning of the sharp look Napier gave him. I thought it must have been a hidden insult to goad him to recklessness, because Donovan responded by coming down the wicket in what looked like an attempt to smash the ball back into Sydney, but only succeeded in missing it entirely and was clean bowled for naught: 66 for 7.

"Why the fuck did you do that?" I demanded, but he avoided my eyes and made his disconsolate way back to the others.

Young David Trumper walked bravely to the wicket - both he and his brother had been coached a little by their father and he saw out the over, playing Napier well, to the admiration of the crowd. But it couldn't last. I took a single off Carter's first ball, his next bounced off the pitch at an unexpected angle and young David was clean bowled: 67 for 8. David's younger brother Jonathan somehow managed to survive the over, so Napier played his final card by bringing back a re-invigorated Hodson. He was even faster than Carter but I managed to sneak a single off his second ball. It was the last run to be added to our total, because Jonathan and a seemingly unconcerned Ben, who'd sauntered to the wicket to hoots of derision, both had their stumps smashed by Hodson in succeeding balls. 68 all out - 87 behind.

The band struck up '*See the Conquering Heroes Come*' as Napier led his team off the field to celebrate in the marquee with more of Levey's champagne. The convicts slumped disconsolately on the ground outside as Bradman and Evans locked their fetters back on their ankles.

"We still might have stood a chance if it wasn't for that bastard umpire - he'll never give a decision our way till hell freezes over," lamented Miller bitterly, as Crowe re-bandaged his foot. I spied an extra strong dose of Crowe's tincture of rhubarb in his open bag and had a moment of inspiration. I lifted it unnoticed and slipped inside the tent. Boyle was standing haw-hawing with a group of officers, holding a near empty glass of champagne behind his back. I'd just replenished it with something a good deal stronger, which I hoped would make the stuck-up macer* spend the night and most of the morrow spewing and skittering, when I noticed Levey beckoning me. He looked extremely flustered.

"Things are not going well, my dear," he whispered frantically. "There is now so much money on Napier and his team, that I will be bled dry."

"What about your man Croft? I thought he was a genius with the odds?"

Levey shrugged: "He is not so great a genius as I thought. Perhaps I spent too much time admiring the beauty of Mrs Napier and did not pay enough attention to my business." He shook his head mournfully in the way Fagin used to. "I do not understand this cricket business. Can you still win?"

"Can pigs fly? Napier bends the rules as he pleases and half our team is crocked." I spied Boyle draining his glass in a greedy quaff. "Even if we had a fair umpire we're still too far behind."

"You have Ben."

"What could he do? He's been bloody useless all day."

"What if I told him I needed you to win?"

"He'd have to perform a bleeding miracle."

"He might be able to if you make sure that he throws - what do you call it? - Yes, bowls. It's my only hope, my dear - I'll be ruined else."

"You'd have to find a new umpire - one that would do us some favours." I could see Boyle stuffing his face with pork pie. "Something tells me that crooked bastard won't be up to it tomorrow." I winked, showed Levey the empty tincture bottle and he took my meaning. "Yes, my dear. Don't worry - that can easily be arranged. I know the very man. He is due on this evening's packet."

"What about poor Harper? He can't play now the match has started, but he's in no state to fight again - use your influence - get him back."

"Of course, my dear, of course. I'll make sure he is safely returned by morning."

He was so desperate - I sensed an opportunity to turn things further to my advantage: "What's in it for me?"

"If you win, Ben will take you to your father. I give you my word."

Warnie and the others had already been marched to their barracks by the time I got outside, so I went back with Crowe to the hospital. He seemed a broken man. I decided to leave mentioning Ben and the new umpire till later - the situation still seemed so hopeless.

A few hours later I was in Crowe's room, soaking my bruised hands in vinegar to hardened them for the next day's pounding, whilst he wrote a report to the authorities in England - fat lot of use it would have done, when there was a faint tap on the door. I opened it and Sarah Trumper hastened in, pale with anxiety.

"Mr Crowe, my mistress has sent me - but no one must know I've been here."

"Don't worry Sarah, there's no one in this block – my colleagues, Adair and Hampton, are busy celebrating with Napier and his supporters," Said Crowe bitterly.

"That is why I've come. My mistress went home as soon as play finished - she was extremely upset by the way our team was treated. I was going down to the study to fetch a glass of brandy to help her sleep, when the front door opened and Captain Napier came in with a man called Monks - the master of Sam and my boys. Do you know him?"

Crowe nodded: "I've seen him lurking around - I would say he's suffering from epilepsy - he shows all the symptoms."

"They were deep in conversation and didn't notice me in the shadows on the bend of the stairs. I would have either announced my presence or gone back to my mistress, but I caught the drift of their talk…I couldn't believe what I heard…" She stopped and shook her head, close to tears.

"Yes?" Crowe almost pleaded: "You can tell me."

"They were talking about the cost of keeping the captain's horses and sheep at Monk's farm - Monks is short of money and wanted instant payment. The Captain said, I can remember his words distinctly: *'I owe you nothing. The tip I gave you was worth a fortune - if you'd had the sense to lay the bet whilst the odds were favorable'*. Monks then asked him why'd he'd been so certain of winning and the Captain, he'd been drinking otherwise I'm sure he wouldn't have revealed it, said he had a man in your team making sure you'd lose. Then they went into his study and I couldn't hear any more. I went back and told Mrs Napier - she said I was to tell you at once."

Suddenly everything was clear: "It's Donovan!" I exclaimed. "He deliberately ran out your husband, made sure we dropped catches, didn't score a run, and then gave his bloody wicket away."

Crowe nodded sadly: "I think you're right, Dawkins. It's a pity we didn't know this before the game."

"We can still do something before tomorrow," I said.

Crowe shrugged: "It's too late. We're too far behind and the fault is entirely mine - I was too concerned with getting one over on Napier, I lost sight of everything else."

I got up and went to the door: "I'm going to tell Warnie. He must know."

"You can't get into the barracks at night."

"Can't I? I too have undisclosed talents, Mr Crowe."

Twenty minutes later, I lurked in the shadows as a couple of drunken soldiers rattled the iron barrack gates demanding entrance. Whilst the duty sergeant was admonishing them, I stole in behind him and crept across the yard to the main building: a brick-built barn on three floors, which very much resembled a workhouse. I was all too familiar with the layout of workhouses and quickly found a half-open window to climb through. Warnie and the rest were in the long dormitory on the first floor, which that night was more like a dressing station after the Battle of Inkerman. Kidman's head, Warnie's privates and Miller's foot were swathed in bandages; O'Neil and Lindwall were black and blue with bruises. Only Donovan appeared to be unscathed. They clustered around me in surprise.

"What yer doing here, my little mate?" Warnie whispered.

"I've got some news Mrs Napier thought you ought to hear," I said meaningfully.

The mere mention of her name changed his demeanour at a stroke: "What is it?"

I told them all what Sarah had heard. There was a shocked silence, as if they found such cruel betrayal impossible to believe. O'Neil spoke first: "We all know who it is, don't we lads?" The others nodded as Donovan hung his head in shame. "I'm going to tell the other Irish fellows - we have our own way of dealing with traitors - gouging's too good for the likes of him. He must have betrayed us on the boat as well - five men died because of that damn'd villain."

O'Neill turned to go but Warnie stopped him: "Let's hear what the bastard's got to say for himself first."

All our eyes fixed on the wretched Donovan, who merely whispered in a hollow voice: "Kill me, I deserve to die. I've wished I was dead every day this past year. If God did not forbid it, I'd have killed myself long ago."

"But why did you do such a terrible thing?" demanded Warnie. "We were your mates, your fellows in suffering."

Donovan still couldn't look at us - each word he uttered, in the lowest of voices, seemed to cause him the deepest pain: "I was a rebel, out with a pike along with the boys of Wexford, when we came up against Napier and the damn'd hussars. We hadn't a chance. I was taken along with the others and sent to rot in Kilmainham gaol. Then Napier discovered my mother and father were tenants on his cousin's estate in Galway. He threatened to evict them if I did not give him certain information. They were old and I knew they would starve. I tried to resist him - but he persisted as only he can - had me hanging on a wall for days on end without sleep - telling me how my poor old ma and pa would die in the gutter because of me. At last I broke. I couldn't bear it any more - I told him what he wanted - names and whereabouts of the leaders - from that cursed moment I've been completely in his power."

"How many poor souls have died because of you, you bastard?" growled O'Neil.

"I dread to think. My only wish is for a priest - I have much to confess."

"You can rot in hell with all your bloody sins un-shriven."

O'Neil grabbed at Donovan's collar but Warnie restrained him again. "What have you got to gain if you kill him tonight? Napier will know we did it and he'll hang us for sure. What harm can he do? We've lost anyway."

"Levey says that Ben can still win it for us if you let him bowl," I said.

Warnie turned to me with a glint in his eye. "I've thought we could win it with spin all along - despite what Crowe said - but the lazy black bugger was useless today."

"That's because Levey told him not to try. Levey thought he'd make more money if Napier won - he was involved in getting rid of Harper but now the odds have changed - he's promised Harper will be back by the morning and now he's desperate for us to win, Ben does what Levey tells him."

"That foul fart of an umpire would never let Ben bowl; he'd say it was Black Magic."

"I think he's farting his arse off at this moment, Warnie. I slipped him an overdose of Crowe's rhubarb, he won't last more than five minutes at the crease."

Warnie chuckled and rubbed his chin: "Even if we get 'em out cheap - we've still have to get more than a hundred runs."

"Give me another chance," Donovan whispered. "I swear by all that's holy, I'll stay in until you get them."

The others protested bitterly at the mere suggestion, but Warnie pondered before offering Donovan his hand: "Very well. What have we got to lose? You certainly can defend - you proved that today - but if you even think of betraying us again, I'll cut your bloody throat myself."

Challenge Match

Sydney Racetrack
January 26th 1829

First Day

Officers and Gentlemen
First Innings

Captain Napier	**Not Out**	**83**
Right Hon. Henry Dumaresq	**bowled Miller**	**0**
Captain Charles Sturt	**caught Trumper D. bowled Miller**	**2**
Major Fredrick Chidley Irwin	**caught Dawkins bowled Miller**	**3**
Right Hon. George Macleary	**stepped on wicket**	**15**
Captain Chisholm Frazer	**bowled Lindwall**	**22**
Mr Charles Darling	**bowled Kidman**	**12**
Lt Alan Nettleton	**caught Warne bowled Miller**	**4**
Lieutenant Attenboroug	**hit wicket bowled Miller**	**0**
Sergeant F. Hodson	**caught Warne bowled Lindwall**	**14**
Private H. Carter	**bowled O'Neil**	**0**
	TOTAL	**155**

Felons & Others
First Innings

Trumper S.	**run out**	**22**
Kidman	**retired hurt**	**0**
Warne	**caught Capt Napier bowled Carter**	**8**
O'Neil	**bowled Hodson**	**13**
Donovan	**bowled Capt Napier**	**0**
Lindwall	**bowled Capt Napier**	**9**
Miller	**stumped bowled Carter**	**8**
Dawkins	**Not Out**	**4**
Trumper D.	**bowled Hodson**	**0**
Trumper J.	**bowled Hodson**	**0**
Aborigine	**bowled Hodson**	**0**
Extras	**byes**	**4**
	TOTAL	**68**

10. Second Day

The crowd was smaller. Many emancipists, feeling that the match was lost, had stayed away, and there was an air of anti-climax around the ground. I'd sneaked back to the hospital for the remainder of the night and was waiting with Mr Crowe and the returned Harper, who seemed unharmed apart from a few cuts and swellings, when Warnie and his party arrived. Ben was with them, listening intently to Warnie as he laid out his plans. Even though the others were limping, bruised, and swathed in bandages, there was a firmer resolution about them all. As Bradman removed their fetters, Crowe, me, Trumper and his boys joined them on the grass. Ben stood one-legged as usual.

"I made mistakes yesterday - I made a military blunder by sticking rigidly to my original plan and not adapting to changing circumstances. But today is a new day and we can turn the present situation to our advantage," said Crowe briskly. "They have been celebrating all night and we will attack them in a manner they will not expect."

"Ben and me are going to spin the ball, baffle 'em, frustrate the bastards," explained Warnie more mundanely. "Yesterday we let Napier win too easily - today they'll be over-confident, and we'll take 'em by surprise. Yesterday you played like gentlemen - today fight and cheat like the rogues and villains you are."

At that moment Levey marched towards us with a stoutish person, of late middle-age, in tight-fitting white flannel jacket and black trousers. The stranger carried his straw hat in his hand, there was no more hair on his head than on an egg, a vivid red egg, fried in the sun. He peered at us through a quizzing glass, which he held up to his extensive face - although his squinting signified that he saw very little. There was a jaunty but kindly air about him.

"May I introduce my esteemed acquaintance," purred Levey, "Wilkins Micawber, Esquire, Magistrate of Port Middlebay, who has sailed down the coast to our fair city to witness this match?"

"Welcome to our antipodean paradise, the fair land of promise," said Micawber in a genteel voice, as he held his glass even closer to his eye, "I hope I see you all well and ready for the fray?"

"We are indeed fortunate that the Magistrate is with us," Levey continued. "I have had the distressing news that the good Colonel Boyle is suffering vehement spasms to his stomach. He is being ministered at this moment by Doctors Hampton and Adair, but sadly will not be fit to stand today. Mr Micawber has agreed to stand in his place."

"Ahem! As a life-long student and disciple of the noble game - many the afternoon I have sat under a spreading tree by a village green, in our favoured native land, nursing a flowing tankard of brown English ale, beholding the upright yeomen at their honourable sport," Micawber wiped his eyes nostalgically, "I deem myself fortunate indeed to partake, however small a part, in this momentous encounter...."

He undoubtedly would have continued but a trumpet blast signified the arrival of Napier, and his team. Crawley was with them and threw up his breakfast the moment he got out of the coach. Most of the others looked distinctly jaded and green about the gills, and hurried into the tents, intending to sleep off their overindulgence whilst Napier fashioned another huge innings to add to their invincible lead.

"May I crave your forbearance, my good Captain?" called Levey, as Napier was about to follow the others.

Napier frowned and swaggered over. "Make it sharp. What is it?" he demanded surlily.

"May I introduce Mr Wilkins Micawber, an esteemed local magistrate, who will be taking over the official duties of the unfortunate Colonel Boyle?"

Napier surveyed Micawber with utter disdain: "What the devil d'you mean?"

"Unfortunately Colonel Boyle has been taken violently ill and is at this moment being administered to in the hospital. I have already presented Mr Micawber's credentials with the officials - he is fully qualified to preside."

"There are some landmarks on the road to the tomb, which a man would never wish to have passed," said Micawber with a comprehensive and condescending roll in his voice, "and such an occasion is this clash of titans. It will be an honour to pass judgement - I have as long acquaintance of the art and mystery of the noble game of cricket, as I have of the law itself: having applied myself to the Commentaries of one of the most eminent and remarkable of our English jurists."

Napier eyed him incongruously - if he'd not been so certain of victory he probably would have objected - but he simply nodded coldly and went to join his team.

"Will you sample a glass of punch, Mr Micawber, before you attend to your duties?" inquired Levey.

"Hem! Punch, like time and tide, waits for no man," responded Micawber, putting his hands in his pockets and nodding his head as if to say the case was very clearly put. "Farewell, gentlemen. We will meet again when the God of Day is high upon the mountain tops."

I wondered how on earth Levey had managed to discover such a strange cove. They left us to make our final preparations: Crowe applied fresh bandages to Miller's foot and Kidman's head, I pulled the gloves over my raw palms, whilst Warnie and Ben whispered together, turning the ball with their fingers. Bradman brought word that Darling was attending to business at Government House and was not to be expected until lunch, so we were to commence play without him. Warnie called us all together for a final word: "They think we haven't got a hope in hell - surprise is everything. Don't let 'em know the black feller's going to bowl till the very last minute. We've got to get Napier cheaply. Don't give away a run in the field, make very catch count - we can still win."

Micawber and Crawley made an unlikely pair as they led the way to the wicket. Crawley, bent, white and nauseous, Micawber, walking upright, humming a tune, with his straw hat very much on one side, and his sleeves loosely turned back at the wrists, as if he was ready to lend a hand in any direction.

We walked out on the field to derogatory applause. Warnie surreptitiously nodded his thanks to Mrs Napier, who had joined Levey, then threw the ball to Lindwall, who began turning over his arm as if to prepare himself, as Napier and Dumaresq strolled confidently to their respective ends. Napier asked for his guard: Micawber trifled with his eye glass before nodding his approval. He then settled his chin in his collar and cried 'Play' with exceeding gravity.

Lindwall immediately tossed the ball to Ben, who was standing beside him. Ben carefully put his fingers around the battered stitching then spun the ball up into the fresh morning air. Napier watched in complete disbelief as it turned and twisted and turned again, before landing on a bald spot of earth, spinning around his upraised bat and knocking over his middle stump.

"How is that?" screamed Warnie in ecstasy.

"Out!" pronounced Micawber, sticking up a finger in the most resolute manner.

"I can't be out! That's illegal," Napier protested. "I've never seen anyone bowl like that."

"There are more things in Heaven and Earth than are dreamt of in your philology," said Micawber, with an air of extreme satisfaction.

"I refuse to be out! That was an unfair ball!" screamed Napier.

Micawber fumbled in his waistcoat pocket and took out a well-thumbed note book: "According to the Code of the Marylebone Cricket Club - Laws 9 and 10 - the ball was delivered with one foot behind the bowling crease and the bowler's arm was below shoulder height. In short - you are out. May I suggest you commence your peregrination from the wicket?"

"No you may certainly not, you damned idiot! Crawley you're our umpire, say something, you blasted fool!"

Crawley smiled weakly: "Can't see what I can do, old chap. It's his call."

"In the words of Cato: it's all up now. You can protest no more!" intoned Micawber, in a pulpit sort of voice.

There were now raucous cries of "Out! Out! Out!" emanating from the emancipists and a few of the soldiers; Napier glared at Ben and Micawber a final time and stamped reluctantly from the wicket, to the levity and raucous rejoicing of the toughs and larrikins. Captain Sturt was taken so much by surprise that he was still doing up the buttons of his pea-green shirt as Micawber gave him his guard.

Sturt watched mesmerised, like a rabbit about to be swallowed by a snake, as Ben spun the ball towards him. He managed to get the faintest of touches, which sneaked off his bat - I dived to catch it but it was just too wide and flew past me. They ran a hasty single before young Jonathan Trumper had thrown the ball back from long stop. Henry Dumaresq, quite ashen-faced, now faced his first ball. As wicket-keeper I had the best view of anyone and I swear it was like watching a magician perform at Drury Lane. This time, instead of spinning the ball with his finger, Ben seemed to throw the ball out of the back of his hand - Dumaresq followed it with his bat as it appeared to break to the right, only to see it turn in the opposite direction and flatten his leg stump.

"I say...that ain't cricket...what?" he bewailed.

"Out!" declared Micawber, with an air of exceeding satisfaction, sticking a thumb in each of his waistcoat pockets. The Judge Advocate's Assistant, who'd only just arrived, hastily chalked up 1 for 2.

Dumaresq was still shaking his head in utter disbelief as he passed Major Irwin on his way to the wicket. Major Irwin was made of sterner stuff and advanced boldly to attack the ball. He hit it with great force and it soared higher and higher into the blue simply begging to be caught, but to my consternation, I saw that only Donovan was near enough to get beneath it. The ball came down so slowly - I closed my eyes, waiting to hear the groan as Donovan dropped it - but there was the sound of leather smacking flesh and a triumphant shout. I looked and saw the Irishman brandishing the ball over his head. I shot a glance towards Napier at the officer's tent - he was shaking his head furiously in utter disbelief. Ben had finished his first over: 1 for 3! But not all the emancipists were cheering - some began to feel a trace of concern over their re-laid bets - others were uncomfortable seeing such a despised creature as Ben, lording it over white men, even if they were gentlemen.

George Macleary came in as Sturt faced Warnie, who naturally was nowhere near as bewitching a spinner as Ben. Sturt hit a four and three twos off Warnie's four balls: 11 for 3 - with their 87 run lead from the first innings they were already 98 ahead. We were very relieved when Ben took over the bowling again - and even more relieved when he bowled Macleary with his first ball. 13 for 4.

The cream of Napier's batting had gone without a run between them. Young Charlie Darling swung his bat and missed his first ball completely, but it pitched wide and failed to hit the stumps. He swung again at the next ball - this time managed to connect and ran four - to the relief of Napier and his supporters; only to be bowled comprehensively by another of Ben's bewildering off-breaks. 17 for 5.

Sturt faced Warnie again and thumped him clean over his head for two. Whilst Sturt and Frazer, the new batsman, were running their runs, Warnie gave me a wink, signalling he was about to try something special.

"Capital stroke - well played, sir!" I enthused as Sturt took his guard again.

He turned and smiled - he wasn't such a bad bloke really: "Thank you, boy. Glad to see that cricket is teaching you how to behave like a gentlemen."

He turned back to face Warnie, who delivered an artful lob that seemed to swing slowly in both directions. Sturt, now full of confidence, advanced down the wicket intending to dispatch it in similar fashion to the previous two, but the ball somehow spun round his bat at the last moment and landed smack into my gloves. His foot was way out of his crease as I smashed the stumps down.

"How is that?" I cried.

"Not out!" drawled Crawley, without a second's thought.

Before we could protest, Sturt put his bat under his arm and turned to me again: "You got me fair and square, boy. Always walk if you know you're out. That's the true spirit of the game. It 'ain't Cricket else."

The pale young man shook his head in total disbelief as he chalked up: 19 for 6.

Napier stood by the tent hopping in fury - but there was nothing he could do. Frazer was clean bowled by the first ball he faced from Ben: 19 for 7. Nettleton followed after getting an edgy two. Attenborough and Hodson managed to score three runs between them off Warnie's next over, but Ben duly polished them off as soon as he took back the ball. They were all out for 24. (If you think the score ridiculously small - you only have to remember that as recently as 1877 a MCC side, containing the great Grace himself, was bowled out for a paltry 19 runs by the Australians at Lords.)

We walked off to desultory applause. The gentry couldn't believe their eyes - the soldiers and ex-convicts were fearful for their bets - many of them were now pouring into Croft's tent to lay money back on us - although we still had to get the huge total of 112 to win. The Governor arrived at that moment and was first astounded, then mortified to learn that the cream of his military had been wiped out by a black. Whilst Darling partook of an unexpectedly early lunch with the officers and gentlemen, and Micawber refreshed himself with brandy and water - I again managed to pilfer some beer and vittles for Warnie and the rest. They ate and drank in silence as Crowe bound thick bandages around Trumper's and Donovan's forearms and legs, in preparation for the cruel pounding we all knew would come.

Napier led his team out after a hearty meal which had restored his confidence of victory - but his face darkened when he saw Donovan walking out to open the batting with Trumper. He stormed over and whispered something to him with great vehemence and agitation, but Donovan merely shook his head and continued his way to the crease.

Hodson was shining another brand-new ball on his thigh as Micawber took his place at the wicket. He then puffed up his chest so that he looked half as broad again, before pronouncing: "Play!"

Trumper got behind his bat and played Hodson with ease. Batting seemed so natural to him, he timed his strokes, scored runs all round the wicket and had put twelve on the board by the end of the over. Donovan then faced Carter, who let the ball fly as high as he could manage, hoping to fell the Irishman with yet another blow to the head; but though he took savage hits on his arms and shoulders throughout the over, Donovan did not so much as wince.

Hodson then came charging back at Trumper - in fact he charged so hard and fast that he released the ball when he was almost half down the wicket.

"No Ball!" exclaimed Micawber sonorously.

That counted as an extra run bringing the total we needed down to 99, but the ball had hit Trumper a nasty crack on the hip, where there was little flesh to protect the bone. I rushed on immediately with Crowe, who administered his soothing balm, but when Trumper tested his leg he collapsed in agony: "It's no use, Mr Crowe, I can't run."

Napier marched over with a foxy smile. "What's the matter? Get on with the game."

Micawber had been gravely contemplating the injury; his face turning every possible colour whilst an endless procession of lumps followed one another in hot haste up his throat: "What is the matter?" he screamed at Napier, "what is not the matter? Villainy is the matter; baseness is the matter, deception, fraud, conspiracy, is the matter. That 'No Ball' was deliberately aimed at invalidating the batsman, contrary to the laws and ideals of the noble game."

"How dare you address me in such a fashion? I am an officer holding the King's Commission."

"And so was I," steam seemed to rise up from beneath Micawber's collar. "I had the honour to serve as lieutenant in the Royal Marines at Trafalgar, under the immortal Nelson himself, and know an interminable cheat and liar when I meet one. The batsman shall be provided with a runner."

"A what?" expostulated Napier.

"The batsman is unable to run because of an illegal ball - then someone shall be appointed to run his runs for him."

"There is no provision for that in the rules," Napier protested.

"Then I will compose a petition to Marylebone praying for an alteration in the law regarding to that matter.* Procrastination is the thief of time." He turned to Crowe, "May I suggest you select a person swift of foot and quick of mind, so the game can follow its ultimate course." Micawber clasped his hands tightly behind his ramrod back and went back to his position at the wicket, whilst Crowe called for young Jonathan Trumper to come out to run for his dad.

Donovan came down the wicket and slapped Trumper on the shoulder: "You stay that end where the umpire will give you protection. I'll keep the other and take whatever they throw at me."

Trumper valiantly took guard again and deftly wielded his bat for the remainder of the over, whilst young Jonathan ran four runs with extreme enthusiasm. That brought Donovan back to face Carter once more, without the safeguard of Micawber. Crawley made no protest as Donovan was subjected to a savage pummelling - the Irishman was felled twice in the over, but each time got up and fearlessly took guard again. This pattern of play continued for several overs: as Trumper cut and drove and young Jonathan scampered our score past thirty. The game seemed to be swinging our way, more and more bets were being switched in Croft's tent, and Trumper may well have got all the required runs on his own, had not Napier, becoming increasingly infuriated and sensing Jonathan's excitement and eagerness, played a dirty trick. He pretended to misfield as the ball was driven past him. The boy, seeing him fumble, called for an extra run, but before he was half way down the wicket, Napier had recovered the ball and shattered the stumps with Jonathan yards from the crease. The boy was broken-hearted: he'd run out his father and our best batsman. 35 for 1.

Warnie came in and play continued as before. Donovan's knuckles were bruised and bleeding where the ball had caught him time after time - but still stood his ground. Warnie began to attack Hodson and took our score past fifty - we were almost half way there. Napier's face was like thunder when he took over the bowling from Hodson. He hurled the ball at Warnie's head with all his might. Warnie swayed out of the way and clipped it for four.

"Beautiful stroke, my boy! Beautiful stroke! Splendid, splendid! Stick to it!" Micawber enthused without impartiality.

Napier was always most dangerous when he was angry and he had the cunning of a fox. He snarled and made as if to make a similar delivery; Warnie made ready for it, but was completely fooled - the ball was a slow one - it hung momentarily in the air, Warnie was caught between strokes and hit a simple return catch. He'd fallen for his own trap.

"A slower one if I'm not mistaken," sneered Napier triumphantly as he plucked it out of the air. "I recalled your comment on the ship that morning. Thank you for your unsolicited advice."

The pale young man was printing 58 for 2 as Warnie came back, humiliated and dejected under Mrs Napier's pitying gaze. O'Neil was in next and after he'd made half a dozen runs Napier took himself off and changed Hodson and Carter's ends. Carter gripped the ball in his huge hand and squeezed it with all his considerable strength as he advanced menacingly towards O'Neil: "A pair of Irish pigs. Donovan is too dumb to feel pain - but this time I'll really make you squeal."

"You sir, are an unmitigated Ruffian, you will not threaten a batsman in that manner - it undermines my authority as an umpire. Kindly desist!" exclaimed Micawber severely.

But Carter had the last laugh - O'Neil's dander was up. He swung ferociously at the first ball Carter bowled him and missed completely. His wicket was shattered: 64 for 3. We only needed 46 to win but Lindwall was our last uninjured batsman - apart from Tom and us boys. The mood of the punters swung again, but when some went to lay more money back on Napier's team they found, to their consternation, that Croft had closed his books. Donovan continued his heroic defence as Lindwall added another ten runs before being beaten by Carter's pace: 74 for 4.

Miller was next in. He got up reluctantly and gingerly put his bandaged foot to the ground: "I'd sell my sister for a strong pair of boots."

"Borrow mine. My boots not my sister," Bradman made a rare witticism. "Me bunions could do with an airing." He pulled off his boots and tossed them to Miller. "Want 'em back mind. Best Toledo leather; followed Wellington all over Spain in 'em."

The freshly shod Miller marched resolutely to the wicket, smashed his first ball way beyond the ropes and managed to run four. He lasted a couple of overs before he was caught by Napier on the boundary rope for fifteen. 89 for 5.

Kidman's face was as white as the new bandage that Crowe had applied to his head, as he made his tentative way to the wicket, but something strange was happening. The spectators no longer seemed to care about their bets or their prejudices, but were beginning to appreciate the convicts' pluck and endurance and resent Napier's ruthlessness. When Carter made his first ball bounce past Kidman's head there were prolonged boos from all parts of the ground - which was filling up as news spread of the day's turn-round. Kidman, though weak, cut and drove and added another four to our total before a savage ball flew off the handle of his bat into the grateful hands of Charlie Darling behind the wicket. 94 for 6 - only another sixteen needed - and I was the next man in. Sixteen seemed as impossible as sixty. I could see defeat in the eyes of Warnie, Crowe and the rest. Mrs Napier had her head resting on her hand, looking completely downcast - Sarah Trumper was near tears, but Bradman remained resolute and clapped me firmly on the back: "Don't get in a funk, young 'un, you'll do famously," he said encouragingly, as if I were a drummer boy at Badajoz. "There's a gap between slip and point - lift your bat in a beeline with Carter's arm and you'll snick him for four."

My guts were churning as I walked out. The sun was so bright; it seemed hotter than ever, the flies were buzzing about the sweat dripping into my eyes. Donovan came to meet me - his hands and shins were bleeding, his face and arms and shoulders, bruised and swollen. "I'm going to go for runs now - there's no point in my hanging on - someone's got to get them,." he whispered.

I'd one more ball to face in the over. I did what Bradman had told me and watched Carter's arm - I lifted my bat in line with it and felt the faintest nick - the ball went streaming towards the ropes. We ran four to the cheers of the crowd. Only twelve more to get.

Hodson took the ball once more and tore in ferociously, intending to give Donovan another pounding, but the Irishman took him completely by surprise. He literally danced down the wicket and hit the bully clean over the marquee. We scrambled four more. Just another eight, paltry, runs and we'd won.

In all my encounters with him, I'd never seen Napier in such a taking until that moment. He called Carter and Hodson together and hissed urgently with them. Carter seized the ball, glared at Donovan, spat: and said: "Fuck the Pope!" He then bowled a slower ball which Donovan furiously slogged over his head but, as he began to run, Hodson came crashing into him, falling heavily on top of him so that he was unable to get up. In the meantime Napier recovered the ball and smashed down the wicket.

"Out!" screamed Crawley.

"That was sharp practice," protested Micawber, bursting into a state of extreme excitement and turning pale.

"It's not your call! He's out," Napier snapped.

"Scoundrel! You are the most consummate villain that ever existed..." he was cut short by a bottle, which had been hurled at Napier but managed to miss Micawber's strawberry of a nose by a hair's breadth. Louder boos were coming from all around the ground; some of the more inebriated emancipists were showing their displeasure by invading the pitch, at which Napier's team armed themselves with the stumps and formed a square, intending to defend the wicket with as much defiance as the Guards at Waterloo. The 'on duty' soldiers nervously un-slung their muskets and looked towards Governor Darling who'd become purple with rage, whilst the ladies outside the marquees paled with fear. It seemed we were only a minute away from a gory affray, an Antipodean Peterloo*, but at that moment Micawber advanced upon the invaders, with puffed out chest and thumbs stuck in waistcoat."

"In my esteemed office of Magistrate of the salubrious metropolis of Port Middlebay," he bellowed mellifluously, "I order you to return to your places on the non-active side of the rope and allow this epic sporting contest to play out to its ordained conclusion. Britons shall never raise their arms against each other - even in this distant territory, the King's law is to be obeyed."

And the funny thing is they obeyed him. I'm sure if Governor Darling had tried to restore order there'd have been a bloody riot, but there was something about that eccentric old codger that commanded respect. The emancipists retreated somewhat reluctantly to their places on the grass; Crawley and young Darling replaced the stumps; Bradman barked a command and all Brown Besses were slung back on shoulders unfired; and Levey signalled the waitresses to begin serving tea.

Donovan made his painful retreat from the wicket passing little David Trumper coming in. "For pity's sake go easy - he's only a boy!" cried Mrs Napier - and her sentiments were echoed all around the ground. But they fell on deaf ears.

Carter bowled a particularly nasty ball, which young David missed completely, and then followed up with another even more vicious, which spread-eagled the boy's wicket. Cries of 'Shame!' and 'Blaggards!" came from all sides, but it didn't alter the fact that we were 102 for 8.

Jonathan came in - his eyes still red with the shame of causing his father's dismissal. I had the bowling and nicked Hodson for a single. Poor little Jonathan lasted two balls without scoring before being bowled. 103 for 9.

There was a breathless hush around the ground as Ben sauntered out in his lackadaisical manner: '*Seven to make and the last man in*'- to quote young Henry Newbolt, my favourite poet. We all knew what Ben could do with a ball - if he tried - but what would he be able to do with the bat? I stole a look at Levey - expecting to see him gnawing his finger nails, like Fagin when he was fencing dodgy goods. To my surprise he seemed strangely calm and contented, but Monks, the foul rogue, standing beside him, was biting his bleeding hands in frenzied agitation. Croft stood behind both of them with a satisfied smirk on his ugly face.

I had the bowling and repeated the stroke that Bradman had advised and we managed to run three - the Judge Advocate's Assistant's face was now pink with excitement or brandy or both - I watched him chalk up 106 - only a pitiful four more needed. One hefty strike from Ben and against all the odds we would be triumphant - Warnie and the rest would get their tickets of leave and Levey would have to keep his word and get me to my father. The crowd were now with us to a man - Governor Darling could sense it and grew even purpler in the face. As Ben took his guard, I caught him looking across at Levey - as if seeking instruction. - Levey shrugged enigmatically but Croft raised a thumb. Ben gave a lazy smile and made ready to receive.

"Play!" intoned Micawber, who was positively white with anticipation. I heard Hodson come thundering in behind me, my mouth was dry with excitement, I saw the ball fly from his hand as he passed me but, to my almighty consternation and utter disbelief, Ben made no attempt to play it. I heard the smack of leather on wood and watched in shocked despair as his off-stump went flying.

"How is that?" screamed Napier.

Micawber raised a very reluctant finger. We'd lost by four beggarly runs, with all the fearful consequences that it entailed. I was close to tears with rage and disappointment - but then I became aware of the noise. The crowd - soldiers, emancipists and some of the gentry even, had risen to their feet and were heartily applauding and cheering like we were all Grimaldis at Covent Garden. The record books says the first Test match between England and Australia was played at Melbourne in 1877, but I believe the bitter rivalry, together with a sense of Australian nationhood, began that day in Sydney in 1829.

Challenge Match

Sydney Racetrack
January 27th 1829

Second Day

Officers and Gentlemen
First Innings

Captain Napier	**bowled Aborigine**	**0**
Right Hon. Henry Dumaresq	**bowled Aborigine**	**0**
Captain Charles Sturt	**stumped Dawkins bowled Warne**	**12**
Major Fredrick Chidley Irwin	**caught Donovan bowled Aborigine**	**0**
Right Hon. George Macleary	**bowled Aborigine**	**0**
Captain Chisholm Frazer	**bowled Aborigine**	**0**
Mr Charles Darling	**bowled Aborigine**	**4**
Lt Alan Nettleton	**bowled Aborigine**	**2**
Lieutenant Attenboroug	**bowled Aborigine**	**1**
Sergeant F. Hodson	**Not Out**	**2**
Private H. Carter	**bowled Aborigine**	**0**
Extras		**1**
	TOTAL	**22**

Felons & Others
First Innings

Trumper S.	**run out**	**34**
Donovan	**retired hurt**	**4**
Warne	**caught and bowled Capt Napier**	**20**
O'Neil	**bowled Carter**	**6**
Lindwall	**bowled Carter**	**10**
Miller	**caught Capt Napier bowled Carter**	**15**
Kidman	**caught Mr Darling bowled Carter**	**8**
Dawkins	**Not Out**	**8**
Trumper D.	**bowled Carter**	**0**
Trumper J.	**bowled Carter**	**0**
Aborigine	**bowled Hodson**	**0**
Extras		**1**
	TOTAL	**106**

11. Repercussions

We stood defeated in a forlorn line. I was numb with grief. I can still see Napier's triumphant sneer, Warnie staring dejectedly at the ground, trying to avoid Leticia's pitying eyes, and Crowe biting his lips with fury and frustration. Micawber growled his disapproval before disappearing within the marquee to console himself on the remains of the punch. Monks, shocked and ashen-face, looked almost as desolate as we all felt, but Levey, the oily rogue, was smiling like a ginger tom-cat after a night on the tiles. I learnt later that Croft had closed the books at the perfect moment and that our defeat had made his boss a fortune on the day.

Darling, after congratulating each gentleman fulsomely, eventually turned to us, his pompous, chubby face becoming forbidding and humourless: "Whatever you may have heard, I must inform you that I only allowed this match against my better judgement, and never had any intention of lightening your well-deserved sentences. In the eye of the law which I uphold, you remain incorrigible convicts. Those not already assigned will be conducted to the penal settlement at Moreton Bay in a matter of days, where you will remain until you have proven yourselves capable of reform."

There was even more dismay and consternation all round, but it was too much for Warnie: "What have we got to fucking prove? Didn't you tell him how we saved his rotten ship, Mr Crowe?"

Darling's face grew blacker than Ben's: "How dare you utter profanities in my presence!" He caught Bradman's eye: "Corporal, give the rogue thirty lashes when you get him back to the barracks."

Bradman stared incongruously before shaking his head in anguish. When he spoke it was as if the words were being dragged up reluctantly from the depths of his very soul: "I will do no such thing, sir. These are good men. I've been with them since they sailed from England and know only too well the injustices they've endured."

There was a shocked silence. We all looked at Bradman with incredulity, admiration and no little affection - he was one of us at last.

Darling gaped like a fish in astonishment before exploding in rage: "I have never heard such blatant insubordination in my entire military career," he expostulated. "I'll have your stripes for that and more. Captain Napier, see where your folly has led us? Put that man under close arrest!"

Napier, perhaps remembering Bradman's past service and loyalty, hesitated for the slightest moment before turning to Evans: "Assume command of the detail and take Bradman back with the convicts."

Evans, the dirty little sheep-shagger, looked agonizingly between Bradman and Napier before making the most heroic decision of his murky life: "Afraid I can't do that, sir. Everyone knows Corporal Bradman is the best soldier in the regiment."

"Clap him in irons as well!" screamed Darling. "Captain Napier, your regiment is a bloody disgrace! Captain Frazer, call over a detail from the 37th."

Frazer, somewhat reluctantly, summoned a grizzled sergeant, who called together an armed escort, whilst fetters were bolted on the ankles of Bradman and Evans.

Crowe, who had been gazing disbelievingly in a mixture of fury and self-reproach, found his voice at last: "This is a gross injustice, your Excellency. Corporal Bradman is one of the finest men I've ever had the good fortune to serve with. We would have lost the ship without him."

"It is your fault, Mr Crowe that he finds himself in his present position - you have fostered radical and seditious illusions amongst these misguided men."

"I have only encouraged them to believe in their basic rights. Englishmen have enjoyed freedom and justice since Magna Carta. If you will not grant them that, I will return to London and take this case to Sir George Murray* at the Colonial Office. I will demand that this colony has fair trials by jury and rule by a legislative assembly"

"I'll see you ruined, Mr Crowe, if you embark on such a harebrained course."

"At least I will have tried. I owe these men that at least. One day enlightenment will prevail."

"Mr Crowe, you are an even bigger fool than I took you for." Darling turned and made towards his carriage.

"Let's have three cheers for Mr Crowe, lads," cried Warnie defiantly.

Darling turned in fresh fury as the lusty cries rang out, and they came not only from the convicts: many of the emancipists and some of the soldiers joined in.

The clamour brought Micawber out of the marquee with an empty glass. He surveyed the defeated convicts with a melancholy eye: "A man must take the fat with the lean," he sighed. "I, like you, have walked the earth like a vagabond - tossed in all directions by the elephants - I beg your pardon - I should have said elements - but this is a land of opportunity, fear not you will prevail." He gave us all an encouraging nod then lurched back into the marquee in search of yet another glass of punch.

Crowe and I watched with Harper, Trumper and his boys, as Warnie, Bradman, Evans and the rest were marched away.

That evening Crowe knocked on my door and sat heavily on my bed. He looked down at his clasped knuckles before he spoke: "Dawkins, I've decided to take you back to England with me."

You could have knocked me down with a feather: "What about that bastard Darling? I'm still a convicted felon. He'd never let me go."

"You're assigned to my care - I intend to make myself your legal guardian."

I was even more flabbergasted: "Why would you want to do that?"

Crowe spoke with difficulty, as he always did when expressing his feelings: "I've grown very fond of you, Jack. I don't suppose I'll ever marry - I'm not the sort to take a wife - I find myself ill at ease with women - but I'd like a son."

I didn't know what to say. This man had been more than a father to me - he would always have a place in my heart - but something - I couldn't describe it - but something stopped me from taking his hands and tearfully thanking him for the inestimable gift he was offering me.

"I can't go with you, Mr Crowe - I've got a father and he's somewhere out here in this God-forsaken land."

His eyes grew wide in astonishment: "What do you mean? A father? You've never mentioned it - I supposed you were an orphan."

I then told him my story - every last drop of it. He listened silently looking at the floor. It wasn't until I'd finished that he looked up at me again: I could see the hurt. "I wish you had informed me earlier of your proper circumstances - I thought we had no secrets from each other." He sighed deeply: "But blood is thicker than water and you must do all you can to find your father. In any event my offer will still stand when I return. I beg you one thing however - keep away from Moreton Bay, especially if that cruel rogue Napier is there - he will gladly kill you."

A few days later Crowe and I watched as the 57th assembled silently on the parade ground. We'd hardly spoken since the night of the defeat - there was a distance between us that hadn't been there before. After what seemed like an eternity, the awful silence was broken at last by a solitary bugle blast. Then the guardroom door swung open and the prisoners appeared - their heads shaved, their ankles shackled. Just as cruel was the sight of that vile bastard Carter swaggering along with Bradman's stripes on his arm. The snare-drums beat out a harsh tattoo as Bradman and Evans made their painful way towards a cluster of officers, adorned in their finest red and gold, where Napier, sour-faced as ever, was waiting to read their sentences:

"By order of His Excellency, the Governor, you have been found guilty of gross insubordination and negligence of duty. You have been deemed unfit to serve and are therefore condemned to be drummed out of his Majesty's Service and sentenced to seven years hard labour." He turned to Attenborough, standing stiff and rigid as if he'd a broom stick up his arse: "Lieutenant, you know your duties. Take over."

Attenborough's hands trembled as he cut off Bradman's badges and stripes, removed the epaulets from the old soldier's shoulders and tore the brass buttons from his faded scarlet tunic. He then repeated the process with Evans before ordering both men to strip off the remnants of their uniforms and put on the despised convict garb of yellow and black. Crowe shook his head in fury when he beheld their bloody backs. We watched as the regimental blacksmith hammered a spiked collar round their necks and attached it by heavy chains to the leg irons around their ankles. Finally, as the band broke into *The World Turned Upside Down,* Corporal Carter barked his orders and led the way, swaggering with malevolence, as the two prisoners were marched out of the military camp to their solitary cells in the convicts' barracks. Bradman, ever the soldier, marched proudly, ignoring the cruel impediment; but poor little Evans, never the most robust of men, could hardly stand unaided. Bradman quickly saw his predicament and pulled his comrade's arm around his own shoulder, and bore Evans tenderly away, as if he was walking wounded from the bloody field of Salamanca.

Tears of frustration trickled down Crowe's cheeks: "Evans was in no fit state to suffer punishment. I requested permission to examine him, but Darling refused. I swear I will turn over every stone in Whitehall - I will petition the Colonial Office, the commander-in chief - King George himself, to get those men released - no matter how long it takes or how much it costs."

Evans didn't have to wait long. It only took five days for death to release him from his torment. A few days after that Bradman, Warnie and the rest were put on a convict ship and taken up the coast bound for the Brisbane River, under Napier's sole command. Meanwhile Monks, the villainous fool, having persuaded himself to put a fortune on us to win during the second morning of the game, had lost his stables and farm to Levey. The Jew was no fool and wisely left Trumper in control. Crowe, ever mindful of my welfare, assigned me to Levey's care. I was safely ensconced at the farm with Harper, Trumper and his boys when, in early March, 1829, dear old Crowe began his voyage back to dear old England. I ran along the banks of Sydney Cove, as his ship ebbed out with the tide, waving to his broad-shouldered figure standing solitary at the stern. I followed his progress all the way out to the point by Fort Macquarie. At that moment I wished I'd gone with my noble benefactor - and I doubted if I'd ever see him again.

But I soon began to enjoy my life on the farm. Trumper taught me to be aware of the strange birds and creatures of our new home: I woke each morning to the screeching laugh of the bleedin' Kookaburra, which reminded me of the sound dear old Nance made whenever you pinched her bum. I became fond of the spiky little Echidnas - with snouts even longer than Fagin's -and the pretty Koalas, who scudded up and down the gum trees with more velocity than I'd ever managed with a Bow Street Runner on my tail. I discovered I'd an understanding with horses and soon learnt to ride - I even had my own mount, a sweet-natured little mare, whom I couldn't forbear but name Nancy. Harper quickly recovered from his abduction and grew contented and ever stronger with the healthy outdoor work. Trumper's boys, David and Jonathan, became like brothers to me - it was one of the best times of my life.

But in spite of all this, every week that passed I never failed to beg Levey to allow Ben to take me across the bush to seek my father, but every week he managed to find some prevarication. He spent a great deal of time overseeing the construction of a concert hall at the back of his hotel - where he intended to launch Mrs Napier's music upon Sydney society. Now that her cursed husband had departed, Levey spent most evenings in Leticia's company, planning her first concert, which he promised would be the most glittering social event in Australia's short history. Leticia allowed herself to be swept along with his excitement - I suspect she was only too glad to be rid of Napier and had put Warnie completely from her mind; she seemed happy enough with the company of her little son and the devoted care of Sarah Trumper. I'm not sure if she noticed the growing scorn of the ladies in the Governor's circle, scandalised at her close liaison with a Jew.

One sunny day in May, I was riding with Harper in the southern grazing when I spied a black figure waving from the boundary fence. I rode over with Harper following, and soon distinguished Monk's haggard features and chewed, bleeding knuckles. He was obviously down on his uppers - his clothes were worn and shabby.

"Hallo my flash companion! What's the row?" I demanded in my best Smithfield manner.

It was that that gave me away - I'd never addressed the rogue before. He looked at me with great astonishment - then went white with rage or fear or both. "You? How could I have mistaken you?" he rasped between clenched teeth. "I know you now - many's the time I've seen you lurking in that stinking London tavern - Fagin's sneaking, snivelling pickpocket. I thought you'd been hung alongside your treacherous damn'd master and long screwed into your coffin."

It was his voice, his harsh, cruel voice saying those very words '*sneaking, snivelling pickpocket,*' that stirred some distant memory I couldn't fully recall. However I gave the rogue no hint of my perplexity and doffed my straw hat: "Well my covey - your own peepers prove how wrong you are. What in damnation are you doing trespassing on my master's property? Be off - or I'll call the traps on you, you rogue."

"Your master's property - this is my property - I've been cheated out of it by that damn'd Jew, but I'll get it back never fear."

I put on an impish expression to annoy the villain the more: "Be off, I say! Me and my colleague, Mr Harper, are very busy gentlemen - we cannot afford you to partake of any more of our valuable time."

His bloody lip quivered with rage: "A murrain on you, you foul young devil - it's that Blackamoor I've come to seek. Is he fit and strong? I've arranged a match at the end of the month. This time I'll make sure it takes place. I shall recoup all my losses and more."

Harper understood only too well what the rogue had in mind and looked fearfully at me, like a faithful dog pleading not to be put down. I quickly put him out of his misery: "Mr Harper ain't going to mill no more, never. Mr Crowe has pronounced his head can't take another pounding."

"The black dog is bound to your master. If that foul Jew smells profit he'll agree to anything."

I shook my head scornfully, winked reassuringly at Harper and we rode away, although I suspected that the foul rogue could be right and that Levey would again prove false. I was unsure what course to follow, but fate once more directed my path. I'd become as much attached to Levey's horses as Magwitch had been to Napier's Merinos. The following night was hot and close and I'd gone to the stable to water them. I was watching the cool dark water swirl into their trough when I became aware of a dusky head behind me. I thought it was Harper but turned to see Ben.

"Miss Sue says you should come."

I'd no idea why she should want me – I'd long forsaken any hope that she might desire another visitation of my eager little member, but despite my constant questions, the obstinate brute would say no more as I followed him into town to Levey's hotel. The adjoining concert hall had come on apace and was almost completed, apart from the roof. The bar was full and hot with sweating noisy men. I scoured the room twice before I made out Sue sitting at a corner table, where a sun-blackened bald head was whispering sweet nothings into her ear. I recognised the pate as belonging to the miner from Newcastle - I scudded over - he turned - his eyes were glazed with drink.

"Hello, Shorty." He stared at me intently, as if debating with himself, before mumbling: "I've brought a message from yer pa."

My heart thumped rapidly against the inside of my chest: "He's still alive?"

"Just about – if you can call it living," he swallowed the rum in his glass then motioned Sue to refill it. "I've just got back from a trip up the Brisbane River. I've seen sights and such there as you'd never dream in your foulest nightmare. Those damn'd officers can't stop 'emselves exploring and having their cursed names immortalised in outlandish places. There's this officer there, a real bastard, by the name of Napier - he sailed up a tributary and discovered a quarry full of limestone and decided to make his convicts dig it out of the earth with their bare hands. I've mined some foul mines in my time, but I couldn't believe men could live as those poor bastards do. They work and sleep in irons, day after endless day. Some are forced to work though they can barely stand – the soldiers prick 'em with their bayonets and the overseers cut 'em with their cats. There's one brute, a giant of a man, the chief overseer – Bamber – claims to have once been a noted pugilist in England – they say washes the blood off the thongs of his cat in a bucket of water then drinks it. The other punishers are nearly as bad. Such a herd of cruel tyrants never gathered together in one place before." He shook his head as if trying to disbelieve the horror of his own words and poured himself another rum before continuing. "But they are as nothing compared to Napier himself. He's the very devil incarnate – there's no torture or punishment that man can devise that he doesn't delight in putting those poor buggers through. I saw him sitting on his thoroughbred, with a smile on his face, sentencing a dozen men to 50 or 100 lashes, for no reason but to gratify his pitiless entertainment." He drained his glass, wishing to wash away the memory.

"What about my father?" I whispered fearfully.

"I sailed up from Newcastle on a barge to bring back a load of stone. I was leaning on the bulwark, watching the poor devils stumbling up the gangway carrying huge rocks in their bleeding hands, when this old bloke staggers up, near naked he was, and calls my name. Begging me for water. Didn't recognize him at first," he broke off and gazed at the portrait behind the bar, "he'd aged thirty years – but then I realized it was yer pa. Told him I'd seen you – that you was seeking 'im. He broke down and cried at that. Cried like a baby he did – thanked God that there was someone in this cursed world that cared for him – couldn't believe why you should, as he'd never done nothing for you. But he made me swear on my life, to beg you not to go up there looking for him. He said whatever you do, keep away from Napier and the Brisbane River – it'll be the death of you – he reckons he's only got a few months left him now – he says make a life for yourself and say a prayer for him."

I was stunned – it was odd to feel love and pity for someone I'd never seen. I was close to tears and hurriedly changed the subject: "What about the other convicts that Napier took up with him – my mates, Warnie, Bradman and the rest, what about them?"

"Those that played cricket against him? – Napier's got a special hatred for 'em all, 'specially that fair haired bloke with rosy cheeks like apples – he's the only one that stands up to him. His leg got infected through rubbing against his iron and the poor sod could hardly walk, but Napier had him dragged from his bed and flogged in his crutches. His mates took him away in a wheelbarrow - still Napier couldn't break his spirit. They say Napier intends to flog him until he's whipped the last spark of life out of him and then bury him like a dog."

I turned to Sue whose eyes were welling with pity. "Where's Levey?"

"Upstairs with Napier's wife."

I became aware of soft piano music above. I knew Leticia was Warnie's only hope.

I rushed up the staircase to Levey's private suite and pushed open the door. Leticia, no longer shy, stopped playing and smiled warmly at the sight of me, but Levey's eyes flickered with annoyance:

"What do you want, my dear? We are busy choosing pieces for the concert. Who is attending my horses?"

"I've fed and watered 'em – they're snug and comfortable for the night. That's more than can be said for the poor souls up at Moreton Bay."

Leticia's smile faded. "What do you mean? Have you any news?"

"There's a bloke down there in the bar that's just come back from that hell hole. Your husband is near flogging 'em all to death – especially Warnie." I then repeated what the miner had told me – her face grew more and more anguished as she listened. When I finished she turned to Levey with tears streaming down her cheeks:

"Barnet, do something I implore you."

"What can I do my dear? I cannot challenge the Governor's authority."

"You promised you'd let Ben lead me across the bush and help my father escape," I interjected. "I've waited for weeks and you've fobbed me off time and time again. Give us two of your horses and let us go – we'll get help from Ben's tribe up there and rescue Warnie as well as my father."

"What you are advocating is little short of a rebellion – treason. I have no intention of losing all I have and suffering a traitor's death."

"You'll not be involved. You can report that we've stolen your horses and buggered off. There's bushrangers a plenty in the outback – a few more will make no difference."

Levey shook his red locks: "It is better to wait for a new Governor; Mr Crowe will be in London by now pleading their case."

"Mr Warne will be dead within weeks – you know it. He can't wait for any decision made in London," Leticia's face was flushed. "If you wish our understanding to continue, at least let the boy try. Give him any help you can."

Levey sucked on his teeth before reluctantly nodding his head. "Very well, my dear, but I fear we are sending this young fool to his death." He looked toward the closed door and softly called "Ben!" The door opened immediately and the stone-faced rogue was in the room, arms folded, regarding Levey with a look such as you'd see on a faithful spaniel. "Ben, you will go tonight with this boy and do the thing we have discussed. Only you will bring out more than just the old man."

Ben broke into a rare grin, "You mean I bring out the one with the red face? Whose eyes never leave this lady?"

"Yes!" said Leticia vehemently, without a trace of a blush.

Levey frowned and turned to me. "Take two spare horses and take your father and this Warnie west into the new colony. They can buy land cheap and assume new identities there." He went over to a safe and drew out a bag of gold. He tossed it me and looked at me not unkindly: "I think I can trust you with my money. Is there anything else you need?"

I sensed another opportunity: "Can we take Harper with us, Mr Levey? He'd be a hell of a help if it comes to a fight."

He frowned again: "I have received a fresh offer to match him. He can still make me money."

"How can you think of money when good men are suffering such torments?" demanded Leticia scornfully. "If the boy thinks Harper can aid them in the rescue he must go."

There was such vehemence in her eyes that Levey had to acquiesce. He shrugged and forced a smile: "Why not, my dear? The black villain's prize-fighting days are probably over and he costs me a fortune to feed."

Leticia gently kissed my cheek, my nostrils were filled with Levey's expensive French perfume: "May God protect you, Mr Dawkins, and deliver Warnie from his torment. Tell him he is constantly in my thoughts."

Levey's smile faded as she spoke.

12. Into The Outback

I told Harper of our plans to rescue Warnie and my father and also of the farm we would share between us. I'm not sure how much he understood but he joined us with a nod of his ugly head. We hastily gathered some supplies and weapons, bade a tearful farewell to dear old Trumper and his boys, then rode through the night along the bleak road Darling was building to the north. Ben led the way, trailing the two spare horses; Harper on a strong black gelding; and me on sweet little Nancy, with Levey's gold and all my accumulated wealth tucked securely into my saddlebags, following behind. After a few miles we passed the flickering campfires of the chain gangs; the poor buggers who were forging this new road, foot by agonised foot, across the hard and pitiless land. Ben was ever alert, sniffing the air like an animal, wary of patrols of Darling's mounted police, the hated Dragoons. It was illegal to travel without a ticket of leave or travel pass, and we were armed to boot. They'd probably shoot us on sight - especially as my two companions were black. As dawn broke, I was relieved when Ben swung away from the coast and headed towards the distant mountains.

Escape had been easy but I could see survival would be a different matter. Every now and then whitened bones of runaway convicts lay littered on the barren landscape. In the early days of settlement benighted fools believed the legend of a large wide river to the north, on the other side of which was a back part of China - where slanty-eyed people would treat you kindly. Many died trying to find it, others returned even more broken than before and so starved that the crows wouldn't have bothered to pick their carcasses. The very grass looked famished;

only solitary trees and meagre bushes grew on the waterless, pale-yellow plain, defying the relentless sun. Innumerable kangaroos and wallabies fled at our approach, we saw big birds called emus and little koalas, hanging from lonely gum trees. Then as we drew nearer the mountains everything changed. The air became cool and the grass a vivid green. We rode through rich farmlands, part of the vast estates of the favoured aristocrats and officers, who'd acquired the best land at giveaway prices, from fortunes made by rum and convict labour. Ahead of us, all along the mountainsides, as far as the horizon and beyond, stretched a thick forest such as I'd never seen before.

Ben stopped his horse, took in the view and smiled: "The Dragoons never dare enter the forest. We will travel north along the mountain tops."

We were about a mile or so from the safety of the forest when Ben halted and pointed to some riders standing beneath some trees on a far-off hill. The roasting sun glinted on something flashing, as if sending a signal. "Bloody Bushrangers," Ben muttered, brandishing his musket. "They spy us through their magic glass. The buggers will pinch our horses. Hold up your fire-stick, big man. Let the sods see we are warriors - most are like dingoes, they will not attack if they think we fight back."

Harper duly drew his musket, which looked very small and puny in his great fist, and waved it above his head, grimacing fiercely - but even his ugly phiz didn't scare 'em. Three horsemen left the group and galloped down towards us. As they drew nearer I could see the leading rider was a squat little fellow, little more than a youth. He was dressed like a swell, in black hat; superfine blue cloth coat lined with scarlet silk, light cord trousers and laced boots. He had an altogether remarkably clean appearance. A pistol was stuck into the top of his trousers and three pairs of pistols were fastened to the belt under his jacket. His companions were a little older but far less stylish. One, carrying a blunderbuss, had a sallow complexion. His boots were half worn out and he had a sweat-soaked red handkerchief around his neck. The third, who wore a broad brimmed straw hat, was a cross-eyed cove, with a rather melancholy cast of countenance. His black silk-velvet waistcoat was in vivid contrast to his ragged trousers: four pairs of pistols were stuck in the belt that held them up. He rode with one hand on his reins - in the other was a long, double-barrelled pistol. Out of the corner of my eye I could see Ben and Harper had levelled their muskets. It looked like being a bloody encounter. I thought of the riches I had with me, especially Levey's gold, and for the first time in my life was apprehensive that I might be robbed. I decided to adopt a conciliatory attitude and raised my hands.

The young dandy drew up his horse barely a few yards from us and doffed his hat: "Top of the morning mates. I'm glad to see you're of my mind: you'd rather roam these hills like a fucking dingo or kangaroo, than work one hour for that bugger, Darling." He smiled. He'd a freckled face and a soft Irish brogue. I noticed a scar on his lip under the left nostril. I knew then who he was - he'd been the talk of Sydney a few months back, when he'd miraculously escaped from custody on his way from the Court House to the gaol in Sussex Street. I don't believe even Jack Shepherd, the most noted jail breaker in the entire Newgate Calendar, could have managed a feat like that. Sue had often spoken of Donahue very fondly indeed. I suspect he might even have ranged in her parts as well.

I doffed my own straw hat: "Is it the bold Jack Donohue*, the second Napoleon, a model of muscle and bone, I've the pleasure of acquainting?"

"Indeed it is. 'Tis an equal pleasure to meet someone even shorter than meself. Whom would I have the honour of addressing?"

"Another Jack. Dawkins is me surname - known among me professional colleagues in the great metropolis of London, as 'The Dodger'." His two companions continued to glower menacingly, so I decided there was need to impress them further. I pointed to Harper, who was glaring back at them with equal menace, "This noble savage here is Harper, the noted pugilist. A veritable gamecock who has milled with England's finest. Ain't he a caution?" There was a faint spark of recognition or something in their eyes. "And this other fine fella is Bennelong, King of the Turrbals. He's escorting us on a mission of mercy through their lands."

Donohoe, for it was indeed he, smiled even wider as he took in the muzzles of the two muskets levelled at his breast and doffed his hat again. "'Tis an honour and privilege to encounter both of you two fine gentlemen, I'm sure. May I introduce my associates, Mr Walmsley and

Mr Webber?" * The surly brutes nodded reluctantly, whilst Donohoe continued to scrutinise me and Ben closely. "Are you not the young shaver I saw at that cricket match? And is he not the black fella that did such wondrous things with that little red ball?"

I was truly astounded: "You were there? With Darling offering money for your head?"

"Indeed I was. Seated in the midst of the Irish Emancipists - it would take more than Darling's money for them to betray me. It was a great fight you boys put up - nearest thing anyone's got to giving that bugger Darling a bloody nose."

"Fat lot of good it did us. He sent most of the boys to the penal camp on the Brisbane River. That's the purpose of our mission of mercy - we're hoping to spring a few."

He whistled. "You're bold fellas indeed, but you'll be dead meat if you try it." He took out a flask of rum and took a swig before offering it to me. I declined and was relieved, knowing their weakness for it, when Harper and Ben did the same. "Why not join my little band?" he continued. "We can always use useful fellas, and all three of youse look like you can handle yourselves."

"We'd make bloody good use of yer spare horses, that's for sure," growled the sallow brute with the blunderbuss. "They'll be fucking wasted on such a fool-arse enterprise."

"We don't rob our own kind, John Walmsley; we find our horses in the stables of the rich." Donohue's smiled faded momentarily: "But I wish you fellas would re-consider. There's safe pickings a plenty down here, between the Illawarra and the Hunter Rivers. The free settlers will never betray us - we keep 'em supplied with all manner of goods."

For a moment I was tempted. He was the sort of bloke I could easily follow. Mr Crowe had read me stories of Robin Hood, and I'd often thought being one of his Merry Men would suit me fine. This would be the nearest thing to it, but even so, I reluctantly shook my head: "My poor old father is up there too. He's dying. I've never seen him. This is my only chance."

Donohoe's eyes grew soft with a suspicion of a tear: "I know how you feel, Dodger boy, it is my own dear Da I left behind in Dublin that I shall never see again." He shot a glance at his companions, who somewhat reluctantly lowered their weapons. He smiled at me again: "Best of luck, me boy. If the Holy Virgin sends a miracle and you ever get back - you'll always have a friend in Jack Donohoe."

He raised his hand in a sort of salute and with another stern glance at his companions, swung his horse around and galloped back to his waiting band. Walmsley gave me a final surly look before he followed. I never liked the rogue from the beginning. I was right - but we were not to know that then.

We watched until Donohoe and the other riders had melted away beneath the trees, then Ben scowled, pointed north to a break in the hills and kicked his horse into a canter. The spare horses, Harper and me followed after. Once in the forest we entered a moist green luxuriance such as I'd never seen. Birds of all colours: rainbow-hued lorikeets of orange, purple and blue; pure white cockatoos, yellow-winged honey eaters and crimson rosellas, swirled noisily in the tree tops above - Trumper's dear old heart would have been lifted by the very sight of 'em. That night Ben made us shelters of tree bark to sleep under, and hunted down something that looked like a huge fat rat, a wombat he called it. We had it for supper. It didn't taste too bad, a bit like gamey mutton, better than Fagin's old sausages at any rate. I told Harper more about the farm we'd share with Warnie - he gave the suspicion of a smile and I sensed he was happy.

We travelled north for days, along what is now called the Great Dividing Range - sometimes coming out of the trees into canyons and gorges, where Ben pulled strange plants out of the rocks and crammed them into his ugly great mouth together with live grubs he dug out of the earth, saying we should eat them too, to give us strength. I'd never been a one for veg and salads, but I chewed on a few bits of green, although I could never learn to palate a wriggling worm. Other times we were more fortunate and feasted on roasted cockatoo (as fine as any capon) and emu, which tasted not unlike tender young beef. We were never short of water; Ben had a piece of bone that he waved over the earth that could find any hidden spring. Ben was the third great teacher in my life after Fagin and Mr Crowe: he taught me about plants and snakes, lizards and insects, and at night, as we sat around the fire, which he miraculously ignited by rubbing a stick into a piece of wood, he told me legends of his primitive people. How the sun was a woman, who is awakened each morning by the laughter of the kookaburra bird and rises to bestow light and heat to the world; and the moon a man who chases her across the sky. Even poor, dumb Harper listened in awe-struck fascination. Ben also told us tales of the Mamandis, evil spirits who lurked in the darkness waiting to destroy unwary travellers, and of the giant malevolent serpents to be found at the bottom of the rivers and waterholes. He had no use for possessions - apart from the tobacco and rum which Levey supplied him with - he considered the whole land was his and he was part of it. After a while I realised that savage though he was, he knew far more than most civilised men of my acquaintance. He even taught me to throw his bloody boomerang.

I'd always been intrigued how such an independent, wild soul could be so obedient to the commands of Levey. I asked him one night as he gazed solemnly into the fire:

"Mr Levey, found me naked and drunk. He treat me as a man, not just a bloody black savage, like all the others. He will always be my boss."

After a week or so we quit the mountain range and descended onto a straw-coloured plain dotted with trees that stretched as far as even my sharp eyes could see. Ben told me it was waiting for the winter rain, which was late that year, then it would become rich farmland - there's enough land in that vast continent to provide estates for all the poor of London, and Manchester and Birmingham besides. The air became hot and humid and we were soon soaked with sweat and plagued with flies that flew up my nose and into my ears and eyes. In fact there wasn't a single orifice the buggers didn't attempt to explore. The following night Ben found a waterhole surrounded by bushes and a small clump of chestnut trees, and left Harper and me with the horses and went off to seek out his people. I was glad big Harper was with me - we heard dingoes howling and saw shadows moving under the distant gum trees. I remembered Ben's tales of the Mamandis and began to fear a bleedin' giant serpent might indeed be lurking under the muddy water. I was therefore relieved when Ben returned before dawn with Beppo, one of the Turrbal Tribe, whose naked body shone with stinking fish oil. Ben said the new convict settlement was barely ten miles from where we were, and that Beppo and his fellows were angry because the strangers had come uninvited and violated their hospitality. They were a generous people and would always invite a stranger to partake of their women's charms, but they objected to them being taken forcibly and stolen. Their sacred land was also being defiled. A huge hole had been dug in the earth, the ancient stone torn out and smashed into pieces, and was borne away by big boats on the river. Many men wearing iron chains laboured there throughout the day and into the night. The guards were lax and Beppo knew how to get me and Ben to the convicts undetected. I could then find the exact whereabouts of Warnie and my father, if they were still alive.

We rested throughout the hot, burning day, under the shade of a spreading chestnut tree, eating fish that Beppo somehow conjured up from the muddy water. When the fiery sun began to set we rode east, with Beppo trotting effortlessly at our side, until we came to a river. The water was low because of the drought and we followed the meandering flow for several miles. Beppo eventually stopped by a small clump of trees and motioned us to dismount. We left Harper with the horses whilst Beppo led me and Ben, with two muskets slung across his back, towards a glow in the eastern sky. Not the glow of the dying sun, but the glow of fire, arising from a giant pit about a mile downstream. As we got closer I began to see into it and thought I was beholding the Pit of Hell itself. Great galleries had been hewn out of the stone and on every level, ant-like men, clad in yellow and grey, were hammering lines of holes into the perpendicular rock. Others were beating wedges into the holes - pounding with their weary arms until the stone split and cracked as if in pain. Mixing with the incessant thud of the hammers was the sharp swish of the lash, as black-clad overseers stalked around like ministers of death, inflicting pain wherever their fancy took them. The only way in or out of this pit of torment was a corkscrew path cut out of the rock on the far side. A few bored-looking soldiers stood guard as yet more convicts loaded the split rock into carts, which they then heaved up the corkscrew path to the nearby river, where other poor wretches hauled the heavy boulders into a barge with their bare, bleeding hands. A horse neighed - I looked back into the pit: firelight glittered on gold braid - a scarlet figure on a black horse - my mouth was dry - it was Napier, as arrogant and proud as ever. Beside him stalked a monstrous brute, swinging his curling whip over every back that passed within its range. It had to be Bamber, the cruellest of the cruel.

We waited until the labour finally ceased and the convicts were led to the fires where some sort of gruel awaited them. Napier and other officers retired to one of several stone buildings, the overseers and most of the soldiers to tents. A hut was unlocked and two naked black women were dragged to the officer's quarters, other women were pulled towards the tents. Soon there were cries of foul ribaldry as pleasure was taken and rum was drunk. Only a few sentries remained, wandering desultory around, and they appeared to have little interest or trepidation for the chained wretches in their care. I glanced at Ben. His black hands were firmly gripped around one musket, the other lay loaded by his side. He made double sure none of the sentries were looking in our direction and checked with Beppo, before finally giving me the nod. I licked my cracked lips, pushed my pistol firmly in my belt, made sure the rope was tied firmly around my waist, and my bent nail was safely stowed in my deepest pocket, together with a large flask of Levey's finest rum and a phial of Beppo's most pungent fish oil. I gave Ben a wink and then slid over the edge into the pit. I climbed down silently, finding easy footholds, keeping in the shadow of the overhanging galleries and, almost before I knew it, was very much relieved to reach the bottom. I looked anxiously about me, half expecting to hear a sentry's challenge - but none came. Fires were still burning, around each one lay tattered, exhausted shapes. In spite of my fear, it was the thought that one of those shapes could be my father that made my heart beat all the faster. But which one? And where too was Warnie?

I made my way across the bottom of the pit, a thousand times more furtive than on any pick-pocketing mission of Fagin's. I avoided the firelight but anxiously scanned every face I could make out in the glow. I was half-way across when to my left a tent flap opened and the lamp's gleam finally shone on a familiar face - the ugly, engorged face of Corporal Carter - and the brutal bastard, was coming directly at me. I lay flat on the earth, praying he wouldn't see me in the blackness. His boots crunched ever nearer - I was sure he'd tread on me with his next step - but then the bugger stopped. I thought he'd seen me and prepared my body for the vicious kick I was sure would come. I heard a fumbling above - was he getting out a club to beat me? I screwed my eyes tight and waited for the thudding blow. Suddenly a hot torrent of stinking liquid splashed down on the back of my neck. The bastard was pissing on me! I was be soaked and dared not do a thing to evade it. God knows how many pints of rum the rogue had drunk that day - he must have emptied at least a gallon over me. He completed his efforts by shaking out the last reluctant drops and emitting a satisfied belch. It seemed an eternity before his heavy footsteps crunched away - I looked up through dripping eyebrows to behold his fat rump disappearing into the tent. I shook my head like a dog and cursed him ten-fold, before continuing my tentative way through the fires. I was beginning to despair I'd ever find them, when in a flicker of light I made out a face, a tough, knowing face - staring thoughtfully into the embers - as calm and assured as that morning we entered Corunna.

"Corporal Bradman!" I whispered.

He turned and saw me. Recognition, amazement and concern rapidly intermingled across his granite-like features: "What the devil are you doing here, lad? Be gone you young fool before the bastards see you."

Although he spoke in barely a whisper, heads rose immediately from around the fire. Miller, Lindwall, O'Neil and Kidman were rubbing their eyes with astonishment. This was no time or place for greetings: "I've come for my father and Warnie. I've heard word Napier's killing him."

"Warnie is in the punishment hut with Donovan - your Pa's over there, least I think he's your Pa. The old devil never stopped asking us about you." Miller pointed to a heap of rags on the periphery of their dying fire. They watched dumbfounded as I crawled over and tentatively lifted a rag. Beneath it was a face - as thin and ravaged as any skull - but it was a face I knew as mine. Small dark eyes opened and blinked - full of wonderment - incomprehension. I think the poor old bugger reckoned at that moment he'd passed into some after-life.

"Father, I've come," was all I could manage to utter.

His dirty, scarred hand reached up and gently touched my face as if ascertaining I was flesh and blood. "My boy…Are you really my boy? I thought I'd never see you…" His eyes were now streaming tears, making little pink lines down his filthy cheeks. "But why have you come? I sent word. We're all dead meat here…there's no escape."

"I've come to get you out…you and poor Warnie," I was already busy with my bent nail unpicking his cursed shackles. "I've got help and spare horses." His thin old bloody ankles were free. I turned to Bradman and the others: "Do you want me to free you as well? I've only got two spare horses…do you want to risk it on foot?"

Bradman shook his head: "No lad, we wouldn't stand a chance. Napier would ride us down like foxes and delight in killing us all. We'll wait and trust Mr Crowe succeeds in London." Miller and Lindwall looked disappointed at this. I suspect they fancied giving it a try, but Bradman still held his old authority over them.

I pulled the flask of rum from my pocket and poured a draft down my father's throat. The gratitude with which he imbibed indicated a life-long appreciation for the beverage. I looked at him with incredible fondness, feeling that even if all else failed this moment would have made it worthwhile. Our eyes met: "Father, I don't even know your name."

There was a small twinkle: "Private Robert Skinner of the 44th Foot. I fought at Waterloo, you know."

"I had heard rumours pertaining to that fact," I retorted. "I'm Jack, Jack Dawkins. Known by some as the Dodger."

"I know. Your pals have told me of your exploits." He held my hand and kissed it. "God bless you, my dear boy."

I wiped a tear from my own eye and passed the flask to the others: "Look after him. I'm going to get Warnie. Which hut is he in?"

Bradman gave my shoulder a comradely squeeze and indicated a solitary building some fifty yards away. I winked and crept towards it through the dying fires. My heart sunk when I discerned a sentry outside, sitting on the ground with his back against the wall, but as I got nearer I could hear he was snoring like a Trojan. I stole past him, took out Beppo's oil and rubbed it deep into the hinges, praying the stink wouldn't wake the bastard up. I slipped my trusty nail into the lock. To my delight the heavy door swung open without the slightest creak. I crept inside and pulled it shut - all was dark as pitch. There was a rustle in the far corner:

"Who's there?"

It was the same whispered voice I'd head that first night on the hulk - it seemed an age ago although it was little more than a year and a half. "Warnie, it's me - Dodger."

"Why in damnation have you come here? Get out you young pillock before the guards discover you."

"I've come to get you out... Leticia sent me."

"Leticia?" There was a silence then he began to sob. My brave, defiant, proud Warnie began to sob like a girl. I hated Napier even the more for reducing him to that.

I moved closer, my eyes becoming accustomed to the dark. In the faint light coming from the small barred window, high in the wall above, I made out two forms lying face down on the bare earth floor. Both their backs glistened black with blood, they were chained to the wall by their ankles. I immediately set to work with my nail. The other form, which I took to be Donovan, hadn't stirred. "How is he? Is he strong enough to come with us? I've only got horses for you and my Dad. Perhaps Donovan could share a horse with me."

"It's no use, Dodger, old son." I distinguish his face now; it was covered with a matted beard. "He's dying. Napier has flogged the poor sod to death - he's taken even more lashes than me." At that Donovan stirred, painfully raised his head and began murmuring some Roman prayer. "Poor bugger doesn't know where he is - I don't think he even feels the pain any more - I pray he doesn't anyway." Warnie was now free and rubbing circulation into his raw ankles.

"Shall I free him?"

"Yes. We'll carry him outside. Let's hope he can die in God's fresh air. He was the bravest of us all."

"Will you be able to climb the cliff? Ben's at the top waiting for you. He'll carry you from there to the horses."

His blonde head nodded in the faint light. "I can manage. No man need carry me. What about your Pa? I fear the poor old rogue is not far off death himself."

"He's not much bigger than me. I'll carry him up. Let's go."

I crept back to the door, carefully pushed it open, and was relieved to hear the sentry's continued snores. I stole back to Warnie and between us we tenderly lifted Donovan from the ground. Warnie was so weak he tottered unsteadily, but we somehow managed to get the Irishman outside and round to the blind side of the hut. We laid him face down, the terrible wounds and lacerations on his back gleaming damp in the starlight, whilst Warnie mumbled a prayer over him. I hoped with all my heart that there was such a thing as Heaven and that poor Donovan would find salvation there, although I couldn't comprehend how any God could allow his creatures to endure what that poor fellow had suffered. I prayed with all my heart that he'd die before Napier discovered him.

We were about to crawl away when he stirred, raised his head from the earth and looked at me. "Turn me over. Let me die looking at the stars."

Despite the terrible gashes on his poor abused back, we did as he bade us. I expected him to cry out in anguish and pain, but he smiled beatifically and waved us farewell. We left him gazing lovingly at Heaven, which I hoped he'd enter soon. I then crawled back furtively towards my father and the others, feeling Warnie's breath on my ankles. The sounds of debauchery had largely ceased but sad music was coming from one of the tents. Someone was playing a fiddle whilst his companions sang a song from home. Most of the sentries were now clustered around a fire on the far side of the pit. Things were working out better than expected.

We reached our friends but there was no time for words of fond farewell. My Dad had managed to purloin the lion's share of the rum and had drifted into a stupor. Bradman helped me lift the little man upon my back, and strap him securely to me with the rope. We nodded our goodbyes and then, with Warnie lurching behind, I made my cautious return to the rock face. The music and song continued; even a few convict voices joined in - a sad song affects friend and foe alike. My father stirred behind me.

"Close your eyes and remember Waterloo. Don't make a bloody sound," I whispered, and began to climb. Small and emaciated as he was, my father became ever heavier as I scrambled upwards. I glanced behind and saw Warnie labouring beneath me. His blonde hair was so visible I couldn't understand why no one had spotted us, but by some providence, the enervating effect of the music perhaps, nobody did. I was halfway up and my strength was ebbing fast, when my keen nostrils became aware of a noxious stink. I looked up and was comforted to see Beppo's naked arse descending rapidly towards me. I rested on a ledge whilst, in a trice, Beppo freed me of my father, slung him over his shoulder and scampered up with him as nimbly as one of those apes on the Rock of Gibraltar. I waited for Warnie before we began to ascend the last few feet together. We'd nearly reached the top and safety, when a sharp cry echoed from below:

"Who goes there?"

A sentry must have cast a sentimental eye to heaven and seen something move. We scrambled up even more frantically.

The cry came again - sharper and more urgent: "Turn out the guard."

I couldn't help but look down - lamps and dark figures were emerging frantically from the huts and tents. Then, suddenly, Ben's musket cracked from above. There were fresh cries and even more movement - men scuttled for cover in all directions. Ben fired his second musket.

Napier emerged from the hut with his trousers round his ankles. His haughty voice screamed through the quarry: "Beat to arms! The savages are attacking. We'll teach the villains a lesson they'll never forget!" A drummer boy had tumbled from his cot and began a sharp tattoo, whilst everywhere, soldiers and overseers ran back to their tents to grab their weapons.

Stones were dislodged as I pulled Warnie over the edge. They clattered into the pit causing Napier to glance up. The cruel scoundrel spied us immediately: "Look! There they are - it's only damn'd convicts trying to escape. Fetch the horses - Attenborough! Crawley! Mount up - we'll have sport and hunt 'em down!."

The bastard had no idea we'd horses of our own and I knew we'd a chance of getting to them before he caught up with us. Napier and his fellow officers would have to pull on their boots and saddle their mounts and then ride up the winding path on the far side of the pit - if we ran fast enough we might just be able to mount up and get away with moments to spare, then hopefully lose them in the darkness of the bush. Beppo was already running back towards Harper and the horses, with my old Dad bouncing on his back like a sack of flour. Warnie could hardly walk, let alone run. Ben threw me his two muskets, pulled Warnie's arm around his shoulder so that his feet barely touched the ground, and swiftly made off behind Beppo. I brought up the rear, constantly checking to see if Napier and his fellows had yet come out of the pit. We'd covered just half the distance when I saw Napier lead them out on the far side. They still had to circle the pit, but I doubted now if we would reach our horses in time. I ran for all I was worth, weighed down by the heavy muskets - I stole another look and saw our pursuers swirling around - as if uncertain direction we'd gone. There were four of 'em - the three officers and a giant of a man, it had to be Bamber, who was whipping his horse in a frenzy of fury.

Perhaps it was my pale face that attracted his attention for at that moment Napier pointed in our direction: "There they are! The damn'd villains! Over there! Tally Ho!" He drew one of his long-barrelled pistols, dug in his spurs, and set off at the gallop. I looked despairingly towards Ben - Beppo had already reached the trees with my father - but there was no way Ben would get to safety supporting Warnie, and they would be on me in an instant. The hooves were thundering ever nearer. I heard the sharp crack of Napier's pistol and earth stung my face as the bullet hit the ground ahead to my right. I felt like one of Trumper's Sabine Gulls and remembered the accuracy of the shot that did for poor old Boswell. My guts were churning - I was certain the cruel blackguard was now aiming his second pistol at the middle of my backbone - anticipating the dreadful pain, when the flash of a musket exploded out of the darkness ahead. A horse was charging towards us with a black phantom on its back. It was Harper, brave, faithful Harper, urgently waving Ben and Warnie to continue towards the trees. He flashed past me in an instant and rode straight towards Napier, swinging his musket like a club. I continued running and heard a thundering crash behind. I looked back again and saw Harper and Napier on the ground together. Harper got swiftly to his feet, picked up a dazed Napier by his throat, and mashed him a mighty blow to the jaw, knocking him senseless.

Attenborough and Crawley, following behind, reeled back their mounts in alarm, but the brute Bamber kept coming. He hurled his bulk off his horse, threw himself at Harper and wacked him back to the ground. I was now only a few hundred yards from the woods and escape, but something made me stop. I sensed I was about to witness something remarkable. But Harper's final fight was more than remarkable - it was epic - such stuff as legends are made of.

Harper was back on his trotters in an instant - with a gleam of battle in his eyes such as I'd never seen before. He tore off his shirt to reveal the well-tuned muscles under his shiny black hide, spat defiantly on the ground and raised his fists. I never realised until that moment how nobly moulded he was. Bamber got slowly to his feet. He'd lost his flat-brimmed hat and I viewed the brute clearly for the first time. He had a broken nose, short cropped hair with a considerable tract of bare and sterile country behind each mangled ear, and a malevolent smile on his cruel ugly face. He took off his shaggy black coat and slowly and deliberately undid the buttons on his shirt, revealing a forest of thick matted hair on his huge chest. He was as tall as Harper but so broad as to appear almost squat. He then raised his fists, which looked as hard as iron hammers, and beckoned Harper on.

Attenborough was trying to revive Napier, Crawley was running around vainly trying to retrieve Napier's horse - I was the sole spectator as Harper got up on his toes and virtually danced in with bewildering speed. If Bamber's fists were hammers - Harper's were pistons. He shifted, feigned and drove Bamber backwards with a mixture of straight lefts, crosses, half-arm digs and muzzlers. I've seen the mills of Sayers and Heenan, Sullivan, the Boston Strong Boy and Gentleman Jim Corbett, but none of 'em could have stood up to Harper's opening attack that night in the bush. There was no ring to limit the contest and Harper had driven Bamber half way back to the quarry before a ferocious upper-cut finally dumped the brutal bugger on his arse.

Bamber glared malevolently up at his opponent and spat a tooth from his bleeding mouth: "I'll tear your ears off, you black dog." With that he grabbed a handful of dust, flung it in Harper's eyes, and threw himself back into the attack. Prize-fighting still followed Broughton's* rules then, (that vindictive scoundrel, the Marquis of bleedin' Queensbury hadn't even been born - poor old Oscar will always wish he'd never seen the light of day, but that's another story) - but Bamber didn't intend to follow any rules. He swung his left arm around Harper's neck and then held him in Chancery as he pummelled him savagely to the head. Poor Harper was unable to retaliate - I feared for his addled brains and vainly tried to think of a way to help him. The terrible pummelling continued, Harper's black face was now a bloody red mess - I was about to reach for my pistol - I'd have done anything to stop it - when he swung out his fist and thumped it mightily into Bamber's bollocks.

Bamber howled like a dog and immediately released Harper from his grip. Harper shook his head as if to clear his mangled brains - saw his opponent was still doubled up with pain and smashed a huge down-cut on his cheek. Bamber staggered backwards and the titanic contest resumed. This time, although Harper constantly drove him back, Bamber counter-attacked on the retreat. They were both meeting out and receiving dreadful punishment - there were no rounds, no second's knee to crawl back to - occasionally they broke off in their exhaustion and glared defiance at each other before resuming their gory battle. Harper's chest and sides were heaving, he was getting slower and Bamber was finding him easier to hit, as he backed ever closer to the edge of the quarry. Another furious rally and Harper's face was a mass of flowing claret, one eye was half-closed, the other completely, and there was no second to lance the swellings. They broke off again in dire fatigue - although I saw with sinking heart that Bamber now appeared the stronger. I will never know if Harper thought that too, if his poor battered head could think anything at all, or if he could even see how close Bamber was to the edge, or that Corporal bloody Carter was fast approaching up the path out of the quarry with a squad of soldiers; but I believe this was one contest in which Harper was determined not to be defeated. He summoned up the last of his strength and with a final savage cry, hurled himself at Bamber, wrapped his arms around him and carried him over the edge. Bamber's scream echoed to the bottom of the pit and then all was still.

No one would have survived such a fall. For a second time that night I hoped with all my heart that there was a Heaven, and brave Harper had gone there to join his Betsy. Cries and shouts swirled up from below. Above, Attenborough and Crawley were coming towards me leading Napier, slumped senseless over his saddle like a dead pig. Carter and the soldiers were advancing rapidly from the opposite direction. It was time for me to scud off in the darkness and confusion.

I ran sobbing through the night back to the clump of trees by the river, where I found Ben and Beppo waiting with my father and Warnie.

"Harper's gone," was all I was able to say.

"The poor bugger died for me - two of the best of fellows gone in a single day," said Warnie bitterly. He was in a terrible condition: his exertions had caused the map of scars on his back to bleed afresh.

Private Robert Skinner, on the other hand, had regained his consciousness and gave me a warm greeting: "Oh, How de do? There ain't no drain of another drop of rum handy, is there?" I couldn't speak with grief but proffered him the last flask from my saddle bag. He proposed the brief sentiment, "Towards us!" before emptying it into himself as into a cask.

I looked at Ben: "What do we do now? Warnie must rest."

He nodded: "The fuckers won't track us in the dark - we'll go back to the water hole."

Next morning after Beppo had applied one of his foul oils to Warnie's lacerated back, we breakfasted on a nourishing soup that Ben had concocted out of a white cockatoo and a couple of crows. Ben and Beppo then went off hunting kangaroo, for meat for our journey, and Robert Skinner took a post-prandial nap. All was quiet and peaceful in contrast to the night's turmoil, as Warnie and I sat by a tree stump, roasting some chestnuts and contemplating the muddy water.

"What do we do now?" Warnie asked, peeling the burnt skin from a yellow kernel.

"We go west into the new territory and buy land. Levey's given me gold. We'll have our own farm. Work it between us: you, me and my Dad - poor old Harper was supposed to come with us too. Wait for a new Governor and trust that Crowe can win us our pardons."

He ruminated for a while before he spoke again: "How is Leticia?"

"Don't fret your eyelids on that score - Levey takes well care of her." He bridled at this so I quickly added, "Not that he has his way with her or anything - they're just friends."

He shook his head, "No man ever does anything for nothing."

Behind us there was a jingle of harness and a horse champed on its bit: "And no villain will ever escape my custody."

We spun round astounded to behold Napier on his stallion with heavily bandaged head and his silver-butted pistols levelled at our breasts. He was dressed as for the hunt in black riding coat and white stock. Tied to his saddle, with a rope leashed around her neck, was a naked Abbo girl. Corporal Carter was mounted a few yards behind, holding his reins in one hand and aiming a musket at us in the other.

"Oh, bugger me!" Robert Skinner had woken and was slowly raising his hands.

"Did you fools really presume I'd give up so easily? This creature," Napier gestured towards the girl looking sullenly at the ground, "with a little persuasion, can track as well as any hound." I noticed the red weals across her back. The Captain glowered at Warnie with hatred stamped all over his stuck up phiz. "How dare you discuss my wife as if she were a common trollop? I noted the disrespectful way you eyed her on the voyage and thrashed your back to ribbons for it. Yet you still continued with your damn'd insolence. You dared to challenge me at cricket and, in spite of all that fool Crowe's seditious efforts, I thrashed you again. Now I'm going to drag you back to the quarry like the dog you are, where I'll thrash you and this old villain as you've never been thrashed before. Five hundred lashes and double chains is the proscribed punishment for an attempted escape. As for you…." he then turned his cold eyes on me, "you have been a thorn in my flesh ever since I first clapped eyes on you at Gravesend. You have rebelled against the Governor's authority in aiding the escape of prisoners and causing the death of one of the Governor's servants. You will be hanged."

"Have mercy, Your Excellency," pleaded Robert Skinner, "he's just a lad. I'm his father - he did it for me."

"All the more reason to hang him…"

I noticed Carter's eyes wandering to the water where our horses were tended. A look of concern spread across his face: "There's four horses Captain…. There must be another one!"

At that very instant a spear flew from a clump of bush and pierced Napier's side. Simultaneously a musket blast blew Carter off his horse. Beppo charged out of the bushes, dragged Napier to the ground and furiously belaboured his bandaged head with his club. Ben emerged from behind a gum tree and ambled over to where Carter was croaking. He slowly reloaded his musket and coolly fired another blast into Carter's chest. The cruel brute arched his back, shuddered, and was still. Warnie, who'd been standing in shocked silence since Napier first appeared, now gave a terrible scream, as if releasing all the suffering and cruelty he'd so long endured. He grabbed one of the silver pistols from the dust where it had fallen, and was about to join Beppo in making the back of Napier's head a bloody mess, when my old father frantically pulled him back.

"Don't have murder on your conscience, lad. We've enough to answer for when we meet our Maker."

His words had no effect: Warnie shook his arm free and raised the silver mounted handle as a hammer. I'm often surprised at the depths of my sagacity, which at that moment made me cry: "Stop! You can't kill the father of Leticia's son."

Warnie halted in his tracks and lowered his arm as my forewarning struck home. He said nothing but hurled the expensive weapon into the middle of the muddy water, then, with a dreadful look upon his face, continued to watch as the savage pounded Napier's skull. At last the sickening sound of cracking bone ceased, and Beppo, covered with blood and fragments of brain, rose from his prey. I looked down at the bloody red mess, unable to fully comprehend that this vile tyrant, who'd tortured our existence for so long, had truly gone. Beppo said not a word, but went to Napier's trembling stallion and cut the rope from the young girl's neck.

Ben nodded in satisfaction: "She is his daughter."

After that things happened very fast. Ben and Beppo hurriedly stripped Napier naked and buried him face down in a shallow grave - Ben said he should be buried because he was a chief. I took grim satisfaction in seeing Napier's white arse being slowly covered with black earth. They stripped Carter too, but left his carcass in the bushes for the dingoes. I considered gaining some sort of revenge by emptying my bladder over him, but decided the foul brute wasn't worth it. Warnie and my dad had dire need of the boots and breeches, but Beppo was soon arrayed in the rest of Napier's togs. Before we knew it, he'd taken Napier's remaining pistol and Carter's horse and jogged off with his daughter seated upon it like some black Lady Godiva. I realised I'd forgotten to thank him - the savage had saved my life twice.

Ben sniffed the air: "We must go. Others will be following."

We set Carter's proud stallion free and slapped its rump. It galloped back towards the Brisbane River as we headed north-west into the bush. *

13. Change of Plan

We cantered across the outback throughout that day, putting as much distance we could from any pursuers - for pursue us we knew they would - our speed only limited by the weakness of Warnie and my father. Indeed it was their frailty that forced us to make an early camp in a thick clump of bush. In the flickering flames of the smallest of fires, whilst Warnie brooded and Ben listened awe-struck, Robert Skinner told me, without his usual elaboration, some of the story of his eventful life. How, having been made an orphan at twelve, he'd joined the army as a drummer boy and had followed King George's colours throughout Flanders, Portugal, Spain, and France and to the Indies and back. I then told him some of my adventures, and was somewhat touched when he wept and lamented that he'd not been able to protect me from such evils. I must confess I did not consider myself worthy of such pity, or that my lot had been so bad compared to what I'd seen others suffer: but then I've never been one for feeling inordinately sorry for myself.

The following morning we were much perturbed to spy some red-coated riders behind us to the east, but had lost all sight of 'em by the time we reached the foothills of the Great Ridge. Nevertheless we didn't make camp until we were well into the safety of the forest. Warnie had hardly spoken a word since Napier's death and was sitting staring into the fire, his kangaroo stew uneaten.

"Ain't this a queer fix?" I asked, trying to hearten him.

He turned and looked at me with anguish in his eyes: "I'm going to Leticia."

You could have knocked me down with a sparrow's feather. "What? Are you mad? She's in the middle of Sydney. It's a guinea to a gooseberry you'll be taken as soon as you set foot in the place. You'll be wanted for Napier's murder as soon as they find his body."

"That's it. Napier's dead. But she doesn't know. She's free now. She's rid of him at last. If I can get to her quickly, before the news of the bugger's death reaches Sydney, they won't be looking for me. I'll take her with us into the new territory. With her boy - I'll bring him up as mine even though the poor little sod has Napier's cursed blood is in his veins."

"Don't be a bloody fool, Warnie. We're safe now. We'll buy land far away - have our farm. Ben will tell her what happened - in a few years things may change."

"In a few years she'll marry another or return to England. I have to see her now."

Ben had been listening intently: "Mr Levey be very angry. He told me to take you west."

Warnie stubbornly shook his head: "I'll not travel west until I've seen her."

"What about my poor old father?" I glanced affectionately at Robert Skinner, who lay in an exhausted sleep on the opposite side of the fire, "I won't put him in danger of being taken again."

"You don't have to come with me. I'll go alone."

"You're not strong enough to travel alone and you'd never find the way without Ben. Besides you've no ticket of leave or travel pass - you'll be taken by the first troop of Dragoons you meet. We're still heading south-west towards Sydney - for the moment let's stay together. Don't fret your eyelids - you'll soon see sense and change your mind."

Warnie said no more and during the following days I hoped that he'd indeed changed his mind, as Ben led us westwards, on a more direct but more dangerous path, on the lower mountain slopes. On the fourth day the black fellow said we'd come within reach of Darling's Dragoons' patrols, and it would be safer to cross over to the far side of the range. We followed him uncertainly up through a narrow pass, over treacherous shale. On two occasions it was only my sure-footed little Nancy that prevented us sliding over the precipice on to the rocks below. I constantly looked anxiously back at my father, but he was a far better horseman than I'd perceived. He told me later a dubious tale of how he'd served as a trooper in the Light Horse under the Duke of York in the Low Countries in 1793. Warnie though, was never at ease on a horse and it was only Ben's firm hand constantly on his bridle that saved him from disaster. We were all greatly relieved when we eventually left the mountains and descended to a green, endless plain. We galloped across it for hours and my backside had been chaffed raw when, towards evening, I heard dogs barking. I raised my weary eyes and spied a flock of familiar looking woolly sheep grazing outside a solitary wooden hut. Smoke was wafting lazily from its chimney. Outside the hut, smoking a black pipe, was a big, fierce looking man. I knew at once it was Magwitch.

As we drew nearer I saw the same dark little eyes that had so frightened me that first night on the hulk and heard that same click in his throat as he recognised me: "You, young devil. What brings you here? By God, I'm glad to see you. For months I've seen no faces but the faces of sheep - I'd half forgot what men's faces were like."

He made us welcome and we feasted that evening on roast mutton - an old ewe whose broken leg even Magwitch hadn't been able to mend. He told us that the sheep run stretched for more than thirty miles - his master, Provis, was tending a flock on an even bigger run further to the west. All this land belonged to them. The rams had done their duty and the lambing season would soon begin. Their flocks would multiply and in a few years these plains would be full of their sheep. After supper we sat around the fire, drank rum, and Magwitch, my father, and I, lit our pipes. Magwitch nodded grimly as I recounted our adventures, but when I described Harper's heroic end a sentiment of sort glimmered in his eye. "He were a brave 'un," was all he managed to say. The news of Napier's death affected him less - he merely took the pipe from his mouth, and spat out black juice:

"What do you plan to do?" he asked after a while.

"We're making for the new territories - we've got gold and we're going to buy us a farm..." I began, but Warnie interjected:

"I'm going into Sydney and beg Napier's wife to come with me."

"Don't be a fool - I thought you'd put that harebrain scheme out of your head," I remonstrated. "You don't stand a chance of getting to her."

"But I've got to try. You're too young to understand, Dodger. It's the thought of her that's kept me alive. I saw her face and heard her piano even whilst the lash was cutting into my spine. "

Magwitch slowly rubbed his large brown venous right hand over his cropped head: "Lord strike me dead, but I believe a man should go for whatever he wants. Mayhap he may prosper wonderful - if he don't try he'll spend the rest of his days regretting it."

"But he's no ticket of leave or travel pass. The first bunch of Dragoons he runs into will hang him."

"Man shouldn't believe in death until he meets him in the face." Magwitch went over to the fireplace and took worn documents out of a small wooden box. "Might as well take my papers and pass - if they stop you say you're Abel Magwitch, assigned to Provis, going into the town for supplies. Drop 'em off back when you return with your lady."

"I go with you". We turned to Ben who'd not uttered a word since we entered the hut. "I have to tell my boss, Mr Levey, what happened. He be fucking mad you got his gold and don't buy the land. Maybe he think you a thief, Mr Dodger."

I'd never bothered if anyone had considered me a thief before, in fact I'd have thought it an insult if they hadn't; but on this occasion, despite my fears and trepidations, I knew I should put the record straight. I reasoned if I accompanied Warnie and Ben to Sydney and explained things to Levey before the news of Napier's death and the escape arrived, I'd have nothing to fear. It might take several days before the body was discovered in the bush and then they'd have to get word to the main camp at Brisbane, where there might be a further delay before a ship sailed. Even though I'd no pass or papers, I was still officially assigned to Levey - if he had reported the theft of his horses and the disappearance of me and Harper - I would swear to any authority that the poor black rogue had forced me to accompany him and that Ben had rescued me and was bringing me back.

I found myself saying that I would go as well, if Magwitch would provide shelter for my father until I returned. Magwitch agreed instantly.

He'd already struck up some kind of understanding with Private Robert Skinner, who'd regaled us all with tales of his exploits at Waterloo - where, surprisingly, we learnt he'd managed to be present at the simultaneous actions at Hougoumont and La Haye Sainte, and furthermore had played a vital part in the defence of both. Having sampled Magwitch's plentiful supply of fine rum, Private Skinner announced he'd be quite content to remain at the little hut for a week or so; and thus our new plan fell into place.

The three of us set off as dawn was breaking, leaving my father in Magwitch's tender care. We galloped over yet more leagues of lush green plain until Ben led us up over the Blue Mountains again. The black villain was in a sullen mood - I'd witnessed his devotion to Levey, remembered how he'd lost us the cricket match at a toss of Levey's head and, despite all we'd gone through, I was uncertain what his real intentions were, indeed I was somewhat apprehensive as to whether he would bring us to Sydney at all.

We spent two days and nights in rocky gorges until, on the third morning, we rode along a ridge with the measureless plains spread beneath us and blue mountain tops all around. We then entered a forest, passing through the most beautiful glades I'd ever seen: Ben told us it was a sacred place for his people. After watering our horses in a huge lake, we descended a steep path by the side of a mighty fall of water at the bottom of which was a solitary weatherboard hut, which proclaimed itself an inn. Although I was desperately craving a glass of hot gin, I didn't dare to stop, and we soon found ourselves on a rutted track, with the vast farmlands of the wealthy settlers on either side. We made cautious progress, no longer a frantic gallop; our poor horses were too spent anyhow. Ben halted constantly and scoured the horizon with his dark, sweepy lashes. We saw distant labourers working in the fields and stockmen with the cattle, but thankfully no trace of a scarlet or blue coat. As dusk was falling, we skirted the pitiful convicts labouring on their road, which had edged forward barely a mile or so in the intervening weeks, and were just outside Parramatta, thinking all had gone well, when a sharp cry of "Halt!" came out of the trees and a troop of horsemen rode onto the road before us. But they were not Dragoons - I saw green facings on their uniforms - they were soldiers of the 39th - the Green Linnets. There were eight of them all told, led by a huge-shouldered sergeant, who regarded us with extreme suspicion and disapproval. "Where's yer fuckin' passes?" he demanded.

My heart sunk even lower when I recognised his ugly phiz - it was Hodson. The great brute who'd mangled Miller's foot and peppered Warnie's baubles. Even though Warnie's face was now covered with a luxuriant golden beard there seemed scant hope he wouldn't recognise him - Magwitch's papers would be useless. I had to act quickly. I felt in my saddle bag for my own purse, containing all the Yankee dollars I'd filched from the slaver.

"Oh my wig, Sergeant Hodson! What a jolly game! I've never been so glad to see a red jacket in my life. Don't you know me?" I reached out and desperately shook his hand, palming the purse into it. "I was bloody abducted so I was, and these two fine gentlemen have saved me and are bringing me back to my assigned master, Mr Levey. I'm sure he'll reward you further if you would kindly escort us back into town."

Hodson squeezed my purse, into his enormous hand, feeling the weight of the coins, before surreptitiously slipping it into his tunic. He glanced back at the troopers, making sure this action had been unobserved, then turned back to me with a sneer on his face. "None of yer lip, short arse. We've got more important duties than to tend to the likes of you. Tell that damn'd Jew, your master, he can thank me next time I look into his hotel."

"I will indeed. He'll thank him properly, won't he Ben?" I turned to the black devil, who nodded non-too enthusiastically. Warnie was staring at the ground with an old hat of Magwitch's pulled over his eyes. "I'm sure Mr Levey will provide grog for all of your brave men," I continued. The brave men pricked their ears up at this and began to look thirsty.

Hodson patted his chest, feeling my hard-won bag of coins bulging beneath his tunic. "We're out after that Irish bastard, Donohoe and his gang. The damn'd villains get bolder by the week. They were in Regent Ville this morning. Robbed two tenants of Sir John Jameson. Seen any trace of the buggers? You might have passed them on the road."

I shook my head inconclusively.

He spat derisively: "Wouldn't expect you to tell us even if you had. You convict scum never grass on yer mates, do yer?" He looked at Warnie for the first time. "Who the hell are you anyway? Haven't seen you around Levey."

Warnie didn't raise his eyes but thrust his papers under Hodson's snub nose and spoke in a gruff voice: "Abel Magwitch. Assigned to Provis, coming into Sydney for supplies…"

"Yes, we met him at the inn by the falls. We all stayed the night there," I offered brightly.

Hodson glanced at the papers with an attitude that told me the bastard couldn't read.

"Thought you said he'd saved you from abduction?"

I cursed myself for my carelessness. I was beginning to forget all Fagin's lessons on the delicate art of lying. "Indeed he did. It's a long story which I will be more than happy to recount," I took out my pipe and was on tenterhooks as I racked my brains for a suitable explanation. I decided to change tack: "But his cove Donohoe, would he be a short little fellow like yours truly, flashy dresser, smart togs, with a bit of a scar under his nose?"

Hodson shoved the papers back into Warnie's hand: "That sounds like the very bastard himself. Where did you see the villain - was he alone?"

I tamped some of Magwitch's tobacco into my pipe with my dirty thumb. "He had a couple of ugly brutes with him - one was a real miserable-looking bloke, with pistols sticking out all over his belt…" I got no further.

"By God! That's them. Where did you see the devils?"

I sucked out some black juice from the stem of my pipe and spat it in the dust. "I saw 'em resting their horses under the trees, a few miles back, as we came through Kurragong."

Hodson turned in the saddle and waved his men on: "On your way, you damn'd rogues. We'll waste no more time on the likes of these. Governor Darling has put a hundred pounds on that Irish rogue's head."

"Any chance of yours truly partaking of the reward?" I inquired innocently; but they'd all galloped past us towards Toongabbie. I cursed myself again. I'd given the rogue all the wealth I had - I'd only Levey's gold now. I'd grown soft - Fagin would turn in his grave.

It was well into night when we reached the outskirts of Sydney. The racecourse, where we'd waged our valiant fight, was white under the moon. As we entered the town, to my relief, it was empty and quiet as the grave until, as we rode into George Street, the delicate notes of a piano wafted on the air. To my surprise and consternation the concert hall beside the Royal Hotel was a blaze of light. A large poster proclaimed:

30th June 1829
The Grand Opening
Of
Mr Barnet Levey's Royal Concert Hall
Before an Esteemed Invited Audience
Recital of the Finest Music
Performed on the Pianoforte
by
Mrs Patrick Napier

I cursed myself the third time that day for being a fool. I'd forgotten all about the damn'd concert - we'd ridden into a trap - Darling himself would be present - the place would be surrounded by his guards. But when we drew closer I spied no carriages or sleek thoroughbreds tethered outside. No waiting grooms and coachmen were seated on the steps. We exchanged puzzled looks before we dismounted and pushed open the door. In the vestibule, bedecked with flowers, were tables laden with uneaten delicacies and untouched wine. I saw Sue among the girls waiting to serve a non-existent audience. They looked up expectantly as we entered. When Sue saw me her expression changed rapidly to one of concern. I winked at her and laid a finger to my lips. Warnie wandered across the lobby as if in a trance. The music was enticing him on, like those charmers do to snakes in India. He made for the entrance of the hall where Croft was sitting morosely on a chair. The rogue looked up and glowered and would have barred Warnie's entrance, but Ben whispered in his ear. We crept past him. Croft followed us in, locked the door, and leant against it.

On the stage at the far end Leticia, dressed in a pale blue silk gown, was seated at a huge gleaming black piano. Her dark ringlets tossed in the candlelight as she fervently played, what I now know to be *The Emperor Concerto*, to rows of empty seats. I thought she was completely alone until I spied Levey seated in a box, stroking his beard in great agitation, and Sarah Trumper in the front row with little Horatio asleep on her lap.

Warnie froze as soon as he saw Leticia. Ben made to go towards Levey, but I held him back. We remained in the shadow for several minutes as Warnie listened, drinking in every single note his beloved played. She ended the piece with a fine crescendo and then sat with her head bowed over the keys. Levey rose to his feet to applaud. Warnie applauded too - his claps echoing round the empty hall. Levey started and looked fretfully in our direction.

"Who's there?"

We walked into the light. Leticia raised her head, saw us, and gasped. Her cheeks were wet.

"Why do you come here, you damn'd fools?" Levey climbed out of his box and stormed towards us, in a foul mood such as I'd never seen before. "Ben, you black fool, how dare you disobey me?"

"Sorry Boss," Ben mumbled. "Things happen not as we planned."

Warnie pushed past Levey, clambered on to the stage and took Leticia by the hand. "Leticia, your husband's dead. You're free. There's no time to waste, bring the boy and come with me."

There was a long silent pause as her expression changed from surprise to utter shock. I thought she was about to burst into tears but then, I swear, a look of relief mingled with happiness passed over her lovely face. She withdrew her hand from Warnie's. "Dead? Patrick is dead?"

"Yes...but not by me...."

Before Warnie could explain any further Levey had forced himself between them and pushed Warnie aside. "Be off, you idiot. How dare you intrude? I've saved your worthless life and given you gold enough. You think this exquisite lady would consider a beggar like you? Go while you can and leave her alone." He attempted to grab Leticia's other hand: "My dearest, never fear, I will protect you. I will make you the finest lady in all Australia."

She snatched her hand away, her expression changing to fierce disdain, "You would make me the finest lady in all Australia and you cannot even cajole a shopkeeper's wife to listen to me play? Even my cursed husband did not humiliate me as you have done tonight. I allowed myself to become the scandal of Sydney because of your vulgar attentions, but I have no further need of you now."

Levey gulped and spluttered; "Leticia, my love... my dearest.... There can be no scandal if you are my wife...."

"Your wife?" she whispered, as if she were ashamed even to mention the possibility. "Do you honestly think I would marry a Jew? That I would allow you to bring up my son?"

Levey looked so crest-fallen at that moment that I almost felt pity for the rogue.

Warnie came forward again: "I love you Leticia, it was the thought of you that kept me alive. I'll devote every day of my life to you and your boy."

"Where? In a hut? Living on an earth floor, plagued by snakes and drought and famine? My son was born a gentleman and gentleman he shall be." She tossed her curls defiantly. "Now that I am a widow, my wealth is my own. Horatio and I will return to England on the next sailing." She saw the pain in Warnie's eyes and softened her tone. "I will always remember you. You have been a true and gallant friend, but that is all you can ever be."

Throughout my long and varied life I've never completely fathomed the intricacies of womankind, and Leticia had fooled me as much as poor old Warnie, who looked as if he'd been thumped in the bread basket by one of Harper's mightiest blows. I knew I had to act quickly before

Levey asked for his gold back, but was mightily perplexed as to what course to follow. At that very moment the boom of a cannon came to my rescue and reverberated around the hall. We all froze and gazed at each other in consternation.

Croft was the first to speak: "It's the bloody alarm from Fort Macquarie."

Levey rubbed his beard. I saw the fear in his eyes as he turned savagely on Warnie: "It must be a ship from Brisbane with news of Napier's death and your escape. We are all dead if you are found here. Go in the name of Hell. I have risked enough for you. Your insane obsession with this lady is common knowledge - this will be the first place they will look."

Warnie was still staring disbelievingly at his lost love, who had turned her back on him and was taking her sleeping son from Sarah's arms. Napier's lash had not been able to induce a single tear, but now the poor cove's eyes were full of pain.

Levey turned on me. "This is your fault. I was insane to listen to you. How dare you bring him here? Artful Dodger? Fagin's best hand? You are nothing but trouble and a fool. Give me back my gold and never come near me again."

"No! Let them keep it." Leticia looked up from her sleeping child. "I owe Mr Warne that." Levey was about to protest but she silenced him with a flicker of her lashes, "Don't fret, Mr Levey, I will repay you as soon as I have access to my money."

I tugged at Warnie's sleeve, wanting to get well away before she changed her mind. "Come on, we've got to get back to my Dad." But the obstinate fool wouldn't budge. He continued to look disbelievingly at Leticia, like a calf at a butcher's knife.

"Get them out I tell you," Levey screamed, turning to Ben and Croft. "Throw these villains off my premises." Ben dutifully raised his gun level with Warnie's breast. "Go now or I'll order Ben to shoot," Levey threatened. "As far as the authorities are concerned you have escaped and murdered an officer of the crown. It is my civic duty to capture you dead or alive. There will be no questions asked."

"Please go, both of you, whilst you have a chance," Sarah Trumper pleaded, speaking for the first time.

Leticia laid her hand on Warnie's arm, "There will only be more scandal if you are found here with me. I beg you go, for the sake of my son."

Warnie began to sob, deep huge sobs. So big and violent that his back heaved; the strain opened the lacerations and blood began to seep through his shirt. Leticia didn't notice as she'd returned her attention to her sleeping boy.

I pulled the poor, love-sick dupe towards the door: "Come on, big wig. We've got to get beyond Parramatta whilst it's still dark."

Croft had a triumphant gleam in his eye as he unlocked the door. I was no threat to his position now. "Artful Dodger? More like Bloody Fool," He gloated as his kicked my arse and booted me into the lobby. Sue and the other girls, having heard the alarm, looked anxiously towards us. "Clear up and go to bed, you trollops," Croft snarled. "You've seen nothing. These two rogues were never here."

Striving to maintain my customary dignity, I winked at Sue and whispered, "Here's a jolly life," then scudded past her, quickly helping myself to some pies, a few legs of chicken and a bottle of wine. Croft slammed and barred the front door behind us. Our tired horses were tethered as we'd left them. Warnie was still sobbing as I pushed him into his saddle. I climbed quickly onto my faithful little mare and thrust the victuals into my saddle bag together with Levey's gold. I swung Nancy's head westwards, pulled on Warnie's bridle and we were away - his gelding automatically following the scent of my pretty mare. There were more people in the streets now: soldiers were running frantically out of whorehouses and gin shops towards the castle, where flickering torches and a constant tolling bell signalled an emergency. Such was the general consternation that no one noticed or challenged us until, as we were approaching *The Fox and Hounds* in Castlereagh Street, a solitary figure stumbled out into the road before me. He was a tall man with a lurking walk, looking back angrily over his shoulder, so he failed to see me until I was almost on him.

"Watch yer bleedin' step!" I screamed. "You want to be run down, you stupid cove?"

He gave a frightful curse and looked up with hate in his eyes as my little Nance danced round him. I recognised the withered, haggard face with teeth marks around the lips - Monks recognised me at the same instant.

"Rot you!" he cried, shaking his fist in a horrible passion. "You sneaking, snivelling pickpocket, I'll grind your bones to ashes. I should have done it as soon as I realised you were here." *Sneaking, snivelling, pickpocket!* Those very words again; but I'd no time to think: his scarred hands were tight around my leg, dragging me from the saddle. I was certain the bastard had got me until there was a sound of hooves behind and the blur of a swinging arm. Warnie had galloped up and struck the back of my assailant's head with the butt of his pistol. The fiend crumpled to the ground without another murmur. I hoped the action had helped galvanised Warnie to his senses, but he still sat slumped in his saddle.

I slapped him gratefully upon the shoulder, "Thanks, old pal. That'll put the villain out for an hour or two. My popularity has definitely waned in this metropolis; let's make all the distance we can before he tells 'em we were here. Come on! Move yer arse, Warnie!"

I kicked Nancy's heaving flanks with my heels and galloped back up the road to Parramatta, with Warnie's tired gelding in tow. Warnie, himself, looked as though he'd lost all interest in life, and I realised that our course of action would have to be determined by me alone. There was no Fagin, Crowe, or even Ben to guide me: I felt very lonely indeed. I decided not stay on the North Road for long, as I knew fresh patrols would shortly be leaving the fort and our spent horses would be no match for them. Warnie had told me long ago he'd learnt to navigate by the stars when he was a fisher lad, so I hoped he could lead us north-west over the Blue Mountains yet again. But, even if he'd been his normal self, I'd foolishly forgotten that even the bloody stars were different on this side of the earth and we were soon hopelessly lost, deep in thick bush. I recalled those whitened bones of lost runaways and was beginning to despair, when I spied a minute gleam of light. I pulled up my spent little Nancy and screwed up my peepers and made out the glimmer of a hidden fire.

"It might be some poor bolter hiding up, or a local black," I whispered to Warnie, who remained deep in his dumps. I drew my pistol and slipped to the ground. "Whoever it is, the bugger will be able to put us on the right course. Besides, our horses must rest for an hour or so and I could do with some hot grub."

Warnie didn't say a word but slid out of his saddle. I crept forward, leading Nancy by her nose. As we drew nearer I made out a dark blanket spread over some low branches and a small fire beneath it. A billycan was set on the flames with the mouth-watering aroma of frying bacon wafting from it, but there appeared to be no sign of life. My hunger got the better of my caution. I crept closer to the fire; the bacon smelled more and more enticing. I was about to help myself to a sizzling rasher when I heard the click of metal behind:

"Put up yer hands, and don't move a frigging muscle. I've two pistols trained in the middle of each of yer backs," said a soft Irish voice. A hand reached out of the dark and removed the pistol from my grasp. In an instant Warnie had been similarly disarmed. "Now walk into the light of the fire and let me see yer phizes." We stepped closer to the flames as a figure flitted past us to the other side of the blaze. It was a small fellow, not all that much taller than me. I got a glimpse of scarlet silk lining his coat, a multi-coloured waistcoat and light cord trousers tucked into fine black leather boots.

"Would it be the famous Mr Donohue, whose supper we're interrupting?" I enquired pleasantly.

He stepped a little closer and recognised me instantly: "Indeed it is. And is not yerself the famous Dodger from the fair city of London? And is this the father you were seeking?"

After I'd corrected him as to the true identity of Warnie, he led us to a secluded hollow through which ran a little creek, where we tethered our horses alongside his. We were soon seated around the fire eating hot bacon together with the grub I'd divested from Levey's buffet. Warnie remained morose and silent whilst I informed Donahue of our present situation. The Irishman appeared to have lost the confidence he so bravely displayed at our previous meeting, and as I passed him the bottle of Levey's wine I inquired where the rest of his band might be.

"They've left me. The cowardly dogs," he sighed pulling out the cork with his teeth. "I've learnt too late that every man has his price: no settler will harbour us now Darling has levied a hundred pounds on me head. The bastards would betray the Pope himself for half that sum. The convicts themselves want to see me swing: Darling has ruled he'll issue no more tickets of leave until I'm taken. Even that bugger Walmsley has deserted."

"I heard you were busy at Regent Ville this very morning," I remarked encouragingly, licking hot bacon fat from my fingers.

"Yes and what brave pickings we had! We robbed two old men of this very bacon, a pound of tea, some flour, a little sugar and two pairs of tattered trousers. Walmsley was in so vile a mood he endeavoured to burn their hut down with them inside it - it was meself that thwarted his cruel intention with a bucket of water. He rode off in a rage. I found meself apologising to the poor old critters. Gave 'em back half of what I'd stole so they'd have a good breakfast."

"Why not rob the farms of the swells? You'd get richer pickings there."

"Indeed it is a great pleasure, robbing from the rich, but they've all invested in bull dogs which bark as soon as they smell us, and armed servants who would be delighted to blast me to smithereens for Darling's reward. I'm afraid my time is up, Dodger, me little friend. I'm a dead man now."

We bedded down by the fire, all huddled under the thin blanket and fell into an exhausted sleep. We were rudely woken by the blast of a musket and then a harsh, sneering voice:

"Come out Donohoe, you fucking carrion. Come out with yer hands above yer ugly head. Yer pal Walmsley has led us to yer. We knows yer there!"

I knew the voice at once. It was Hodson.

"We've got yer surrounded, with nine loaded muskets. Yer haven't a chance. Come out you damn'd Irish pig before we blast yer to pieces!"

Dawn was beginning to glimmer in the sky and when we peeped through the bushes we could just make out Hodson's burly figure, with the fading moonlight gleaming on the barrel of his musket, and the handcuffed Walmsley seated disconsolately on his horse behind him.

"That bugger has betrayed me," Donohoe sighed. "We've often hid out in this place."

"They don't know we're with you. That's two more pistols," Warnie seemed to have woken up at last. "Let's give the bastards a surprise."

Donohoe shook his head. "It's me they're after. I told you, I'm a dead man now. I've given 'em a good run. Slip down to the creek whilst I keep 'em busy. You'll be under cover most of the way. Get on yer horses and ride as fast as shit flying off a shovel. Keep yer heads down, follow the creek and it will lead you directly up to the Blue Mountains. Cross over them Dodger, and find yer Da." I made to protest but he stopped me with his pistol under my sniffer. "Go! Damn yer! Live yer life. Have fun and never let the buggers grind you down." He turned and hurriedly laid all his seven pistols on the ground, checking each was loaded and primed before stuffing five back into his belt. "I'll take some of those redcoat bastards with me - Walmsley too, if I can get to the traitorous dog."

"Come on out, you little Irish fucker!" Hodson yelled. "Or I'll blast you all the way to yer Popish Hell. Throw out all yer pistols. Yer pal Walmsley has told us how many you have. I'm going to count every fucking one."

I pulled my pistol from my belt and laid it beside his. "Here's one more - he won't be expecting that." I patted bold Jack on the shoulder, "Mother Ireland will be proud of you."

"Sure, and she'll be singing songs of me tomorrow. Don't move until I start shooting," he whispered, peering into the gloom for traces of scarlet coats, "then run for yer horses. Don't look back until you're on the other side of the mountains."

"I'll stay with you," Warnie primed his pistol. "I've got nothing to live for. I still owe that big bastard for what he did to my balls."

"Go, you damn'd fool and find yerself another woman. Mind you look after that wee fella as well - he's got a lot of promise." said Donohoe with a tremor in his voice.

There was a sharp crack and a musket ball violently shook the bushes around us. "Start throwing out yer pistols. We'll all fire next time. You'll be blasted to pieces, you stupid Irish bugger."

"Go now. Run like the devil himself with a hot spit up his arse. I'm going out the front door - they won't be expecting anyone to run out the back." Donohoe leapt to his feet and fired both the pistols in his hands. "You rot in hell yerself, you red-coated coward. One Irishman is worth the whole rotten nine of yer." With that he drew a second pair of pistols, duck's foot with splayed barrels, and stormed out towards the sound of Hodson's voice. The very bushes seemed alive with terror as muskets blasted from all directions. I grabbed Warnie's sleeve and ran, bent double, towards our horses and the creek. An astonished trooper rose out of a bush as we swept past him, but disappeared twice as quick as Warnie's pistol shot off his shako. Trees and scrub flashed past. Small birds rose out of the grass, squawking in fear. We heard more shots behind and fresh shouts of defiance from Donohoe. Then another volley, a scream of anguish and Donohoe's triumphant shout. Bold Jack had taken at least one redcoat with him. Our faithful horses were waiting where we'd left them. We loosed the reins and were on their backs in an instant, galloping along the creek with water splashing around us. I feared once more for Warnie's lack of horsemanship, but he managed to cling on, and we were already some distance away when we heard two more pistol shots, then another volley of musket fire, followed by shouts of triumph. I knew then that stout-hearted Jack Donohoe had gone to meet his maker. But he'd given us enough time. The sides of the creek were high and we rode on with our heads pressed into our horses' flying manes. I guessed that as Hodson hadn't yet heard of Napier's death, he'd be so gratified with poor Donohoe's head and the reward that went with it; he wouldn't bother to pursue us.

I was right. We crossed back over the mountain range that night and rode east throughout the following day, until we came back at last to Magwitch's lonely little hut. Old Provis had ridden over to see his partner and we found them both drinking rum alongside my father, who was deeply engrossed in giving them a detailed account of how he, single-handed, had managed to capture an Imperial French Eagle at the battle of Salamanca. I felt gratified and warm inside to see the old rogue again. I suppose, until then, apart from my obsession with Molly, it was the nearest feeling I'd ever had to love. Magwitch looked at me through the smoke of his pipe with a glint of tenderness in his small black eyes: "You've come back for yer father, have yer, you infernal imp?" He laid a hand upon the old soldier's knee: "You've a faithful boy there, Skinner, my friend. I thank God I've one meself back in England that'll be a fine gentleman yet."

I told them of the developments in Sydney and Provis decided the safest course for us would be to move as far west as possible, where Darling's mandate hardly reached. He told us that magistrates in small towns in the new territories were permitted to issue warrants for land. He thought they wouldn't ask too many questions if their fees were paid in ready gold.

We rested our horses for two days during which we had a real Irish wake for bold Jack. I mourned his brave soul and also that of Harper: they'd both sacrificed their lives for me.

14. The True History Of Private Robert Skinner

We left with Provis at sunrise on the morning of the third day, with rum-befuddled heads and furry tongues, then travelled south-east across plains of great extent, free of timber and brush, watered by clear streams which Provis assured us were teeming with fish of fine size and flavour. He told us that this had been the land of the Wiradjuri people until they had been driven off it by Governor Brisbane's campaigns. At noon, after pointing out a distant peak as our course, he left us to make his way to his own lonely hut. Warnie remained silent throughout the rest of the day, but Private Skinner more than made up for him in loquaciousness. He told tales of France and Spain, the heat of the Indies and the freezing cold of Canada. He regaled us with accounts of rowdy nights in taverns and cantinas, of cruel sergeants and brave captains, of the anguish of bloody battles and the sweet remunerations of victory. But there was one subject he never spoke of. I'd forborne to mention it as I didn't wish to distress him; but on the sunlit morning of the following day, as our horses were gently climbing a long verdant accession, my curiosity could restrain itself no longer.

"Tell me about my mother."

He drew up his horse and looked at me with fearful pain in his eyes. "She was the most beautiful creature that walked God's Earth and I wronged her even more than I wronged you." He kicked his horse on and contrary to his nature, remained silent for the rest of the day. I'd a hard time of it, I can tell you, riding between two such sullen and dispirited companions. That night, after he'd drunk a great quantity from the flagon of rum that Magwitch had provided, and had made certain

Warnie was gently snoring under his blanket, Robert Skinner beckoned me over to his side of the fire.

"Your mother was a dancer, small and delicate as a doll and light as a fairy," his eyes softened at the remembrance. "I loved her from the moment I first saw her the early spring of 1809, dancing in a bloody draughty barn in Barnstable. My regiment was billeted in the town on our way to Plymouth and embarkation to Lisbon. I'd gone with some mates to see a play, *The Grecian Daughter*, I think it was called. Bleedin' boring thing it was too. I didn't go much to plays, but there was nowt else to do in bleedin' Barnstable. My pay had almost gone. I hadn't enough to get drunk, or bed a whore, which were my main forms of relaxation, so I paid me penny, sat on a hard bench, with me feet sunk in dirty straw and watched those pitiful rogues declaiming some nonsense I couldn't for the life on me understand. At first my mates and I had great sport tormenting the poor fool actors: booing and hissing and throwing nut-shells and anything else that came to hand. Then I spied a little creature at the corner of the platform they called their stage, banging a pair of snuffers against a candlestick, trying to produce the sound of something or bleedin' other, horses hoofs or thunder, I can't remember what. But I'll never forget the perfect beauty of that little face or the golden curls that framed it. Then in the interlude she danced in a little white costume, whilst an old actor played a fiddle and a fat woman puffed into a flute. I had never seen such grace as in her movements in that cold and dirty barn. My mates soon departed to the nearest inn, but I remained until the conclusion of the evening's entertainment and sought her out.

I found her helping to take down the make-shift stage, whilst the fat woman squatted beside her noisily filling a chamber pot. She told me her name was Dora, she had no other. She thought she was twelve years old but couldn't be sure. Mr Latham, the manager of their motley troupe had obtained her from a foundling's home in Wolverhampton - he'd been seeking a little fair-haired creature, his previous dancer having recently died of a consumption in Bridgnorth. Dora looked frail and undernourished herself, so I helped her with her tasks then took her to a respectable tavern and spent my last pennies on a plate of cold beef.

Whilst she ate I bragged of my exploits and bravery, and her beautiful eyes filled with tears when she learnt I was about to face the French yet again. I took Dora back to the barn and sought out Latham as he was packing his cart. I vowed I'd kill him if he ever ill-treated her. I kissed her pretty cheek and never thought I'd ever see her again.

I spent five long years in Spain and wenched and whored my way from Fuentes de Onoro to the Siege of Badajoz, but never found a soul that could stir my heart. Then, in the summer of 1814, back from France, with that bugger Napoleon, as we thought, defeated and in exile, my regiment, the 44th Foot, spent the night under canvas near Ashford in Kent. I wandered into town and saw a young lad handing out play bills outside the Town Hall. I took one and have kept it with me until this day. As I'd not found time to acquire the skills of literacy, I was forced to ask a fellow soldier to read it for me."

He pulled a yellowing piece of paper from his pocket. I took it and read:

Mr Latham's Company of Comedians
This evening will perform in the courtyard at the King's Head
A celebrated historical play never performed here

CHARLES THE FIRST
The Characters to be dressed in ancient habits
According to the fashion of those times
Between the Acts of the play will be presented
A series of musical interludes
With the noted danseuse
Miss Dora Siddons-Garrick-Kemble

"Needless to say," he continued, "I hastened to the aforementioned hostelry, paid the princely sum of sixpence and placed myself at the centre of the front row. The play was no better than *The Grecian Daughter* and I feared it might not be the same Dora, but the moment she danced onto the stage at the interlude I knew it could be no other than she. The old fiddler was even older and the fat flutist was even fatter, but Dora had blossomed into the most beautiful creature I'd ever seen. Her skimpy dress succeeded in displaying to advantage her shapely legs and firm young bosom. She flew through the smoky air and sang '*Robin, Sweet Robin*' as prettily as any bird you've ever heard. As soon as the so-called entertainment ended, after the turnip representing King Charles' head had fallen into the bucket, I pushed aside the curtain and hurried backstage to seek her out. I feared she'd long forgotten me and couldn't believe that such a beauty would not have a lover, but as soon as she saw me she flew into my arms. This time we dined in style in the tap room with a bottle of fine French claret. To my great joy she told me how she'd constantly prayed for my safe return. I told her of my adventures and suffering, with slight embroidery here and there, and in the words of that Shakespeare fellow:

'She loved me for the dangers I had passed,
And I loved her that she did pity them.'...."

He took a long swig of rum and lit his pipe. "She then told me of her life and it weren't no bed of roses neither. Trudging from village to village through hot dusty lanes in summer and muddy cold roads through the rest of the year. Stumbling along behind Latham's top-heavy, overloaded wagon over never-ending hills and snow-swept moors, in the company of tippling, improvident bleedin' actors, who each night, in some flea infested barn, would attempt to force open her legs. But she swore she'd never succumbed, not once, she'd always been waiting for me to return, like the hero in those God-forsaken plays they performed each night.

I had money at that time - there had been good looting in France - and that night we lay together for the first time in *The Red Lion's* finest chamber. I clasped her to my breast and begged her to leave Latham and follow me like any soldier's wife. She readily agreed and next morning trudged proudly behind the regiment with the other women. She never complained and gave me love such as I'd never imagined any soul would bestow on such as me. For a few happy months we were comfortably quartered in Bedford, where the 44th was based. You were growing resolutely inside her belly, and I'd fully determined to marry her, when Boney caught us with our breeches down and scarpered back from Elba. The 44th was ordered post haste to Flanders, and my sweet little Dora was too near her time to stumble behind us. I gave her the few shillings I had and promised to wed her on my return, though in my bones I feared I would not. I'd danced with the devil too often, I thought this time a French bullet or cannon or cruel long bayonet would find me."

He took an even bigger swig, wiped his mouth with the back of his hand and watched the fire for a moment or two. "I've told my story of Waterloo a thousand times, it has brought me drink enough to float a man-of-war, but I've never told it as it really happened. I think it's time to tell it now." He gave a pitiful sigh before continuing. "We marched out of Brussels on a wet morning in June and around noon heard a distant rolling like the sea. I'd heard it all over Spain: the damn'd French artillery; the bastards always had more guns than us. We soon met wounded streaming back to Brussels - telling us the French had attacked with superior numbers and that Wellington himself was endeavouring to hold his position until re-enforcements came. When we joined the battle at the cross roads at Quatre Bras in the early afternoon, my heart was full of foreboding. True we'd licked the French enough in Spain but we'd never faced Boney himself. To make matters worse I could see there were very few redcoats around us, and half of them were new recruits. We were lined up alongside Dutch and Belgians, I didn't believe they'd stand beside us for long, some were already running into the nearby woods as we arrived. We were up against that mad red-haired bugger, Marshal Ney, not Napoleon, but we were soon taking a hard pounding from the French cavalry, especially the dreaded Cuirassiers, with their plumed helmets and polished metal breastplates, riding us down on their great black horses. Even so we stood firm in our square, I managing, as was my wont, to find a safe place in the rear rank, and eventually our raking musket fire drove them off. We rested exhausted where we stood, but in the night came rumours of the defeat of our allies, the Prussians, and at first light the Duke ordered us to fall back ten miles to a village called Waterloo. We retreated throughout the day under a torrential downpour, it was as if water was being tumbled out of heaven in tubs, but at least the sodden fields prevented Ney's cavalry attacking our flanks. That night, as we lay dead beat in a muddy field, we heard never ending shouts of '*Vive L'Empereur*', and knew that on the morrow we would be facing Bonaparte himself and his invincible Old Guard. I couldn't face another battle - one we were bound to lose. Even though I was loathe to leave my old comrades, I told myself I'd done my duty and more, and crept away like a cowardly dog in the pitch-black night. I stole back up the road towards Brussels and found a roofless barn in the village of Saint Genese. I spent all that long day cowering under stinking straw, as I heard the cursed French cannon relentlessly pounding our poor lads in their squares, the fearful rat-tat-tat of Napoleon's drummers and the terrible chant: '*L'Empereur recompensera celui qui s'avancera,*'* as his Old Guard moved in for the kill. As darkness fell I was certain that we had suffered a bloody defeat and crept out to offer my surrender to the first Frenchman I met. You can imagine my shock when I beheld red-coated couriers galloping to Brussels triumphantly proclaiming the news of Wellington's great victory. In the chaos and drunkenness it was an easy matter for me to rejoin the remains of the 44th without anyone having noticed my desertion. There was no elation - the field of Waterloo was a sea of bloody bodies, 40,000 men and 10,000 horses, dead, dying or screaming in agony: piled on top of each other where the fight had been fiercest. I wandered down to the village of Rossomme, looted a bottle of fine brandy from the Emperor's abandoned baggage and drank myself to sleep."

He wiped tears from his eyes. "The rest of the story I learnt much later from various soldiers, who met your poor mother in her search for me. Within days the London newspapers were full of reports of the magnificent victory, the heroism of our soldiers, and the terrible suffering of the wounded - most of whom were still lying unattended in the fields. Your mother, like me, couldn't read or write, but she heard all the dreadful stories and had a fearful premonition that her valiant lover, steadfast, as she believed, in his square, was laying among the wounded. She was certain I would die without her care. You had been delivered well and strong, and she resolved to leave you at the workhouse and return for you as soon as I'd recovered from my wounds. How she managed to get to Brussels I'll never know, but she was scouring the gruesome battlefield within a week. By then the 44th had advanced on Paris. It took her days before she finally convinced herself I was not among the wounded, but she was now obsessed in finding me alive. She'd spent the little money she had, and on her long walk to Paris she went back to her old profession. She danced each night in wayside taverns, earning enough for a bed and her supper. When she arrived in Paris all was disorder and confusion. She could not speak a word of French, and it was several days before she met some fellows from the 44th, who told her of my miserable fate. I'd never had much problem with the drink before Waterloo, but after that bloody day I poured it down my throat at every opportunity in a vain effort to forget my shame. So many of my old comrades had died resolute and loyal in their ranks, and I loathed myself for being a bloody coward, a cheat and impostor. One night the colour-sergeant discovered me drunk on sentry duty outside the Louvre: I was sentenced to fifty lashes and three months penal duties in the guard house. When your mother found the regiment at last they told her of my fate. So my faithful little Dora decided to wait for me, and she was soon dancing nightly in the cafes and taverns. As well as us British there were Russians and Prussians aplenty, and one night a bored Russian Prince, Nikolai Dmitrievich Kiselev, I'll never forget the villain's name, decided to enter a low tavern where he spied the most delightful little dancer he'd ever seen. He sat drinking bottle after bottle of champagne, watching her graceful movements and pretty legs, before inviting her back to the palace where he was quartered. He was deeply insulted when a common little dancer had the effrontery to refuse him. The blaggard was used to having anything he wanted and late that night, as my pretty little Dora made her way to her mean lodging along a dark alley in the Marais, some rogues threw a sack over her and brought her to Prince Dmitrievich. She was never seen in Paris again; although some troopers of the Scots Greys told me they spied her, frantically pulling aside the curtains of a black coach heading east. She is in Russia if she is still alive."

"Didn't you ever try to find her? I'd have gone to Hell itself for such a woman." Warnie had been listening. His ruddy cheeks were wet with tears.

My father shook his head. "How would I find her in that savage land? If by some miracle I did what power would I have against a Prince? Besides, you know now I am a worthless coward." He threw back his head and emptied the remains of the flagon down his throat.

I couldn't speak. A terrible yearning filled my heart. I'd found my father and now knew my mother's fate: how carefree I'd been before I had knowledge of either. I remembered Fagin's advice: "Only care for number one." Not for the first time, I believed he was right.

15. The District Magistrate and The Settlers from Yarmouth

I cannot remember how many days we continued south along what is now known as the Great Dividing Ridge, the lush grasslands gradually giving way to snowy mountains and icy cold lakes. Even I could sense the beauty around us. Finally, one crisp morning, we caught a glimpse of a faraway sea and decided we'd travelled far enough. We followed a serene river down through heavily forested ranges into fertile flats that stretched eastwards towards the distant ocean. We passed small farms whose rich and fertile pastures overflowed with cattle and sheep, crops of wheat and orchards heavy with fruit. The farmhouses themselves were little better than huts, but the bare-footed children who ran through the fields to watch us pass, were as hale and hearty as you could wish to find in the grandest of mansions. Then, after an abrupt bend, the river mingled at last with the sea, into which the evening sun was falling like a flaming ball. We rode towards a collection of wooden buildings clustered around a solitary pier from which the British flag flew. A pair of small fishing smacks was pulled up onto the shingle of the beach, where a rough-looking man was mending a net.

"Beg yer pardon, sir," I enquired as we drew nearer, "what would be the name of this fair place?"

He looked up and regarded us with suspicion. "Why, this be Port Middlebay, any fool knows that."

Port Middlebay - I knew I'd heard of that place before but couldn't remember when, until I noticed a familiar figure coming out of a large hut by the pier. Although his face was partly hidden by a straw hat with a very low crown, I recognised at once the upright stance, a shirt collar of formidable dimensions, and the manner in which he nodded his head as he perused us through a mariner's telescope. He was accompanied by a thin and faded lady, holding a young child by the hand; two elder children of equal size and opposite sex, who I rightly assumed were twins; a youth a few years older than myself and a good-looking young lady, who I supposed was his sister.

I took off my hat and waved it above my head, crying: "Good evening, Mr Micawber,"

He was quite taken aback and perused me further before exclaiming: "Good God, the valiant little keeper of the wicket." He swept off own his hat in greeting, revealing his sun-burnt, egg-like head. "It is indeed a meeting which is calculated to impress the mind with a sense of the instability and uncertainty of all human..." he waved his hand expansively as he sought to express his sublime sentiments, but on this occasion he could not quite reach the heights he aspired to. "In short, it is a most extraordinary meeting. What brings you and your fellow travellers to this salubrious habitation?" Without waiting for a reply he turned to the faded lady: "Emma my dear, take our eldest daughter and prepare refreshment and hospitality for these valiant souls, who suffered one of the most perfidious miscarriages of injustice ever to be witnessed upon the field of sporting conflict." He then addressed the youth, who was waiting in keen anticipation, with the sleeves of his shirt loosely turned back at the wrists, ready to lend a hand in any direction, "Wilkins, my son, I would command thee to kill the fatted calf, if we had one: nevertheless pluck the partridge and light a fire beneath the grid-iron." He finally surveyed the smaller members of his family who were now dancing around him in joyous anticipation: "Children, lay the board with our finest silver and heat the water for the punch." They disappeared into the hut with squeals of delight. He passed his hand complacently over his head with an air of exceeding satisfaction, before bending low and offering his open door with a generous sweep of his arm: "Enter our hearth and home, where I will prepare a generous quantity of that beverage which is peculiarly associated in our minds with the Roast Beef of Old England."

Without more ado he swept us past a brass plate engraved, *'Mrs Micawber's Boarding Establishment for Young Ladies'* into his humble abode, where cooking pots were bubbling contentedly over a cheerful fire. The furniture consisted of nothing but a plain wooden table, two chairs, a bench and a dresser containing the minimum of chipped crockery and a collection of well-used books. On one wall was hung a coloured print of good old St Paul's. Even though its famous dome was a delicate shade of pink, it nevertheless aroused a ripple of homesickness which ran through my exiled breast.

Mr Micawber swept his hand over his simple domain: "The luxuries of the old country," he said, with intense satisfaction in their renouncement, "we have abandoned. The denizens of the Bush cannot expect, at present, to participate in the refinements of the Motherland, but in this distant outpost I have been fully understood and appreciated for the first time. England gave me birth but not employment, but here there are openings for a man who conducts himself well and is industrious." This observation failed to elicit much interest from my father, though a sparkle seemed to return momentarily to Warnie's eye. "I prophesy," Micawber continued, clearing his throat in a magnificent way, "that within a few years this little habitation will be a beacon of industry and learning. My dear wife herself stands ready with her scholastic establishment." Mrs Micawber turned and nodded graciously with a healthy-looking fish in her hand. Her husband motioned us to sit on the bench whilst he began peeling lemons with his long clasp knife, which he occasionally wiped, not wholly without ostentation, on the sleeve of his Guernsey shirt. Mrs Micawber and her children busied themselves in preparation of a feast, whilst Micawber threw the lemons into a steaming pot to which he liberally added two bottles of rum and large spoonfuls of sugar.

Private Skinner watched and sniffed in keen anticipation and appeared to have thrown off his melancholy at last: "I've haven't smelt a decent punch since I left old England."

Micawber appeared to notice him for the first time: "My dear sir, I do not think I have had the honour..."

"Private Robert Skinner of the 44th," he thrust out his hand, "I fought at Waterloo, you know."

"Indeed it is an honour to welcome such a hero under my humble roof. To quote the immortal Shakespeare: *You have done well by land, and I by water.*" Micawber began to ladle the steaming liquid into a series of villainous little tin pots. "I had the privilege of serving as an officer of Marines in the mighty conflict at Cape Trafalgar under the immortal Admiral himself." The mention of the word officer infused a slight air of discomfort in the private soldier, but he quickly relaxed as he began disposing of Micawber's potent brew.

As Mrs Micawber gutted the fish and Miss Micawber sliced a large sausage, and Wilkins Junior plucked the final feathers from some sort of fowl, and the three youngest Micawbers clustered around on the floor, I told their father our long and tragic story. He listened with rapt attention, only interrupting when he became too moved or excited, with sighs of sorrow and gasps of excitement; but when I described the part played by Barnet Levey he could restrain himself no longer.

"He is indeed a usurer and a rogue, but there are far greater villains in the City of London. I would have walked the earth like a vagabond, floated like a straw on the surface of the deep without him."

"But I would never have deserted you, Wilkins," exclaimed the good lady of the house, chopping the head off the now fully mutilated piscatorial vertebrate.

"Emma, my angel!" cried her husband, running to her and taking her into his arms, "I am perfectly aware of it." He appeared to be deeply affected by her devotion and took two long gulps of steaming punch before continuing: "All my life I had been pursued by creditors, they followed me even here like ravenous leeches, and it was the aforesaid member of the Israelites who finally freed me of their chains and found me this humble position." He nodded his head appreciatively as he swept his gaze around his home and family. "I had sailed up to Sydney on the packet ship, with the final payment of the debt I owed him, on the first day of your valiant contest. I officiated the following morning at the aforesaid Levey's request, and was honoured and delighted to assist you in the victory he required and you fully deserved." He took out a large yellow handkerchief and vigorously wiped his eyes before loudly blowing his nose. "But alas the odds changed unexpectedly and Levy could not resist the siren call of pecuniary profit. I regret that I could not do more. I will do all I can to make amends."

"We still have his gold to buy land; I reckon he owes us that. What do you advise we do?" I asked.

Micawber sprawled back in his chair, thrust his hands deep into his pockets and raised his eyebrows whilst he ruminated: "Any warrant of land I assign is sent on the packet to Sydney for confirmation. Any names I put down which are not on the official list will attract suspicion. My advice would be to lay low for a while until matters simmer down. '*Now is not the day or the hour,*' but the foul tyrant Darling will not continue in office long. Nearby lives an old and loyal friend, who is, if you will excuse the simile, as good as gold and as true as steel. Due to his heartfelt generosity, his farm is the abode of a preponderance of the gentler sex, which though they add greatly to the beauty and gentility of the property, leave too much heavy toil even for his strong and willing back. I have no doubt he will be happy and relieved to offer you sanctuary and employment."

I almost wept with the relief and happiness at the prospect of a potential saviour. Micawber then led us outside to demonstrate a new method of cooking which he claimed to be ideally appropriate to the Australian climate. Hot embers were glowing beneath a large grid-iron upon which Micawber tossed the dismembered fowl, filleted fish and slices of sausage, which he covered with pepper, mustard, salt and cayenne. He then turned them over again and again with a fork as they sputtered and blazed, at the same time heating a quantity of spicy mushroom ketchup in a saucepan. We spent a merry and convivial evening feasting on the appetising result, together with an apple pudding with lashings of cream from Miss Micawber's very contented cow. After which Mr Micawber entertained us with renditions of some well-known strains of '*The Immortal Excise Man nurtured beyond the Tweed*', as he described his favourite poet, Burns. Then his son, Wilkins Junior, sang several sentimental ballads in a truly affecting tone, causing Mrs Micawber and her daughters to weep copiously. I astounded the gathering with several of my card tricks and Private Skinner, after Micawber had concocted an even more potent second jug of punch, contributed to the festivities by lustily singing *The British Grenadiers* and *Over the Hills and Far Away.*

Only Warnie remained sad and distant in his thoughts.

Early next morning, after bestowing such tender farewells upon his wife and his children that you'd have thought he was departing to fight another Trafalgar, Mr Micawber mounted his mule, with the all determination of a steeplechaser, and bade us follow. He sang cheerfully for a while about '*bonny banks and braes*' as we rode through the rich pastures by the river, but soon fell silent as we entered the Bush, complaining his throat was becoming as harsh and arid as the land itself. After an hour or so, without sight of a single habitation, he led us into a canyon which opened into a hidden valley where, among majestic trees, stood a solitary house and outbuildings. An old woman sat knitting on a stool outside the portal with poultry running about her feet. A hale, grey-haired man, ruddy and strong in his old age, was ploughing one of the adjacent stony fields, whilst a slight young woman was watering sheep and cattle in another.

"Behold the hearth and home of Daniel Peggotty, a truer and nobler friend no man could ever wish to have," proclaimed Micawber proudly and loudly.

The old man looked up from his toil and his face immediately shone with uncommon satisfaction. I thought him as handsome an old man as ever I'd seen. He laughed with all his might as he ran towards us holding out his rough hands wide open: "Why Lord love my heart alive, if it ain't a treat to see you, Wilkins my dear old friend." He then bowed to we three strangers, chuckling and tucking in the ends of his neckerchief at his breast: "Glad to see you genl 'men. You're welcome indeed. You'll find us rough, but you'll find us ready." He shook our hands vigorously whilst he called back to the watching women: "Em'ly, and Gummidge, old dear, prepare vitals for these genl' men."

At that moment a piano struck up from inside the house. I recognised it immediately as a soft, uplifting tune Mrs Napier had often played in the roughest nights at sea. I now know it be Beethoven's Sonata No 20 in G-major. (Heard Arabella Goddard play it once at a concert in the Crystal Palace - though not nearly as delicately.) Warnie froze. His face then ran through an abundance of emotions before he jumped from his saddle and made for the door. Daniel Peggotty went to speak but I hushed him with a finger to my lips - I was as much bemused as Warnie. I slid off Nancy's back and followed him into the house. In my mind's eye, I can still see the inside of that simple dwelling as if it were yesterday. Everything was beautifully clean and as tidy as possible; the very floor boards gleamed with polish. There was an immense cupboard by the door, a long table, a Dutch clock, a shining black oven with a pot of mouth-watering stew steaming upon it, and a chest of drawers, on which rested a quantity of blue cups and saucers and a tea tray with a painting on it of a lady with a parasol, taking a walk with a military-looking child who was trundling a hoop. The tray was kept from tumbling down and smashing the crockery by a large black bible. On one wall there were a pair of coloured pictures, framed and glazed, which I later learnt were of Abraham in red going to sacrifice Isaac in blue, and Daniel in yellow cast into a den of green lions. On another wall was a painting of a small ship with a brass plate stating that it was *The Sarah Jane, Built at Sunderland*. But above all I can still see and hear the piano, which was set by an open window, over-looking the bright pasture. It wasn't a gleaming polished one, but distinctly worn and battered, but it sounded non-the-less sweet for that. Seated at the piano with her back to us, her fingers floating delicately over the keys was a young woman. Although she was silhouetted against the light I could discern that her hair was the same colour as Mrs Napier's and pinned up in the identical manner; her dress looked familiar, her figure was lithe and still youthful.

"Leticia!" Warnie rasped in a low voice.

She didn't hear him but continued playing, the music becoming more and more defiant and exquisite - even to my ears. Warnie, completely overwhelmed, walked hesitantly towards her. Daniel and the others were now watching from the door in absolute bemusement. Warnie stood stock-still directly behind her: as if he was frightened to touch her in case she vanished into thin air like a fairy. She began to play softer, gentler, as if expressing infinite love and sorrow. Completely entranced by the music, Warnie hesitantly raised his hand and rested it tenderly on her shoulder. The keys struck discordantly: there was a startled cry and a fair-complexioned young woman spun around in alarm.

Warnie's apple cheeks crumpled in disappointment, "Please forgive me," he mumbled, "I thought you were someone else." The young woman stared at him fearfully, and searched his face, as if he were indeed someone she'd once known, before turning timidly away.

"Why, Lord love my heart alive, that's our Martha," exclaimed Daniel Peggotty, his honest eyes fired up and sparkling as if their depths were stirred by something bright, "you've certainly taken the wind out of her. Gentl'men," he continued, "we're truly honoured by your company. Tis not often we see such fine gentl'men here. Let us offer you some refreshment; my friend Micawber here, says you have a tale to tell."

The old lady, who was not as I had presumed Peggotty's wife, but the impoverished widow of an old friend, brewed us a kettle of tea, to the inordinate disillusionment of Private Skinner who'd been expecting something a good deal stronger. We were soon all sitting around the long table, drinking tea like gentlefolk from the blue cups, whilst Micawber took it upon himself to narrate, in his inimitable fashion, a brief history of our predicaments. Emily, the other young woman, had a worn quality about her. She had sorrowful blue eyes, a delicate face, a pretty head, which she leant a little down as she listened; Martha, still throwing anxious glances at Warnie, was nevertheless wide-eyed with pity; Mrs Gummidge, for that was the old lady's name, whimpered fretfully and wiped her eyes with an old black silk handkerchief; whilst Daniel Peggotty drank in every word with a patient gravity stamped on his face. When Micawber finally completed his dissertation by violently blowing his nose, Daniel Peggotty, gave the table such a mighty thwack with his strong right hand that it almost split in two. He rose to feet, so moved that he did not know what to say or do, except to shake our hands, over and over again. First my father, then Warnie, and then with me, finally exclaiming, "Mates, I'll be Gormed if I let you wander any further. I'm as rough as a Sea Porkypine, but my heart is truly touched by your suffering. My house ain't much to see, but it's hearty at your service."

So began another happy interlude in my long and varied life. We lived with these good people for more than a year, labouring under the burning sun, breaking the stubborn earth with pickaxe and plough, building fences, digging ditches and splitting stone. I helped the gentle Emily bring her feeble young creatures into the world and held her hand, whenever Daniel slaughtered a pig or sheep. Daniel had been a Norfolk fisherman with his brother, Emily's father, and Mrs Gummidge's husband, both of whom, according to Daniel, had been 'drowned dead.' Emily was the delight of Daniel's life. He'd brought her up as his own child, but lost her when she ran off with a worthless rake. Daniel spent several years looking for her before he eventually found her, broken-hearted and abandoned, and brought her home. Because she was then considered a fallen woman, he'd decided to start life afresh at this far end of the world, where no reproach could reach her. Because of her experience, Emily seemed to have no interest in men - something had been drained out of her. Even though I was now fourteen years old and sex was forever on my mind, there was something about Emily that doused my lust.

I could see that Martha was different. She'd been Emily's close friend at school but had somehow drifted into Nance's old game. Daniel had found her one night in London, on the cold banks of the Thames, about to throw herself in and, out of the pure goodness of his heart, had brought her out to Australia as well. She still bore the signs of her trade upon her and became fretful and suspicious whenever men were around, but I often caught her gazing at the still weak Warnie with a soft look in her eye. Daniel had also taken poor old Mrs Gummidge into his care, but she didn't always make herself as agreeable as she might be expected to under the circumstances, especially on those occasions when she caught me spying on Martha taking a bath.

Every week or so we were visited by Micawber, sometimes bringing us news from Sydney and the world in general, that he, in turn, had received from the packet ship or the occasional whalers and sealers that put in to his humble port. Warnie had been anxious about the fate of the companions he'd left behind in that Brisbane hell-hole, and was mightily relieved to hear that Attenborough had taken over the camp and had established a gentler regime. Following the death of Bamber, and knowing his value and worth, he'd even freed Bradman of his chains and installed him as his chief overseer. I knew then that there was some justice in the world after all.

My father gradually recovered his strength, not that he had much strength to recover. To my surprise the old rogue began to take a fancy to the 'lone lorn creetur,' as Mrs Gummidge described herself. He seemed oblivious of her miserable nature, especially after he'd been dipping into Daniel's supply of grog. One pleasant evening he came up to her as she knitted in her usual place on her stool. "Well my dear," he said, sitting on the ground beside her, "and how are you?" She sniffed at the fumes on his breath and shook her head despondently over her knitting. "What's amiss?" he asked with a clap of his hands. "Cheer up, old girl." She gave him a very depreciating look and took out her black silk handkerchief and wiped her eyes, then wiped them again. "What's amiss?" he repeated.

"You've been at the grog again, ain't you?" She returned.

"Why, yes. I had a little sip to take the dust from my throat at the end of the day," he smiled winningly.

"Sorry I should drive you to it," she said acidly, clicking her needles like a pair of Chinese chop sticks.

"Drive, I don't need no driving," he laughed, "I've always been ready for a drink."

"Very ready," said Mrs Gummidge, shaking her head and wiping her eyes again. "Yes, yes, very ready. I'm sorry it should be along of me that you're so ready."

"Along of you? It ain't along of you!" protested Private Skinner." Don't you believe a bit of it." Maybe it was the grog that befuddled my father's sensibilities, but without more ado he planted a smacking wet kiss upon her withered cheek. She screamed as if she'd been bitten by a snake and seizing the adjacent milk pail, laid it over Private Skinner's head, again and again, until the hero of Waterloo sung out for help and had to be rescued by the combined efforts of Daniel and myself. His ardour cooled somewhat after that. Most evenings he would sit in the shade of a big Beech tree, which grew by the little creek that flowed through the farm, smoking his pipe and drinking his rum, telling me stories of his battles and campaigns, and I pretended to believe them.

Warnie's recovery was slower. He'd been broken inside as well as out. Although he threw himself into his labours on the land, he still remained downcast and reticent. At meal times he never raised his eyes from his plate, ignoring Emily as she served him his food, though I sometimes caught him stealing a sidelong glance at Martha. One day, after we'd been there a month or so, Warnie was digging up the obstinate root of a gum tree in the field behind the house. It was a blazing hot day, as only Australian blazing hot days can be, and he'd taken off his shirt. Martha, seeing him labour, left off playing her piano and came from the house with a pitcher of water. It was then that she saw the weals and furrows on his back for the first time. She gasped and only just managed to prevent herself from crying out in horror.

"How could any man inflict such suffering to another? she asked.

Warnie took the pitcher and drank gratefully. "The world is full of such men," he said gently, wiping his mouth with the back of his hand, "it is good not to hear their voices. Only those of the singing birds and your piano." Their eyes met and he gave a rare smile.

She lowered her eyes immediately, "My soul bears more terrible scars than your poor back. I have walked the streets of London and done such things as even now I dread to think on. Before dear Daniel found me, I thought I was only fit for the filthy Thames - it springs clear and clean in the country, but the city pollutes it, as it did me."

He gently put his hand under her chin and raised her head, "We will heal together."

I spent my first and only Christmas with my father, although he was hardly aware of it, having imbibed prodigious quantities of Daniel's grog. Warnie had shot a crane with the old musket Peggotty kept in the cupboard by the door, and we pretended it was an English goose. Mrs Gummidge cooked it and a plum pudding, whilst Martha played carols and Emily sang. The remembrance of the child born in a stable made me in turn think of my own pitiful nativity and the agony of my poor mother leaving her child in the hope of saving its father. I wondered if she'd ever spent a merry Christmas. I prayed a rare prayer that she had.

The months and seasons passed. In spite of my pleasant life at Peggotty's farm, I began to miss dirty, stinking, old London something dreadful. Micawber continued to supply us with the latest news: more settlers were arriving in the environs of Port Middlebay; one of the huts by the pier had become a rough tavern and general store, and there were even a couple of pupils attending Mrs Micawber's school. Sometimes he brought old newspapers from England, which I found engrossing, especially the legal notices and reports of the trials at the Old Bailey. I remembered that bright young man, Charles Dickens, who took down my defiance in shorthand, and wondered if some of them came from his pen.

One morning in an edition of the Times, more than two years old, I read how a certain Mr Brownlow, of Craven Street, London, was endeavouring to establish the claim of an illegitimate boy, known as Oliver Twist, to the fortune of his natural father, Edwin Leeford, and of the strange proviso that the boy's inheritance would be forfeited and go to his elder half-brother, if the boy fell into crime or dissolution. You could have knocked me down with a feather. Suddenly the memory of that night in London, almost four years past, became crystal clear. It all came back at once: I was asleep in the downstairs front room with Charley and the other boys when I was awakened by the sound of the front door slamming up above. That was unusual: Fagin always closed it softly. Then a sneering voice said, "Look sharp with the light or I shall knock my brains out against something in this confounded hole." I heard someone creeping down the stairs and a match struck to light a candle. Through my half-closed eyes I saw Fagin's ugly old head in the flickering light, peering in to check we were all asleep. The crafty villain closed the door gently, locked it and went back up the stairs. I heard whispers and then footsteps go up to the top of the house.

I stole out of bed, turned the lock with my trusty bent nail, and crept up two flights to where the candle was glimmering on the floor by an open door: there were holes in the shutters of that room and Fagin was always loathe to show lights to our neighbours. They talked in whispers, I could hardly hear but it seemed that the stranger was berating Fagin. I heard him say: *"I tell you again it was badly planned. Why not have kept him here among the rest, and made a sneaking, snivelling pickpocket of him at once? Haven't you done it, with other boys, scores of times? Couldn't you have got him convicted and sent safely out of the kingdom; perhaps for life?"*

I heard no more because at that moment Nance came creeping up behind me - she'd let herself in with her own bent nail - and urgently gestured me to go back to bed. I'd forgotten all about it, but now I understood everything: *sneaking, snivelling pickpocket*! The voice had belonged to that vile rogue Monks, or Leeford to give him his real name and Oliver Twist must be his younger brother. Monks, or Leeford, had been paying Fagin to lead dear little Nolly astray so that he could inherit the entirety of his father's fortune. He was an even bigger villain than I'd taken him for. I tore out the article and folded it carefully in my pocket.

Towards the end of that year, it must have been 1830; Micawber appeared on his mule with a black crepe scarf tied around his battered top hat. He looked down and shook his head sorrowfully before covering his face with his pocket handkerchief, which had more snuff on it that he was aware of. His subsequent sneeze was so violent that it almost blew him from his saddle. "The blossom is blighted, leaf is withered," he intoned with exceeding gravity, once he'd recovered himself. "Our sovereign, King George, the Fourth of that name, is dead. Take him for all in all, we shall not, in short, make the acquaintance, probably, of anybody else, possessing, at his time of life, the same legs for gaiters and eyes to read the same description of print without spectacles." After he had dismounted and partaken of a brimming glass of rum to assuage his grief, he informed us that George's brother William, or Silly Billy, as he was more popularly named, was now our monarch. Micawber was certain that things would turn up for the better in the new reign.

Then one morning, in March 1831, Micawber came again with the news that Wellington's government had fallen and Lord Grey and the Whigs were now in power: Darling was being recalled and the more liberal Sir Richard Bourke* was to be appointed Governor. Pardons would surely follow. Everything appeared to be turning out well, especially as Micawber added that new land grants had just been released in the distant bush, and suggested that Peggotty should buy a few thousand acres in his name on behalf of Warnie, my father and myself.

It seemed an excellent stratagem and the following day Peggotty and Warnie rode north to inspect the possibilities of the new territory, leaving me and my old Dad to tend the farm. I must admit I'd begun to feel restless, having been confined to the limits of the property for more than a year, and heartily wished I could've gone with them. Peggotty expected to be away four days at least and was fretful at leaving the women, especially Emily, but Private Skinner assured him that he'd guard them with his life.

At around midday on the third day following their departure, as I was endeavouring, somewhat unsuccessfully, to induce a pair of Peggotty's placid cocks to fight by tickling their arse-holes with straw, I spied two red-coated figures riding into the distant mouth of the valley. I blinked and rubbed my eyes and checked again before I scudded into the house by the back door at a more than rapid pace. I found my father smoking his pipe, listening to some country tunes that Martha was playing. Mrs Gummidge was darning socks and Emily was cutting up vegetables for a stew. It broke my heart to disrupt so homely a scene.

"Plummy and Slam! Up on your pins old fellow! Burn my body if the bloody traps ain't coming!" Private Skinner turned a greenish colour and was in the back room in an instant, cowering under Mrs Gummidge's bed. I, after beseeching the women to stand firm and get rid of the bastards double sharp, dived into the large cupboard by the door, where I took deep breaths and tried to still my frantic heart. I peeped through a chink and watched Mrs Gummidge and Emily attempt to compose themselves, whilst Martha began to play a peaceful lullaby with trembling hands.

All too quickly I heard the harsh rattle of harness outside and then an ominous shadow fell across the sparkling floor boards from the open door.

Martha looked up from the keys and stopped playing. Emily shrieked with fright, but Mrs Gummidge, playing deaf, continued to conscientiously darn a particularly hole-ridden sock of my father's.

"Where are yer men?" demanded a harsh voice.

I knew the voice but couldn't quite place it.

"Hunting," Martha replied evenly. "Why are you here? We've done nothing wrong."

"Don't fret yer pretty eyelids. We're just checking there's been no bolters round here." A second shadow appeared in the doorway. "How about a drink? I've a terrible thirst; we've had a long ride," said the first voice, which was becoming increasingly familiar. The two shadows moved into the house and the wide arse of Sergeant Hodson waddled past my hiding place and plonked itself heavily on Daniel's big chair at the table. A slighter figure followed him and sat opposite. He had a thin rat-like face.

"Give us some rum," Hodson demanded, laying his shako upon the table and wiping his sweaty brow.

Martha hastily got up from her piano and fetched a bottle from the dresser. Hodson studied her closely as she poured out two cups. "I've seen you somewhere. You been in Sydney of late?" Martha shook her head, placed the bottle on the table and stole back to the dresser.

"Pity. We could do with a few good-looking bints. What about a bit of grub?" Martha hurried over to the larder and took out a loaf of bread and butter and cheese. She placed them with pewter plates and knives upon the table. Hodson cut himself a wedge of cheese and stuffed it in his great ugly mouth. "You play that piano a treat. Give us something a bit more livelily." Martha still averting her eyes, crept back to her piano where after a moment's consideration, she began to play an extremely jolly Irish jig. Hodson poured himself another glass of grog with one hand whilst beating on the table in time with the other. "That's more like it."

Rat Face hadn't yet spoken. He too, availed himself of more grog before he turned towards Emily and smiled. He'd hardly any teeth and not a single white one. "What about a little dance, sweetheart?"

Emily gasped with fright and backed away into the furthest corner. Rat Face got up and stole menacingly after her. "No, please! I can't dance," she implored. But he grabbed her by the wrist and put his grubby hand around her tiny waist.

Martha stopped playing. "Leave her alone, I beg you! She's too delicate."

"Delicate?" Hodson laughed. "What in the Devil's name does delicate mean?" He got up and walked menacingly over to the piano. "You're not delicate are yer? I've always been able to smell a whore and you're a fuckin' whore as sure as I'm a soldier." He took another swig of grog and eyed her maliciously. "I remember where I saw yer now. I've got a bloody good memory. There was an establishment in Wapping where we soldiers used to go when we were in the Tower. You used to play the piano there too, didn't yer? Only there you did it with yer tits hanging out and with a private's hand up yer skirt."

Emily watched, frozen with terror whilst Rat Face leered lasciviously.

"Perhaps we'd better give those tits another airing. I haven't seen a nice pair of tits since I crossed the Equator." With that Hodson grabbed Martha's dress at the throat and ripped off the bodice.

She screamed as her white breast tumbled out. "Please! I beg you! I have finished with that life!"

"A whore will always be a whore!" the brute snarled, holding her by the wrist with one hairy hand and lifting up her skirt with the other. "I paid over the odds for you last time. I'll have this one for free!"

Rat Face had now locked Emily in his arms and was plunging his dirty face into her pretty neck. I was desperately racking my wits as to what to do, but at that very moment Mrs Gummidge, who'd still been feigning to assiduously darn her sock, rose from her stool, with more speed than I'd thought possible, picked up the sharp knife Emily had been using on the vegetables, and sank it, with unbelievable force, deep between Rat Face's shoulder blades. He screamed in anguish and astonishment as Hodson spun round.

"Damn you! You murderous old bitch!" Hodson snarled, hurling Martha aside. He stormed across the room, kicking aside Peggotty's heavy chair, which fell against the door of my cupboard, and knocked Mrs Gummidge to the floor with a ferocious blow with the back of his hand. He hauled her up, like an old sack of rags, to administer further violence, just as Private Skinner tore out of the back room and threw himself onto the bully's huge back. I watched, half frozen in terror, as Hodson shook my father off as if he were a fly. The little old fellow hit the wall and slid to the floor. Hodson snarled even more viciously and proceeded to furiously lay into my father with his thick boots. In an instant my father's face became a mass of blood. All my fear vanished. My only thought was to stop the brute killing my poor father. I could hear ominous sounding cracks whenever those steel-capped boots struck his ribs or stamped on his chest. I pushed and kicked frantically against the cupboard door, straining to get out and fling myself upon that murderous brute's back, but it was firmly wedged by the fallen chair. Meanwhile Rat Face was spewing out his life blood on the floor, Emily and Martha were clinging to each other in fright, and Mrs Gummidge was lying still and silent beside her teeth. It was only then that I felt Peggotty's old musket, standing hard and cold in the cupboard beside me, where Warnie kept it primed and ready for any game that should pass by. I strained against the door yet again. It edged open an inch. I took up the musket. It was heavy and unwieldy but I managed to push the muzzle through the small crack so that it was pointing towards Hodson's back. I put my finger around the trigger, closed my eyes, and fired. There was a mighty blast but Hodson squealed louder than the pig we'd slaughtered the previous week. I opened my eyes and saw that the shot had caught him in the base of the spine. His backbone was shot through. His dirty hands flew frenziedly and helplessly to the dark patch that was spreading rapidly like water spilt from a bucket. He turned round in his agony, kicking the chair aside. The cupboard door swung open and for the briefest moment he recognised me with an astonished look upon his ugly face. Then he tottered around, like a puppet whose strings had been cut, before crumpling on the boards of Mrs Gummidge's polished floor.

Three men were dying in what a few minutes before had been such a peaceful home. Hodson and Rat Face screamed and gurgled and kicked, but the hero of Waterloo lay still and silent. I lift up his poor, old, battered head and wiped the blood from his eyes. He opened them, saw me and gave a rueful smile. "It looks as though we won't have that farm together after all, Jack." He coughed up blood before enquiring, "You wouldn't have a spot drink to give me afore I go?" I looked towards Martha, who'd pulled her torn dress back into place. She went round Hodson's writhing body to the table and poured a cup of grog which she put into my proffered hand. I lifted it gently to my father's swollen lips. He drank and winced in pain, as the liquid passed through his ruptured innards. "Thankee, son. I'm sorry we had so little time together. Forgive me for not being a better man."

"I wouldn't have wanted any other father but you," I answered tearfully.

"At least I've got you off my conscience now. I can see Jack that you're more than able to take care of yourself - better than I've ever been able to, fool that I've always been." He held my hand and squeezed it tightly as he coughed up more blood mixed with rum. Emily was now tending Mrs Gummidge, but Martha was still standing fretfully above us. She handed me her white lace handkerchief which rapidly turned red as I held it before my father's mouth. The spasm passed and he looked at me again before pulling the old playbill from his pocket: "If by the faintest of chance your mother is still alive, and if by the one chance in a hundred million you ever find her, tell her I loved her and beg her to forgive me, coward that I am."

"You are the bravest of men. You are a hero. You sacrificed your life protecting us," Martha said softly.

The old rogue looked up at her and winked and died.

Warnie and Peggotty returned that evening to find the three dead men. As I told the story, Peggotty's face and lips went quite white. When I'd finished, he wrapped his strong arms around Emily's slender body and said in a tremulous voice: "Whoever killed these men, I bless them for saving my child." Warnie's only concern was that no blame should fall upon Peggotty and the women. Whilst Peggotty comforted them and my dead father lay stiff on Mrs Gummidge's bed, Warnie and I stripped the two soldiers and burnt their uniforms and equipment on a great fire. I, naturally, had retrieved my bag with the Yankee dollars and a good deal more from Hodson's pouch during the afternoon. This time, unlike my attempt to poison Deplidge, I had no doubt I'd killed a man; but I felt no remorse, the cruel bastard had kicked my poor old father to death. Warnie resolved that the best course would be to bury the naked bodies deep in the outback, giving the impression, if they were ever found that like Napier, they'd been killed by local blacks. We therefore wrapped their carcasses in blankets, tied them to the backs of their horses, and rode north throughout the night. We buried them in thick bush, covered the grave with stones and used eucalyptus branches to wipe away all traces of our tracks. The horses were poor jades with no distinguishable marks, but Warnie said it was too dangerous to keep them, and reluctantly decided they had to be shot. The dingoes and kites would soon pick their bones clean. I felt far more remorse at the untimely death of those poor creatures than I have for many a man.

When we approached the farm late in the afternoon we spied Micawber's mule tethered outside and a freshly-dug open grave under the big beech tree by the creek. Micawber had come to warn us of the arrival of a detachment of soldiers in Port Middleton, but had stayed to oversee my father's burial. Mrs Gummidge, much affected by Private Skinner's demise, had dressed him in what remained of his uniform, and after we'd all stood around him, whilst Micawber took care of the religious consolation by intoning a solemn prayer, the old soldier was borne to his rest on the shoulders of Warnie and Peggotty. Micawber walked behind the corse, his large head bowed down like a horse, reciting a heartfelt admixture of his two favourite poets:

"In his narrow cell forever laid
The rude forefather of the outback sleeps.
Should auld acquaintance be forgot
And never brought to mind
We'll take a cup of kindness yet
For this village Cromwell

Guiltless of his country's blood."

I followed, doing my best not to blab, and the three weeping women brought up the rear. I comforted myself with the thought that my father would rest among these good people. All he had bequeathed me was the old playbill with my mother's name upon it. But that was enough. That night at his wake, Martha played soft soothing music and Emily attended to Mrs Gummidge's gums; whilst we men decided what course to take. It would only be a matter of days before there would be a thorough search for the two missing soldiers, and Warnie believed we would undoubtedly be considered guilty and hung on the spot if we were found. He therefore proposed that in the morning, he and I went as far away as possible: start a farm hundreds of miles north in the far distant outback and trust that in time things would be forgotten. I didn't fancy this at all. Much as I loved Warnie I couldn't contemplate spending my life with him as my soul companion. Now that my father was dead I had no reason or desire to remain in Australia - London was calling me. I was now almost 15 and had an ever growing itch to become better acquainted with the more exotic parts of the female. I reasoned that the slaver's dollars I'd retrieved from Hodson would be more than enough for Peggotty to buy Warnie a grant of land. I could then keep the rest of the bastard's money for myself, and if I gave Levey back his purse it might persuade him to vouch for me again. Then if Crowe returned with my pardon, I could perhaps work my way back to England. The problem would be Leeford - if he were still around. There were a lot of 'ifs' but I decided it was a gamble worth playing.

Warnie looked surprised and hurt when I informed him of my intentions. "It'll be lonely without you, little mate," was all that he could find to say.

There was an awkward silence. Martha had stopped playing. She had raised her eyes from her piano and was looking at Warnie with tender affection.

"I'll go with you,"

Warnie's look was equally tender. "I couldn't ask you to do that," he replied in a low voice. "It will be a solitary life. Hundreds of miles away from any voices but mine and the singing birds."

"I want to go with all my heart," she almost whispered, "besides my piano will break the silence."

Early next morning, after we'd loaded the cart with the piano, tools, and all the spare farm implements, Micawber, in his office of District Magistrate, married Warnie and Martha under the great beech beside Private Skinner. The rest of us then stood and waved as the man and his wife headed north, with a couple of cows and a pair of sheep trailing behind and a sow, big with litter, in the cart. I almost changed my mind and ran after: Warnie had been my true friend ever since that first terrible night on the hulk. I didn't want to lose him as well as my father, but an insatiable desire for life was burning in me and I had to follow that desire.

16. Back To Sydney

After taking tearful farewells of Peggotty and the women: Mrs Gummidge promising to attend to my father's grave every remaining day of her life, I accompanied Micawber back to Port Middleton. The packet was due that evening and I was determined to be on it. Micawber, the eternal optimist, had no doubt that things would turn out well, and resolved that I would travel with papers declaring myself to be his eldest son, Wilkins Micawber Junior. As well as magistrate he was also the official customs officer and landing waiter, and had no doubt he could get me safely aboard. After more than a year in semi-isolation, the bustle of the small conurbation of Port Middleton came as a shock, especially the sight of red-coated soldiers. I knew from the green facings on their tunics they were from Hodson's Regiment, the 39th, some of whom I may have well encountered on the Parramatta Road. I kept my head down in case any should recognise me. Throughout the rest of the day I remained in Micawber's house with his wife and family until the *Henrietta* came in from Hobart on the evening tide. Young Wilkins Micawber, who would be taking over the duties Warnie and I had shared on the farm, made me a gift of his Sunday clothes, much turned up at the ankles and sleeves. In return I presented him with my faithful little Nancy, whom he promised to cherish whilst there was breath in his body, and for several happy hours young Wilkins rode proudly around the field at the back of the Micawber residence, displaying his equestrian skills to his appreciative siblings. The eldest Miss Micawber had come on apace since I'd seen her last. She'd a knowing look in her eye, and I was a little frustrated when her father sonorously announced that the packet was at last in sight. I made tearful farewells for the second time that day, giving Miss Micawber an especially tender kiss and squeeze, then followed her father to the pier.

We found it crowded with soldiers of the 39th, idly watching the loading. I scanned their faces and muttered nervously to Micawber that I thought I recognised a couple of the rogues.

The Magistrate put his head to one side, settled his chin further in his collar, raised his eyebrows, and perused me with his eye glass: "H'm. Though the years have undoubtedly given you wisdom, they have not, alas, added many inches. Your migration trembles in the balance: even with my son's identity, your stature may yet give you away. I will provide a distraction to assist your safe departure." He then shook my hand, most vigorously for a final time, declaring most solemnly: "Our knot had been tied forever at the sacred alter of friendship. May you forever be a pattern and a bright example and treasured among the muniments of our noble race. My foot will never return to my native heath but I wish you God's speed to England, home and beauty. Now's the time and now's the hour!" He pushed me behind a large barrel, raised his stick to attract the attention of the soldiers and began practising broad sword drills with great alacrity and vigour. The soldiers, quite bemused at the sight, drifted away from the ship and clustered around Micawber, as he burst into song:

"If I had a beau, for a soldier who'd go
Do you think I'd say no?
No, no not I!"

He made sure all eyes were firmly on him and my way was clear, before giving me a surreptitious nod of farewell: his voice soaring ever higher as I crept from my hiding place towards the gangplank:

"When his red coat I saw, not a tear would I draw
But I'd give him éclat for his bravery
If an army of Amazons e'r came into play,
As a dashing white sergeant, I'd march away!"

He threw his stick triumphantly into the air and caught it the very moment I gave the ticket he'd provided me with to a surly boatswain and slipped safely aboard. Even after all these years I can still see the remarkable Micawber standing on the pier, raising his hat in a final farewell, the setting sun glistening on his egg-like head, as we sailed out of Middleton Bay. I can still hear his lusty voice floating over the waters:

"When my soldier is gone
Do you think I'll take on
Or sit moping forlorn
No, no, not I!
His fame's my concern
How my bosom will burn
When I see him return
Crown'd with victory!"

I waved back until he was a distant speck, and then feeling quite lonely, found a quiet corner of the deck and settled down for the voyage. I quickly discovered the entire vessel reeked of the fishy smell of dead seal. There were indeed piles of freshly slaughtered seal skins in the hold together with a dozen or so unfortunate convicts from the punishment settlement at Hobart. There were several other passengers aboard, including a plump, lubberly Major with gold ticker and chain flapping on his belly. I found I'd not lost my natural instinct to steal - my very fingers itched at the prospect - but for the moment I was Wilkins Micawber Junior, and I had no wish to sully that good name.

The following afternoon we sighted the lighthouse, built by the convict architect, Francis Greenway, and sailed into Sydney's great harbour behind a stiff south-easterly breeze. We tied up at the Commissariat Wharf, at almost the same spot where *Enterprise* had docked almost three years before. I pulled Wilkins' cap down over my eyes, put my tongue in cheek, and swaggered boldly down the gangplank. I was a little perturbed to spy the Superintendent of Convicts, who'd grown even uglier in the interim, standing on the dock waiting for his new arrivals. I nevertheless scudded quickly past him and handed Micawber's papers to a customs official, who perused them with a simple nod of his head.

I made my way directly to George Street and the Royal Hotel. I was surprised to find the concert hall had been pulled down and a half-finished, much bigger, structure standing in its place. There was no sign of activity, apart from Ben sitting by the door, fast asleep, an empty bottle beside him. I crept past and slipped inside, thankful that there was no sign of that bastard Croft. All was quiet and still, indeed there was a distinct air of neglect about the place. I was pleased to see Sue behind the deserted bar. She looked up, her pretty face apprehensive at the sight of me. I must admit that all sorts of carnal feelings began to arise in my nether regions on seeing the firm shape of her breasts again, but I merely winked and laid my finger to my lips to prevent difficult questions.

"Did you find yer Dad?" she asked softly.

I nodded in reply, a lump coming to my throat as I gazed up at his battered old phiz which was still hanging on the wall behind her. "Where's the boss?" I whispered.

She pointed towards the frosted glass door of the office at the far end of the lounge. "He spends most of his time in there. He's not the man he was since that woman left. The business has gone to pot - he's sold the flour-mill and the granary - he's even mortgaged this place, not that anyone comes anymore."

"Why ever not?" I asked, putting my pipe in my mouth.

"He fell out with the damn'd Governor after supplying liquor to ticket-of-leave men. Darling put the Royal out of bounds to his officers. The Southern Cross in Bridge Street is where they all go now. Even that sod Croft has buggered off and left him." Her voice was tinged with pity. "That Napier bitch broke him, Art. Barnett never touched a drop of liquor before, but now he drinks more than a fuckin' fish. He's up to his neck in legal problems and is obsessed with some mad dream of building a bleeding theatre - somehow thinks that will make him respectable again. If you're as bleedin' artful as you say you are, try to talk some bleedin' sense into him"

A bottle of gin was on the bar. I pulled the cork out with my teeth. "I never thought you cared much for the rogue," I said in a low voice.

Her cheek coloured into an unlikely blush: "He was kind to me before she came with her damn'd piano. I give him what comfort I can."

"You're a good and faithful girl." I took a swig of gin, blew her a kiss, then scudded over to the frosted door and pushed it softly open. It was dark inside with curtains drawn, but in the candlelight I beheld Barnett Levey sitting at his desk with a leather-bound volume in his hand. He was no longer sleek and shiny but distinctly dishevelled.

He looked up in utter astonishment: "You! The artful one! Come back yet again? Have you not brought me enough bad luck?"

I threw the bag upon his desk. "I've brought you back your gold. I hear you're in parlous need of it."

His hand closed over it like a drowning man grabbing a rope. He felt the weight before shooting me a dubious frown: "You returned my purse before: you never do anything without wanting something for yourself. What is it this time? I should warn you that at present I have not the means I once had."

"Assign me back into your service. If anyone asks where I've been - say I was kidnapped by Harper and escaped and have just managed to find my way back."

He gazed at me thoughtfully with his big dark spaniel eyes, "Where is your father?"

"Dead."

"I am sorry." I think he really meant it.

I tried to affect my old nonchalance: "Stow the gammon - at least I found him - and now I've got a fearful itch to get back to London. Let me work on the farm with Trumper and his boys until Crowe returns."

"The farm?" he sighed. "The farm? My dear, I will no longer have it after tomorrow."

"Why ever not? Have you sold it as well?"

"If I had, I would at least have money. No, my dear, that villain Monks has fallen in with a recently transported lawyer, named Uriah. Uriah is a Hebrew name - priests and prophets and valiant warriors bear it in our Holy Book, but this Uriah is nothing but a rascally shark and leech. He has concocted a deed which states I signed the property back to Monks." He gave a mournful sigh: "I have seen the document, the rogue is a skilful forger, I have to admit that the signature looks like mine. The Governor will decide in the morning. They also claim I had no right to the farm in the first place, because I won it in an illegal wager."

"Illegal wager? There's no such thing. You may have cooked the result but the wager was legal enough. I thought it was beneath an officer's honour to welch on a wager?"

"Darling holds there is no honour involved in dealing with a Jew. It was ever thus, my dear." He picked up the book; sunlight stole through a chink in the curtains and glistened on its gold-edged pages. "Before I fell into this financial difficulty, I ordered a consignment of novels from London. I was hoping to establish a lending library here, but in the present absence of funds and participants, I am availing of them myself. Knowledge is a precious thing, my dear. For instance in this novel, *Ivanhoe* by Sir Walter Scott, Isaac of York, raises money from the Jews in England to pay the ransom of King Richard himself. Isaac thinks, poor fool, that it will make his people accepted, but it did them little good. A few years later hundreds of Jews were burned alive in Isaac's very own city of York. Although they no longer burn us, we are still despised and have no rights in England - that is why I came here, my dear. I was the first free Jewish settler in the colony. I thought, fool that I was, a new country might treat all men the same." He threw the book aside and went over to a huge bookcase heaving with volumes, on one shelf of which rested the welcome sight of a bottle of London Gin. He poured two full measures, added water and handed me a glass. "I tried everything to win the acceptance of the gentry. I became a Free Mason, a founder member of the Sydney Bank, wined and dined them at every opportunity - but to them I was still Levey, the Jew. So I decided to take as much as I could from them through their wagers, I even attempted to take one of their wives." He smiled ruefully, before unfolding a large sheet of white paper with drawings all over it. "Since Leticia left I have devoted myself to a new stratagem, a new way to gain respectability. There is no reason why

Sydney should not have as fine a theatre as any in Covent Garden. If I build it they will come fawning on me again - Darling is implacably opposed to the idea but he will be replaced in a few months. I commissioned Francis Greenway to draw up these plans for my *Theatre Royal*, it will seat a thousand, and I intend to present opera and the works of the immortal Shakespeare himself. I have sunk all my finances into the venture and I need the money from the sale of the farm to complete, but if Darling gives the verdict against me - I am ruined, my dear."

"Doesn't Darling know what a white-livered villain Monks is?"

"He only cares that he professes to be a Christian gentleman."

"Christian gentleman, my arse! He was a consort of Fagin and a bigger villain to boot. I know things of him that he thinks no living person knows. Let me speak at the hearing tomorrow - I'll show the damn'd rogue in his true colours."

The hearing was set for 10 o'clock in the Governor's office. I knew it was imperative that Monks be caught off guard, and therefore told Levey to go ahead alone and begin his plea, then call me in as a surprise witness. At a quarter to ten I hid in the shrubbery whilst Levey made his uncertain way up the long drive to Government House. He looked so forlorn. I suspect he'd little faith in me, indeed for all my bravado I was uncertain how much faith I had in myself. I'd scarcely squatted down when I heard the crunch of approaching feet on the gravel. I peeped out and beheld Monks, as pale and withered as ever, his eyes sunk even further in his head, his lips still discoloured and bitten by the marks of his teeth. But if the sight of him was foul, that of his companion was fouler. The rogue had a cadaverous face and red hair, cropped as close as the closest stubble, hardly any eyebrows and no eyelashes. His eyes were red brown and so unsheltered and unshaded, that I remember wondering how he went to sleep. He was high shouldered and bony, dressed in a mouldy-looking black, with a white wisp of a neck cloth, buttoned up at the throat. He was rubbing his chin with a long, lank, skeleton of a hand and holding a legal-looking document in the other.

"Remember we must be very 'umble," he muttered to Monks in a wheedling voice as they passed.

I waited a few minutes more, then rechecking for the umpteenth time that the dog-eared piece of newspaper was safe in my inner pocket; I marched boldly to the house and entered the anteroom. An orderly looked up from his desk. The same cove as when Crowe and Napier had been summoned here by Darling before the cricket match all those eventful months before. He recognised me at once but I lay my finger to me nose and winked: "Just got back from the Bush, my covey. About to be summoned as special witness."

I could hear voices through the door, especially the unctuous voice of what I took to be Uriah: "In all 'umbleness, your Excellency, you must take written proof and the sworn word of a gentleman. My client is an Englishman of impeccable pedigree; his oath must count tenfold against that of an 'ebrew."

"I must protest, I am a respectable business man who has contributed much to the colony." Levey's voice didn't have much conviction about it.

"You contributed to the consumption of alcohol and encouraged the vice of gaming, all to your own profit," came Darling's sour reply. "Moreover you attached scandal to the name of the wife of a noble officer, brutally murdered whilst carrying out his duty. Your word has no value as far as I am concerned."

"I 'umbly concur with your Excellency. This signed deed is a melancholy confirmation of the Israelite's perfidy," Uriah wheedled.

I ascertained that poor Levey would lose his case before he'd the chance to summon me. I therefore gave the orderly another wink, knocked on the door and scudded in. Darling was seated at his desk, with two armed soldiers behind him. Levey and Monks stood before him whilst the obsequious Uriah sat perched on a chair, like some black bird of prey, squeezing his bony hands, laid palm to palm, between his bony knees.

"How dare you push your way into my presence whilst I am determining a case?" Darling exploded, angrily tapping his large office ruler upon the top of his polished desk.

The sentries made a move to throw me out but I interjected quickly, purloining one of the rogue lawyer's favourite words. "I most humbly beg your pardon, your Excellency, but I have evidence vital to this case."

There was a look of amazement and fear on Monk's haggard face. "Your Excellency, this vile brat is a convicted pickpocket and runaway. Put him in irons and send him back where he belongs."

"Do you redress yourself to me, my man? That's a case of deformation of character surely," I queried, with all the innocence I could muster.

Darling peered at me, wrinkling his nose as if I were a particularly bad smell. "Weren't you the young rogue who played in that damn'd cricket match?"

"Indeed I was your Grace. I was then assigned to Mr Levey but was abducted by some runaways against my will. I managed to escape from their vile clutches and have only just returned after suffering months of privation in the Bush."

"That is true, Your Excellency. He was a good worker and loyal servant. He came back of his own free will," Levy interposed.

Darling sniffed inconclusively and tapped his ruler against the palm of his hand with some irritation.

"May I 'umbly propose that this mongrel whelp, this scum of our fair colony be ejected forthwith," protested Uriah, frowning to such a degree that he almost closed his small eyes.

I took the yellowing piece of newsprint from my pocket and laid it on Darling's desk beside Monk's forged deed, smoothing it out with the back of my hand. I knew that I'd no tangible proof of his villainy; my only chance was to take him by surprise and provoke his wrath so that he would undo himself. I could see I had the gimcrack worried: the hurried raising of his gnawed knuckles to his chin betrayed his trepidation.

"I trust your Excellency can recall the case of Fagin and Oliver Twist," I inquired demurely.

At that, Monk's cheeks lost what little colour they had and an unwholesome paleness overspread them. "You cannot prove anything against me," he stammered and made a sudden dart for the paper, as if to tear it to pieces - but with more dexterity than I thought possible, the

Governor caught his advancing knuckles with the ruler. It was a mighty blow and looked to have disabled the rogue's right hand. Leeford bit his bleeding lips and writhed in pain.

"How dare you attempt to destroy evidence that is placed before me," Darling snapped. "What have you to say for yourself, boy?"

I took off young Wilkins's cap and held it in my right hand and laid my left hand contritely on my breast. "Before I had the opportunity to reform myself, thanks to the benevolence of His Majesty, I am ashamed to confess I misspent my youth in London where I consorted with all sorts of rogues and vagabonds, including the infamous Fagin himself. I found a lost boy, a meek-looking, hungry, boy who had run away from the workhouse," I blinked my eyes as if to stop my tears, "I took pity on him and brought him to Fagin. Fagin could always find a home for lost boys. This rogue and scoundrel," I pointed to Monks, tightly holding his rapped knuckles under his arm, "whose real name is Leeford, recognised the little lad by chance as his own half- brother. He paid Fagin to teach him every villainy he knew, and promised him more, should the boy be condemned as a criminal and so lose his inheritance. I can remember his exact words: "*make him a sneaking, snivelling pickpocket like all the rest.*"

Monks fell back as if he'd been struck or stung and wiped the sweat from his forehead with his chewed hand: "It's a lie! A murrain on you! I'll tear the life out of you, you cursed imp!"

"I heard you threaten to do the same thing to your brother, poor little Oliver Twist," I taunted, looking up with an air of innocent abstraction.

"Rot him!" Monks exclaimed in a horrible passion, between his clenched teeth. "If only I'd had the courage to say the word, I might have been free of him. I wish the brat were ground to ashes or screwed down in his coffin"

Darling looked shocked at this, causing Uriah to give a sickly smile, "Your Excellency, as my client's 'umble and learned advocate, may I 'umbly suggest that this matter has nothing to do with the case in question."

"It damn well has everything to do with the case in question," snapped Darling, putting on his half-moon spectacles and perusing my article from *The Times.*

"Do you still give more value to his word than mine?" enquired Levey softly.

"You are all rogues and villains, infesting this colony like a plague of rats," snapped Darling testily, "but some of you are viler and more pestilent than others." He laid down the newspaper, picked up the bogus deed and waved it beneath Monk's nose, "If this document is indeed a forgery, Mr Monks or Leeford or whoever you are, I promise, both you and your so-called lawyer will be bound for the delights of Brisbane."

"What a spree! Won't they be glad to see you up there?" I chortled. "I hear the climate is very conducive to a person's health."

Monk's lip quivered as he turned all his fury upon me. "The devil take you, scum that you are! May you rot in hell where you belong!" He lurched toward me with the intention of striking me with his bloody knuckles, but I dodged nimbly out of his way, giving him my most chirpy wink. He stamped his foot upon the ground in a perfect frenzy of rage, "Come here you born devil! I'll tear your very life out!" But in that instant his face became distorted and black. There was a rattle in his throat and a startled look in his eyes before he collapsed violently on Darling's Turkish rug.

I was overcome by a burning desire to put his lights out. I knelt beside him and whispered in his ear: "I've seen how things are where you're going. I'll make sure I tell little Oliver what you're suffering when I get back to London." At that he writhed even more and foamed in an uncontrollable fit.

"Here's a merry-go-rounder!" I chuckled.

Darling's face was now purple with outrage. "Don't spew on my damn'd carpet, you infernal rogue! It's the finest weave - I brought it with me from Mauritius." He turned to the guards behind him. "Don't just stand there gawping, you oafs! One of you get an orderly with mop and bucket; the other run to the infirmary and fetch one of those fool doctors."

Monks continued to splutter fearfully. He was choking himself to death. I'd killed him as surely as I'd killed Hodson and felt an equal lack of remorse. I made a great pretence of consternation, vigorously applying my hands to his chest, as if to ease the strain on his heart. I was gratified to discover that my old skill had not left me: under Darling's very nose, I extracted the villain's wallet together with some papers from the inside pocket of his coat and transferred them into my own, long before my old shipmate Doctor Hampton arrived and pronounced the scoundrel dead. My triumph was complete when the Governor ordered Uriah, who'd been staring in frozen dismay, to be shackled and await the first boat up to Moreton Bay.

"The Devil take you - one day I'll be even with you!" He whispered in my ear as the soldiers dragged him away. Those words and his hateful face would haunt my dreams for months to come.

That evening alone in my room in Levey's empty hotel, I opened Monk's wallet. I was disappointed at first to find that it contained little money - a few silver pieces and three gold sovereigns - but two other items proved far more intriguing. One was a sheet of paper, torn and tattered with age and constant handling. The writing was unsteady and with many crossings out, but I made it out to be a letter to a girl, in which someone who signed himself Edward Leeford, pleaded forgiveness for deceiving her and promised to provide for their child. He wrote in such pitiful terms that it touched even my hardened young heart. The second item was a minute portrait of a man, such as would be put in a locket. The fellow was about thirty, thin and weak-looking, but there was something in his pale face and fair hair that reminded me of someone I knew. I looked harder and saw the sad eyes of Oliver Twist.

Darling had no choice but to declare in my master's favour, but despite my misgivings, needing instant cash, Levey sold the farm to a retired officer, Captain Lindsay. Lindsay was a good-natured old bachelor and Sarah, long free of her duties to Leticia, became his trusted housekeeper and cook, whilst Trumper and his boys ran the farm as if it were their very own. Levey kept me in his service as boot boy to the hotel, although there was precious little for me to do, apart from teaching Ben the rudiments of whist. It proved a mistake. Within a few days the savage had mastered the art of perusing an opponent's hand even better than me, and regulated his play accordingly. That black rogue won more from me than any London sharp or New York trickster ever did.

All the while the colony was growing. Each month brought fresh arrivals of convicts and an ever increasing number of free settlers. With the sighting of each sail at the entrance to Sydney Cove, I would dash down to the Commissary Wharf in the expectation that Crowe had returned with my pardon, but I was always disappointed and began to fear that he might never come. One morning in August, I arrived at the wharf later than usual and beheld the poor wretches from the convict ship, *Eleanor,* already waiting in line to be assigned, like we had done two years before. There was no sign of Crowe but as I turned sadly back to the Royal I heard a familiar cry:

"Plummy and slam! Is that you Jack?"

I swung round at once. Among the throng of faces - some hopeful, some fearful, some plain perplexed - I recognised a pair of small twinkling eyes, beneath a pock-marked forehead.

You could have knocked me down with a feather. "Tom Chittling!" I cried.

The poor dupe was almost dancing in his shackles with delight. "I knew it was you, Jack. I never saw such a feller as you. Where's Bet? Do you know where she is?"

"Tommy! What are you doing here? I thought you were too fly to be lagged."

"Indeed I am, Dodger. But I was so uncommon sweet on Bet that when I learned she was lagged - I got lagged on purpose so that I could join her. Where is the old gal? Is she well?"

It was one of those rare occasions when I was lost for words. "You've been a long time coming, Tommy, old son. Bet was bound for Botany Bay more than three years ago."

"I know she was, but try as I might the buggers wouldn't lag me. I was milled and sent to retirements all over England and did villainies I never dreamed of, before a beak found it in his heart to give me what I wanted. But I wouldn't mind going through it all again so long as Bet is alright. Now I'm here at last I going to do what I always intended - marry the dear girl. How is she?"

I could prevaricate no longer. "She's dead, Tom. She's dead."

He looked at me in utter disbelief, like Tiny Tim when I told the little sod that there weren't no Father Christmas. Though Tommy was some five or six years older than me, back at Fagin's, I'd always sensed a degree of deference in his deportment towards me, as if he were conscious of a slight inferiority in point of genius and professional acquirements; but now he crumpled like a little kid.

"No, Jack, no! She can 't be!" he sobbed.

Though I'd never been particularly fond of the poor half-witted dupe, Tommy was part of my old London life and I didn't like seeing him in such a state, particularly in front of his fellow prisoners, some of whom were sneering at his discomfort in a derogatory way. At that very moment the Superintendent of Convicts came out of his office. The bastard had a malicious grin on his brutal phiz as he surveyed the chained wretches before him. "Well, you lazy brutes," he said with a jeering laugh, "I expect some of you have heard of the good times we enjoy in this fair land and are looking forward to an easy life, but I'm happy to inform you that there'll be no soft assignments for the likes of you. You're all bound for the road gang. You'll make more than five hundred miles of road out of the hardest rock, and your backs will be truly broken before any of you damn'd blaggards are rid of yer chains."

Tom turned to me, with an even more pitiable look in his eyes, "Jack, help me I beg you. I can't bear another day with this iron on my leg."

I knew only too well the agonies that awaited him on the road gang, and was therefore relieved to see Levey on the other side of the Circular Quay. Whenever a boat arrived he would scour the newly-arrived passengers in the hope of tempting some of them back to his empty hotel. He presently earnestly engaged in conversation with a mean-looking man and his even meaner-looking wife, whilst a couple of Abbos were loading their heavy trunks upon a handcart.

"Be stout-hearted, Tom," I whispered softly, and scudded over as if the Runners were at my heels.

Levey turned from the sour-looking couple at my approach and smiled. "Ah, young Mr Dawkins, my Boots. What can I do for you, my dear? I have just been informing these esteemed gentlefolk of the refinements and luxuries of the Royal."

I'd no time for niceties: "Mr Levy, an old pal of mine has just arrived and is bound for the road gang. Please get him assigned to you."

The mean woman sniffed. "Fine sort of establishment you keep, if your boot boy consorts with criminals."

"I'll have you know I was top japanner at the Golden Cross at Charing Cross before I decided to take a voyage here for my health. I've polished the trotter-cases of many a judge and lord, not to say a few ladies," I retorted, giving the bitch a knowing wink.

"Indeed, I have been a frequent guest at that establishment for many years and don't recall seeing the likes of you there," sneered the sour-faced man. "In any case, we already have bookings at the Southern Cross and I am pleased to inform you that we will have no need of your hotel, Mr Levey." Having assured themselves that their entire luggage had been loaded upon the cart the sour pair departed in the direction of Bridge Street.

Levey shook his head mournfully. "Two more customers lost. How long can we go on, I wonder?"

Tom and the other convicts were being formed into a desultory line to march away to the barracks. "What about my pal? He'll die on that road, I know it."

Levey stroked his red beard and shrugged apologetically, "Alas, my dear, I have not enough work for you. How can I afford to feed another unprofitable mouth?"

"Tom Chittling is an excellent cook," I lied. "He can bake a rabbit pie so that the very bones melt in your mouth, so you have no occasion to pick 'em. He'll bring in a whole tribe of new patrons."

"You are not so artful, my artful one. We have no rabbits here." He pondered for a moment before his eyes twinkled, "But perhaps I should send for a few from England. They breed fast - like Jacob's flock - it could be a profitable business." (Maybe if he hadn't been so distracted by his damn'd theatre he might have done so and earned a fortune. The Honourable Alexander Macleay, the Colonial Secretary for New South Wales, did so a few years later. Now, I'm told, there are millions of the little buggers nibbling their way across Australia.)

Levey had essentially a soft heart and that night Tom was duly installed as Pot Boy at the Royal, where he enjoyed, amongst other treats, one of Sue's finest kangaroo steaks. Indeed I was a little surprised how quickly the sight of Sue's ample dugs seemed to alleviate his grief for Bet.

Next morning I came down to the kitchen for my breakfast of coffee and ham rolls, Levey allowed the forbidden flesh in his establishment although he never partook of it himself, and beheld Tom's raw and bleeding ankles sticking out from beneath the oven. I thought for a moment he'd topped himself. "Tom! What the devil are you doing under there?

He gingerly extracted himself from beneath the hot stove, very red in the face. "Here's a merry-go-rounder!" he exclaimed sheepishly. "Just checking the Jew don't keep his gold in the same place as Fagin."

"You are an utter blunder-head, Tom Chittling. If you steal from Levey you'll be on that chain gang in double-quick time. Besides, Fagin kept his pretty things in a box in a trap under the floor of the top room at the old place in Saffron Hill. Every one of us knew that."

"Indeed he did, Jack. But not on that last day - the day that he was took. It was just after dinner time, about two in the afternoon. Me and Charley was with him when we heard the officers beating on the door and the people screaming and raving. I followed Charley up the chimney to do a 'lucky' over the roof, but lost my footing and fell back into the hearth. It was then that I saw Fagin stowing his box under that oven he kept for smelting down the gold. He'd only just got it under when they burst in. The women were worst - they were screaming they'd tear his heart out, snarling with their teeth and making at him like savage dogs - he was so terrified of the bitches that he clung to the officers as if they were his dearest pals. Then people began to fight the officers to get at Fagin. They were all too pre-occupied to notice me creep back up the chimney."

I was thunderstruck, stupefied and befuddled, and could hardly manage to speak: "Tom, you damn'd dunderhead, do you mean that Fagin's pretty things are still there? Under the oven at Saffron Hill?"

Tom went even redder, his devil-may-care-swagger gone. "There's no standing against you, Jack: I never thought of that."

"Who else have you told?"

"I haven't blabbed to anyone else about it, Dodger. I wish I might be busted if I have."

Fagin's treasure might still be there - waiting for me. I'd more than earned my share of it. London was calling me stronger than ever.

Darling finally relinquished his office in October 1831 and there were few signs of regret amongst the populace when he sailed back to England on *Hooghly*. Deliverance came at last on the 2nd of December, when a ship was sighted sailing behind a stiff south- easterly breeze, into the mouth of Sydney Cove with the Union Jack floating at her mast head. The signal was recognised by the duty officers and the colours were instantly hoisted at Fort Macquarie. When *HMS Margaret* cast anchor in the cove, a royal salute from Dawe's Battery signalled the arrival of the new Governor, General Sir Richard Bourke. I heard the gun fire whilst drinking a glass of gin and scudded down to the Commissary Wharf - there, standing on the poop, amongst a throng of red-coated officers and officials, waving papers in his hand, stood my dear good and kind friend - Mr Crowe. He'd kept his word, as I knew he would. All the colony seemed to be rejoicing with me: that night Sydney was illuminated with bonfires.

Mr Crowe had come back with tickets of leave for all the convicts that had taken part in the saving of *Enterprise*, together with a full pardon and promotion to Sergeant for Corporal Bradman. Lindwall, Miller and the rest were back in Sydney within a fortnight and I ensured that Warnie's ticket-of-leave was sent to Micawber on the first packet to Port Middlebay. Governor Bourke wanted Crowe to resume control of the hospital but my dear friend had other ideas. One evening as we looked out upon the great Southern Ocean from a headland near the mouth of Sydney Cove, he asked me if I had reconsidered his offer of adoption.

"I intend to go on to New Zealand," he said, laying his hand on my shoulder. "They have great need of doctors there. I'm told it is a beautiful land, greener and more fertile than Australia. Now your father has gone, there is nothing to keep you here. Will you come with me, Jack?"

The idea of journeying even further from my beloved London was beyond my comprehension, especially with the prospect now of finding Fagin's treasure, and I had no doubt that Crowe could persuade Governor Bourke to turn my ticket-of-leave into a full pardon. "I want to go home, Mr Crowe."

He looked at me incredulously: "Home? What home have you got to go to, Jack?"

"The streets of London are home enough for me. With the knowledge I have acquired from you and the lessons life has taught me here, I've little doubt that I shall prosper. Besides there are tidings I must take to my erstwhile companion, Oliver Twist."

So it was, a few weeks later, on the 14th April 1832, that I boarded *Isabella,* bound for Cape Town and London, with my pardon, signed by the Governor himself, safely stowed in my pocket. Though I'd spurned his offer of adoption, dear old Crowe was determined that I should not starve. He assured me that he'd written to his lawyer, a Mr Spiker of Chancery Lane, and had made arrangements for my future well-being. Lindwall, Miller, Trumper and his boys, stood on the wharf alongside my benefactor, waving goodbye with their tickets-of-leave. They, with Sergeant Bradman, were among the bravest and truest companions I've encountered on my long and adventurous journey through life. I regret that I never saw any of them again, although I've firm knowledge they all prospered. Unlike my old master Barnet Levey, who also stood on the wharf with Sue, my first and more than accomplished teacher in the subtle art of sex, together with Tom Chittling and black Ben, who gave me a parting gift of a boomerang. Levey also had something for me: my father's portrait tightly rolled in oilskin. The Jew's fortunes had taken a temporary upward turn, and he'd recently acquired 1000 acres of fine land in the Blue Mountains. He'd proudly named his new estate, Mount

Zion, and was building the Pilgrim Inn upon it. I'd begged him to concentrate on his businesses and land sales, but he was still obsessed with his damn'd Theatre Royal. It opened later that year, with a melodrama entitled *The Miller and his Men,* with Governor Bourke himself sitting in the stalls. The theatre flourished for a time but it would ultimately bleed Levey dry. Even old Sir Henry Irving himself went broke running the Lyceum, Macready made very little out of Covent Garden, and the Theatre Royal broke Levey's heart as well as his pocket. He eventually lost it and all his other interests, and died penniless and worn out in 1837. Faithful Sue stayed with him until the end and married Tom Chittling the following year. They, together with Ben, ran the Pilgrim Inn for many years. I always thought there was something heroic about Barnet Levey, rogue though he was. Perhaps if I'd had stayed with him things might have turned out different.

I had a pleasant voyage on *Isabella,* Captain Wiseman was aptly named and was humane to boot, and the Surgeon, Mr Galloway, was an old friend of Crowe's. I assisted him as I had Crowe on the journey out, for which I was allocated my own small cabin. Although there was little to do, as our cargo consisted only of returning officers and their families, together with a hold full of fine merino fleeces. We sailed north up the eastern coast, past Newcastle and Brisbane into the Coral Sea. We passed through the Torres Strait, took on spices, pepper and tea in Timor, then made our way along the islands of Indonesia before dropping south-east across the Indian Ocean.

We docked in Cape Town in early June. Many times throughout the voyage I'd unwrapped the oilskin and gazed tenderly at Private Skinner's battered phiz and felt a strong urge to tell the melancholy Dutch artist, Jan Peeters, that thanks to his picture, I had found him. This time I stepped boldly down the gang plank a free man, and man I considered myself now that I was almost sixteen. Cape Town, like me, had grown in two years; the streets were more crowded, the Boer language sounded louder and uglier, although more English voices mingled with it. There was a different atmosphere about the place, I suspect those sullen Boers were already planning their Great Trek of 1835.* I found the tavern at the end of the closed yard, as dirty as before. The bar was still crowded with whores and their would-be customers. I was considering availing myself of the services of a particular raven-haired beauty with a dirty look in her eye when, in a corner, shining like a beacon, I spied a familiar strawberry nose. I turned to the bar to buy two large glasses of gin when something else caught my attention. My body trembled as if I'd seen a ghost. I stared transfixed and could not take my eyes away. Above the bar was a life-size painting of a naked girl, lying on her side among seaweed-covered rocks. Her breasts were ripe, her belly taut, one arm rested behind her head, the other was draped across her body with her hand nestling, so provocatively, in a cluster of gold. There was a knowing look in her eye, a look that suggested she was revelling in her nakedness, delighting in the desire she was arousing in the artist, whose hand must have trembled as he held his brush. It was my Molly.

It was several minutes before I had composed myself enough to join Jan Peeters at his table. "Did you paint that girl?" I rasped in a low voice, sliding the gin towards him.

It took a moment for his sad eyes to recognise me. "Ah, the boy that was seeking his father. Did you find him?"

"Yes, I did, thanks to your picture - but however did you paint her?"

He raised his eyes up to the painting; his face grew even more melancholy. "Ah, her! My sea nymph, my siren of the ocean. Did you know her as well?"

"I did. Her name was Molly. She drowned."

He took up the glass of gin and drained it in one swallow. "Some creatures the sea cannot digest, it throws them up on the shore."

I pushed the second glass towards him. "How did you find her?"

"As well as Rembrandt, I studied the great Dutch seascape painters: Backhuysen, Verbeeck and Van de Velde. On days when my existence here becomes intolerable, I take my easel, paint and brushes, and trek up the coast to find a bay that reminds me a little of home. A few days after you had sailed I came upon a lonely bay I had not discovered before. I climbed down to the beach and, to my amazement, there laying among the rocks, half-naked, her arms wrapped around a spar, was a beautiful girl. I thought for a moment she was a Nereid - blown from the purple waters of the Aegean." He drained his glass and looked at me for more. I scudded to the bar and returned with a full bottle. He filled the glass to the very brim before continuing. "At first I thought she was drowned, she was so cold, but I poured some brandy down her and I felt a flicker of life. When she opened her eyes she thought at first she was in hell and I was some sort of devil. When she came to her senses she made me swear I would never tell how I had found her. I wrapped her in my coat and brought her here. She never told me a single word about her past, or how she came to be in the sea. I called her Amatheia - I find great solace in Homer - and she became my muse." He pointed to his bag, bulging with sketches. I could see they were all of Molly. My hand trembled as I pulled them out and devoured her with my eyes. He'd drawn every part of her from every conceivable angle. The dark enticing divide between the small round cheeks of her buttocks, the line of her back, the firmness of her thigh, even her delicate ankles. I wanted her then more than ever. He looked up from his gin and gave a sad smile. "I can see you lust after her as I did. She knew her power over me but never let me so much as touch her."

"Where is she now?"

He raised his mournful eyes to the painting over the bar. He found it hard to speak: "She would sit here every night and watch the faces of the men as they looked up at her. They were aroused as you are now, and I think she despised them all. I sold many sketches of her. I had money at last and needed only a little more to buy my passage back home with her. I told her of my plans, but one morning I awoke and she was gone with every penny I had. A ship had sailed for London on the early tide."

I studied her lovely face and tried to fathom her: she'd justly killed the evil bastard who'd violated her, but robbed the poor sod who'd saved her. Angel or devil, she was all I desired. I wanted to tell her that I was not the coward she thought me and was planning her escape the very night she plunged the knife into Deplidge's spotty back. I gazed and gazed at her whilst my companion finished the bottle of gin. His head was resting on the table when I slipped five pieces of gold into his pocket, and made off with a dozen sketches.

That night I hung them on nails around the walls of my small cabin, and lusted achingly at my beautiful Molly.

Years later I sold them to a rich young student called Freddy Leighton. The crafty bugger copied them into his paintings and made a fortune. Queen Victoria loved him - the old girl likes a bit of bare flesh - she knighted him at Windsor and later made him a Baron; although Lord Leighton didn't enjoy his title long: the poor sod dropped dead the very next day.

17. London Again

I will not dwell long on the final leg of my voyage home, apart from recalling my frequent borings of the bored young wife of an old Boer merchant. (Beg pardon. Found it hard to resist.) It all began on my sixteenth birthday, whilst her old dullard of a husband was drinking schnapps at the captain's table. It was a choppy afternoon and Mr Galloway sent me to the lady's cabin to administer a tincture to allay her sea-sickness. I knocked on the door and being invited to enter, was quite taken aback to discover her smiling at me, with her naked shoulders and legs protruding from beneath the flimsiest of sheets. Disraeli wrote in his youth, before he became respectable, that there is no fascination so irresistible to a boy as the smile of a married woman. The crafty old devil was right. The treatment I administered was not that which good Doctor Galloway had prescribed, but much more effective. I slipped off my clothes in a trice and joined her under the sheet. She said not a word, but jogged me up and down on her soft belly to the motion of the waves, crying out in such frenzied delight at my youthful potency, that the boatswain on the deck above thought we were sailing over a school of bloomin' mermaids. It was a very rough crossing and my medicinal visits were called for frequently, sometimes half a dozen times a day. Old men forget and all shall be forgot, but I remember, with advantages, the feats I did those seaborne days.

We sighted Old England at last one bright August morning, the fields on the white cliffs golden with ripe wheat and corn. As we sailed up the Thames the orchards of Kent, bursting with fruit, were clustered around pretty churches and fertile farms: it truly seemed the blessed plot that Shakespeare described. But as we approached London the sky gradually became covered in smoke. The docks had grown even more enormous in the five years of my exile. Where a hundred masts had anchored before, an innumerable multitude now bobbed on the tide.

We berthed in the New East India Dock and after giving my farewell and profuse thanks to Doctor Galloway, and administering a final treatment to my rapacious sea wife, I slung my knapsack, containing my money, the spare shirts Crowe had bought me, my father's portrait, the sketches of Molly, Ben's Boomerang and a few other pickings, over my shoulder, and descended the gangplank to set foot on London soil once more. Although I'd promised Mr Crowe I'd visit Mr Spiker on my arrival, and was most anxious to give Oliver the mementos I'd retrieved from Monks, and was fervent in my determination to look for Molly; my first concern was to see if Fagin's precious things remained where Tom Chittling had described. Indeed it was more than a concern - a positive fever gripped me, a fever I've since experienced many times, not least in the California Gold Rush, the Klondike stampede, and here recently, in the diamond mines of Kimberley.

Evening was falling and it was beginning to rain as I made my way west along the Ratcliff Highway. After my years in pristine Australia, the squalor of my native land came as a bit of a shock. Indeed as the rain fell heavier I mused that it would take a deluge to wash away even a portion of the filth and slime. A black noxious stream was leaping along the gutter, bubbling and seething, towards overflowing drains, where it was swallowed up in a maelstrom of liquid mud and worse. Mariners, in their long sea-boots, walked along the slippery pavement with me. They seemed to come from every part of the globe: Negroes from the Gold Coast, lithe, active, tiger-cat Malays, rough, weather-beaten men from the Artic Seas, bushy whiskered and broad-chested fellows, with faces like elaborate carvings in the very darkest mahogany. Every squalid shop, opium den, penny gaff or dram-house was trying to inveigle them over their thresholds and strip them of their hard-earned pay. Some establishments had ill-painted signs of merry sailors dancing hornpipes or carousing with their 'mollies'. Others displayed announcements such as: *"Grand Concert held here every evening, admission 2d."* Others, professing to be *Sailor's Lodging Houses*, or *Dancing Rooms,* had drunken, bloated-faced drabs at their doors, begging the passing men for a drop of gin. When I reached the bridge in New Gravel Lane and gazed into the stagnant inky water, disturbed only by the falling rain, I was overcome with such gloom and depression, that if the craving and excitement for Fagin's treasure had not gripped me, I'd have been sorely tempted to make my way back to the docks to sign up for the first ship bound for the Baltic and seek my poor mother in Russia.

I eventually came into the more salubrious air of East Smithfield and passed the newly built Mint on my right, as the grim, black outline of the Tower appeared on my left. The streets were no longer crowded and all was dark when I passed through Eastcheap, apart from a solitary light burning in the window of '*Scrooge and Marley*'. Through it I spied a thin clerk, who I later knew as Bob Cratchit, plying his pen with great assiduity in a musty ledger. I made my way up Cannon Street, past huge warehouses and the London Stone, towards Mansion House, little thinking one day I would often frequent its imposing doors. Then dear old St Paul's arose before me and, I swear, at that very moment, a rare beam of moonlight gleamed on the golden cross on top of the dome, as if to welcome me home. I took it for a good omen and my heart was pounding with hope and excitement as I quickened my pace and went down Ludgate Hill. I then turned right, past the plaintive cry of the debtors, calling for relief through the grille of the Fleet Prison, and then, through the shuttered shops of Fleet Market, towards Clerkenwell. (Farringdon Road and the Holborn Viaduct were yet to be conceived.) I could hear the wretched, doomed animals bleating and mooing in Smithfield as I slipped into the dirty, muddy, narrow street off Saffron Hill. I ignored the stink, the drunken men and women glaring malevolently from their doorways, the young infants playing in the filth; all I could think of was running my fingers though Fagin's treasures. Gold rings, jewelled watches, diamond bracelets and pearls: enough to set me up to live life as a young gentleman, like Magwitch's Pip. I turned the corner at the bottom by Field Lane, expecting to see the door of the familiar tumbledown house, wondering who would open it on my whistle, and if the old password '*Plummy and Slam*' still stood, but then stopped dead in my tracks. Nothing was there. Nothing apart from blackened ruins, a brick chimney stack, an old, rusty, dented saucepan, and the remains of an iron oven. The entire house had been burned to a cinder, whether by accident or the fury of the mob, I knew not. I remained transfixed, refusing to believe my own eyes, until, almost sobbing with bitter disappointment, I forced myself to creep across the charred earth and, hoping against hope, fell to my knees and reached tentatively under the oven. I drew out a handful of dust, a large, black spider and a small piece of iron. Whilst the spider angrily scuttled away, with all the malevolence of Fagin himself, I examined the cold metal and recognised it as part of the clasp of the old Jew's precious box. There was nothing else. Someone had been there long before me. I squeezed the dust in my hand and it ran between my fingers - all our skill and thievery had ended in this.

I suddenly felt very lost and lonely. All I could think of was to make my way to *The Three Cripples*, the only place where there might be a familiar face. But who was left? Fagin and Bill were both choked, poor Nance battered to death, dear Bet was beneath the waves, and Tom Chittling transported in Australia. That left Charley and the boys, but I had little hope they would have remained now their home had gone. Then I remembered Barney, the waiter. I quickened my pace: if anyone knew anything it would be Barney. I was quite relieved to find *The Cripples* still standing, though it was smaller and dirtier than I remembered. The bar, lit by a flaring gas-light, was empty, apart from a surly young man, reading a dirty newspaper with his elbows on the counter. He looked up and eyed me with unveiled hostility.

I summoned up what civility I could muster: "Hullo, my flash companion. Where's young Barney?"

"Barney?" The young man wasn't very bright and it looked as if it was painful for him to think. "What that Jew-boy? Used to be the waiter here before me? Nobody's seen him in years. They say he buggered off one morning and never came back."

The last ounce of excitement and expectation drained from me. I now knew, without doubt, who'd purloined the treasure. There were no flies on Barney. All at once I felt very tired. "Have you got some grub and a bed for the night?"

"Yes. If you've got money."

I slapped a half crown from my pocket on the counter. "Give us a bit of cold meat and a quartern of gin. And make sure the bed's got no fleas."

My home coming hadn't been the triumph I'd expected. Half an hour later I was laying on a foul-smelling mattress, with my knapsack as my pillow, dreaming of Molly and the Blue Mountains.

I woke next morning and decided to forgo the apology of a sausage that *The Cripples* offered for breakfast. I still had the faded cutting from *The Times* with Mr Brownlow's address upon it, and thought I'd give him an early morning visit and present my old pal Nolly with the mementos of his Dad. I was thinking of my own poor old Dad at a stall by the new Waterloo Bridge, partaking of a mug of hot coffee and a slice of bread and butter, when, pushing through the crowd of donkey carts and coster barrows making towards Covent Garden Market, I spied chestnut ringlets bobbing under an expensive bonnet, a yellow silk dress, a full bosom and a slim figure. There was singing in my ears, and my heart fluttered like a young bird about to fly: I was sure it was Molly. I called her name and hurried after her as she weaved through the crowd: her yellow dress bursting out now and then among the sober-dressed Londoners, like a flash of sun in a black and grey sky. The pavements were covered with sieves and sacks full of apples and potatoes, mountains of turnips and cabbages, the flag stones were stained green and made slippery with the leaves trodden underfoot. Men and women pushed past me with their arms bowed out by the cauliflowers under them, or their faces red with the weight of their loaded head baskets. In spite of all these obstacles, I'd nearly reached her when, outside the fruit-covered steps of the Theatre Royal, I bumped into a snub-nosed, flat-browed, common-faced boy, as dirty as one would wish to see. He looked up at me with little, sharp, ugly eyes.

"Watch where yer going, you damn'd clod-hopper!"

I frantically tried to push past him but he persisted to block my way until I delivered the little bastard a sharp box on the ear. As he broke away howling, I spied another boy come from behind me and they ran off together. I forgot them immediately and continued to press my way desperately towards Molly but, like in a bad dream, she got further and further away. I called her name louder, but she didn't turn round, and to my great consternation, by the time I reached the top of Bow Street, she'd vanished in the pulsating throng. My anguish and frustration were indescribable. I made a vain search of Long Acre before I eventually cut down to the Strand and made my sad way towards Craven Street. Having imbibed a quartern of gin in *The Golden Cross* to re-ignite my spirits, I enquired of a passing buxom milkmaid where the residence of one Mr Brownlow might be, and was pointed towards a fine house, four stories high, with a door painted shining black. I rubbed my shoes against the back of my trousers and did what I could with my collar before pulling the bell handle, let into the left-hand door post. The door was opened almost at once by a motherly old lady, very neatly and precisely dressed.

"What can I do for you, dearie?" she enquired kindly.

"I have things concerning Oliver Twist, that might be of interest to Mr Brownlow," I replied, as politely as I was able.

Her countenance underwent a very great variety of odd contortions, before she managed to utter, "Wait there," and shut the door in my face. She reopened it almost immediately and signaled me to follow her into the house. She led me over the black and white stone floor of the hall into a small room at the back, quite full of books and dark treacley paintings, overlooking a pleasant little garden. An old gentleman, dressed in a bottle- green coat was waiting to greet me. In spite of his concerned expression, he had a benevolent appearance with his spectacles pushed up on his forehead. I recognised him immediately as the old cove whose pocket I'd picked outside the bookshop in Clerkenwell all those years ago. He was about to offer me his hand before he abruptly changed his mind:

"Who are you?" he demanded sharply.

I attempted my old devil-may-care swagger: "I'm an old friend of young Oliver, that's arrived sooner than was expected from foreign parts."

"And I wager you are far too modest to want to be presented to the Judges on your return!" said a sarcastic voice. A stout old gentleman in a blue coat, striped waistcoat, nankeen britches and gaiters, was sitting in a high backed chair by the fire place, eating a plate of buttered muffins. His head was screwed on one side as he munched, and he looked out of the corners of his eyes at the same time in the manner of a parrot. "Take care, Brownlow, old friend. I'll eat my hat if this mealy-faced young gutter-snipe is not an outright villain."

I affected a look of shocked outrage; no one had described me as 'mealy-faced' before. "I beg your pardon sir, are you addressing me?"

Old Brownlow was examining my phiz more carefully. "Were you not one of Fagin's tribe of pickpockets? I thought the entire gang had been executed or transported."

"I have my pardon in my pocket," I retorted, patting my breast with great aplomb, "together with certain items concerning Oliver Twist, or should I say Leeford?"

Old Brownlow blanched at this. "What do you know of Leeford? Edwin Leeford was my dearest friend."

"I know he had two sons and one was a damn'd villain."

"The little blaggard has been sent by Monks to entrap Oliver, and make him forfeit his inheritance. Have nothing to do with him, Brownlow. Throw him out or call the police," exclaimed the stout old gentleman in a malicious voice.

"My wig! Don't go on so!" I retorted. "Fret not. Monks is dead and buried. I watched the foul scoundrel die."

They both started at this and before they could say more, I drew the folded portrait and worn letter from my pocket, and laid them, with a flourish, on the table drawn up before the window. The stout gentleman wiped his buttery fingers on a well-worn wiper, which I'd never have deigned to lift, opened a double eye-glass, which he wore attached to a broad black ribbon, and waddled to the table. Brownlow joined him and they both proceeded to pour over my offerings, nodding their pates like old bald crows.

"It is a perfect likeness of dear Edwin," exclaimed Brownlow, at length. "And this sad letter is undoubtedly his. I know his hand as well as my own."

"I still damn well don't trust this young villain. He's out to deceive you, my good friend; he positively reeks of falsehood." said the stout old man with a provoking sneer. "How much do you want, you rogue? Is blackmail your game?"

This, together with all the other disappointments I'd suffered since my return, made me more than angry. I was tempted to lift his ticker, but perceived the chain was made of steel with nothing but a key dangling loosely at the end. "I only came here to give these to my one-time companion, Oliver Twist. Where is he?" I demanded, smiting my fist upon the table. "I want to see him before I go."

"Do you honestly imagine that I could let you, a convicted felon, the ultimate cause of so much of poor Oliver's suffering, ever meet with him again?" exclaimed old Brownlow, sadly. "If he so much as consorts with a convicted felon his inheritance is in jeopardy, and the very sight of you, bringing with it the remembrance of all he suffered under Fagin, might cause his fever to return." He rummaged in his pocket and extracted a five-pound note, "Please accept this for your trouble, and never try to see dear Oliver again."

I'd suffered bigger rebuffs in my time but for some reason, tears were welling in my eyes. "Keep yer damn'd money. I never came for that."

I turned on my heels and swept out into the hall just as the front door opened and a pale, slim young fellow, several inches taller than me, entered, accompanied by a rather plain girl, a few years his senior. The pale young fellow and I stood transfixed, staring at each other in the same manner as that first morning in Barnet years before.

"Hullo, my covey! What's the row?" I said softly.

But there was no warmth in his eyes, only a trace of fear. "What in damnation are you doing here? I want nothing to do with you." The young lady looked puzzled. She put a lace handkerchief beneath her nose as if to keep out my smell. "Oliver, who is this young person?"

"A sneaking, snivelling pickpocket," he replied, still looking at me with extreme distaste. "He was Fagin's top hand. He enticed me into joining that den of thieves."

"You'd been walking for seven days and would've starved if I'd not bought you a four- penny bran. You'd have died in the street if I hadn't taken you to Fagin. You survived as best you could, just like the rest of us."

An arch little smile had stolen across the countenance of Oliver Twist. "I was never like the rest of you. I was born a gentleman."

I stormed past him out of the house but immediately ran into a tall, stern-looking man in a blue tail coat with big brass buttons and high top hat, who was progressing up the street in a most stately fashion. He seized me by my collar and held me up as if inspecting a fresh-caught fish.

"What's a young rogue like you doing in Craven Street? Up to no good I'll be bound."

It was my first encounter with one of Peel's obnoxious new Bobbies - I was to have many more bitter dealings with the bastards in the years ahead.

"It's alright, officer. He has just delivered something." Mr Brownlow had followed me to the door.

The policeman dumped me on the pavement like a sack of potatoes. "Don't let me see you hanging round here again, young gallows. I've got a nose for the likes of you."

I rearranged my coat and collar and walked away with what dignity I could muster, as Oliver regarded me disdainfully from the sanctity of Mr Brownlow's hall.

Things were definitely not turning out as I'd expected. I got to the top of Craven Street and watched the workmen heaving huge lumps of stone in the new Trafalgar Square, before deciding it was time to pay a visit to Crowe's solicitor, Mr Spiker, and see what he had to offer.

My spirits rose as I made my way back along the Strand, through the wonderful restlessness of London. Dandies, in their dark blue morning-coats and poet's shirts, mingled with courtesans and washer-women; costermongers with their barrows of fruit pushed against the carriages of the gentlefolk; hawkers were selling fried fish, baked potatoes, ginger beer and sherbet, and by the time I'd pinched the bum of a cheeky, nutty maid selling curds and whey, my confidence had been fully restored. I came into Fleet Street and admired the wooden Highlander outside Hardman's snuff shop and marvelled at the clockwork witch with her broom at the door of Mrs Salmon's waxworks. I lingered at a toy shop's window, wide-eyed at the brightly painted sailing boats, wooden horses and tin soldiers. A plump, pink boy came out with his doting father, greedily clutching a big wrapped box to his chest, and I realised, with no little regret, that I'd never been given a toy in my life. Micawber had told me tales of Sweeny Todd and other preparers of cannibalistic pasties, which he claimed did a lively retail business in the metropolis, but there was no sign of a barber shop as I passed through the old muddy gates of Temple Bar; although an old crossing sweeper did come out of Bell Yard eating a particularly savoury and well-filled meat pie. I left the roaring street at Fetter Lane and entered the stone gateway into the yard of Clifford's Inn, swarming with lawyers, with wigs perched on their heads like thrushes' nests. I searched through myriads of painted names before I discovered Mr Spiker's and went inside. The place smelt of cat's piss and damp. I climbed up three flights of stairs before I found his office at the top of the building and knocked sharply upon the door. It was opened by a timid looking clerk, who ushered me into an inner chamber at the back, lit by a skylight only, where sat a man who looked so stern and cold that his head, instead of being grey, seemed to be sprinkled with frost. Mr Spiker, for it was he, looked up at me, pursed up his mouth and frowned.

"You must be the boy that Mr Crowe has instructed me on." He leant back in his leather chair, with rows of brass nails round it, and motioned me to sit in the cliental chair opposite him, which was greasy with the sweat of innumerable hands. "It is my client's desire that you should be brought up a gentleman. To that end he considers that you must be better educated. He has lodged in my hands a certain sum of money to pay for your board and education at a suitable school. You are very fortunate that I have found the ideal establishment. I presume you can read?"

He rummaged among the papers on his desk and tossed me an advertisement, cut from a newspaper. I kept it for many years and can remember every word:

"EDUCATION - At Mr Wackford Squeer's Academy, Dotheboys Hall, at the delightful village of Dotheboys, near Greta Bridge in Yorkshire. Youth are boarded, clothed, booked, furnished with pocket money, provided with all necessaries, instructed in all languages living and dead, mathematics, orthography, geometry, astronomy, trigonometry, the use of globes, algebra, writing, arithmetic, and every other branch of classical literature. Terms, twenty guineas per annum. No extras, no vacations, and diet unparalleled."

Spiker tossed aside the paper and played with his watch chain, in a comfortable, prosperous sort of way. "I have written to Mr Squeers and he expects you. A coach leaves for Yorkshire from the Saracen's Head at six tomorrow morning. My clerk will purchase you an outside ticket."

I was dumbfounded and crestfallen. This wasn't at all what I'd been expecting. It sounded more like another transportation. "Beg pardon, sir, but I will not be going."

It was his turn to be dumbfounded. "Not going? You are refusing Mr Crowe's most generous offer and have no desire to better yourself?"

"The world's taught me all I need to know."

He shrugged dismissively. "It is immaterial to me. I have already deducted my fees from my client's account. Mr Crowe's financial assistance is dependent on you obeying my instructions. If you ignore them, I will do nothing for you and save my client a good deal of money."

I got up with all the swagger I could muster: "Don't fret yer eyelids on that score. I've money enough to last me for a while; in fact I'm on my way to the bank to deposit a considerable sum."

I swept out of a room for the second time that morning. I was half way down the stairs before I heard "Mr Dawkins!" being called softly after me.

I stopped and turned and beheld Spiker's clerk. On closer examination I saw that he was a tall man of late middle age, with two goggle eyes, a rubicund nose and a suit of clothes much the worse for wear. He descended until we stood on the same stair before addressing me in a low voice.

"My name is Noggs, Newman Noggs. I've known Mr Crowe since he was a boy. I read his letter and I perceive he has only the best intentions for you. I have his antipodean address, and will write and inform him of the outcome of your meeting. Spicer has sent other boys to Squeers, unwanted boys for the most part. Squeers is a villain - he ill-treats them - you made the right choice. You mentioned a bank - may I recommend Child's by the Temple Bar? They are a small bank, but my dear friend Mr Tellson is a clerk there. Reams of bank notes have been shuffled over by his practised thumbs. He will instruct you how as best to deposit what little wealth you have, and will act as intermediary between us if I receive any communication from Mr Crowe. Farewell for the present. I must return to my desk before my absence is noted." He crept swiftly upstairs without another word.

I went uncertainly back into the street. I'd been bluffing about the bank, but on reflection it didn't seem a bad idea. I'd intended to cash in the few tickers and trinkets I'd acquired as soon as I found a decent fence, but the cash was too precious to carry around for long. I therefore decided to take Newman Noggs' advice - he seemed to be the only friend I had at present in the whole of London. I made my way back to Fleet Street as the giants on St Dunstan's clock were striking noon, and immediately spied Child's Bank in the shadow of the Temple Bar. It was not imposing - indeed was very small and very dark. A grim-faced, red-eyed man, wearing an old fashioned three-cornered hat sat on a stool outside, with a grisly urchin squatting beside him. They regarded me silently, like a couple of suspicious monkeys, as I pushed open a stiff door, which creaked as if in protest at being disturbed, and went down two steps into what seemed little better than a miserable little shop, lit by the dingiest of windows, crisscrossed with stout iron bars. It had a musty odour. Behind two cramped counters, two very old men looked up at me from their scratching pens.

"Can I help, young sir?" enquired the elder.

"Yes, if your name be Mr Tellson," I replied. "Mr Newman Noggs has recommended you to me."

"That is indeed my name. What service do you require?"

I glanced at the other old cove, who was now holding up a cheque and painfully examining the signature in the feeble light. "I have a considerable sum to deposit with you. Can I be certain of the soundness of this House?"

Tellson gave a dry chuckle: "We may be small, old and incommodious, but we are undoubtedly sound."

"Very well, you shall have my custom." I slung the knapsack from my shoulder with assiduous condescension. It was then that I saw the slit at the side, a clean slit such as a quick slash with a sharp knife would make. I reached inside but only felt my father's portrait, the sketches of Molly, Ben's Boomerang and a few other worthless odds and ends. The purse, containing all the money and other valuables had gone. I cursed myself. I knew at once who'd done it - that ugly, sharp-eyed urchin and his pal outside the Theatre Royal. I'd been too pre-occupied chasing Molly, and had had done to me what I'd practised so often on others in my younger days. How could I have been such a fool? Me, the Dodger, Fagin's top hand, who'd survived transportation, defeated Napier and outsmarted Governor Darling himself? I realised that old Tellson was still looking enquiringly at me.

I drained up my last ounce of swagger: "I appear to have left my purse in my lodgings, but having satisfied myself of the soundness of your establishment, I have every intention of becoming your client. Good day to you."

He watched with a kindly twinkle in his eye as I went up the two steps back out into Fleet Street. The man and the urchin were sitting as before, I sensed derision in their eyes. I walked westwards cursing myself yet again. I'd grown soft and stupid. I'd forgotten all Fagin had taught me. I hadn't been thinking of number one. I'd been duped by a couple of gutter-snipes, and had ended up with little more than a few shillings in my pocket. I'd even tried to do Oliver Twist a favour, and look at the thanks the little toad had given me. I'd no idea where I should go or what I should do. I even briefly considered going back to that mean old sod Spiker and taking up his offer for Dotheboys bleedin' Hall. At least that would guarantee a roof and food. But then I thought again. My skill at dipping hadn't left me. The street I walked on was full of prosperous-looking coves with bulging pocket books. I'd never go hungry. But why should I be content with that? Fagin always said I possessed the talent to rise to the very top of the thieves' lexicon. I determined at that moment to devise yet unthought-of crimes and misdemeanours and become the most ingenious and most heartless thief in London - if not the world.

These thoughts were whirling through my feverish brain as I passed the entrance to the old Roman bath. A slim, good-looking young chap was coming up the stone stairs, his long dark hair still wet from his cold plunge. He looked to be about twenty, not much older than me. There was something vaguely familiar about him. He was obviously in a great hurry for he dashed past me without a glance and made off in the direction of Westminster. As I gazed after him, still trying to place him, I spied something that looked like Mrs Napier's shining piano with two brass pump handles on the top. On closer inspection I discovered it was one of the new ginger-beer fountains. I purchased a ha'penny glass, lit my pipe, sat on the kerb and contemplated further. My hopes and expectations had gone up in smoke like the last of my tobacco, together with my hard-won pickings - all I had left was Molly, if it had indeed been her that I'd spied in Covent Garden. I decided to retrace my steps and look for her again; there couldn't be many young women in yellow silk dresses.

I retraced my steps into the Strand and paused to look at the bills outside the Olympic Theatre, where Madame Vestis,* who was reputed to have the finest thighs in Europe, was performing one of her breeches roles in the extravaganza, *'Faint Heart Never Won Fair Lady'*. I was admiring a coloured depiction of the aforesaid thighs, when a flash of yellow to my right disappeared into Wych Street. By the time I got to the corner the vivid dress was vanishing around the curve of the narrow lane. I rounded the bend just in time to see a trim figure going into a turning on the left. I followed it into a nest of dark, irregular alleys, where projecting eaves and arched doorways of ancient decrepit buildings afforded every facility for unforeseen attacks and easy escapes for members of my former profession. I was in Clare Market, the 'New Sodom,' where more than a hundred pleasure houses kept their doors open night and day. I became aware of hard-faced harlots patrolling and guarding their territory, as vigilantly and jealously as any Tory Squire. The figure in yellow stopped to exchange sharp words with one of them. She turned her head a little in an agitated manner and in that instant my heart rose to my mouth: it was the unmistakable profile of my beautiful Molly. It really was her - I'd found her at last. I surged eagerly forward but, at that very moment, was stopped by my arm being pulled by a street hawk. He endeavoured to thrust prints under my nose, of erotic coupling and views of female parts, such as I hadn't seen since my blimp hole on *Enterprise*. By the time I'd freed myself of the insidious patter coming from his foul smelling mouth, Molly had vanished into yet another side street. I wandered vainly through the filthy warrens until, when I'd almost given hope; I came to a hemmed-in, miserable churchyard near the top of Drury Lane. At the far end, through the iron bars, a yellow dress was floating through the aged lichen-covered tombstones. I called her name, but she was too far away. I ran as fast as if I'd had Sir Robert and half his bloody 'Peelers' on my heels. I raced through the graves, leaping over the bumps of the newly interred, and had nearly reached my quarry when she turned into Macklin Street. I got to the corner in time to see her enter a neat, bow-windowed house. I paused and collected my breath and my thoughts, wondering how she'd receive me. Would she still despise me for not helping her escape the clutches of Deplidge? Had she found a lover? Or a husband? The house she'd entered looked clean and decent, its bowed window was modestly screened by a green curtain. The step was nicely scoured and sanded.

My heart was thumping rapidly, whether from running or excitement, I did not know or care, as I licked my lips and knocked on the door. It was opened immediately by a brute not less than six feet high, broad and strong in appearance. Though he was well-dressed, in a light, loose, grey tailcoat, a white waistcoat and sandy kerseymere breeches, there was a villainous threat about him. He looked at me maliciously through his small eyes:

"What d'yer want?" he growled in a deep voice.

"Molly."

"You can't have her. But there's others on offer. If you've got the cash."

I was taken aback by this, but I wasn't going to let this clod-pole see it. "Tell her it's Jack. The Dodger. Her old crew mate from *Enterprise*."

He shut the door, re-opened it within a minute, and reluctantly nodded me in.

I entered a comfortable room with teapots on the dresser and shelves full of plates, dishes and tea-ware. Molly, my beloved Molly, was sitting in a bow-winged chair by the fire, on which a kettle was boiling. She'd taken off her bonnet and her beautiful chestnut hair was hanging about her shoulders. I held out my hands and made towards her, my heart beating faster than ever, until she turned and I recoiled in horror. One side of her lovely face was disfigured by a jagged scar, the flesh around the corner of her mouth had been cut away into a sneer, and one eye was completely white.

She fixed me with her one good eye, as blue and beautiful as I remembered: "Never thought I'd see you again, short-arse. Didn't think you'd got the spunk to find your way back from Botany Bay."

Tears were rolling down my cheeks; "Who did that to you?" was all I could say.

"A pimp who tried to force me on the game. He paid for it with interest." She turned her one eye to the brute standing at the door. "Sam saw to that."

"I sliced the bastard's balls off and shoved them down his throat, before I cut it," Sam replied with grim satisfaction.

At that moment agonised cries came from the room above.

"What the Devil's going on?" I managed to mumble.

Molly raised her mutilated head and listened: "Screams are indispensable to their delight. Some call it defloration mania. Respectable elderly gentlemen like nothing better than a girl of tender age. Some idiots even believe it can cure 'em of the pox. They're willing to pay well over the odds."

Sam chuckled evilly at this.

"You let them have children?" I gasped. I don't know why but it shocked me even then.

"Why not?" She took the kettle off the fire and added the boiling water to two half-filled cups of gin. "I seem to remember this was your tipple." I took a cup from her and gulped it down, my mind and emotions, whirling in so many directions. "How did you find me, by the way?"

"I saw your picture in Cape Town. That poor old painter, who you duped, told me you'd sailed to London. I saw you in the street by chance and followed you."

"Got anywhere to live?" she asked, looking at me intently with her one good eye.

I shook my head. She glanced up at Sam behind me as if seeking his approval.

"I think you could be of use here."

"Doing what?"

"Sam and me keep a nice dress house here. That bugger Deplidge took away my taste for men when I lay every night in his stinking bed. But every time that old whore, Greere came in to give him his share of her takings, I listened to every word they said. It was a perfect education for this trade. I made plans. I waited until we were near to land and then I stuck Deplidge like the pig he was and slipped over the side. Didn't know I could swim, did you, Dodger? My poor father taught me in the mill race as soon as I could walk. He was so afraid that I might drown." Her face softened at the memory but hardened immediately. "That drunken Dutch fool found me on the beach. The money I took from him was mine. I earned it, sitting naked all day, with me legs apart, whilst he painted and drooled. I took what was mine and arrived back here with just enough to start myself up with a couple of girls." She gazed reflectively into the fire and raised her hand to her cut mouth. "But the bastard who did this tried to force me on the street and pocket the earnings. I realised double quick that I needed a protector, someone who appreciated my business skill but didn't want to have me. Not that many would now with a phiz like mine. I found Sam. You wouldn't think it, but though Sam's big and strong, he doesn't like women or girls, do you Sam?" Her twisted mouth smiled provocatively: "You'd better watch that tight little bum of yourn Dodger, my boy." She refilled my cup with more gin and hot water. "Trouble with Sam is though; he looks too much like what he is. He stands out for a ruffian in any crowd. I need someone more subtle, Jack."

"To do what?" I asked again.

"We need unspoilt young doxies all the time, as I said there's a great demand for them." As if on cue another cry came through the thin floor above. "I want someone to go about London and find girls, young girls lost without a home, just as you used to find the boys for Fagin. Sam frightens 'em and they're reluctant to go with him, but a younker like you could use your charm and have no trouble in persuading 'em." She rummaged among some papers on the small table beside her and perused a list of addresses with her one good eye. "I also want to advertise any fresh supply in the clubs in St James. Sam wouldn't be let inside their doors, but you could slip in easily and give particulars to the porters. Those greasy spongers will be only too willing to co-operate for a cut."

I was looking at her in disbelief. This was not the girl who'd sat sewing on deck of *Enterprise*, speaking so tenderly about her father. She noticed my consternation.

"Cat got yer tongue, Jack."

"How do you keep 'em from running away?"

She laughed: "That's easy; they wear my clothes and the bits of cheap jewellery I give 'em. I feed 'em and give 'em all the drink they can take. If any of the silly cows did a runner I'd have 'em arrested for theft and transported. But that will be another of your duties, Jack; you won't let them run away. When they promenade in the evening along the Strand, you will make sure they talk nice to every toff they pass and pocket every penny they earn." She chuckled evilly, "Sam, take Jack into the back and introduce him to the girls."

The brute pushed open a door and beckoned me into the room within. In contrast to the neatness of Molly's parlour, all was dirt and disorder. Four young girls were sitting around a deal table drinking gin and beer. Although it was now afternoon they were still in their night gowns and slip shod. Their faces were unwashed and heavy from lack of sleep, any allure or fascination they might once have possessed was fading fast.

Sam laughed; "They don't look too fresh do they? But what can you expect? They all had eight or nine tricks last night. Say hallo to Jack, girls. He's going to be yer new tout."

The girls looked at me as if the vulture of misery was gnawing at their vitals. They were entrapped like animals, devoid of will or hope. I couldn't think of anything to say and backed into the parlour. Molly's eye was fixed upon me. It was hard, mean, and avaricious. "You can't treat girls like that," I stammered.

She gave a ferocious laugh: "I thought you were a man of the town, with all your talk of being Fagin's top hand. You're nothing but a milksop. Those bints are bloody lucky. There's houses in this street with rings on the ceilings, where gentlemen pay to hang up naked girls by their wrists and whip 'em with birch whips and holly branches till they bleed all over. Me and Sam don't go in for that, it damages the goods and they're not fit for use for days on end."

At that moment a door creaked open on the floor above and a stout old gentleman in a blue coat and striped waistcoat came down the stairs, adjusting his nankeen britches. I instantly recognised Mr Brownlow's morning visitor. The wicked old charlatan recognised me as well, for his mouth dropped open and his several chins wobbled.

"What in the name of Hell are you doing here? He gasped.

"Spying for the Society for the Protection of Juvenile Prostitution, my covey" I found myself replying. "Is your friend Mr Brownlow aware of your predilections? I wouldn't like you to spoil young Oliver's expectations"

At that moment I received a mighty thump to the side of my head and sank to the floor. When I regained my senses the foul old rogue had hastily departed and Sam was standing menacingly over me, ready to inflict another blow.

Molly was still sitting in her chair. "I would let Sam kill anyone who upset my customers and interfered with my business. It's only for old time's sake that I'm letting you go. You're nothing but a useless loser, Jack Dawkins. Don't ever come near me again or Sam will skin you alive."

Sam kicked me viciously out into the street and I made my painful way back to the Strand. Everything I'd expected to find in London had now blown apart. I had nothing - no friend, no hope. Maybe I was a thief, but there were some things I knew I could not do. I'd believed that the sights I'd seen on the hulk, the convict ship and in Australia had hardened me for life. I thought I'd come back to London knowing the ways of the world. But there was still so much I didn't know. London was full of hypocrisy and corruption and evil. I wanted to tell the world about it, but how?

The late afternoon crowd in the Strand was thicker than ever. Senior businessmen, in search of pleasure, were quitting their offices early, leaving the mundane work to their poorly paid clerks; officers swaggered along the pavements in their scarlet and dark blue uniforms, mingling with hawkers, chimney sweeps, painted trollops, fire-eaters and sword swallowers, whilst vendors shouted their wares and street musicians sang out of tune and played a multifarious assortment of instruments. Amongst all these, I spied him, putting a coin into the box of the old blind woman playing the hurdy-gurdy. The same long-haired young fellow that I'd seen coming out of the Roman Bath, but his hair was now dry and floated about his shoulders. He attempted to dress like a swell, but his worn shoes and cuffs and collar let him down. He was holding a large envelope in his hand. He turned and noticed me staring at him.

"Do I know you, young fellow? You look familiar."

His look reached into my very soul. I knew then who he was. "You were in court that morning when that mealy-faced old beak lagged me for life."

A look of surprise then recognition spread across his handsome features. "My God! I remember you now. I am blessed with a strong perception of character and oddity. The chirpy little pickpocket! I captured you in shorthand and kept a description of you somewhere in my papers.

You've grown a bit, but how on earth did you manage to get back from that outlandish place?"

"That's a long, long story," I replied.

His keen eyes swept my face. "I would guess it is and one worth the hearing without doubt." He looked at the envelope in his hand. "I'm on my way to drop this, my first literary effort, into the dark office of a new publication up a dark court in Fleet Street. Accompany me, and after I've dropped it, with fear and trembling into the dark letter box, I'll treat you to a mutton chop and a tankard of extra-creaming stout in my favourite tavern."

I walked beside him through the crowded London street as he told me of his present occupation, reporting the Reform Bill's passage through Parliament, and how his whole future trembled in the balance on the success of the humorous essay he was submitting to *The Monthly Magazine*. We crept up Johnson's Court together and posted it through the aforesaid letter box, then went up a covered way into a little lop-sided, wedged-up establishment called *The Cheshire Cheese*, where I began to tell Charles Dickens my story....................

End of first volume

I could never have told Dodger's story without the assistance of two great works on early Australia:

The Fatal Shore by Robert Hughes and *The Commonwealth of Thieves* by Tom Keneally.

Also *Dancing with Strangers* by Inga Clendinnen, *Mayhew's London*, and of course the immortal works of Charles Dickens.

My heartfelt thanks to David Beresford for his invaluable editing and cover design and to Andrew Lownie for his constant support.

Notes

Chapter 1: Farewell To Fagin

* Dickens was at this time perfecting his skill in the Gurney Method of shorthand.

* Penny Gaff: a low music hall.

* Dickens didn't always follow this principle. He gave *Great Expectations* a happy ending on the advice of Bulwer Lytton.

Chapter 2: The Hulk

* Foogle: a handkerchief.

Chapter 3: *Enterprise*

* Ticker with seals: watch and chain.

*. Tom Cannon: British Heavyweight Champion 1824-1825.

Chapter 4: The Voyage Begins

* Bluchers: leather shoes with open lacing.

* Buzz-gloaks and rum-hustlers: practised criminals.

* Jepan his trotter cases: polish his shoes.

* In 1840, the convict Charles Cozens, describes in his diary, being instructed to dance to the cask for his ration of port wine as a: '*purpose of exercising and as preventive to disease...the steps as various as the performers, formed altogether a most amusing ballet.*' Dodger may have been influenced by Dickens' description of Mr Fezziwig's Ball, or vice versa.

Chapter 5: At Sea

* Britain had abolished the slave trade in 1807. Slavery throughout the British Empire was not abolished until 1833.

* Oakum: fibre made from tarry ropes and cordage, used in ship building for caulking the joints of timbers.

Chapter 6: Across The Southern Ocean

* Very similar to a speech of thanks given by convicts to Captain Alfred Tetens on the *Norwood* in 1861.

Chapter 7: Sydney

* General Sir Ralph Darling. (1772-1858)Governor of New South Wales 1825-1831

* Major General Lachlan Macquarie. (1762-1824)

Governor of New South Wales 1810-1821. Known as 'the good governor'.

Chapter 8: Wild Colonial Boy

* Francis Greenway (1777-1837). Bristol architect transported for forgery in 1808.

* Barnet Levey (1798-1837). First free Jewish settler in the colony. Entrepreneur and founding father of the Australian Theatre. Dec 26th

1833 produced *Richard III* at his Theatre Royal, Sydney. First professional Shakespeare production in Australia.

* Nee Elizabeth Dumaresq. (1798-1868) Unlike her husband she was very popular, and presided over many benevolent committees.

Chapter 9: First Day's Play

* 4 balls an over was the standard rate until 1881

* Charles Henry Darling. (1809-1870) Lt-Governor of St Lucia 1847, Cape Colony 1851, Newfoundland 1855. Governor of Jamaica 1857, Victoria 1863-66.

* Rt. Hon. Henry Dumaresq.(1792 -1838) Brother to Darling's young wife Eliza.

He had been severely wounded at Waterloo.

* Captain Charles Sturt. (1795-1869) Veteran of Wellington's Peninsular Campaign.

* Major Frederick Chidley Irwin. (1788-1848)

* George Macleay. (1809-1891) Member of New South Wales Legislative 1857. Keen Zoologist.

Chapter 10: Second Day's Play

* Micawber may well have written his letter although the rule allowing a runner for an incapacitated batsman was not in fact introduced until 1861.

Chapter 11: Repercussions

* Sir George Murray. (1772-1846) Conservative Secretary of State for Colonies: 1828-1830. Crowe was not to know that Murray would be out of office on his return.

Chapter 12: Into The Outback

* Jack Donahue. (1804-1830) Irish born bushranger and folk hero.

* Jack Walmsley. Escaped convict.

Bill Webber. Bushranger. Executed in Sydney 1831.

* Jack Broughton. (1703-1789) Champion of England 1738-1750.

First to codify a loose set of boxing rules. Buried in Westminster Abbey.

* Napier's death has many similarities to that of Captain Patrick Logan. (1791-1830) Commandant of Moreton Bay Penal Colony 1826-1830. Though a fine soldier and intrepid explorer, he was the most savage and brutal of all camp commandants, and was known as 'The Beast of Brisbane'. His murderers were never found.

His widow was named Leticia, but there is no record of her having any association with Barnet Levey, though they undoubtedly met.

* Dodger's account of the death of Jack Donahue largely follows the report in the Sydney Gazette.

Chapter 15: The District Magistrate And The Settlers From Yarmouth.

* Sir Richard Bourke. KCB. (1777-1855) Governor of New South Wales 1831-1837.

An avowed Whig.

* Mass migration away from British rule to found new Boer republics in Natal and Orange Free State

Chapter 17: London Again.

* Lucia Elizabeth Vestis. (1787 - 1856) First female actor-manager in the history of London Theatre.

David Weston
123a Grosvenor Road
London SW1V 4BE
02076305026
David@dcweston.freeserve.co.uk

About the Author

David Weston was born in London and educated at Alleyn's School Dulwich where he was taught by Michael Croft and became a founder-member of the National Youth Theatre. After National Service, where he was commissioned in the Royal Artillery, he won a scholarship to RADA. He has been a working actor for more than fifty years, doing everything from starring in Hollywood films, many seasons at the RSC and the National, appearing in twenty nine of Shakespeare's plays – to Eastenders and Doctor Who.

His first book, Covering McKellen, described as 'Hugely enjoyable' by the Daily Telegraph and 'Salty, evocative and informative' by the Daily Mail, won the Theatre Book of the Year Prize for 2011.

Dodger - Down Under, his first novel, follows the adventures of Jack Dawkins, aka the Artful Dodger, following his transportation to Australia.

David lives in Pimlico with his wife and dotes on four grandchildren, a cocker spaniel and Chelsea FC.

22711561R00196

Printed in Great Britain
by Amazon